W9-BMY-539

Dallas's hold subtly tightened and any thought of talking slipped away.

By the time the song was over, he was holding her snugly against him, and her arms were around his neck. Patience couldn't help noticing how good he felt, how perfectly they fit together.

He reached up and tucked a strand of her hair behind an ear. "I'd really like to kiss you. I haven't been able to think of anything else since the moment I saw you tonight." A corner of his mouth edged up. "You won't slap me again, will you?"

Slap him? When he looked at her that way, hitting him was the last thing on her mind. "No. I'll just kiss you back."

Something flashed in those blue, blue eyes. He didn't wait, just lowered his head and captured her lips. His were warm and softer than they looked, sinking in, molding perfectly to hers. He tasted her, kissed her more deeply, started over and did it all again . . .

Also by Kat Martin

THE SILENT ROSE

THE DREAM

THE SECRET

HOT RAIN

DEEP BLUE

MIDNIGHT SUN

Published by Kensington Publishing Corporation

KAT MARTIN

DESERT HEAT

ZEBRA BOOKS
KENSINGTON PUBLISHING CORP.
http://www.kensingtonbooks.com

ZEBRA BOOKS are published by

Kensington Publishing Corp.
119 West 40th Street
New York, NY 10018

Copyright © 2004 by Kat Martin

All rights reserved. No part of this book may be reproduced in any form or by any means without the prior written consent of the Publisher, excepting brief quotes used in reviews.

If you purchased this book without a cover, you should be aware that this book is stolen property. It was reported as "unsold and destroyed" to the Publisher and neither the Author nor the Publisher has received any payment for this "stripped book."

All Kensington titles, imprints and distributed lines are available at special quantity discounts for bulk purchases for sales promotions, premiums, fund-raising, educational, or institutional use.

Special book excerpts or customized printings can also be created to fit specific needs. For details, write or phone the office of the Kensington Special Sales Manager: Attn. Special Sales Department, Kensington Publishing Corp., 119 West 40th Street, New York, NY 10018. Phone: 1-800-221-2647.

Zebra and the Z logo Reg. U.S. Pat. & TM Off.

First Printing: May 2004
ISBN-13: 978-1-4201-3136-9
ISBN-10: 1-4201-3136-2

First Electronic Edition: May 2004
eISBN-13: 978-1-4201-3419-3
eISBN-10: 1-4201-3419-1

10 9 8 7 6 5 4 3 2

Printed in the United States of America

To the men and women of the West. To my grandmother, Ruby Adelaide Kelly, who was a real cowgirl and relay racer in the early rodeos between 1910 and 1920 and whose split-leather riding skirt now belongs to me. To my uncle, Joaquin Sanchez, one of the great rodeo clowns of all time.

A special thanks to Jamie Olson, Brian Wooley, George Wilhite, and all the rodeo riders, clowns, and contestants who helped me over the course of this book.

And a grateful thank you to my editor, Kate Duffy, for all her hard work on this book.

CHAPTER 1

She tried not to be frightened. She told herself it was co-incidence. He hadn't followed her there. He had only come to the supermarket for groceries, just like everyone else. She wasn't afraid, she convinced herself; she simply refused to be.

But Tyler Stanfield wasn't like everyone else. He was the man who had made her life miserable for six long months. The man who had spied on her, followed her for hours on end, phoned her at all hours of the day and night, and written her dozens of letters, some professing his undying love, others warning her that if he couldn't have her no one would. She had been forced to get an unlisted number and a new e-mail address, but that hadn't stopped him.

Night after night, he watched her apartment from the street below her house. By day, he followed her around the Boston University campus, making it nearly impossible to concentrate on her work. He had hassled her, embarrassed, and harassed her.

Finally, he had broken into her apartment, using a key to the back door she hadn't known he had. He needed to talk to her, he had said, tears in his eyes as he approached where she lay nearly paralyzed in bed. Fortunately, she had told one of her neighbors about the trouble he had been causing. The woman heard the commotion and called the police, who were patrolling a few blocks away and arrived before things got any further out of hand.

Patience wanted to press charges but Tyler's parents were important people who made heavy contributors to the school. It took the help of two of her college professors, her parents, and one of her girlfriends to finally get a restraining order against him. Tyler Stanfield, an above average graduate student, was forbidden to have any sort of contact with her. He was ordered by the judge not to come within a hundred yards—the length of a football field.

Still, the area just off campus where she lived while she studied for her Ph.D. wasn't all that large and she was bound to run into him on occasion. Just as she had today.

Patience shifted the bag of groceries from her right arm to her left, dragged her keys out of her purse, and unlocked the trunk of her gray Nissan coupe. Her palms were sweating, the brown paper bag soaking up the moisture as she looked over her shoulder, trying to spot Tyler's silver BMW.

Six months ago, she had thought he was attractive. Nearly six feet tall, a well-built, blond man in his late twenties, Tyler was intelligent; they both went to B.U.; and she was intrigued. She rarely dated. When Tyler asked her out, at first she had said no, but needing a break from her thesis, the third time he asked, she said yes.

He took her to dinner at the Top of the Hub where they could look out over the city, and she had to admit she had fun. His family had money and Tyler always had a pocketful. He had expensive tastes and a brand new car, and in the beginning, he showed her a very good time.

She had slept with him. It was a terrible mistake. The sex wasn't good and she suspected it wasn't going to get any better. And there was something about Tyler . . . something she couldn't quite put a finger on. A few weeks into the affair, she told him she didn't think the relationship—such as it was—was going to work. She refused to see him, tried to make him understand she simply wasn't attracted to him.

That's when her nightmare began.

Patience put the groceries in the trunk and closed the lid. Tyler's car no longer sat in the parking lot. She should have been relieved but she wasn't. Tyler had never gotten physical, but she thought that if the right buttons got pushed, he very well could, and she didn't want to take any chances. She wasn't the same naïve young woman she had been six months ago. She was wiser now, more wary, even a little paranoid, she supposed.

She'd get over it. Once she left Boston. Patience wished she were heading for the airport right now, instead of going back to her apartment.

The phone was ringing when she stepped through the door. Patience set the bag of groceries down and reached for the receiver, hesitating only a moment before she picked it up. Her sister Hope's voice reached her from the other end of the line.

"Hi, sis. How's it going?"

She knew why her sister was calling. Hope was the eldest of the three Sinclair sisters. Patience had been eight when their mother died and Hope, eleven, had taken over the job of raising them. They were grown now, but nothing had really changed. And ever since her problems with Tyler, Hope had been calling more often.

"Everything's great. How 'bout you?"

There was a long moment of silence. She'd overdone the cheeriness, she could tell.

"You saw him again, didn't you?"

Patience sighed. It was impossible to keep secrets from Hope. "He was getting into his car in the parking lot of the B&P Market. I couldn't tell if he had followed me there or he was just there buying groceries. There's no law against that, you know."

"No, there isn't. Still, it's pretty hard to believe."

Patience made no comment. She had thought the same thing herself.

"So, when do you fly out?" Hope asked.

Patience reached into the bag, pulled out a cold Diet Coke and popped the tab. "First thing in the morning, and to tell you the truth, I can't wait to leave." With women in western history the focus of her dissertation, she planned to do the final portion of her research over the summer, combining a study of early women in rodeo with those of the present day. After her months of battling with Tyler, it posed the perfect escape.

"I'd say your timing is right on the money. You'll be away for the summer and good ol' Tyler won't have a clue where you've gone. The only ones who'll know are your family and they sure as hell aren't going to tell him."

"Maybe by the time I get back, Tyler's fixation will be over."

"Let's hope so. Be sure to check in with Dad and Tracy. If you don't, they're bound to worry."

"I will. Thanks for the call, sis."

"Have fun."

"It's supposed to be a working summer."

"True, but it's all right to mix business with a little pleasure."

"I'll remember that."

Hope hung up and Patience began to unload the groceries she had bought, setting out a chicken breast, a small head of lettuce, taking a sip of her Diet Coke. Aside from what she had bought, the refrigerator was pretty much bare. Her luggage was packed and she was ready to leave. She had a 7:18 flight in the morning.

She thought of Tyler Stanfield and ignored a faint shiver. She was getting out of Boston. Patience could hardly wait.

CHAPTER 2

Maybe it was the heady sense of freedom she hadn't known in weeks. Maybe it was leaving Boston, leaving the last six troubled months behind. Or perhaps it was simply the wide-open Texas spaces. Whatever it was, she found herself driving the bright red Hertz rental car, a low-slung Chrysler convertible she had indulged herself in at the airport, faster than she should have.

Patience braked the sporty red car only a little as she pulled through the rodeo gates and headed toward the arena. She was enjoying the warmth of the sun, the wind in her face, looking straight ahead, thinking of the exciting summer she was about to begin, when a horse and rider jumped up from the ditch at the edge of the dirt road directly in front of her.

She slammed on the brakes, throwing up a cloud of dust, and her heart slammed into her ribs. The little boy on the horse never gave her a second look, just flapped his boots against the sides of what had to be his daddy's heavy leather saddle and kept on riding.

Patience leaned back against the seat, trying to catch her breath. She hadn't noticed the boy or his horse. Or the two tall cowboys on the opposite side of the road now bearing down on her, one of them with murder in his eyes.

She looked up at him as he reached the door of the convertible and braced his legs apart in an angry stance.

"I'm really sorry," she said. "I didn't realize I was going quite so fast. The rodeo is about to begin and I didn't want to miss the start. I should have slowed down. I really do apologize."

The bigger of the pair shoved back a wide-brimmed black felt hat. "Yeah, well, the rest of us would like to be around to see the show, too. Use some common sense, lady. You'll spook one of these horses and someone will wind up getting hurt."

Patience raised her sunglasses up on the top of her head, beginning to feel a tug of irritation. "I didn't see the horse, all right? I'll be more careful next time."

"That's a damned good idea."

She didn't like his tone. She refused to let him ruin her very first day. "Look, cowboy. I said I was sorry. What else do you expect me to do?"

"Like I said, try using—"

She didn't let him finish. She was hot and tired from the hours she had spent on the road, and after Tyler Stanfield, sick to death of pushy men. She slammed her foot down hard on the accelerator and the convertible leapt forward. The cowboy cursed as the car sped off toward the arena, throwing up a thick cloud of dust. She couldn't help a smile as she watched the men disappear in her rearview mirror and the thought occurred that lately she hadn't smiled all that often.

This summer, she vowed, she was going to make a point of it.

"Sonofabitch." Dallas waved his hat to fan away some of the choking dust floating in the air. "Damned woman. Ought to know better than to drive like a maniac with little kids around."

His best friend, Steve "Stormy" Weathers, just smiled. "Maybe you should have cut her a little slack. You can tell she's new to these parts." His gaze followed the flashy red car as it disappeared in the dust. "Probably some rich gal out for a good time on Daddy's money. But man, she sure is a looker."

Dallas just grunted, recalling the woman who had glared at him through a pair of wraparound tortoiseshell sunglasses. She was wearing a brand new straw cowboy hat and a white western shirt with red flowers embroidered across the yoke. Shiny pearl snaps curved over a pair of nice-size breasts. She had honey blond hair smoothed into a coil at the nape of her neck, and her lips were full and a softer shade of red than the flowers in her shirt.

She was pretty. Damned pretty. But lots of pretty women hung around the rodeo. Buckle bunnies, the cowboys called them, groupies who swooned over the riders, women who got their kicks out of having a fling with a "real live cowboy." Dallas figured she was probably just another one of them.

Whoever she was, even the western clothes couldn't hide an air of class or disguise her sophisticated eastern voice. He wondered where the hell she had come from.

"We better get goin'." Stormy started off toward the arena, leather chaps flicking against his boots. "Like the lady said, the show's gettin' ready to start." Stormy was a calf roper, six feet tall and sandy-haired, a lean, lanky cowboy with an easy grin and an unflappable disposition.

Dallas fell in beside him. "I drew Cyclone. I need to start limbering up."

"Man, you got that right. That horse is as tough as they come." Like Dallas, Stormy was a Texas cowboy. They'd been friends for years and hauled together as often as they could. "Cyclone's a two-time Finals horse."

"He's one helluva bucker, but if I stay aboard, I'll have a good chance at finishing in the money."

"You'll stay aboard," Stormy said. "You always do."

Not always, but enough times that Dallas Kingman was the current reigning, World Champion All-Around Cowboy on the professional rodeo circuit. He was a saddle-bronc rider, but he also competed in the calf roping whenever he could.

As they walked toward the arena, Dallas began to think of the ride ahead, to mentally prepare himself and envision a successful outcome. He walked behind the chutes to make a final check of his gear and caught sight of the blonde.

She was taller than he had first thought, maybe five eight or five nine, with legs that seemed to go on forever. She was wearing a new pair of jeans and fancy red cowboy boots—a true buckle bunny if ever he had seen one. Since another groupie was the last thing he needed, Dallas began to check his gear, carefully going over the straps and stirrups on his bronc saddle. Once he was satisfied, he started his stretching exercises, limbering up his legs, loosening the muscles in his arms and shoulders, getting ready for the tough ride ahead.

"Excuse me." Patience approached a cowboy in dusty jeans and worn out, mud-covered boots. "I'm looking for Shari Wills. Can you tell me where I might find her?"

The cowboy pointed toward a petite woman brushing a shiny sorrel quarter horse. "Shari's that little redhead standing over there." She was an attractive woman in her twenties with a compact body and nicely feminine curves.

"Thanks." Patience gave him a grateful smile, turned and started walking. "Shari Wills?" Patience asked. Her horse was impressive, lean yet solid, with excellent conformation and a bold white star in the middle of his forehead.

The brush paused mid-stroke and the woman's head came up. "That's me."

"I'm Patience Sinclair. It's great to meet you. I've been looking forward to this for months."

Shari wore dark green riding pants, a matching sequined

shirt, and a green felt hat, the flashy clothes of a barrel racer. "Same here." She stuck out a small, callused hand and Patience shook it. "You're taller in person. Short as I am, we're gonna look a little like Mutt and Jeff, but I'm happy for the company."

Patience returned the smile. "I can't tell you how grateful I am you agreed to let me join you for the summer."

Shari shrugged. Patience had found her with the help of the PRCA—Pro Rodeo Cowboys Association—over the Internet. Shari was a barrel racer, a modern-day cowgirl who would be an important part of the dissertation Patience was writing on women of the West for her doctorate degree.

"Show'll be startin' soon," Shari said. "Let me introduce you to Charlie before he gets tied up." Charlie Carson was the owner of the Circle C Rodeo Company, a business that produced rodeos all over the southwestern part of the country. Like Shari, he had agreed to help Patience with her research, allowing her behind the scenes whenever she attended a Circle C show. While Shari had done it in order to split expenses and defray costs for the summer, Charlie had said that if Patience was going to do a paper on the sport, he wanted to make darned sure she got it right.

Falling in behind Shari, she followed the smaller woman toward the announcer's stand behind the chutes. The place hummed with activity as the start of the performance grew near. Shari nimbly wove her way through half a dozen cowboys in worn chaps, battered hats, and dusty boots, a couple of rodeo clowns in baggy jeans and face paint, and several members of the press with cameras or notepads in hand, finally stopping at the bottom of the wooden stairs leading up to the announcer's stand.

"Hey, Charlie!" Shari waved at a barrel-chested man who looked to be in his early sixties. "Somebody here I'd like you to meet."

Charlie ambled toward them down the stairs, shoving his sweat-stained straw hat back off his forehead. Though a slight paunch hung over his big silver buckle, there was an air of authority in his stride. Charlie Carson looked like a man who got things done.

Shari made the introductions and Charlie stuck out a meaty hand. "Welcome to rodeo, Ms. Sinclair."

"Patience," she corrected, accepting the handshake.

"Good, 'cause I'm just Charlie to everyone who knows me." He seemed not to notice the hubbub around him—big broad-backed bucking horses milling in their pens, massive Brahma bulls pawing the ground, bellowing and tossing up dirt. Western music—Willie Nelson warning mothers not to let their babies grow up to be cowboys—played in the background over the loudspeakers mounted on the announcer's stand.

"I don't know how much you know about rodeo, Patience, but I can tell you one thing for sure—whatever time you spend with the Circle C, you ain't gonna be bored—not for a minute."

A thrill shot through her. No, she wouldn't be bored. Just standing behind the chutes as she had dreamed of doing, sent a shot of excitement through her. In college, her focus had been on western history, and though she lived in Boston, she knew everything there was to know about the West. She especially loved rodeo, but there was a second reason she had come.

Along with Hope and her middle sister, Charity, Patience had made a pact—each of them had vowed to have one great adventure before she married or settled into her career. Last year, Charity had set off for the Yukon, her own personal dream. Not only had she had a fabulous adventure in the untamed Northwest, she had met McCall Hawkins and fallen madly in love. Charity was married now, starting to think of having a baby, and happier than Patience had ever seen her.

"Come on, little lady, and I'll introduce you around." Charlie caught her hand and tugged her over to a cluster of cowboys all working to limber up. Some of them wore T-shirts and she was treated to an array of impressive biceps. Two of them had their boot heels propped on a section of pipe fenc-

ing, using it like a ballet bar to stretch out the muscles in
their legs. These men were athletes, most of them in fantas-
tic physical condition.

"This here's Wes McCauley. Wes is one of the best steer
wrestlers in the business."

He was tall, at least six-foot-three, a big, beefy man in his
early thirties with the kind of muscle it took to bring down a
five-hundred-pound steer.

Wes tipped his hat. "A pleasure, ma'am."

"This guy here is Cy Jennings. He's a bullfighter—one of
the best there is." Charlie slapped the clown on the back.
"Having a good man in the arena can make the difference between livin' or dyin' when a rider comes off his bull."

She couldn't really tell what Cy Jennings looked like under
all the bright-colored face paint, but his body was lean and
wiry. He wore a pair of red tights beneath a short pair of red-
fringed chaps, a bold, red and white striped shirt, and cleated
running shoes.

"Nice to meet you," she said.

"Same here." Cy smiled but she could tell he was distracted, his mind on the upcoming show.

"And this is my nephew, Dallas Kingman." Charlie grinned,
making no effort to hide the pride in his voice. "World Champion All-'Round Cowboy and the finest damned saddle bronc
rider you're ever gonna meet."

Her gaze swung to the third man in the group. When he
lifted his head, she could see his face beneath the brim of his
black felt hat and for an instant she couldn't think of a single
thing to say.

She knew the name, of course. She had been studying rodeo
for months, reading anything and everything she could get her
hands on and watching every telecast on TV. She should have
recognized him, probably would have if he hadn't been so
darned rude. But who would have thought the top rodeo rider
in the country would turn out to be the same arrogant, overbearing cowboy she had run into on her way to the arena.

She stiffened, tried not to let her annoyance show. The cowboy's gaze ran over her, skimmed her breasts, made a slow perusal of her hips and the length of her legs.

A corner of his mouth edged up. "I've already had the pleasure." He was handsome, even better-looking in person than he was on TV, with a lean, athletic build and shoulders that stretched the limits of the fabric in his pale blue western shirt. Dark brown hair, trim hips, flat stomach, and he was tall for a bronc rider, around six-foot-one. Most of the best riders were shorter, their center of gravity lower. But Dallas Kingman was also a calf roper, which was generally a bigger man.

The simple fact was the man was a good enough rider it didn't matter that he was tall.

She gave him a frosty smile, the best she could manage, determined to be polite to Charlie's nephew. "That's right. Our paths crossed out on the road."

He was wearing hand-tooled, black and gold fringed chaps over a pair of worn jeans, and black boots. When he turned, she saw that he had one of those round, muscular behinds that rodeo riders developed over the years. The guy had the carved, rugged features of a Marlboro man and the bluest eyes she had ever seen.

As much as it galled her to admit it, Dallas Kingman was an incredibly good-looking man. Too bad he had an incredibly big ego to match.

"You'll be seeing Patience around quite a bit," Charlie told the men. "She's working on an article about the history of women in rodeo. I want you boys to help her any way you can." She had asked him not to mention the dissertation for her Ph.D. She wanted to fit in and she doubted that someone from the academic world would be readily accepted. Aside from that, after her troubles with Tyler Stanfield, she had simply become a more private person.

"You a magazine writer?" Dallas asked.

"No," she replied with false sweetness, figuring he was looking for more publicity than he got already.

"She'll be haulin' with Shari." Charlie flicked his nephew a glance, picking up the faint trace of hostility that arched between them. "Like I said, if Patience needs anything, I hope you boys will help."

Wes McCauley gave her a smile that actually looked sincere. "You need anything, ma'am, anything at all, you just let me know."

"Me, too," said the lanky, sandy-haired cowboy she had seen with Dallas earlier that day, but she thought the remark was aimed more at Shari than at her. Dallas, she noticed, didn't bother to offer. They didn't like each other and both of them knew it.

"Thank you," Patience said to the other two men. "I'll remember what you said."

"Hey, Charlie!" One of the cowboys ran toward him down the alley behind the chutes. "We got trouble! You better get over here!"

Charlie sighed. "Gotta go. See ya after the show." Charlie took off and Dallas left with him.

"Poor Charlie." Shari shook her head, moving the ends of the red bandana tying back her shoulder-length curly red hair. "He's sure had his share of bad luck lately."

"I'm sorry to hear it. He seems like a really nice man."

"Charlie's the best." She glanced off in the direction the men had disappeared. "You know what they say—trouble always comes in threes. I wonder what it is this time."

The trouble turned out to be a blown PA system. As Charlie scrambled to find a substitute, one of the clowns went into the arena to stall for time.

By the time the problem was corrected, the show was half an hour late getting started and Charlie was out the cost of a new PA system. Still, once the events got underway, the audience got into the spirit.

Patience felt a hum of excitement as she stood in the staging area where the cowboys got ready to perform. There was movement all around her. One of the clowns adjusted the red suspenders holding up his baggy jeans while a cowboy buckled on his fringed leather chaps. A man walked his dogs, three Australian shepherds, the stars of a contract act slated to perform in the middle of the show. There were a number of press people—the group she had been tossed into—as well as the wives, children, and girlfriends of the contestants, though they were mostly in a small set of bleachers reserved for their use.

Rodeo was big, bold, flashy entertainment, an extreme sport that offered chills and thrills, excitement and danger. The sport had begun in the late eighteen-hundreds, growing out of the ranching and cattle industry, and still carried an aura of that time.

Tonight was an indoor, night performance beginning with the usual mounted salute to the Stars and Stripes. Riders on two big pinto horses, each carrying a massive flag, galloped full speed around the ring, spurred on by the audience singing "there ain't no doubt I love this land," the lyrics of "God Bless the U.S.A." The national anthem and the Pledge of Allegiance followed, then the competition began.

The opening event, bareback bronc riding, was a tough and dangerous event. A dark-skinned cowboy in a steel-reinforced vest worn to keep his ribs from being crushed if the horse stepped on him wrapped his neck to keep from getting whiplash and climbed up on the chute. Several other riders helped him get settled and keep from falling into the chute beneath the horse's thrashing hooves.

The gate opened and the horse charged out. The cowboy managed to stay on the cantankerous little pinto named Wildfire who leapt and twisted but couldn't seem to shake him, and wound up making a high-scoring ride.

The steer wrestling followed, a big man's event. It took a good deal of brawn to lean down from a horse galloping at full speed, grab hold of a pair of horns, and bring down a five-hundred-pound steer. The first man out was Wes McCauley, who thundered down the arena next to his hazer, the man who rode on the opposite side of the steer to keep him running straight ahead. McCauley brought the steer to a halt in the deep black dirt in the middle of the ring, but his time wasn't all that fast and as he rode out he didn't look happy about it.

The dog act followed, giving the contestants time to get ready for the saddle-bronc event.

"You ever see Dallas ride?" Shari asked, standing next to Patience behind the fence.

"Only on TV." Her gaze fixed on the cute little dog in the arena standing two-legged on the handle of a broom.

"You don't like him much, do you?"

She managed a nonchalant shrug. "I hardly know him. Why would I dislike him?"

Shari grinned. "Stormy said the two of you got off to a rocky start."

Patience watched a second clown in a gigantic pair of Wranglers rush into the ring. "I guess you could call it that. He's all right, I guess. If you don't mind a guy whose ego is as big as his hat."

Shari laughed. "Wait till you see him ride."

More excited by the prospect than she cared to admit, Patience followed Shari up to the fence in the area set aside for the riders' families.

"Ladies and gentlemen," the announcer called out. "Please turn your attention to chute number three. Two time World Champion All-Around Cowboy Dallas Kingman on a horse called Cyclone."

There was a racket in the chute, the jingle of spurs as Dallas settled himself in the saddle and words of encouragement from the cowboys hanging over the gate, helping him get ready to make his ride. He pulled his hat down low across his forehead, settled himself even deeper in the saddle, and nodded for the gate to open.

"My friends—this is a horse that can buck!"

An instant later, the powerful buckskin leapt out of the chute and straight up into the air. Black and gold fringe went flying, spurs flashed in the arena spotlights, saddle leather creaked, and hooves pounded as the massive horse crashed back to earth. The animal spun to the right, then bolted up and twisted, kicking wildly to dislodge the cowboy on his back.

Dallas Kingman rode him as if he were on a Sunday outing. It was impossible for a man to look graceful with a horse leaping and bucking, kicking and spinning beneath him. It was impossible, but Dallas Kingman managed to do it.

"When he rides, they call him The King!" the announcer shouted, and Patience knew exactly what he meant.

It wasn't the same as watching a horse and rider on TV. Not nearly the same. As the eight seconds ticked past, Patience found herself holding her breath. Her pulse thrummed and her adrenaline pumped so hard her head began to spin. Then, the buzzer sounded and the crowd went wild. Up in the stands, the arena lights illuminated people cheering, throwing empty popcorn cartons into the air and wildly stamping their feet. Dust drifted into the bleachers, covering the fans, leaving them nearly as dusty as the cowboys.

She returned her attention to Dallas, who grabbed the shoulders of one of the pickup men, slid off Cyclone, and landed neatly on the ground. His chaps flicked against his boots as he made his way back toward the chutes, raised his hat and waved to the crowd. She had watched enough rodeo to know the ride had been spectacularly good. She wasn't surprised when the score came back at ninety-one points, putting Dallas Kingman in the lead.

She tried not to be impressed, but there was no use lying to herself. The man was a champion. She could respect that about him if nothing else.

Shari left her at the fence to watch the rest of the show and went out to the warm up area where Button, Shari's barrel-racing horse, stood waiting. Patience watched the barrels being driven into the arena in the back of a big Dodge truck. Half a dozen cowboys rolled them out to form a triangle in the center of the ring and the racing was ready to begin.

Shari was the third contestant. Button roared off the starting line, Shari leaning over his neck as they headed for the barrel to the left. She took him though the first turn, the sorrel's long body curling perfectly around the barrel without knocking it over—a penalty that would add five seconds to her time—and the horse charged for the second. They made a figure eight, looping around the second barrel, took the third, then the low-running sorrel stretched out for the drive toward the finish line.

Shari made the run in fifteen and nine tenths seconds, placing her in the top three, which meant she would bring home some money. She was grinning as she blazed past Patience out the gate, knowing she had made a great run.

When the rodeo, a one-day performance, was over, Patience walked to where her soon-to-be-roommate stood talking to a group of other barrel racers. Shari gave her a welcoming smile.

"Nice ride," Patience said.

"Most of the credit goes to Button." Shari rubbed the pretty white star on the sorrel's nose, then turned to the other women.

"Gals, this is Patience Sinclair, the woman I told you about. She's gonna be travelin' with me this summer." She turned to the riders, introducing each of them in turn. Two of them were from Oklahoma, attractive women in their bright-colored barrel-racing clothes.

"And this is Jade Egan. She's from Houston."

"It's nice to meet you," Patience said.

The first two women seemed friendly enough. Though eager to get their animals put away, they offered to give her any help she might need with her article and said good-bye with smiles on their faces.

Jade Egan was another matter entirely. "Patience, huh . . .? That's a funny name. I bet your sister's name is Wisdom."

Patience forced herself to smile. "Actually, their names are Charity and Hope."

"No kidding. Shari says you're from Boston." Jade took in Patience's newly purchased western clothes and a smug smile appeared on her face. "A little far from home, aren't you?"

"She's doing research, Jade. I already told you that."

"Yeah, I guess you did." Jade moved closer. She was small and dark-haired, her skin unblemished and paler than most of the other women, as if she made careful use of her sunscreen.

Patience worked to keep her smile in place. "I'm writing about cowgirls—the modern day sort as well as those of the past. Women's barrel racing evolved from the relay races in the early rodeos. It's an important part of my research."

Jade cocked a winged black eyebrow, her smug smile still in place. "You ever tried it?"

"No. No, I haven't."

"I didn't think so."

"It's time we got going," Shari said to Patience, tugging on her arm. "I need to get Button rubbed down and put away. Tomorrow's gonna be a long day."

Shari led Button back toward the livestock barns and Patience walked beside them, thinking about the women she had met. She wished she had gotten off on a better foot with Jade, one of the event's top contestants, but perhaps in time things would smooth out between them.

"Jade's a spoiled little rich girl," Shari said, apparently reading her mind. "Don't let her get to you."

"She's a good rider. She had the fastest time of the night."

"Oh, she can ride. But her daddy pays for everything. Jade is used to getting what she wants and she doesn't like anyone getting in her way."

Patience stopped and turned. "Am I missing something here?"

Shari tied the sorrel to the pipe fence and began to unbuckle the flank strap on her saddle. "Jade and Dallas used to have a thing. As far as Jade's concerned, they still do. She probably saw you talking to him out on the road when you came in." Shari grinned. "Either that or she thinks you might be competition."

"Actually, I think Jade and Dallas are perfect for each other."

Shari laughed. She loosened the cinch and lifted off the saddle, a lightweight barrel style still steaming underneath from Button's high-speed run.

"He's a beautiful horse." Patience ran a hand down the animal's sweat-slicked neck.

"Button's one of the best barrel horses in the business. I wouldn't trust him with just anyone, but my trailer's falling apart and like I said when you called, I need to save as much money as I can this summer so I can go back to school in the fall. The good news is, I found someone to haul him I know will take good care of him."

"Great."

"You met him earlier . . . Steve Weathers? Everyone calls him Stormy. He travels with Dallas unless Dallas is off at some big rodeo. West Wind Trailers is one of Dallas's sponsors. He's got a custom three-horse rig with one of those fancy built-in RV sleepers. Stormy asked him if they could take Button, and Dallas said it wouldn't be a problem."

Patience ran the information around in her head, a sinking feeling creeping into the pit of her stomach. "That means you'll be going to the same shows as Stormy, right?"

"Yeah, which is good, because he and Dallas always hit the highest paying shows."

Which meant her nemesis, Dallas Kingman, would be around a lot more than she had expected.

"I know what you're thinking and you don't have to worry. Once you get to know him, Dallas is a real nice guy."

Patience just smiled.

So far, the first day of her adventure hadn't been her favorite.

CHAPTER 3

It was late in the evening by the time Patience drove back to the Cozy Nest Motel not far from the rodeo grounds and settled into the spartan room she had rented when she got into town. She was tired from the long, exhausting trip. She hadn't flown directly to Texas, but yesterday had landed in Oklahoma City, then driven today the two hundred fifty odd miles to the little town of Rocky Hill.

It was hard to believe she had actually arrived, that tonight she had attended her first rodeo. She had been so excited and in such a hurry to get to the arena, she had left her cell phone on the dresser in the motel room. She picked it up as soon as she walked through the door and punched in her dad's home number, knowing he would be worried if he didn't hear from her soon.

His wife, Tracy, answered. Patience had been eleven when her father had married Tracy, just twenty-six at the time. The two of them had wound up being more like sisters than mother and daughter. Still, Tracy sounded relieved to hear her voice. Patience knew she wasn't the only one who had been changed by Tyler Stanfield. Her family had suffered as well.

Tracy asked if everything was going all right, seemed satisfied that it was, and handed her husband the phone.

"Hi, sweetheart." Ed Sinclair was a little taller than average, with salt-and-pepper hair and dark, square-framed glasses. Kind of scholarly looking, Patience had always thought, but then, he was a professor.

"Hi, Dad. Just wanted to let you know I got here without any trouble." She had gotten there just fine. The trouble had started once she arrived. "Shari's really nice," she continued, careful not to mention Jade Egan or Dallas Kingman. "I think we're going to get along just fine."

"That's good to hear. I'm glad you called. I was starting to worry."

"Dad, you promised."

"I know, I know. It's just . . . well . . . Hope said you saw Tyler at the market and I was worried he might have followed you."

"I was careful. I actually changed taxis twice on my way to the airport. I'm sure I was probably being paranoid, but I figured better safe than sorry."

"I think that was wise."

"How's Snickers?" she asked, not wanting to talk about Tyler Stanfield.

"Snickers is fine." Her father and stepmother were taking care of her black-and-white cat while she was away. "He's in the living room with Tracy, watching TV."

The image made her smile. She loved the little cat. She had worried about her pet every day, afraid Tyler might hurt the cat to get back at her.

The conversation was brief. It had been a long, stressful day and she needed to get some sleep. Tomorrow she would be turning in the flashy red convertible and signing the papers on the Chevy pickup and eighteen-foot travel trailer she had bought over the Internet with the money from a small inheritance she and her sisters each received when their grandfather had passed away.

Unfortunately, even after taking out her contact lenses, indulging in a long hot shower, and putting on her cotton nightgown, once she climbed into bed, she was still running so high on adrenaline she couldn't fall asleep. She didn't doze off until after two in the morning. Since she was scheduled to pick up the truck at seven-thirty, then drive to Llano to rendezvous with Shari, she didn't get much rest.

She was tired when the alarm went off, slapping on the button and nearly knocking the clock on the floor, but she had too much to do to dwell on her fatigue. Aside from the thrill of traveling the rodeo circuit, by the end of summer—God willing—she would have the last of her research finished and her thesis completed.

And there was the added bonus she had stumbled onto a little over a month ago. Last summer her sister Charity had started doing work on family genealogy, which she had continued to do even after her marriage and move to Seattle. Recently, Charity had discovered a little-known great grandmother, a relative on their mother's side of the family, a woman named Adelaide Whitcomb.

Adelaide, Charity discovered, had been an early rodeo performer—an interesting coincidence—though Charity didn't believe Patience's long-time interest in the West had anything to do with chance. More like a calling of the blood, her sister would say.

Whatever the truth, as soon as the information surfaced, Patience began writing to distant relatives that Charity helped her track down, determined to learn as much as she could. Amazingly, several family members answered, including a cousin a jillion times removed who lived in Oklahoma City.

"I'm the one who wound up with Aunt Addie's fringed leather riding skirt and cuff guards," her cousin said when they spoke on the phone. "My father told me she wore them in the rodeo when she was eighteen."

Another cousin in the same city claimed to have part of a

set of journals that Patience's great grandmother had written.

"I'll be happy to loan you what I've got," the woman said. "Why don't you stop by so all of us can meet? I didn't even know I had a cousin in Boston."

The experience had been interesting, to say the least, though her Oklahoma relatives were as different from the Boston side of the family as maple syrup and molasses.

Patience had spent the night with Cousin Betty and her husband, George, borrowed the journal, and set out the next day for Texas, hoping the information between the faded tapestry covers would bring a new perspective to her work.

Patience thought of the journal that morning as she turned in the rental car at a Hertz drop-off station, then walked over to where the man with the '94 Chevy pickup and eighteen-foot travel trailer waited at the curb with the engine running.

The owner, a short, stout, gray-haired man with several gold teeth, turned off the motor and led her back to the trailer for a quick inspection. It was immaculately clean and well cared for, she saw, with a cozy little kitchen and dinette area, a bathroom with a minuscule shower, and a set of bunk beds down at one end. The pickup appeared to be in equally good condition, though what she knew about cars wouldn't fill the toe of her boot.

"They both look great," she said to the owner, Mr. Nelson.

"Always kept her in good condition. You do the same, she'll get you where you want to go."

Patience handed him a cashier's check in return for the vehicle pink slips. Mr. Nelson gave her the operating manuals and a quick lesson in how to fill and empty the holding tanks. Once he was finished, she opened the door and climbed behind the wheel. It wasn't big as pickups went, only a half ton, not one of the heavy diesels, but sitting there in the seat, it felt like an eighteen-wheeler.

"Did a little rodeoing myself in my younger years," Mr.

Nelson said, watching her from the passenger side of the ve-hicle as she gave him a ride back to his house. She had seen the rodeo sticker on the bumper but she didn't ask him about it. She needed to get on the road.

"You ever pulled a trailer before?" he asked, sensing her nervousness.

"No, but I'm sure it won't be a problem." She didn't men-tion she had never driven a pickup truck, either.

Mr. Nelson cast her a look, then began to give her tips on handling the rig. By the time they reached his house, her palms had stopped sweating and she had begun to feel a lit-tle more in control.

"You take care now, you hear?" Mr. Nelson said through the passenger window as he climbed out of the truck.

"Thanks, I'll do that." Taking a calming breath, Patience stepped on the gas and headed for the highway leading south to Llano and her rendezvous with Shari, praying Shari would approve of her purchase.

It was hot in Texas that first day of June, hotter than Patience was used to. There wasn't a cloud in the sky and she figured the temperature had to be in the nineties. The collar of her long-sleeved western shirt scratched the back of her neck and her new jeans chafed the insides of her thighs. She cranked up the air-conditioning and settled herself in the slow lane, grateful for the big ugly mirrors on the side of the truck that helped her keep the trailer inside the painted lines.

She was doing okay, driving a little slower than she wanted, but beginning to get the feel of the vehicle. Then she hit a long, steep incline and had to pass a big rig in front of her. Her pulse kicked into gear and her palms started sweating again. As she pulled up next to the big truck and trailer, it seemed like only inches separated the two of them. Once her trailer cleared, she pulled back in front of the truck into the slow lane where she felt a little safer.

Unfortunately, when she glanced down at the temperature gauge, she saw that the dial was leaning hard into the red.

"Oh, God." Searching the distance, all she saw was cactus and desert and vast stretches of bright blue sky. She sighed with relief as she spotted a wide place in the road where she could safely pull over. Slowing the pickup, she drove off to the side, and turned off the engine.

Dammit, she didn't know a blasted thing about engines. She'd once considered taking a class in auto repair designed especially for women and now she wished she had. Knowing it probably wouldn't do any good, she climbed down from the truck, went around to the front and lifted the hood. The radiator smelled hot, and gurgling sounds came from somewhere down inside. She wondered if she should unscrew the cap, but a little voice warned her not to.

Of all the luck! She had her cell phone, of course, but there wasn't a town for miles and it could take hours for a tow truck to get there. Swallowing an urge to swear, Patience stared up the long stretch of road and walked back to her cell phone, resigned to a long wait in the broiling Texas sun.

Dallas followed the ribbon of highway heading toward Llano. There were other, bigger rodeos, shows that paid a lot more money, and if he wanted to wind up in the top fifteen and qualify for the National Finals in Las Vegas in December, he needed to be competing in those. But he was worried about Charlie and he wanted to be around to help as much as he could until things straightened out.

Charlie Carson, his mother's brother, had practically raised him. Dallas had been twelve years old when Jolie Carson Kingman had died. It was Charlie—not Dallas's father—who had stepped in and helped him through the worst time of his life. It was Charlie and his wife, Annie, who had been there when Dallas needed them, and Dallas would never forget what they had done.

After that, Dallas had spent every summer until he was grown on the Circle C Ranch, eight thousand prime, cattle-raising acres southwest of Bandera, in the fabulous Texas Hill Country. It was Charlie who taught him to ride, Charlie who instilled the love of ranching and rodeo that made Dallas the man he was today.

But lately, things hadn't been going so well for Charlie.

Dallas thought of the string of bad luck that seemed to be following the Circle C Production Company. Stock truck breakdowns, drivers not showing up to haul their loads, the PA system going down. Those things happened, of course. It was just part of the business. Still, the problems were beginning to wear on Circle C finances. Even Charlie's usual optimism was starting to wear thin, and Dallas was beginning to get worried that something more than just bad luck was going on.

Hopefully, things would return to normal and Dallas could get back to serious rodeoing. Some of the biggest shows in the country were coming up this summer and he intended to be there, to win as much money as he could. At year's end, based on their total dollar earnings, the top fifteen cowboys in each event were chosen to compete in the National Finals Rodeo. The big money was paid in Vegas, and as he had for the past two years, Dallas intended to win.

He was thinking of Llano and the rodeo coming up in a couple of days, when he spotted a brown Chevy pickup and little white travel trailer stalled in a wide spot on the road. He might not have stopped if he hadn't seen the sticker on the bumper—RODEO ROCKS—and noticed that the driver was a woman.

Checking his wristwatch, hoping he wasn't going to be late for the show, he pulled over behind the trailer, turned off the engine of his big black Dodge dually, and cracked open the door. In the horse trailer behind him, he heard Lobo whicker and reminded himself to check on the three horses inside before he pulled out again.

He was smiling as he approached the rolled-down window of the Chevy, until he caught sight of the woman's face.

Sonofabitch.

Until that moment, he'd been thinking how pretty she was. Yesterday, her blond hair had been mostly hidden by her hat. Today she wore it loose, down past her shoulders. It wasn't curly, just kind of soft and ripply. Her lips were lush and a nice shade of pink.

But her smile slid away as she recognized who he was, replaced by a look of grudging relief tinged with a hint of irritation.

"I appreciate your stopping. I think my engine's overheated."

"I thought you drove a convertible," he said a little more harshly than he meant to.

She shrugged her shoulders. "I rented it for the drive from the airport. It seemed like a good idea at the time."

He started toward the front of the pickup and she scrambled down from the driver's seat and walked up beside him. He caught a whiff of her cologne, something subtle and expensive, and felt a sudden tightening in his groin.

"Radiator's hot. That long grade we just came up will do that if you aren't careful. You didn't have your air conditioner on, did you?"

She straightened a little, looked him in the eye. "Well, yes. In case you haven't noticed, it's broiling hot out here."

His mouth barely curved. "You better get used to it, darlin'. This is a cool spring day in Texas."

She tried to look at him down her nose, but as tall as she was, he was a whole lot taller. "Maybe so, but it feels darned hot to me."

"You were hot, so you decided to ignore the warning signs. You know, the ones that say 'turn off your air conditioner so your car won't overheat.' "

She bit her lip and he felt that unwanted twinge again. Damn, she was pretty.

"I didn't see a sign. I guess I was concentrating too hard on staying on the road."

He glanced from her worried features back to the trailer and a lightbulb went on in his head. "Let me guess—you've never pulled a trailer before."

"Well, no, but I was doing just fine until I got to that hill."

Dallas sighed. A complete greenhorn—and she planned to travel with Shari. Since Stormy had a thing for Shari and had managed to con Dallas into taking care of Shari's horse, this was definitely not good news. "I don't suppose you thought to bring any water?"

"Of course." She turned and raced back to the truck and he couldn't resist looking at those long, long legs. She was nicely put together, he had to give her that. He watched her disappear inside the truck and come back with one of those little, individual-size plastic bottles of water with half the contents gone.

Dallas sighed and started walking back to his truck.

"Where are you going? You're not just going to leave?"

He'd like to. Stormy would kill him if he did. Instead, he grabbed the five-gallon can of water he carried in the bed of his truck and returned to the hood of the Chevy.

"Stand back. Radiators can be dangerous when they get this hot." But the cap had a steam release and a cloud of mist shot into the air. A few minutes later he had the radiator refilled, which cooled the engine down, and the metal cap back on.

"Why don't you start her up?"

"All right." She climbed behind the wheel and cranked the engine, which fired right up. Dallas slammed the hood and checked to make sure it was tight. She was smiling from behind the wheel when he walked to the driver's window.

"Looks like you did it. The gauge isn't showing red anymore."

He nodded. "Out here, you need to carry water. Only an idiot would tackle this road on a day like this with nothing but that little plastic bottle."

The grateful smile slid away. "I'll buy a jug the next time I get gas."

She didn't thank him for stopping, though he figured she would have if he hadn't made that wise-ass remark. He wasn't sure why he had. Maybe it was something to do with his father and stepmother, big-time in Houston society, all show and nothing underneath, just like little Ms. Boston. Whatever it was, there was something about Patience Sinclair that seemed to rub him exactly the wrong way.

"There's a ravine a few feet in front of you," he told her. "You'll need to back up and swing the trailer a little to the right before you pull back onto the road."

The color bled from her face. "Back up?"

"Yeah—as in put the truck in reverse, crank the wheel, and step on the gas."

She swallowed. "Crank the wheel . . . which way?" Her eyes were big and green, her lashes thick and spiky. He could read the trepidation and found himself reaching for the handle and pulling open the door.

"Move over. I'll do it for you."

She didn't budge. Instead, her hands tightened around the wheel, slim fingers and neatly trimmed, white-tipped manicured nails. "I need to learn. I'd rather you just told me what to do."

"Look, Patience, like you said, it's hotter than blazes out here. If you've never done this before, it isn't that easy. It'll take you half the day."

"What if I have to do it when you aren't around?"

"I'll tell you what. When we get to Llano—I presume that's where you're headed." She nodded. "When we get to Llano, I'll show you how to back this thing up, okay?"

She still looked uncertain. He wasn't sure if it was the lesson she was worried about or the fact that he would be the teacher. He didn't much like the idea himself.

"All right, you win," she said. "It really is hot out here." Patience slid across the seat and he climbed up beside her, trying to ignore her great-smelling perfume and the brush of her thigh against his. It didn't take long to jockey the truck and trailer into a better position to get back onto the road. He left the engine running and got down from the cab.

"I appreciate your help," she said a little stiffly, as if she had to force out the words.

"No problem." He didn't say more, just returned to the trailer, checked on Button, Lobo, and Stormy's horse, Gus, then climbed up in the Dodge. He waited till she pulled back onto the roadway, then drove in behind her. He left her crawling along in the slow lane with her windows rolled down. He needed to get to the rodeo grounds and at the speed she was traveling, she wouldn't arrive before midnight.

He couldn't help smiling at the incongruous picture she made in the old brown pickup, her blond hair damp and sticking to her temples, makeup beginning to run in the heat. But even hot and sweaty and dressed in cowboy clothes, she oozed a sense of class. What the hell was an upper-crust woman from Boston doing in Texas?

Dallas shook his head. One thing he knew, rodeo attracted all kinds of people.

Well, Shari's Mr. Nice Guy, Dallas Kingman, was as big a jerk as ever. Sure he had stopped to help. He hadn't recognized her at first, probably thought she was some poor needy female who would crawl all over him with gratitude. Patience would have been a lot more grateful if the man had been halfway pleasant.

At least she was on her way again. Not moving very fast, but rolling along the highway. She had called and cancelled the tow truck when the engine temperature fell back into the moderate zone, then down the road took a chance and put the air conditioner on again. The rush of cool air revived her spirits and she pressed a little harder on the accelerator, building up a bit more speed.

The terrain changed a little, grew less hilly as she rolled south toward Llano. The Texas landscape was rugged. Mostly tumbleweeds, coarse sand, blowing winds, and sagebrush, which seemed to thrive on the hot dry sun. The only break in the vast brown earth stretching out in front of her was a scattering of wildflowers: a few bluebonnets and some bright orange Indian paintbrush.

She stopped for gas in a town called Cherokee and bought a big plastic jug of water, which made her angry at Dallas all over again. She had hoped he might be friendlier the next time they met, but it certainly hadn't happened today. His soft Texas drawl carried an edge he seemed to reserve just for her and those handsome features held a trace of sarcasm he didn't bother to hide.

Which suited her just fine. She wasn't one of those women who made a fool of herself over a pair of blue eyes. She didn't have time for that kind of nonsense. She had far more important things to do.

And so when she finally pulled into the rodeo grounds in Llano, her thoughts were fixed on her research, on the study she needed to complete and the hope that her new roommate would like the trailer she had purchased. If Shari approved, they would need to stock up on supplies so that when the Llano rodeo was over, they would be ready to hit the road.

"Hey, there!" Shari waved and called out as Patience drove the Chevy toward the place where the guard at the gate had instructed her to park. She had no idea how she was going to turn around and grudgingly surveyed the area in search of Dallas. She didn't see him, but she spotted his fancy black Dodge dually and RV horse trailer sitting not far away.

"I see you made it without a problem," Shari said through the window of the truck.

Patience smiled and cracked open the door. "Actually, the engine overheated or I would have been here sooner. Dallas Kingman stopped and helped me out."

"That sounds like Dallas. I told you he was nice."

Patience managed a smile. "Yes, that's what you said."

Shari cast her a glance, but didn't say more. "Pickup looks good. Can I take a look inside the trailer?"

"Sure, come on." They ducked inside the rig and closed the door. Fortunately, there were enough windows that it didn't feel all that crowded. Still, it was hot inside. Patience reached up and turned on the fan above the bunks to stir up a little cool air.

"This is great." Shari tested one of the beds. "The kitchen has a stove and fridge, which is bound to come in handy, and you've got room in the dining area to set up your laptop."

"Yeah, that's what I figured. I was hoping you would think it was okay."

"Are you kidding? I've stayed in a lot worse places than this. We won't be inside much during the day and it's a lot cooler at night. We can always rent motel rooms if we get to feeling claustrophobic. In the meantime, this will save us a lot of money."

Patience turned off the fan and they climbed down from the trailer. "I was wondering . . . by any chance, have you ever pulled one of these?"

Shari nodded. "Horse trailers. This won't be much different."

"I'm glad to hear it because I'm going to need a lesson in backing up."

"No problem. In the morning, I can—"

"I thought I was supposed to give you a lesson." The edge was gone from the drawl. The familiar deep voice made her stomach flutter. She turned to find Dallas Kingman leaning against the side of the trailer, his black felt hat shoved back, a stem of straw stuck between teeth so white he could have posed for a Colgate ad.

"I guess I won't be needing your help after all," Patience told him, thankful it was true. "Shari can teach me whatever I need to know."

He tossed the straw away and his gaze moved slowly

down her body. "Oh, I don't know . . . I might be able to teach you a few things Shari couldn't."

She didn't say a word. Every spot those blue eyes touched was starting to tingle. She didn't understand it. For heaven's sake—they didn't even like each other!

She couldn't help thinking of Tyler Stanfield. At first, she'd been attracted to him, too. Then she'd found out what a jerk he really was. Her track record with men was so bad it was embarrassing. Another figure appeared at the edge of her vision.

"Well, if it isn't Shari's new friend Prudence." At Jade Egan's slur, Patience clamped down on her temper.

"It's Patience, not Prudence. And your name was . . . something to do with a rock, as I recall."

Jade stiffened, and Dallas tugged his hat down to hide a grin. "I guess you two have met," he said.

"Oh, we've met." Jade's smug gaze traveled over Patience's clothes. "Dressed like that, I figured she was from Hollywood, but Shari says it's Boston." Jade flashed a phony smile. "I still haven't figured out what an easterner who's never been on a horse is doing on the rodeo circuit."

Patience opened her mouth, then closed it again. She had been riding since she was a little girl—English, not western, but so what? For the last three summers, she had worked at Parklands Stables, giving riding lessons to children, but that was none of Jade Egan's business.

"Hey, Dallas!" Wes McCauley walked toward them, taller even than Dallas, and bulkier, heavier through the chest and shoulders. "Hotshot's started limping. Can you take a quick look at him for me?"

"Sure. Where is he?"

"Over by my trailer."

Dallas started following Wes, and Jade fell in beside them. Dressed in a gold lamé barrel-racing shirt, gold britches molded to a perfect derriere, Jade smiled up at Dallas, then tossed Patience a backward glance that held a note of warning.

"I told you she was jealous," Shari said. "She wants Dallas back, only I don't think he's interested."

"Why not?"

"Because Jade is spoiled and selfish and Dallas isn't that way."

Patience watched his long-legged stride and noticed the width of his shoulders. She saw the way his faded jeans outlined the muscles in his thighs. A bunch of fans, mostly women, rushed up to him, swarmed around him and Wes. She watched the women fawn over him and felt a fresh wave of dislike for him.

"You can say what you want. I still think he and Jade are a perfect match."

The remark drew a chuckle from Shari. "What's your middle name?" she asked, her gaze following Jade's retreating figure.

"Jean. Why?"

"Because I'm tired of Jade's harassment. Practically everybody in the business has a nickname. From now on you're P.J. You okay with that?"

Patience frowned. "P.J.? It sounds like something you wear to bed."

Shari snorted a laugh. "I'm likin' you better all the time."

Patience grinned. "You know, it kind of has a western ring. I think I like it."

"Good. And tomorrow we're stoppin' at the Laundromat on the way out of town. We're gonna wash those jeans, get out some of the new. And as for that hat—"

Patience snatched the hat off her head and held it in front of her. "What's wrong with my hat? It's a brand new straw Bailey. I bet yours is the very same brand."

Shari shoved her own hat back on her head. "There's nothing wrong with the hat. It's the crimp that's the problem."

"Crimp? What crimp? I don't see any crimp?"

"That's the problem." Shari plucked it out of her hand and started bending the edges. Patience fought an urge to snatch it back.

"There. Now it looks like it's been worn more than once. Put it on; see if it doesn't look better."

With some reluctance, Patience settled the hat on her head and Shari tugged her over to the mirror next to the driver's window of Dallas's truck. The change was subtle, but . . .

Patience turned to Shari. "You know, it does look better."

Shari stared down at Patience's boots, an extra pair that were brown instead of red.

"Don't tell me you hate my boots."

"Those are fine. Save the red ones for when we go dancin' after the perf. You'll get plenty of use out of them, I promise."

"Dancing? You mean like the Texas two-step? I wouldn't have the vaguest notion how to—"

"You'll learn." Shari flashed her a teasing smile. "Maybe Dallas will give you a lesson."

Color washed into Patience's cheeks. "Dallas? Are you kidding?"

But Shari just laughed, and Patience ignored the little curl of heat that formed in the pit of her stomach.

CHAPTER 4

Towering cottonwoods along the banks of the Llano River stretched out around the rodeo grounds. There was an RV Park in the Robinson City complex, which would give Patience and Shari a chance to try out their newly purchased portable sleeping quarters later that night.

The show began right on time, starting with the usual rousing red, white, and blue salute followed by the introduction of local officials and the rodeo queen. It was a hot, dusty day, without the slightest breeze, but none of the cowboys grumbled. Instead, they busied themselves wrapping once-shattered wrists and sprained ankles, sliding protective vests over freshly pressed long-sleeved shirts.

The events went off without a hitch, first bareback bronc riding followed by steer wrestling, then saddle broncs, barrel racing, and bulls.

Shari's ride wasn't fast enough to make any money, but "The King," as usual, wound up winning first place. As soon as the show was over, Patience and Shari headed into town for supplies, returning a few hours later with bedding and blankets, enough water and food for at least the next few days.

Mr. Nelson, the previous owner, had left pots, pans, and a set of plastic dishes in the kitchen, so that was taken care of. Patience suggested they toss a coin for the lower berth but Shari wouldn't hear of it.

"Age before beauty," she teased, being twenty-six, a whole year younger than Patience.

They had planned to eat in that night, but Wes and Stormy stopped by and said the whole gang was going into town for Mexican food and invited them to come along. Stormy said they could all ride in Dallas's truck, and though Patience tried to decline, in the end, she acquiesced, climbing into the backseat next to Wes.

The big black Dodge was cleaner than she expected, the interior smelling of oiled saddle leather and traces of a man's cologne. Shari sat in the front between Dallas and Stormy, while Wes regaled them with the men's exploits over the years.

"Hey, Dallas—remember that time in El Paso? That was the night you were hitting on that little brunette at the Three Jacks, that raunchy strip club downtown. Then her husband came in and started throwing punches." He grinned at Patience. "Damned near cut off Dallas's head with a busted beer bottle before we got the guy calmed down. 'Course it was the husband who wound up getting carried out of the place."

"I didn't know she was married," Dallas said darkly from behind the steering wheel.

"Then there was that time in Rapid City when you—"

"Knock it off, Wes," Dallas warned. "We can all do without the reminiscing—unless you want me to tell the ladies about that time in Las Vegas when you—"

"Okay, okay. I get the message." Wes chuckled and finally fell silent and a few minutes later, they pulled up in front of the restaurant, a place on Bessemer Street called El Paquito. Several other trucks Patience recognized from the rodeo grounds were already parked outside.

When they walked through the door, the rest of their party was seated at a long wooden table that ran the length of the room. She recognized Cy Jennings, the bullfighter, and a barrel racer named Tammy Stockton sitting next to Jade Egan.

The El Paquito had a rustic, authentic Mexican look with a round fireplace at one end, reed ceilings, and red tile floors. Wes sat down on the bench beside her and Dallas sat across from her on the opposite side, several seats down from Jade. No one seemed to notice Jade's frown, especially not Dallas, who appeared perfectly content where he was.

Wes, as usual, kick-started the conversation. Shari and Stormy had been calling her P.J. all evening and Wes had begun to pick it up.

"Hey, P.J.," he said. "Hotshot came up with a stone bruise this afternoon. Look's like he'll be down for a couple of days. You interested in doing a little sight-seeing tomorrow? There's a place called Enchanted Rock I heard about, maybe fifteen, twenty miles away. Supposed to be an interesting place."

Patience smiled. "Actually, I've read about it. It's a big pink granite boulder on something like six hundred acres. The Indians believed it held special powers."

"Really?" Tammy reached over to pick up a tortilla chip. "What kind of powers?"

"Well, they said lights flickered at the top and they could hear this eerie groaning—which, I guess is actually the rock heating up in the daytime and cooling down at night. The Comanche used to make human sacrifices to appease the gods who lived there."

"You're kidding." Shari dipped a chip into a bowl of salsa. "I thought only the Aztecs did that."

"In the early eighteen hundreds, one tribe captured the daughter of a rival chief and carried her off to the mountain. As the story goes, the woman's betrothed was a young Spanish don. When he found out Rosa had been stolen, he rounded

up men and rode out to rescue her. He found her tied to a
stake, piles of wood stacked around her, ready to go up in
flames. They say the young don went nearly crazy. He rode
into the Indian camp, fighting like a madman. In the end, he
saved his beloved and they rode off together."

Patience smiled, until she realized the entire table had
fallen silent and Dallas Kingman was staring at her as if she
had grown two heads.

"How do you know all that? I thought you said you'd
never been here."

"I-I told you—I read about it." In the fall, when she started
her job as an assistant professor at Evergreen Junior College,
the subject she would be teaching was the History of the
American West. Texas was a particular favorite. Because the
story was so romantic, she had remembered the legend of
Enchanted Rock.

"That's pretty cool," Wes said. "If it's true."

She could have given him dates and names, but she had
talked too much already.

"I'm hungry," she said a little too brightly. "What's everyone having to eat?"

Dallas studied Patience Sinclair. P.J., Shari called her. There
was something incongruous about the woman, had been from
the start. She was from Boston. Enchanted Mountain was thousands of miles away. Yet he would bet his last dollar her story
was true. Apparently, she was smarter than he gave her credit
for.

The waitress appeared and everyone began to order.

"Shari says you've been here before." Patience smiled at
the group. "Anybody got any suggestions?"

A few seats down the table, Tammy spoke up. "We eat
here whenever we're in town. Why don't you let us order for
you?"

Patience closed her menu. "Thanks. That would be great."

"How about a beer?" Wes asked.

"Better yet, how about a Prairie Fire?" Jade suggested. "The first time you come to the El Paquito, you have to drink a shot of tequila. It's kind of a tradition."

Dallas started to say something. He knew what was in a Prairie Fire and it wasn't good. Down the table, Shari caught his eye. Looking resigned, she slowly shook her head, warning him to keep silent.

Patience was studying the others. He figured she could tell by the grins they tried to hold back that something was up. She turned and smiled at Jade. "Why not?"

Bottles of beer, icy margaritas, and a shot glass of tequila arrived, which the waitress set in front of Patience.

Everyone held up a glass. Dallas took a little longer raising his. He wasn't sure how he felt about Patience Sinclair, but he hated to see anyone put to this kind of test.

"Welcome to rodeo," Tammy said brightly.

"Down the hatch!" said Wes, taking a big swig of beer.

Patience lifted the shot glass. "Down the hatch," she repeated and tossed back the drink.

Dallas's teeth clenched in sympathy. A Prairie Fire was a shot of tequila with a dash of black pepper and the El Paquito's famous Hotter-Than-Hot Sauce, made with jabenero chili peppers. Patience's eyes filled with tears and her mouth opened and closed in an effort to drag in air, though none seemed forthcoming. Tears ran down her cheeks, which were the color of Tabasco, and she started to cough and wheeze. Grinning, Wes slapped her on the back while Tammy and the others fell over in gales of laughter.

It was a dirty thing to do to a greenhorn, but it really had become a sort of tradition.

"Bring her a glass of milk," Dallas told the waitress, who raced away the minute she saw Patience's empty drink.

"It'll get better in a minute," Dallas promised, though a

minute with your entire body on fire felt more like an hour, as Dallas and the others knew firsthand.

She was still making a sort of wheezing noise, but the tears had finally stopped. Her water glass was empty, not that it had done a lick of good, but the milk seemed to help. Patience chugged the liquid and set the glass back down on the table, wiping her lips with a paper napkin.

When she spoke, her voice sounded hoarse. "Gee, guys, thanks a lot. That was really terrific, but I'm still kind of thirsty. Maybe I ought to have another one."

The table erupted into hysterical laughter and even Dallas found himself smiling. She was a pretty good sport—for an easterner.

"One's the house limit," he said, and caught a flicker of gratitude in those pretty green eyes.

"Too bad," she croaked. "Maybe next time."

Shari was proud of her, he saw, beaming at Patience as if she had just won an endurance race. Wes and the barrel racer were grinning. Jade's phony smile looked riveted in place.

She didn't like Patience Sinclair. That definitely gave Ms. Boston a mark in the plus column, as far as Dallas was concerned.

He watched her off and on through supper. She intrigued him. No doubt about it. He wondered what her story was and made a mental note to find out. If he didn't think there would be serious complications, he might not mind getting into P.J. Sinclair's very snug, very well-filled-out jeans.

But he had a feeling there would be. Shari and Stormy had been casting long glances at each other all evening. Stormy and Dallas were hauling Shari's horse, which meant Dallas and Patience were bound to be thrown together. With the Circle C problems and having to miss some of the bigger shows, Dallas needed more trouble like a hole in the head.

Fortunately, he didn't think Patience felt the same unwanted attraction for him he was beginning to feel for her, which should have made him happy and somehow irritated him instead.

Dallas watched her scrape the hot sauce off her enchilada and take a tentative bite. A long string of yellow cheese slid past her lips and his groin tightened. Beneath the table, he went hard.

Damn woman. She was definitely a temptation. Dallas was grateful he would be leaving for New Mexico as soon as tomorrow's performance was over. Temptation was always easier to resist when it was kept well out of sight.

Shari was up and gone when Patience rolled out of her bunk the following morning. Her roommate had a horse to take care of and since she had been raised on a farm, she was pretty much a morning person. Shari came from Guymon, Oklahoma, a longtime, major rodeo town. With her dad's coaching, she had started barrel racing when she was ten years old.

Fortunately, her father had insisted she finish high school before she started rodeoing full time. It was good she had. Last year, she had decided to continue her education, get at least a two-year degree then see what her options were.

Shari got up early, but Patience preferred to stay up a little later, then sleep till seven-thirty or eight, a routine which gave them both more room in the tiny RV.

It didn't take long to shower and dress. Patience's freshly laundered, now slightly faded jeans were a lot more comfortable, and, except during performances, instead of the stiff western shirts she'd been wearing, she wore scoop-necked cotton tops, cooler in the Texas heat.

Eager to get back to the research she had been doing before she left Boston, she ignored her contacts, pulled on a comfortable pair of tortoiseshell glasses and spent the morning at her computer. She worked an hour typing the mental notes she had made about the women rodeo contestants she had met, then dug out the information she had collected on early rodeo women, the very first *cowgirls,* the name they gave themselves way back then.

As a student of western history, Patience had read hundreds of articles about these pioneer women and studied dozens of photos. Like the barrel racers of today, they were flashy dressers, their bright satin embroidered shirts and split leather riding skirts outrageous by early nineteenth century standards. They wore bloomers, colored boots, big-roweled silver spurs, and extravagant, wide-brimmed, high-crowned hats that made the Stetsons of today look bland in comparison.

Often competing in the same events as men—riding broncs and bulls, calf roping, and running relay races, they were the feminists of their day, women like Kitty Canutt, Prairie Rose Henderson, Tillie Baldwin, and dozens of others.

Annie Oakley was one of the first, back in the Wild West Show days. Scores of women followed over the years. It was exciting to know that Patience's great grandmother had actually been one of them.

Patience sat down and opened the faded tapestry cover of the journal. The pages were tattered and frayed and a number of them were missing. Though her cousin had never finished reading it, Betty believed there might be at least one more book, since this one seemed the continuation of a story already started.

Patience looked down at the faded blue writing. The first yellowed page was dated June 18, 1912. From Charity's genealogical work, Patience knew Adelaide Holmes, at that time unmarried and using her maiden name, would have been eighteen.

What a day we had. Kitty scored high in the saddle broncs and my team won the relay races, which made

*the colonel happy he had picked us. After the show, I
met a cowboy named Sam Starling. He asked me out to
supper but I said no. Kitty warned me he was a terrible skirt chaser and she ought to know. But he surely
was good-looking.*

Patience laughed. Maybe times hadn't changed as much
as she thought since 1912. For the next half hour, she continued reading the journal. Though the pages were loose, missing, and often not in order, the information was incredibly
valuable to her work.

*One of the girls on the relay team quit today. Said she
was sick of traveling. Said she wanted to go back home.
The colonel's gotta find a replacement. Since we all need
to make some money, I surely do hope she can ride.*

The colonel was Thaddeus Howard, producer of Colonel
Howard's Wild West Show. Patience read on, beginning to
feel as if she were getting to know Addie Holmes. She took
some notes and read some more. As she set the pen back
down on the Formica-topped table, a page fluttered out from
farther back in the book.
Patience's eye caught on the writing as she bent to pick it
up.

*He was out there again today. I saw him when I got
ready to race. I don't like the way he watches me. Sometimes when I go into town with some of the gals, I feel
like he's there behind us. I keep telling myself I'm bein'
a fool. Surely I am. I guess it doesn't matter. It won't do
a lick of good to worry about it.*

Patience's skin crawled as images of Tyler Stanfield crept
into her head. It was silly. The writing was nearly a hundred

years old. The entries didn't have the least similarity to what had happened to her. Still, she searched through the journal, trying to find the spot where the page had come loose, but none of them were numbered. She couldn't help wondering who the man was and what had happened, and started reading madly again.

She read for another half hour, but couldn't figure out where the page fit in the journal and she refused to spoil the fun of getting to know her grandmother by leaping way ahead. Then Shari showed up and it was time to get over to the rodeo grounds. Reluctantly, Patience set the journal and her glasses aside and went to put in her contact lenses.

She wondered if Sam Starling would reappear in the pages, or if perhaps he was the man Adelaide Holmes had begun to fear.

A hot Texas sun beat down, the temperature lessened only by a few clouds drifting overhead. In the distance, ripples of heat rose over the asphalt highway that stretched from the rodeo grounds off toward the horizon. Patience walked into the contestants' area just as the afternoon performance began.

"Ladies and gentlemen, will you please rise for the national anthem." Cowboys paused where they stood, each removing his hat and placing it over his heart. It was the usual flag-waving, patriotic opening and it never failed to bring a lump to Patience's throat.

Shari had told her that Dallas was entered in the calf roping and she was curious to watch him perform. To her chagrin, he looked as good swinging a loop from the back of a galloping horse as he did riding a bronc. The calf shot out of the chute full speed and Lobo bolted after it. Dallas's rope sailed out, floated down over the head of the calf, then Lobo's rein jerked to a halt. The calf hit the end of the rope and swung around to face him. Dallas was off the horse before it came to a sliding stop and raced down the rope.

He downed the calf, jerked the pigging string out of his mouth, gripped and tied three of the animal's feet, then threw up his hands to signal his finish. All the while, the palomino quarter horse worked with precision to keep the calf in place.

Dallas's time was good, but not good enough to win. He walked back to his horse, slid his boot into the stirrup, and swung into the saddle. As he rode out of the arena, Patience noticed the scowl on his face.

The rest of the rodeo rushed past. During the bull riding, one of the cowboys took a bad spill, then the big Brahma gored him in the shoulder before the clowns could get him to safety. The ambulance hauled him away covered in blood, but it looked as if he were going to be all right.

She was tired by the time the afternoon ended. She returned to the trailer to find Wes McCauley standing next to her door. She had dodged his invitation to Enchanted Rock. This time he asked her out to supper. Wes was an attractive man, in a big, beefy sort of way. She told herself she would have a good time, but in the end she refused, thinking of Tyler Stanfield and her rotten luck with men.

Shari arrived a few minutes later, disappointed with her race and a little disheartened. They decided to wait until morning when both of them were rested before they set off on the long drive to New Mexico. According to Shari, Dallas would also be getting an early morning start.

"He won't be coming to Clovis. He's flying up to Canada for a couple of big-money rodeos in Alberta, one in Innisfail and the other in a place called Ponoka. Stormy's meeting up with him again in Silver Springs."

Shari was going out to dinner with Stormy and Dallas and asked Patience to come along but she declined, preferring to spend a little more time with the journal.

It was getting late. The night was clear and black, stars

everywhere—nothing at all like the sky at night in Boston. She pulled on an oversize T-shirt Shari had loaned her that said *Every Woman Loves A Cowboy—Or Will* on the front, looking forward to crawling into her bunk and getting the chance to read. Charlie, the Circle C crew, and all the big livestock trucks had left right after the show.

Most of the contestants had also left, though Dallas's fancy rig still sat parked in the RV area.

Patience had promised to check on Button before she went to bed so she slipped on a pair of Reeboks, checked to make sure no one was around, then ducked out of the trailer.

Tied next to Lobo and Stormy's horse, Gus, Shari's long-necked sorrel nickered softly at her approach. All of the horses munched flakes of hay and looked perfectly content. She gave them each a few pats, then headed back to the trailer, using the flashlight she kept beside the door to find her way. She had almost reached the RV when she heard it, kind of an eerie rattling sound.

Her pulse shot up. She remembered Shari's warning to watch out for rattlesnakes this time of year and a chill slid down her spine. The rattle came again. The flashlight shook in her hand as she frantically searched the ground around her feet, but nothing appeared in the small yellow circle of light and she started to inch her way back toward the trailer.

Almost there, she thought, her heart still pumping. Silently, she berated herself for not leaving on the light outside the door. Instead, just as she took another step, the rattle came again and something brushed against her leg.

Patience screamed and started running. She didn't realize she had dropped the flashlight until she crashed headlong into an object in the path right in front of her.

"What's your hurry?" Dallas drawled, his arms locking around her.

Patience swallowed, looking wildly back over her shoulder. "S-snake," she said, her voice shaking nearly as much as her body. "I h-heard it rattle. It's somewhere right around here."

Dallas just laughed. "I don't think so."

For the first time it dawned on her she was wrapped around him like a warm tortilla, and color rushed into her cheeks. She released her arms from around his neck, still searching the ground for the snake, and Dallas let her go. He bent and picked up the light, shined it across the ground onto a long, odd-shaped animal completely covered in what looked like hammered silver armor.

"Armadillo," he said. "They're harmless. I guess they do sound a little like a rattlesnake."

She felt like a fool. How was it he always managed to do that to her? "I thought you went to dinner with Shari and Stormy," she said a bit defensively.

"I did. I caught a ride back with someone else."

Jade Egan? she wondered. "I promised Shari I'd make a quick check on the horses, but they seem to be doing just fine. Since the snake wasn't a snake, I think it's time I went back in."

"Yeah," he said, his eyes running over her thin white T-shirt, which covered only a pair of white cotton panties. "Looks like you're getting cold."

It was hardly cold. In fact, it was pleasantly warm. But her nipples stood embarrassingly rigid beneath the cloth. She could still remember the way they felt pressed into Dallas's chest.

She turned away from him, irritated by the knowing look in his eyes and his continuing perusal of her body.

"Good luck in Canada," she said, only half meaning it.

He nodded. "See you in Silver Springs."

Silver Springs. As Patience climbed the stairs to the trailer, she thought of Dallas, felt the throb of desire in her breasts, and found herself wishing she were driving the opposite way.

* * *

Charlie Carson drove his white Dodge pickup through the gates of the Circle C Ranch. He'd missed Annie like the devil, and with all the trouble he'd been having, damn, it felt good to be home.

He drove along the tree-lined lane leading up to the ranch house, a two-story white-framed building with porches on all four sides. Dark green shutters hung at the windows and three redbrick chimneys stuck out of the roof. The original house had been built sometime early in the century but he and Annie had remodeled and expanded the place over the years.

He relaxed a little at the welcome sight and smiled at the horses galloping beside the truck as he drove along the fence line, the small herd splashing through the stream that cut through the pasture up ahead.

He reached the house and stepped on the brake, throwing up a cloud of dust. Normally, Annie would have cautioned him to drive more slowly, but today she just shoved open the screen door and ran toward him. Charlie climbed out of the pickup and the moment he reached her, she rushed into his arms.

"I'm so glad you're home."

"Me, too, honey." He held her a moment, thinking that she felt a little thinner than she had before he'd left. She knew he'd been having problems. She was worried, same as he was.

"Come on in. I'll fix you something to eat. You're probably half starved."

He wasn't really hungry but he loved the way she fussed over him. Fact was, he loved darn near everything about her.

She poured him a cup of thick black coffee, set it down on the kitchen table in front of him, then started scurrying around, opening the fridge, taking out the fixin's to make him a roast beef sandwich.

"Any more trouble?" she asked. She was a slender woman

with iron gray hair, but at sixty, she looked years younger. And she had always been pretty.

Charlie sighed. "One of the trucks broke down on the road on the way out of Llano. Had to call a tow truck. Didn't take long to fix it, but it wasn't cheap."

"Seems like if it isn't one thing lately, it's another. But those things happen, I guess."

"We been lucky over the years. I'd say we've had less trouble than most folks. I guess things just kinda started pilin' up."

"I suppose."

"How things been goin' here?"

Annie set a big Dagwood sandwich down in front of him made with homemade bread and piled with thin-sliced roast beef, then sat down in the chair next to his. "To tell you the truth, we been havin' a little trouble of our own."

He set the sandwich back on his plate without taking a bite. "What kinda trouble?"

"Some of the cattle's come up missing. Maybe a dozen head. I called Sheriff Mills. He's lookin' into it."

The sandwich sat untouched on his plate. Whatever small appetite he'd had was now completely gone. "A dozen, you say?"

"That's what Ben says." Ben Landers was his foreman, had been for nearly twenty years.

"I'll talk to him, then drive over and see the sheriff this afternoon. Maybe he's found out who took 'em."

Annie stood up and walked behind him, leaned over and wrapped her arms around his shoulders. "Folks have problems, Charlie. Like you said, we've had less than our share."

He caught hold of her hands, kissed the back of each one. "You and me, we're good at solving problems. We'll get through these, just like we always have."

Annie nodded, straightened away from him. "Tell me about our boy. How's Dallas?"

Charlie grinned. The man he and Annie had raised as a

son was his pride and his favorite subject. Charlie launched into a replay of Dallas's last few rides and for a while his problems were forgotten.

Charlie just wished he could bury them for good.

CHAPTER 5

Dallas kicked ass in Alberta. He drew a horse named Five Minutes to Midnight, a big black, Finals horse, scored ninety points and took home the purse, a fat one in Innisfail, one of the top pro rodeos around.

Then he'd called Charlie in Texas to tell him the good news, and the moment he had heard his uncle's voice he had known that something was wrong. Under threat of torture, Charlie had finally told him about the breakdown on the road and the stolen Circle C cattle. Whoever had done it hadn't taken many head, but Dallas knew that along with everything else, it was badly disheartening to Charlie.

And it bothered the hell out of Dallas. He wished he could be there to help

In Ponoka, he drew a good bucker, lost his concentration and landed facedown in the dirt. It hadn't happened to him in a while. Maybe it was good for him, humble him a little and get him back on track.

After the rodeo, a sassy little redhead he remembered from the year before had invited him over to her place for a drink. He hadn't really wanted to go, but his pride was bruised and he was worried about Charlie. He figured maybe some hot, no-strings sex would help him forget for a while.

Debbie—he thought that was her name—seemed to be up for the idea. Sitting on the sofa in the living room of her apartment, he watched her peel off her clothes.

"Come on, cowboy." She tugged him to his feet. "Let's go into the bedroom. I've always had a secret yen to make love to a guy wearing only his hat and boots."

Somehow the notion annoyed him. Still, he let her drag him into the bedroom and strip away his clothes. It didn't take long to get in the mood. He hauled her down on the bed and came up over her, parted her legs and drove himself inside her.

He should have gone slower. Usually, he prided himself in giving a woman the same pleasure he took for himself, but lately he'd had it with women who seemed to be using him even more than he was using them. The whole one-night stand thing was starting to lose its appeal. He found himself wanting a little of the closeness Stormy had found with Shari but he couldn't afford that kind of attachment. Not at this point in his life, at any rate.

Dallas had goals, plans, dreams. Someday he wanted to own a ranch like the Circle C. From the day he'd quit college and started full time into professional rodeo, he had known exactly what he was after. Since then, he had won a lot of money and saved a good deal. In five or six years, he'd have enough to buy his ranch and retire from the sport—assuming he didn't get hurt.

In the meantime, he would settle for what he had with Darlene, or Debbie, or whatever her name was. Pound into her until he found release, then get up and get the hell out of Dodge. He would leave commitment to guys like Stormy, guys who expected a whole lot less out of life than he did.

He thought of his friend as he got off the little commuter plane that landed in Silver Springs. Inside the terminal, Dallas recognized Stormy's lean, smiling face, lanky build, and slightly bowlegged walk coming down the concourse toward the gate.

"Hey, buddy!" Stormy slapped him on the shoulder. "Glad to have you back." They shook hands and started for the baggage claim to pick up Dallas's gear, including the bronc saddle he felt naked without. He always hated to check it, but when he flew commercial, he didn't have much choice.

"I heard you kicked butt," Stormy said with a grin.

"Yeah. I also got my butt kicked."

Stormy laughed. "Vegas and Reno are coming up. You can make up for it in Nevada."

They picked up his bags and he settled into the passenger side of his truck while Stormy slid into the seat behind the wheel.

"How's Lobo?" Dallas asked once they were headed for the rodeo grounds.

"Pouting because you've been gone. He'll be glad to see you."

His horse would be glad to see him. That was something, he guessed. An image of Patience Sinclair popped into his head. Why, he had no idea, since she was one person who wouldn't be the least bit glad he was back. During his time in Canada, he had tried to put her out of his mind, but thoughts of her kept creeping in. He'd thought of her even when he was in bed with Debbie, which really pissed him off.

Patience was hardly his type. He liked his women hot and wild—the exact opposite of P.J. Sinclair. Or maybe she was just playing hard to get. Still, as he turned off the engine and climbed out of the truck, he found himself looking for her little white trailer.

And the fact that he was irritated the hell out of him.

"Admit it—you're attracted to him." Sitting in the trailer, Shari shoved away her paper plate, crowded with bones from a Kentucky Fried Chicken supper. The Clovis Rodeo had ended last night. Today they were parked in the field outside the arena in the town of Silver Springs.

"That's ridiculous. We've been oil and water since the day we met."

"Sometimes it starts out that way."

"Is that what happened with you and Stormy?"

Shari shook her head. She had tied back her curly red hair and small gold earrings glittered in her ears. "Me and Stormy . . . we were attracted right off. The problem is I've commitments and so does he and they don't fit together very well. Right now we're having fun, getting to travel together more than we normally would. We haven't . . . you know." Her cheeks turned a little pink. "Not all the way, at least. We agreed just to let things go for a while and see where they lead."

"Well, at least the two of you have things in common. Similar lifestyles, similar interests. Dallas and I—think about it. In the fall, I start a teaching job as an assistant professor. Dallas is . . . Dallas is a cowboy."

Shari grinned. "The World Champion All-Around Cowboy."

"Well, it doesn't matter what he is. Dallas isn't interested in me and I'm not interested in him."

Which was good because he had avoided her ever since his arrival in Silver Springs and she had made a point of avoiding him.

He was nowhere to be seen when the rodeo was over late that night. He'd been bucked off the horse he had drawn, then in the calf roping, he had broken the barrier—the string that marked the head start the calf was given—which cost him a ten-second penalty and any chance of landing in the money. He had obviously gone off to lick his wounds and she told herself she didn't care.

Everyone was tired after the evening performance, but it

was Friday night and Shari and Stormy wanted to go out dancing. They refused to let her stay home.

"You came here to learn about rodeo," Shari said. "Well, what we do after the perf is an important part of the life you're writing about."

True enough. And part of her really did want to go, even if she couldn't dance the Texas two-step.

The sign above the door read The High Desert Saloon and the parking lot was so full of cars Stormy had trouble finding a place to park Dallas's pickup. There had to be some secret code she hadn't yet figured out because all the contestants seemed to know where the local hot spot was in each town.

The bar was buzzing, packed to the rafters when they walked in. A lot of the Silver Springs riders lived within driving distance, which meant a number of Hispanic and Indian cowboys were competing. One of the guys she had met was extremely good-looking, a bareback rider named Blue Cody who was part Navajo, with black hair and dark eyes and incredible cheekbones. Shari had introduced them and Patience noticed him tonight as they pushed through the doors of the saloon and wove their way up to the bar.

The place rang with a combination of honky-tonk, old-fashioned western music, hot country, and good ole rock and roll. In Boston, she never listened to country music, but Shari played it in the pickup whenever they were on the road. Patience had to admit she was beginning to enjoy it.

Especially here, in this loud, smoky, low-ceilinged bar that flashed with neon beer signs, had a big wooden dance floor overflowing with couples in cowboy clothes, and everyone laughing. From what she'd seen so far, most of the serious cowboys didn't drink or party much until the rodeo was over, but those who were already out of the money or just wanted to have a good time showed up in the bar after the performance was over.

She found herself searching for Dallas, but Stormy had

his truck, and besides, he would be riding tomorrow. It wasn't likely he would be out on the town. Especially since he had done so poorly today. She didn't believe he took many falls, at least not as hard as the one he had taken that afternoon. She hated to admit it, but it scared her to see him thrown into the fence then get up and rub his injured shoulder. He had picked up his hat a little stiffly then walked with his head down out of the arena.

But Shari had said he was fine, just a little bruised up and mad at himself for making some stupid mistake coming out of the chute.

Dallas wasn't there, but Wes McCauley was and so was that Navajo cowboy, Blue Cody.

As Stormy shoved an icy bottle of beer into her hand, Blue came up to where she stood and pulled off his broad-brimmed black hat.

"Hey, P.J. How about a dance?"

She smiled. "I'd love to dance with you, Blue, but I'm afraid I don't know how to do the two-step."

Blue grinned. "No problem. I'll teach you."

She hesitated only an instant as Tyler's face flashed in her mind, and she realized how paranoid she still was. Blue wasn't Tyler and this was supposed to be an adventure. "All right— if you're sure your feet can stand it."

Blue took her hand and led her out on the floor. Fortunately, the song ended just then and the disk jockey started playing an old Rolling Stones rock song, "Jumpin' Jack Flash," so she didn't have to try to learn anything new. It was fun dancing again, something she hadn't done in years, and she found herself laughing, just like everyone else.

The dance ended and Wes McCauley stood waiting at the edge of the floor. The DJ started playing "Bubba Shot the Juke Box" and Wes dragged her out in the middle of the crowd, determined to teach her his version of the two-step. But the man's feet were as big as his body and mostly he just whipped her around until her neck was sore and her feet black and blue. Patience was eternally grateful when the song came to an end.

She passed on the next cowboy who asked her, returned to the bar, and climbed up on the stool Stormy gave up for her. "I don't think I'm cut out for this."

Shari laughed. "You'll get the hang of it."

Patience sipped her beer. A slow song started, Garth Brooks, "Beaches of Cheyenne," and she felt a tug on her arm.

"How 'bout a dance?" Dallas asked. He didn't wait for an answer, just hauled her off the stool, across the room, and out onto the dance floor. Before Patience had time to prepare herself, she was wrapped in his arms.

God, he felt even better than he had the last time he had held her. He was wearing the same sexy cologne she had noticed in his truck and his dark, neatly trimmed hair teased her hand at the back of his neck. He was holding her so close she could feel the snaps on his western shirt, and it occurred to her she was following his lead as if they had danced together a hundred times.

He was a very good dancer—no surprise there. Dallas was good at whatever he did. The notion struck out of the blue— *he's probably as good in bed as he is on the dance floor.*

Sex with Dallas Kingman. It was a completely unexpected and totally unwanted thought—and a daunting one.

Dallas might be good in bed, but Patience was a complete and utter failure. She could still hear Tyler's mocking words the day she had broken off with him, telling her what a terrible lover she was. Worst of all, as much as she disliked him, she was afraid it might be true.

"I didn't think you'd be here," she said to Dallas, forcing herself to smile.

"Why not?"

"You have to ride tomorrow."

His dark brows pulled into a frown. "If I ride the way I did today, whether I come here or not won't make a fiddler's damn." There was an odd cadence in his voice. For the first time, she realized that he had been drinking. More than just a little.

"You're drunk."

"So?"

"I don't think you should be drinking when you have to ride. You might end up getting hurt."

He drew back to look at her. "And I suppose you'd care."

Patience glanced away. "Of course I'd care. I-I don't like seeing anyone get hurt."

Dallas stared down at her and something softened for a moment in his features. His body brushed hers as they danced. He tightened his hold and she found herself pressed nearly full length against him. When the dance ended, he eased her into the corner, but he didn't let her go.

Dallas bent his head. "I've been thinking about you." His warm breath feathered over her ear and it was difficult to concentrate. Then the hand at her waist slid down to her bottom and he pulled her even closer. "I've got something for you, honey. You want to find out what it is?"

Patience's eyes flew wide. He was fully aroused and he wanted her to know it. He was looking at her as if she were a saucer of cream he meant to lap up, and at least a dozen people were staring at them.

Patience set her jaw. "I've got something for you, too, *honey.*" Jerking away from him, she drew back and slapped his face.

Dallas's jaw dropped in disbelief. Patience turned and started walking, but Dallas caught her arm. "You know what you need, *P.J?* You need a good hard fucking and I'm just the guy to give you one."

It was all she could do not to hit him again. Instead, she grit her teeth against the name she wanted to call him and walked away, grateful the music had started playing. By the time she reached the bar where Shari and Stormy sat, she was shaking. She'd been right about Dallas Kingman from the start. He was an arrogant jerk and she must have been crazy to feel the least bit of attraction for him.

"Anybody going back to the rodeo grounds?" she asked, trying to keep her voice from trembling.

"I'll take you," Wes offered.

"No need for that." Shari got up from the red vinyl bar stool. "We were just about to leave. There's a rodeo tomorrow and both of us are planning to win."

They left the bar and drove straight back to the rodeo grounds. If Shari or Stormy had seen what happened on the dance floor, they made no comment. At least not until they reached the trailer.

"Dallas hardly ever drinks when he's workin'," Stormy said. "He's not himself lately. He's worried about Charlie and it's affecting his riding. He can't afford to keep losing if he wants to make the Finals this year."

"You don't have to apologize for Dallas," Patience said. "It isn't your fault he's a jerk."

Stormy looked embarrassed. "Like I said . . . he ain't been himself lately."

But Patience thought Dallas was exactly himself—rude and overbearing, arrogant and conceited. A man who was used to getting exactly what he wanted.

Well, he wasn't getting anything from her. Whatever she had begun to feel for Dallas Kingman had evaporated completely.

Patience just wished it didn't bother her as much as it did.

Sonofabitch! Dallas rubbed his stinging cheek and watched Patience Sinclair walk out the door of the saloon with his friends. Sure he was drunk. He'd ridden like a beginner today and it was fast becoming a habit. He never drank when he was riding, but after his dismal performance, he just couldn't seem to get his head on straight. When Ritchie Madden, one of the clowns, had shown up, still wearing most of his face paint, carrying a flask of Jack Daniel's and a six-pack of Coors . . . well, things just got a little out of hand.

Dallas turned at the sound of female voices. Three little blond buckle bunnies gathered around him, grinning up at him from beneath white straw cowboy hats.

"Hey, Dallas—could we have your autograph?"

They were young, but not that young. He could take one of them home if he wanted, work out his frustrations the way he had in Alberta.

One of the girls handed him a ballpoint pen, then turned around so he could sign the back of her T-shirt. One of the others was braver, insisting he sign the front, right above her right breast. She was puffing furiously on a cigarette, talking around the end.

"They're playing a really good song," the short one said. She was the prettiest of the three and obviously interested. "Maybe we could dance."

But Dallas kept thinking of Patience and what he had said to her. Damn, he couldn't believe he had behaved like such an ass. He managed to muster a smile but it wasn't that easy. "Some other time, darlin'."

Turning, he started toward the bar, looking for Ritchie to drive him back to the rodeo grounds. As he crossed the room, he kept seeing Patience's face when he'd made those lewd remarks. She looked like a pretty little filly he'd kicked in the stomach, and that was exactly the way he felt. Like he'd done something rotten to someone who didn't deserve it.

He tried to tell himself it wasn't important. Cowboys got drunk and said that kind of stuff all the time. Not him, but still . . . He wasn't sure why he'd done it, maybe because she'd looked so damned pretty and he'd wanted her and he didn't want to.

He tried to convince himself she'd get over it.

But it didn't make him feel any better.

CHAPTER 6

The Silver Springs Rodeo was part of the small town's annual summer festival, which included a big flashy carnival with games and rides. A neon-lit Ferris wheel turned in the distance. Patience walked past the Scrambler, the Hammer, and the Tilt-A-Whirl, remembering times when she and her sisters had gone to the big state fair with their father.

She had always loved a carnival. She loved to ride the scariest rides, would have gladly climbed aboard any one of them that afternoon if she'd had someone to go with her. But Shari was getting ready for the show, and even Wes was busy. Patience wandered over to the section of the grounds where the carnival games were played, tried her luck with a beanbag toss, took a turn at the shooting gallery, then strolled back to the arena.

When she climbed the stairs to the narrow raised platform where the riders had begun to collect for the rodeo, the crew was still setting up, running the broncs into the chutes and the calves into the trough at the end of the arena. A couple of cowboys sat in saddles resting on the ground, their legs stretched out in front of them, boots in the stirrups, an exercise to limber up the muscles in their calves and thighs.

She didn't see Dallas anywhere around, thank God. She didn't want to see him. She had nothing to say to him and anything he might have to say to her was no longer of interest.

It was crowded up on the platform. The holding pens were below, one full of broncs, the other holding a herd of huge, sharp-horned Brahma bulls. Patience watched the bulls for a while, milling and blowing, stomping and slobbering and rolling their eyes. Their muscles lengthened and bunched beneath their thick skin and she wondered what possessed a sane man to climb up on the back of such a big, brutal creature. It was the danger, of course, the adrenaline rush cowboys craved.

From the corner of her eye, she thought she saw Charlie Carson walking in front of a group of riders. He climbed the stairs along with the men, waved at Patience and she waved back. The riders walked toward her, crowding the platform even more. She didn't want to get in their way so she took a step backward. Someone brushed against her, bumping into her as he passed.

Patience heard herself scream as she started to fall. The ground came up hard, jarring her teeth and bruising her hip, knocking the air out of her lungs. She must have hit her head. For an instant, the world went black.

Her skull was pounding like blazes when she opened her eyes. Then it all came rushing back and she knew that she was in trouble. She was lying on the ground inside the pen behind the chutes and five furious Brahma bulls were staring her in the face.

"Don't move," a man's voice said softly. It was Cy Jennings, the bullfighter, and she was never so glad to see anyone in her life.

"Can you stand up?" another, more familiar voice asked, and she realized two men had jumped into the small, fenced area that held the bulls.

She nodded, but had no idea what would happen when she did. She sucked in a breath and started to move. She felt

Dallas behind her, his arms under hers, helping her to her feet, but the bulls were standing in front of the gate and they weren't budging, and there was no other way out. Climbing over the fence wasn't going to be easy with her head spinning and her legs shaking the way they were.

Cy Jennings kept the bulls' attention fixed on him. "Move around behind me. I'll ease them away from the gate."

Dallas urged her slowly in that direction, moving himself a little in front of her, and she had to admit she was glad he was there. One of the bulls lowered his head and snorted at him, a big iron-gray beast with long, sharp horns that started pawing the ground, throwing up dirt with his heavy front hooves. Cy used his hat to regain the animal's attention, working to circle the bulls away from the gate.

One of them, a massive white, banana-horn bull charged at Cy, and Dallas stepped between them, flashing his hat to draw the beast away. As soon as the gate was clear, one of the cowboys pulled it open.

"Go!" Dallas commanded and Patience ran unsteadily in that direction. She stumbled as she made it through and Wes McCauley caught her. He picked her up and carried her away from the pen and Charlie fell in beside them.

"You okay?" Charlie asked worriedly.

She nodded, twisting her head back toward the pen. "Did the guys get out of there all right?"

"They're fine," Wes said.

"God, Charlie, I'm sorry. I don't know what happened. The platform was crowded. Someone walked past and I guess we must have bumped into each other. One minute I was standing there and the next I was lying on the ground." She didn't tell him that for an instant up there she imagined someone had pushed her. It was just her paranoia kicking in. She had Tyler to thank for that.

Charlie looked back toward the platform. "They don't have

the best setup here. I've always been afraid something like this might happen. You sure you're okay?"

"Just a little shook up. And I guess I hit my head."

Charlie nodded to Wes, who set her down on a saddle blanket someone spread out on the grass. Dallas caught up with them and knelt beside her. For the first time she noticed the Ace bandage wrapped around his shoulder. Half the riders in the show rode with some sort of bandage or sling. Like Dallas, it didn't seem to faze them. Rodeo was an extreme sport. The contestants knew it. They considered injuries part of the game.

"The ambulance isn't here yet," Dallas said. "But it's due any minute." Every show had an ambulance parked behind the chutes during the performance.

"I don't need an ambulance. I already feel like a fool. I hit my head, but I'm sure it's nothing serious."

"Charlie's been after them for years to put up some kind of a railing. Most of us have rodeoed here before so we're used to it. What happened wasn't your fault."

He reached up and slid his fingers into her hair, probing the lump at the back of her head. She winced at a quick shot of pain.

"Pretty good-size goose egg back there. You got a headache?"

"No."

He caught her chin and looked into the pupils of her eyes. "Your eyes don't look dilated. Are you dizzy? Sick to your stomach?"

"I told you I'm fine."

"Can you remember what happened?"

"Yes, like an idiot, I had a run-in with a pen full of two-thousand-pound bulls."

Dallas chuckled. He studied her from beneath the brim of his hat. She could tell he wanted to say something but was having trouble spitting it out.

"Patience . . . I, um . . . About what happened at the bar . . . Last night I was the one who acted like an idiot. I behaved like an ass and I'm sorry. I just . . ." For an instant, he glanced away. "My riding's off. I was pissed at myself. I drank too much—not that it's any excuse. Whatever the reason, I shouldn't have taken it out on you. I don't believe in treating a woman that way, and I give you my word it won't happen again. I hope you'll accept my apology."

She was so surprised that for a moment, she couldn't think of anything to say. Dallas Kingman apologizing? Better yet, he looked like he actually meant it.

She remembered the way he'd treated her and wasn't sure she should let him off so easy. Then she thought about the danger he and Cy had put themselves in just now to help her.

In the end, she just smiled. "I guess, after the way you jumped in with those bulls to get me out, we can call it even."

Dallas smiled, too. God, he had the most beautiful smile. "We kind of got off on the wrong foot, you and me. Maybe we could start over."

"Maybe we could."

Dallas stuck out his hand. "Friends?"

Patience fit her more slender hand into his. "Friends."

Across the way, Charlie was returning to where she sat on the blanket. "How's she doing?"

"Seems to be okay," Dallas said. "Got a pretty good knot on her head. I don't think she's got a concussion."

"I'm fine. I should have been more careful."

Charlie smiled. "Don't fret about it. Next time you will be." For a big, rough man he could be surprisingly gentle.

Blue Cody strode up just then, lean and dark, one of the best-looking cowboys on the circuit. "Charlie, we got trouble. Someone must not have closed the gate on those bulls real good. All five of 'em are running loose on the carnival grounds."

"Son of a bitch!" Charlie and Dallas and half a dozen cowboys started running. Patience got up from the blanket, relieved to find her head had stopped spinning. For the first time it occurred to her that it was her fault the bulls were loose.

"Oh, my God!" Patience took off running.

CHAPTER 7

By the time Dallas, Charlie, and the rest of the crew reached the carnival grounds, havoc reigned. People were screaming and running. One of the bulls prowled the midway game alley and had already knocked over several of the booths. The coin toss, filled with shiny glass dishes, was a mass of splintered glass. The police were moving people toward the exits, trying to keep them calm. More black-and-whites pulled in, sirens shrieking.

Charlie motioned for Dallas and the rest of the cowboys to circle around behind the bulls.

"We'll run 'em back this way, in through the gate next to the grandstand. Once we get them into the arena, we can move them into the pen."

It was a good plan and it began to work as the cowboys herded them closer and closer together. More men had come to help, some of them on horseback, using their ropes and whistling. Four of the bulls were moving toward the gate at the side of the arena, but a big, tough, long-horned brindle bull had cornered half a dozen people in front of the Ferris wheel.

Both clowns appeared on the scene, their makeup only

half finished and still wearing their regular jeans. Cy used his hat to turn the brindle bull, while Dallas and Ritchie Madden moved around behind him. Things were looking good until someone in the crowd made a sound and the bull whirled back in that direction. A little girl screamed and started to run and the bull lowered its head and charged after her.

Everything happened at once. The little girl tripped over one of the heavy cables on the ground in front of the ticket booth and went sprawling in the grass. Ritchie stepped in front of the bull, which caught him on the horns and tossed him a couple of feet into the air. Dallas swept the child into his arms and dodged out of the path of the rampaging bull, and Cy tossed his hat in the animal's face. The bull charged Cy, who leapt deftly out of the way, and one of the pickup men got a loop over the brindle's head. Another guy's loop settled over the first.

Amazingly, the bull began to calm. Maybe it was seeing the horses, something familiar in a world that seemed to have gone mad. Whatever it was, the animal didn't resist when the cowboys gave their ropes a little slack and whistled, urging the bull back toward the arena.

One of the guys ran over to check on Ritchie, while Dallas still held the child, a little towhead with huge blue eyes who was sobbing and clutching his neck.

"It's all right, sweetheart. You're safe now."

"Is he gone?" she asked tearfully.

He held her small body a little closer, trying to reassure her. "I promise he won't bother you again."

"My leg hurts so bad."

Dallas silently cursed. Laying the child down on the grass, he knelt to take a look at the leg, oddly angled beneath her ruffled pink pinafore. A crowd had gathered around them and a man shoved through, desperate to reach them.

"Where is she? What have you done with her? What have you done to my little girl?" Her father, a thin man in his thirties with receding brown hair that stuck up all over his head, came racing up beside them, ranting and raving like a lunatic.

"She tripped over a cable when she ran," Dallas explained. "Looks like she broke her leg. The ambulance is on its way. It was already headed for the arena."

The man knelt next to the little girl, then looked up at Dallas, who had risen to his feet. "You're going to pay for this. I'm going to sue you people for every dime you've got."

Charlie strode up just then, and Dallas spotted Patience at the edge of the circle of spectators, her face as white as chalk.

"What's going on here?" Charlie asked.

"Are you the man who owns those bulls?"

"Yeah. I'm Charlie Carson."

"Then I'll tell you what's going on. Your bull nearly killed my little girl and you, Mr. Carson, are going to pay for it. This is an outrage and it's going to cost you plenty. You can expect to hear from my attorney no later than tomorrow afternoon."

There were more threats and shouts, but the ambulance drove up just then and paramedics poured out of the back. Patience crossed the grass to Charlie.

"This is my fault. If I hadn't been careless and fallen into the pen, the gate wouldn't have been left open. The bulls wouldn't have escaped and that little girl wouldn't have been injured." Her hands were shaking, her features tense. Dallas had to force himself not to reach out and touch her.

Charlie shook his head. "This wasn't your fault, girl. In rodeo, things happen. The latch didn't catch, or maybe it busted. Maybe them bulls just pushed on the gate hard enough to force it open."

"I don't know, Charlie . . ." Her hat was missing, her ripply blond hair tumbled around her shoulders. "Somehow I still feel responsible."

"You listen here. You wasn't the guy who closed the gate.

If anyone's at fault, he is." And Charlie looked like he meant to take a piece out of the guy's hide when he found out who it was. "Like I said, this wasn't your fault. If I really thought it was, I'd say so."

Patience nodded, but Dallas didn't think she was really convinced. They walked over to where Ritchie was lying on the grass and Dallas saw that he was in worse shape that it first appeared.

One of the paramedics worked over him, checking his vital signs. "How bad is it?" he asked the clown.

"Couple of busted ribs, I figure. I think I broke my collarbone. Hurts like the holy bejesus." He sighed. "I'll call Junior Reese, see if he can fill in for me for a couple of weeks."

Dallas just nodded. Junior wasn't one of his favorite people. He and Charlie had bad blood between them going way back and Junior rarely worked a Circle C rodeo. As a clown, Junior was mostly a barrel man, but like Ritchie, he could do the funny bits whenever it was needed. It appeared to be needed now.

"Take care, pard," Dallas said to Ritchie, who waved and sank back down on the grass. Walking next to Charlie, Dallas and Patience started back to the arena. They still had a performance to give.

Halfway there, they stepped off the dirt road, out of the way of the ambulance. Red lights flashed as the vehicle passed by them, speeding off toward St. Joseph's Hospital in town. As soon as they reached the arena, Charlie disappeared up the stairs to the announcer's stand and Dallas walked over to get his gear.

"You were great with that little girl," Patience said, walking up beside him.

Dallas shrugged. "I like kids. I'm sorry she got hurt."

"I really feel bad for Charlie."

Dallas thought of the lawsuit Charlie would likely be facing. He had liability insurance, of course, but the policy limits weren't that high and the little girl's father looked like he meant to go for every penny he could get.

"Yeah," Dallas said. "Me, too."

That night, the Silver Springs rodeo wasn't one of Charlie's best. The Circle C was famous for its bucking stock, but these horses seemed edgy and out of sorts. Their rhythm was off or they had trouble coming out of the chutes. Patience found herself rooting for Dallas, who drew a horse called Black Plague, rode the eight seconds, but didn't seem quite together the way he usually was and only scored seventy-eight points. It wasn't enough to win and he wasn't happy about it.

Shari raced well but her time wasn't fast enough to place. Stormy took a second in the calf roping, so at least one of them won. Patience didn't see any of them after the performance. Generally, there were more contestants in each event than those who performed during the rodeo, and the slack— the extra stock and riders—competed either before or after the show. Back in Llano, the team roping had gone till two o'clock in the morning.

Shari and a lot of the cowboys were still over at the arena, but Patience had opted out tonight. She was tired of breathing dust and kicking dirt. She still had a throbbing headache, and after what the bulls had done at the carnival, she wasn't in the very best mood. She figured using her brain tonight wouldn't be easy, but maybe she could handle reading the journal.

She thumbed it open to where she'd left off the last time.

Finally got enough saved up to buy me a split-leather riding skirt. It's a real nice one, too, fringed around the bottom, with little silver beads on the pockets. It was Sylvie's skirt, but she's going home. Said she wouldn't be needing it anymore and sold it to me cheap. It fits me almost perfect.

Patience smiled. She still hadn't found the section the missing page had come from. There were lots of pages missing so it was hard to tell how much time had passed. She caught a reference to Sam Starling and zeroed in on the passage.

> *Sam took me out tonight. We're way up here in Calgary—that's in Canada—and I figured what the heck? We went to this real nice little restaurant and I ate until I thought I would bust. Sam thought it was funny, how much I could hold. He said he liked a woman with an appetite. I didn't tell him I'd spent most of my money on Sylvie's skirt and this was the most food I'd had all week.*

A later entry read:

> *Got a letter today from Whit. Says he misses me every day. We've known each other so long and with him not being around no more, I guess I miss him, too. He still wants to marry me. But I left the farm 'cause I wanted to see some of the world and I just ain't ready to go back. Maybe someday, but not yet.*

Patience thought about the last few lines. Apparently she and her sisters weren't the only ones in the family who craved adventure. She read until she was yawning and her eyes began to burn, then took off her glasses and put the journal away.

That night Shari didn't come home. Undoubtedly, she was with Stormy. Patience thought of Dallas Kingman and tried not to imagine what it would be like to go to bed with him.

Though the National Finals Rodeo in December was the biggest one in the country, paying over six million dollars in

winnings, the Copenhagen Cup in Las Vegas and the Reno
Rodeo the following weekend were among the top ten highest
paying rodeos of the year.

"We'll have to do some hard driving to make it," Shari
told Patience. "But it's good money and I'd damn sure like to
take some of it home."

Dallas would be going, of course. He needed to keep his
winnings up if he was going to make the Finals in December.

He and Stormy were already on their way when Shari and
Patience set off the following morning on the six hundred
mile run from New Mexico to Nevada, hauling their eighteen-foot trailer.

Charlie was on his way to Flagstaff, Arizona. The Circle
C production crew generally stayed as close to Texas as possible. Charlie had a wife on a ranch near Bandera and he
liked to get home as often as he could. Besides, the animals
held up better on shorter hauls.

But Patience was traveling with Shari, whose horse was
in Dallas Kingman's trailer on its way to Las Vegas. Patience
had never been there and though she had seen pictures on
TV, she wasn't prepared for the incredible array of colored
lights that flashed like a neon oasis in the middle of the
desert, the long lines of illumination stretching for miles
across the flat dry sand.

On the outskirts of town, Shari dropped their trailer in a
small RV park called the Palms, and they drove the rest of
the way into the city in the brown Chevy truck.

"Dallas is the big star of the show," Shari said, "so the
MGM comps him a couple of rooms and he's giving us one."
She grinned. "Since I'm staying with Stormy, you can have it
all to yourself." Shari hadn't mentioned the night she spent
with the tall, lanky Texan, but every time she said his name,
her face lit up in a way it hadn't before.

Patience couldn't help a touch of envy.

It was late afternoon when they rolled up in front of the
MGM, a massive emerald glass structure with more than

five thousand rooms. The golden MGM lion ruled from the
street out in front, and the lobby took up acres. The room
they were given on the twentieth floor had double queen-size
beds and a very nice décor.

Shari didn't unpack. Instead, she phoned down to the desk
and asked the operator to ring Dallas Kingman's suite. She
was grinning when she hung up the phone. Picking up her
suitcase, she headed for the door.

"Don't forget, there's a big welcome party tonight; some
rich guy here in Vegas who likes to big-deal it when the rodeo's
in town. Stormy says he lives in a regular mansion. Since the
show doesn't start till day after tomorrow, if we play a little
too hard, we'll have time to recoup before the competition. I
think it'll really be fun."

Maybe it would be. Patience felt a frisson of excitement.
She was in Las Vegas. She was going out on the town. Throwing open her suitcase, she took out her red cowboy boots and
tried to decide what to wear.

In the end, nothing she owned seemed right for a gala
western party in such a sophisticated city. Deciding there
was still enough time to make an addition to her limited ward-
robe, she left the room, went down to the concierge desk in
the lobby, and asked where she might find something suitable
for such an affair. Something sexy but not too sexy. Something
chic, but not too chic.

"There's a mall at the Venetian," said an attractive, well-
groomed man in his thirties whose name tag read *Bobby.* "It
looks just like Venice. Even has canals with gondolas. My
girlfriend loves to shop there. You might try *Cache* for something like that."

The mall turned out to be the perfect suggestion. And the
Disney-style Venice was a hoot. When Stormy and Shari
dropped by to pick her up at eight o'clock, Patience met them
in a red leather miniskirt that matched her cowboy boots and a

sleeveless red silk top with sequins scattered around the scalloped neckline. It was sexy, but mostly just fun, and it showed off her legs and a hint of cleavage and she thought she looked good in it.

Stormy had retrieved Patience's straw hat from where it had landed in the pen. The brim wound up with a few more crimps, which seemed to please Shari, but Patience wisely declined to wear it. Instead, she wore her hair loose, falling in waves past her shoulders, and tried not to wonder if Dallas would approve.

He wasn't with his friends. Shari said his afternoon was booked with TV interviews. He was also filming an ad for Tony Llama boots, one of his biggest sponsors.

"He'll catch up with us at the party," Shari said. "He won't want to miss this one. Roy Greenwood is a major rodeo fan. He owns Westwind Trailers—among about a jillion other companies. He's one of Dallas's biggest sponsors. Besides, this is supposed to be one of the best parties of the year."

They caught a yellow cab out in front of the MGM. The taxi drove west toward the edge of town, turned into an exclusive residential area, then pulled through massive wrought iron gates onto the Greenwood estate.

A huge, lighted water fountain marked the front of the two-story house. The taxi circled around it, stopping at the entrance to the mansion, which had to be thirty thousand square feet of stucco and tile, with acres of palm trees and lush tropical landscaping.

A white-jacketed valet pulled open the taxi doors. "Good evening. Welcome to Greenwood." There were half a dozen valets, busily parking guests' cars and ushering the latest arrivals up broad, red-tiled stairs to the massive carved wooden doors. To Patience's relief, everyone there was dressed western. The thump of boots and a sea of cowboy hats filled the entry, which was monstrous, with double sweeping staircases leading up to the second floor.

"Champagne?" A small, black-haired waiter presented a silver tray before they had gotten five feet inside the house.

"Why not?" Patience accepted a long-stemmed crystal flute and surveyed the golden bubbles. Stormy declined, preferring a drink from the bar, but Shari took a glass and they clinked them together.

"To a good time tonight."

"To winding up in the money," Patience said, and both of her friends echoed the toast.

Stormy looked good tonight, lean and lanky and smiling. He was one of those guys who really looked great in a cowboy hat. She didn't think she'd ever seen him without one. He escorted them toward the rear of the mansion, where the party was already in full swing around a huge triangular swimming pool. A Jacuzzi big enough to accommodate at least twenty people bubbled in one corner and there was a swim-up bar that looked like it belonged in a hotel in the Caribbean.

The pool was bordered with palms, cascading waterfalls, and the lush greenery that thrived in the Las Vegas heat, the whole outdoors lit with soft peach lighting. A warm, cloudless June night surrounded them, though with all the light from the casinos, the stars were obscured. A quarter moon rose over the distant mountains, reflecting on the surface of the pool, and the music of a country western band mingled with laughter and the clink of expensive crystal.

They wandered toward one of three bars set up around the pool. Stormy ordered a Jack and Coke while Patience and Shari sipped their champagne.

"Damn, girl—you sure do clean up good." Wes McCauley walked toward them, a glass of whiskey in his hand. He seemed even bigger out here among the expensively dressed partygoers, his shoulders blocking the light behind the bar. Tipping back his straw hat, he let his gaze run over Patience. "Mama—you got the prettiest legs I ever did see and they go all the way from here to Sunday."

Patience managed a nervous laugh. There was something about Wes . . . something that reminded her of Tyler, but she couldn't figure out what it was. "Thanks . . . I think."

Wes flicked a glance at Shari and gave a nod of approval to her lavender Rockies and white-and-lavender fringed shirt. "You're lookin' good, too, honey."

They talked for a while and each had another drink. The hours began to slip past. A couple of barrel racers she had met in Silver Springs, Bonnie Sweeney and Ruth Collins, joined the group and she talked to them for a while. Jade Egan was there, looking glamorous in a gold miniskirt and matching western-cut, fringed midrift top, but fortunately she was busy flirting with a group of wealthy businessmen and didn't wander their way.

Patience danced with Wes, a slow song, so her feet were still intact when the song ended, then she danced with Blue Cody. She tried not to look for Dallas. He would get there or he wouldn't, and she knew for sure it was better if he didn't.

Shari introduced her to a couple more people, an older man who team roped with his son, Marty, a tall, bookish-looking cowboy who wore wire-rimmed glasses. Marty was kind of shy and she thought he was charming. She was feeling relaxed, feeling the effects of the champagne and having a really nice time when Dallas walked up to the group. He was wearing black jeans, black ostrich boots, a black western-cut sport coat over a pale blue shirt, and his usual black felt hat, though this one wasn't sweat-stained and dusty and was obviously a lot more expensive, something like a twenty X beaver.

He looked good. Too damned good.

"I thought I'd be here sooner. I got tied up with the Tony Llama commercial. Those things are harder than they look."

But she bet he was great in the ad, like the Marlboro man with Paul Newman eyes, only younger and even better-looking.

"So, how's the party?" he asked, his attention swinging to her.

"So far it's been interesting." Patience surveyed the growing array of guests, everyone from wealthy local types to tall, blond showgirls. The Las Vegas night never ended and apparently no one thought a thing about arriving at midnight.

"Greenwood spares no expense," Dallas said, his gaze following hers. "It gets pretty wild as the evening goes on, but it's always entertaining." For the first time he noticed what she was wearing and the drink in his hand paused on its journey to his lips. "Sweet Mother Mary."

Color poured into her cheeks. "I, um . . . wasn't exactly sure what to wear."

His gaze dropped to her boots, slowly traveled the length of her legs, paused a moment on her breasts, then returned to her face. "You did just fine, darlin'. Just don't get too close to poor old Roy. You're liable to give him a heart attack."

Darlin'. It rolled off his tongue as sweet as maple syrup and her stomach floated up beneath her ribs. This wasn't good. Not good at all.

"You want to dance?"

She cast him a slightly wary glance, remembering the last time they had danced together.

As if he read her mind, a corner of his mouth edged up. "I promise I'll be a perfect gentleman."

The area in front of the band was crowded, but they were playing a nice slow Willie Nelson song, and she found herself looking up at him and nodding. "All right."

His hand captured hers and he led her toward the dance floor. He pulled her into his arms, but not too close, determined, it seemed, to keep his word. Couples were moving in a slow circle and Dallas fell into the rhythm with ease. She liked his cologne, something that reminded her of spice and leather mingled with a sexy male scent that was Dallas's own.

Her pulse kicked up. She tried to tell herself the man had no effect on her, but her heart was pounding and she was sure any minute her palms would begin to sweat.

"I've never been to Las Vegas before," she said, hoping to hide her nervousness. "It's really an amazing place."

Dallas's gaze flicked over the throng of partygoers in their psuedo-cowboy clothes. "You can say that again."

"The town hasn't really been here all that long, you know. It was discovered back in 1829 by a man named Rafael Rivera who was looking for water on a trip to Los Angeles. Rivera found an aquifer here. He named it Las Vegas. That means—"

"The meadow." Dallas smiled at the look on her face. "Everyone in Texas speaks a little Spanish." He turned her gently around a corner of the dance floor and pulled her a little closer. "You were telling me about Vegas."

She shook her head. "I didn't mean to get started. I doubt you're really interested."

"Sure I am."

"Really?"

"Really."

"All right. Well, the Mormons came in the 1850s, but the conditions were too harsh and they didn't last long. It was the railroad that finally put Las Vegas on the map." She grinned. "And Bugsy Siegel, of course."

Dallas flashed one of his devastating smiles. "How come you know so much about western history?"

She shrugged and glanced away. "I guess I watched too many John Wayne movies when I was a kid."

"I didn't know there was such a thing as too many."

She smiled. "Western history was my main interest in college."

"Yeah? Where'd you go?"

She didn't like where this was leading. She could imagine the gap it would put between them if he knew she was only weeks away from getting her Ph.D. "Boston University."

One of his dark brown eyebrows went up. Patience turned toward the bandstand. "The song's just about over," she said, to change the subject. But the band didn't pause, just swung into another Nelson tune, equally slow and seductive.

Dallas's hold subtly tightened and any thought of talking slipped away. By the time the song was over, he was holding her snugly against him and her arms were around his neck. She couldn't help noticing how good he felt, how perfectly they fit together. When the music stopped, Dallas steered her into the shadows of the deep, leafy foliage around the pool.

He reached up and tucked a strand of her hair behind an ear. "I'd really like to kiss you. I haven't been able to think of anything else since the moment I saw you tonight." A corner of his mouth edged up. "You won't slap me, will you?"

Slap him? When he looked at her that way, hitting him was the last thing on her mind. "No. I'll just kiss you back."

Something flashed in those blue, blue eyes. He didn't wait, just lowered his head and captured her lips. His were warm and softer than they looked, sinking in, molding perfectly to hers. He tasted her, kissed her more deeply, started over and did it all again. He coaxed her to open for him and his tongue slid into her mouth. He tasted faintly of whiskey mingled with something raw and masculine that made her insides curl.

Patience trembled. Dallas groaned.

He kissed her again and heat tugged low in her belly. Her limbs felt shaky; her pulse set up a frantic beat. Then, he eased a little away.

"I was afraid of this."

"Afraid of what?"

"I was afraid that if I kissed you, I'd want a whole lot more." He bent his head and nibbled at the corner of her lips. "Why don't we can the party and go back to the hotel? I've got a suite there you wouldn't believe. Big marble Jacuzzi, bedroom from here to Texas, the whole bit." He pressed small soft kisses against the side of her neck. "I could order us some supper—"

Patience drew away, though it was nearly impossible to do. She tried to smile and hoped her tingling lips would work. "Part of me would like to say yes. I'm attracted to you, Dallas—there's no use lying about it. But I . . ." She shook her head. "I know you'll probably think I'm old-fashioned, but I'm not into the one-night thing. Right this minute, I wish I were. The truth is, it just wouldn't work for me."

He stared into her eyes. She thought she saw an odd sort of turmoil in his. Then he sighed. "You're right. I just . . . the truth is, I'd really like to make love to you. I know it's a bad idea—we both know it. We've got a long summer ahead of us. We'll be traveling together and I'm not the kind of guy to make commitments."

She moistened her lips, tasting him there. "I know that."

He looked like he wanted to say more, but didn't. In the end, he just bent and kissed her softly one last time. "I better walk you back to the others."

Patience felt his hand at her waist as he guided her toward Shari and Stormy, who stood laughing together beside the bar. Big Roy Greenwood was with them, tall and stocky with a fringe of hair around a nearly bald head. Dallas introduced her, then ordered a Jack and water on the rocks.

Roy gave her a lengthy perusal. "I do admire the man's taste, yes, indeed. Dallas has always had a fine eye for the ladies."

She didn't thank him for the backhanded compliment. Being reminded of Dallas's endless supply of women wasn't something she felt grateful for.

Greenwood turned away. "If you got a minute, Dallas, there's some folks I'd like you to meet."

Dallas sipped his drink. "Sure." He and Roy left to mingle with the guests, who all wanted to meet America's current number one cowboy. Patience watched him disappear into the throng of guests and tried not to remember his kiss. So what if it was soft and sweet and just thinking about it made heat rush into places that had never been heated that way before?

It was getting really late, though the party showed no sign of slowing. Half a dozen people had jumped into the pool, clothes and all, while another group stripped naked and climbed into the Jacuzzi. Everyone was laughing and drinking and dancing, but for Patience, the night had lost its glow.

She thought of Dallas and wondered what it might have been like if she had tossed caution to the wind and gone to bed with him.

CHAPTER 8

Dallas followed Roy Greenwood from one group to the next. It was always a big deal for Roy to introduce him to his friends. A lot of them were women. Roy liked women—any size, any age, any shape—and he didn't mind sharing. Unfortunately, Dallas wasn't in the mood. There was only one woman he wanted tonight and she was *old-fashioned. Not into the one-night thing.*

The weird part was, in a way he was glad. There were half a dozen women who would leave the party with him and climb straight into his bed. It wouldn't mean anything to either one of them. But Patience Sinclair was different. He had known that from the moment she had driven her little red convertible into the rodeo grounds in Rocky Hill, Texas, and left him standing in the dust.

Dallas smiled at the memory. Maybe he had started to want her right then.

The smile slid away. He might want her, but he wasn't going to have her. She didn't do one-night stands and he didn't do anything else.

Dallas sighed. Turning at the sound of voices, he pasted

on a smile, and let Big Roy introduce him to another round of guests.

Time slipped past. He was yawning when he spotted the slender little barrel racer, Ruth Collins, hurrying toward him.

"Hey, Dallas! Can I talk to you a minute?" She was frowning, he saw, glancing worriedly back toward the house, and his senses went on alert. She caught his arm and he let her lead him a few feet away.

"What is it, Ruth?"

"It's Jade. She's in some trouble, Dallas. I was hoping you could help."

His back teeth ground together. The last thing he needed was a problem with Jade. "What kind of trouble?"

"Jade went upstairs with some of Roy's rich friends. She was pretty drunk. They were going to do some drugs. When she didn't come down, I went up to look for her. She's in really bad shape, Dallas. Somebody's got to get her out of there."

Dallas swore beneath his breath. Jade Egan had been a pain in the neck from the day he had met her. In the beginning, he had been so hot for her his brain hadn't been functioning quite the way it should. It hadn't taken long to figure out she was spoiled and selfish, with too damned much money for her own good. And this wasn't the first time she had gotten herself mixed up with drugs.

He told himself she deserved whatever she got, but he couldn't force himself to walk away.

"Where is she?"

"Come on," Ruth said. "I'll show you."

Weaving their way among the guests, making their way back inside the house, Ruth led him up one of the sweeping staircases, then down a long hall past a row of bedroom doors.

"In there." She twisted the knob and shoved the door open and he saw Jade sprawled on the bed. Her midriff top was crooked, exposing the edge of her black lace bra. Her skirt was bunched up and he caught a glimpse of black thong panties.

"You guys back off," Dallas warned the two men who'd been feeding her booze and marijuana, both in their forties and at least twenty pounds overweight.

"Hey, Jade's a big girl," one of them said. "She can take care of herself." Fat boy number one cut a line of cocaine on a mirror, bent his head and sniffed it through a rolled-up twenty dollar bill.

"Maybe so, but right now, she's leaving." Before they had her doing coke on top of everything else. Grabbing Jade's arm, he jerked her up off the bed and she staggered onto her feet.

"Hi, lover." She gave him a lopsided grin and leaned against him for support. "I've . . . missed you."

Dallas just grunted. He took a second to straighten her clothes, then gripped her wrist and started tugging her toward the door.

Neither of the men protested. One glance at the black look on his face warned them what would happen if they did.

"Where are we . . . going?" Jade asked, and Dallas silently prayed she could stay on her feet.

"Back to the hotel. You're staying at the MGM, right?"

"That's right, baby. I've got a suite with a great"—she hiccoughed—"big, king-size bed."

Dallas made no reply. He wanted her to leave without a fight. Until he got her back to the hotel, he would let her believe what she wanted. Cursing his bad luck and the conscience he sometimes wished he didn't have, Dallas headed for the staircase leading to the entry.

The evening wore on. Wes McCauley returned to the group, drunk as seven lords, a petite brunette on his arm. They disappeared inside the house and didn't reappear until half an hour later, when Patience noticed them emerging through the big glass sliders at the rear of the mansion.

The brunette was pissed and shouting at Wes, and Blue Cody was arguing with him, saying something about it being time for him to go home. Wes said something to the girl, whose hair was mussed and her lipstick smeared. She called him a dirty name, turned and walked away.

Patience was ready to leave herself. She went in search of Shari and found her cuddled up with Stormy on the dance floor. She told them she was heading back to the hotel.

"You want us to go with you?" Shari asked.

"Don't be silly. There's a row of cabs parked out front. I'll be fine. Have a good time and I'll see you in the morning."

It was such a warm night she hadn't needed a wrap. Patience slung the strap of her red leather bag over her shoulder and started up the steps leading back inside the house. She picked her way through the crowd and finally reached the entry. In front of the house, valets were dashing around fetching cars for departing guests. A little silver Porsche, a sleek BMW convertible, a low-slung Mercedes-Benz. Just as Patience started down the wide red tile steps toward the row of cabs, a big black MGM limousine pulled up to the curb and a valet opened the door. Patience froze as she spotted Dallas Kingman standing next to Jade, his arm wrapped possessively around her waist.

He urged her into the limo, then slid in beside her on the red leather seat. As the valet closed the door, Patience thought Dallas might have seen her standing in the entry, but he disappeared behind the darkly tinted windows and she couldn't tell for sure.

Patience watched the limo drive away and realized she was trembling. Dallas had said he wanted to make love to her. He had said it in a way that had made her feel special, as if she were the only woman he wanted.

The truth was, all he wanted was someone to warm his

bed and he didn't much care who it was. Patience had told him no. Apparently Jade Egan had said yes. Patience swallowed past the lump that rose in her throat. What was it about Dallas Kingman that always made her think there was more to him than what it seemed?

As much as it bothered her, it was probably for the best. She had always been a failure in the sex department. Her relationship with Tyler had lasted only weeks before it had come to an end—at least for her. She would never forget his parting words.

You think we should stop seeing each other? Well, maybe you're right. The truth is, Patience, you're the worst piece of ass I've ever had. You're an iceberg. In fact, I think you're frigid.

Of course he had apologized a few hours later and begged her to forgive her. That's when he had started calling and sending her dozens of E-mails. She had told herself he'd only said those things to punish her, but their sex life had been bad from the start and secretly she had worried about it.

Patience took a deep, shuddering breath, determined to shove the memory away, along with the hurt she felt when she thought of Dallas. By the time she reached the bottom of the steps, a taxi had pulled up to the curb.

"Where to, miss?" the driver asked as she climbed inside.

"MGM Grand."

"No problem." The cab sped away and Patience leaned her head against the seat. She closed her eyes and tried to block the image of Jade Egan in Dallas Kingman's bed.

The shrill ringing of the phone awakened her. Patience fumbled with the receiver, dropped it onto the pillow, then finally grabbed it up and pressed it against her ear.

"Hello."

"Hi, honey. Sorry to wake you so early." Her dad's voice

reached her from the opposite end of the line. She glanced at the clock on the nightstand. Seven o'clock. She hadn't gotten back to the hotel until two and then had been unable to sleep.

"It's all right," she said groggily. "It's good to hear your voice."

"Yours, too." She noticed it then, the slight hesitation that brought her fully awake. "What is it, Dad? What's going on?"

A pause on the end of the line. "I hated to call, but I thought you ought to know. Someone broke into your apartment."

"Oh, God. What did they take?"

"The television set and your stereo. Some of your photo albums. Your senior high school yearbook."

"Tyler."

"Maybe. The police are looking into it. I imagine they'll be talking to Tyler."

"When did it happen?"

"Your neighbor, Stella Bingham, discovered it this morning, but we aren't sure exactly when it happened. Stella noticed the lock on your back door was broken. She went in to check. Some of your desk drawers were open and it looked as if someone had rummaged through the drawers in the dresser in your bedroom. She called me to come over. The TV and stereo were gone but she wasn't sure what else had been taken. The only other things I noticed were missing were the photo albums on your shelves in the living room and your senior yearbook. I don't think anything else of value was taken."

Nothing but treasured photos of her and her friends and a yearbook filled with quirky comments that could never be replaced. The dark mood of the night before gripped her once again. "It had to be Tyler. Who else would want stuff like that?"

"You live near campus. It could have been another one of the students. I can't imagine Tyler needing to steal a TV."

True enough. One thing Tyler always had was plenty of money. Still, he might have done it to throw off suspicion.

"Do you think I ought to come home?"

"Absolutely not. If it is Tyler, he has no idea where you are. I think it would be best if you kept it that way."

"I can't hide from him forever."

"You aren't hiding. You've had your summer planned for months. You might as well enjoy it. Besides, there's a good chance it isn't even him. In case it is, I'll keep in touch with the police, remind them about the restraining order, make sure they're on top of things."

"All right, then. I'm not going to worry about it." Not much, at any rate. The TV and stereo were old. It was the photos and yearbook she felt bad about losing. "Thanks, Dad."

"I love you, honey."

"I love you, too, Dad." Patience hung up the phone and flopped back down on the bed. Perhaps the thief really wasn't Tyler. He hadn't bothered her in weeks. She hadn't even seen him except for that day at the grocery store.

If it was him, as her father had said, he didn't know where to find her. He had caused her trouble enough already. She wasn't going to let him ruin her summer.

The Vegas show was bigger, bolder, and wilder than any rodeo Patience had attended so far. It was held at the MGM Grand, one of the big show rooms converted to an indoor dirt-floored arena, complete with bucking chutes. Before the performance, mounted cowboys milled in circles, warming up their horses, sending little puffs of dust into the air. A sea of cowboy hats moved behind the chutes with the soft whisper of worn blue jeans. Horses whinnied, and scuffed leather boots made thumping sounds on the portable stairs leading up to the announcer's stand.

Sitting in the contestants' bleachers, Patience wasn't much

in the mood to watch the performance. She hadn't mentioned the phone call from her father or her troubles with Tyler Stanfield, not even to Shari. She didn't want her summer somehow tainted by him.

Instead, she left the bleachers and went to watch Shari's barrel run from the area behind the starting line. Button was prancing, his ears twitching, watching the barrels being placed in the center of the ring with what could only be called anticipation. The long-necked sorrel loved to run. He seemed to thrive on the challenge it took to spin around the barrels without knocking them over, then stretching out toward the finish line.

Patience's excitement began to build as Shari approached the start. At the signal, Button leapt forward, Shari bent over his neck, urging him faster. The horse took each barrel with perfect precision, then flew back over the finish line. Shari was grinning, her dark green cowboy hat flying off with her sliding stop.

"Fifteen and three," the announcer called out. "A time that just might put that little Oklahoma gal in the money."

And it did. Which in Vegas meant a pretty good chunk of cash.

After the show, Patience interviewed some of the other female riders, asking about their education, the age they had started, how they had learned the sport. There were a number of similarities in their answers—the early exposure to horses and riding, having been raised on ranches or farms—but also a number of differences.

Some were college graduates, top students who had started on collegiate rodeo teams. But a lot of them had never finished high school. Some began riding as children, coached by their parents, others were wives of men who competed. Some of them lived hand-to-mouth existences, winning barely enough to pay their entry fees and buy gas to the next rodeo. Others, like Jade Egan, were good enough to earn a respectable living.

Patience made a couple of notes on a small yellow pad,

then tucked it into her shoulder bag. She hadn't noticed Jade's approach till the woman stood directly in front of her.

"I heard you were doing interviews. I'll be happy to give you one."

Patience inwardly groaned just thinking of the hateful things Jade would have to say. "I imagine you're too busy right now."

"Yeah, I am. Why don't you catch me later?"

"I'll do that." Seeing the anticipation on Jade's face, Patience made a mental note to avoid her.

Just as she had managed to keep avoiding Dallas.

Amazingly, he had come to her room late the morning after the party and banged on the door. Her father's phone call had blackened her already dismal mood and hearing his voice only made it worse. She pretended not to be there and he had finally gone away. He had phoned several times and left messages, but she hadn't returned his calls.

She didn't want to see him. She didn't want to hear that silky drawl or look into those lying blue eyes.

She had passed him a couple of times around the rodeo grounds, but he had always been with someone else or getting ready to ride. She had watched him compete, of course. He had drawn a couple of good horses and ridden well enough to come in third in the overall and take home a sizeable chunk of money.

He wasn't around when she and Shari pulled out of Vegas and headed for Reno. They checked into the Silver Slipper, where Dallas had again come up with free rooms, though they all knew Shari would be spending the night with Stormy. Dallas won a little day money in the saddle broncs, took a third in the calf roping, and Stormy took a day money third.

It wasn't what they were hoping for, but in rodeo, there was always another show, another chance to win, and Prescott and Greeley were both coming up. Dallas would also be competing in Cody, Wyoming, Shari told her, then flying on up to the Calgary Stampede.

It was just getting dark when they pulled into Prescott, which still retained the flavor of the old West gold-mining town it once was.

"The guys got in a couple of hours ahead of us," Shari told her as they drove through the gates of the rodeo grounds. "That's Button over there—tied to Dallas's trailer."

Charlie Carson was also there. Patience saw Circle C livestock trucks parked in the staging area, though the animals had already been unloaded.

"They're probably over at Miller's bar," Shari said. "It's kind of a hangout whenever the rodeo's in town. The guys like to play cards there."

Patience felt a little tug of excitement. She loved to play cards. She had played with her dad and sisters since she was a little girl. Occasionally in the evenings, when she wasn't busy with her research or typing on the computer, she and Shari had spent the evening playing gin, but it was poker she enjoyed the most. As a child she had demanded her father teach her as soon as she had seen it being played in an ancient black-and-white Gary Cooper movie.

"You feel like going downtown?" Shari asked.

"Sure. I've never seen Prescott and it's early, yet. And I could use something to eat."

"I'll check on Button and the other two horses, then we'll unhook our trailer and head out."

Sitting at a round table in the back room of Miller's bar, a narrow, smoky little beer joint on the square in downtown Prescott, Dallas leaned back in his chair. "Ante up, boys, I haven't got all night."

Seated next to Cy, who was clowning the show with Junior Reese, Stormy tossed in a couple of chips. Blue Cody sat across from him, next to Reno Garcia, a short, stout, mustached bull rider who had won some money in Vegas. They were playing Texas Hold 'Em, one of Dallas's favorite games, and the pot was leaning his way, though not by much. Stormy was usually a pretty fair player, but tonight he couldn't seem to keep his mind on the game.

Every three minutes, he kept looking at the door, the way he was now, as if he could will that little redhead of his to come walking in.

Dallas kicked him under the table. "Your bet, slick."

"Sorry." Stormy studied the two cards in his hand and the three cards that were sitting faceup in the middle of the table. "I'll check to Blue."

Blue bet and so did Wes. Reno raised the bet, which Dallas met, and Stormy folded. Which Dallas figured had more to do with the fact that Shari was finally shoving her way through the door than the cards that he had been dealt.

Dallas sat up a little straighter himself when he saw the tall blonde who walked in behind her. Ever since Vegas, he'd been torn between wanting to see her and telling himself it was better if he just left things alone—let her continue to think the worst of him.

He knew she did. He'd caught a glimpse of her on the steps as he had followed Jade into the limo after the party. He didn't have to see her face to know she thought he was lower than pond scum. She had refused to have sex with him so she figured he had taken Jade home instead. Like it didn't really matter who he screwed.

Like hell it didn't.

Patience was mad at him for taking Jade home and Jade was still pissed at him for refusing to join her in bed. He had heard her throwing things against the door as he'd walked away.

But it wasn't Jade Egan he wanted.

The woman he wanted was walking straight toward him and just looking at her made him hard under the table.

"Hi, guys!" Shari waved and Stormy got up from his chair.

"I'm out." Stormy tossed down his cards with barely a glance at any of them. He was out, all right. He hadn't seen his lady in what? Six or seven hours?

Dallas damned near smiled, might have, if he hadn't caught the go-to-hell look on Patience's pretty face.

"We got an open seat," he drawled in her direction, just to goad her a little. She was still mad as hell. Why he found that heartening he couldn't quite say. "What do you think, P.J.? Maybe you'd like to sit in."

The other guys laughed. Reno Garcia grunted and Blue Cody grinned. Dallas couldn't believe his eyes when Patience dragged out Stormy's vacated chair and planted her luscious behind squarely in the seat.

The laughter immediately faded.

"We . . . um . . . kind of have a standing rule," Blue Cody said. "We're playing for money—not high stakes but still . . . it wouldn't be fair to take advantage of someone who's new to the game." Translation—they didn't have time to put up with a female who had no idea how to play cards.

Patience just smiled. "I'll take my chances." She opened her purse and took out a fifty-dollar bill. "This enough to buy in?"

Blue sat up a little straighter. "Like I said, this isn't a high-stakes game." He pushed fifty dollars worth of chips in her direction.

"Texas Hold 'Em, right?"

Dallas shoved his hat back on his head and tried to read her expression. He had underestimated her before, but . . . Man, there was no way in hell Little Miss Boston University knew how to play poker good enough to win.

An hour later, he was silently eating his words.

When Patience laid down a pair of aces, which combined with the cards on the table gave her a full house, Reno Garcia threw in his hand and shoved back his chair. "What the hell we got here—a goddamned mechanic?" A card shark. Reno wasn't a guy who liked losing, especially to a woman.

"Beginner's luck," Patience said, smiling as she raked in another pile of chips. But she was hardly a beginner. Dallas had watched her set a bear trap for Reno, hardly betting at all when it was now clear she had drawn a powerful hand. Since another ace lay among those in the shared hand in the middle of the table, she'd had at least three of a kind before she started betting.

Earlier, she had over-bet the pot, making it appear as if she were bluffing, playing like the greenhorn they expected her to be. She had sucked them all in, including himself, then calmly laid down a Jack-high straight and scraped in her winnings.

He might have laughed if she wasn't enjoying herself so much at his expense. Every time she won a hand, she flashed him a kiss-my-ass smile and it was beginning to get on his nerves. Still, secretly it tickled him that she could play so damned well.

They gambled a couple more hours. Patience was clearly the winner when the game finally ended. The men were grumbling but looking at her with a new sort of respect. Dallas wanted to know who the hell P.J. Sinclair was and how she had managed to sucker five poker-playing cowboys out of their rodeo winnings.

Dallas shoved back his chair and came slowly to his feet as Charlie Carson walked in. Though Dallas had called him every couple of days, he hadn't seen him since Silver Springs and he had been worried about him. The last time they had spoken, Charlie said a marshal had served him with a multi-million dollar lawsuit over the incident at the fairgrounds with the bulls.

Charlie'd had to hire his own set of bloodsucking attorneys to deal with the insurance company, which was trying to weasel out of paying any kind of settlement.

Dallas excused himself and went over to talk to his uncle, who was speaking to a couple of other men, one he recognized as Salty Marvin, a grizzled, old-time cowhand who worked for the Circle C, the other, a guy named Lem Wilkins, one of the owners of the Flying S, Charlie's main competitor in the rodeo production business. Lem looked a little like an aging hippie, with the same mustache and sideburns he'd been wearing since the sixties.

Dallas had never really liked him. Wilkins and his partner, Jack Stiles, had been after Charlie to sell out to him for years, even going so far as to pressure Annie about it, but Charlie had always refused. Dallas wondered what the hell Lem was up to now.

"Hey, Dallas!" Charlie waved him over. "Good to see you, son." He clasped Dallas's shoulder and gave it a hearty squeeze.

"It's damned good to see you, too. Hello, Salty. Lem." He glanced between his uncle and the other two men. "What's going on?"

Charlie's smile slipped a notch. "What's goin' on is I'm thinkin' of selling a couple of Circle C bucking horses to Lem. He's offered me a damned good price for them."

Dallas frowned. It wasn't like Charlie to sell his stock unless he absolutely had to. Worse yet, he was selling it to Lem. Apparently money was tighter than he thought.

Dallas drew Charlie aside. "You're not seriously thinking of selling those horses to Lem?"

"More than serious. The truth is, we've pretty much come to an agreement."

"Listen, Charlie. You need money, I could loan you some. You know I've got a good bit saved up."

But Charlie shook his head. "I ain't takin' your money, son. Not now or any time in the future. You worked too hard to get it."

"You've helped me, Charlie. It's only fair that I—"

"I said no and that's the end of it." Charlie tugged his hat down a little lower on his forehead and Dallas didn't say another word.

"Which ones are you going to sell?" he asked, thinking

how often Annie had grumbled about her hardheaded husband.

"Crawfish, Geronimo, and Spitfire."

Dallas was stunned. They were all Finals horses, some of the best buckers Charlie owned. Dallas shook his head, hardly able to believe it. "You sure about this?"

"We got some good stock coming up on the ranch. They'll be ready in a year or two. We got enough good horses to last until then."

Dallas just nodded, knowing there was nothing he could do. He let the men finish their dickering, but he didn't like what was going down. He didn't like it one bit.

"I love it!" Shari laughed as Patience moved away from the card table and sat down next to her and Stormy. "I had no idea you could play poker like that."

"To tell you the truth, it's not that I'm particularly good. It's just that those guys are all pretty bad."

Shari laughed again. "They don't really play all that much. They usually don't have time." The place was filling up with cowboys just getting into town. The jukebox played Garth Brooks's "Friends In Low Places," and a guy and his girl got up to dance. A couple of barrel racers came in and sat down at the bar. A few minutes later, Jade Egan walked in.

She strolled straight up to Dallas, bent and whispered something in his ear.

Patience's stomach tightened. It was ridiculous. The fact that Jade was sleeping with Dallas had nothing to do with her. Still, she didn't have to like it. "I think I'll head back to the trailer," she said to Shari. "That is . . . if Stormy wouldn't mind giving you a ride."

Stormy just grinned. "No problem."

Shari flicked a glance at Jade, who still stood next to Dallas. "You shouldn't let her get to you."

"It isn't that . . . Well, not exactly. I'll catch you later, okay?"

Patience crossed the bar, pushed through the old-time swinging doors, and felt a rush of warm air as she stepped out into the Arizona evening. She started up the walk toward her brown pickup truck.

"Hey, Patience—wait up!"

It was Dallas. Just the sound of that soft Texas drawl made the hackles rise on the back of her neck. Instead of stopping, she started walking faster.

"Dammit—wait a minute! I need to talk to you."

She turned to face him, kept walking backwards. "Whatever you've got to say, I don't want to hear it. Why don't you go back in the bar? Jade's in there. Or if you're tired of her, I'm sure you won't have any trouble finding someone else."

She turned around and kept on walking. A tug on her arm spun her around, then she grunted as Dallas's shoulder connected with her stomach. Hoisting her over his shoulder, he started for his truck.

"Are you crazy? Put me down!" She pounded on his back but did more damage to her fist than she did to him.

"I'm not letting you go till you hear what I have to say."

"Damn you!"

He rounded his truck to the passenger side, clicked his car keys to open the door, then set her down on the black leather seat. "I know you're pissed. I know you saw me leaving with Jade the night of the party."

She bristled. Pissed? He didn't know the half of it, but she'd be damned if she'd let him know. "So I saw you. So what? It's none of my business who you spend the night with."

"Maybe it isn't. But that particular night was different. I wanted to make love to you. I told you that and I meant it. And I didn't sleep with Jade."

"Right." She tried to jump down from the seat, but he braced his arms across the door, trapping her inside the cab.

"The truth is, Jade got wasted that night. She was drunk, doing marijuana with a couple of rich boys in one of the upstairs bedrooms. Ruth Collins came after me, asked me to get her out of there before she really got herself in trouble."

Patience looked at him hard, trying to decide if he was telling her the truth. "So I'm supposed to believe all you did was play Sir Galahad and rescue her?"

"I guess you could put it that way."

"But you didn't sleep with her."

"I'm not interested in Jade. I haven't been for quite a while."

Patience sighed and leaned back against the seat. "It really isn't my business, Dallas. You don't owe me an explanation. I don't have any kind of hold over you."

"I know. And I'm not saying I won't sleep with a woman in the future. I just wanted you to know the truth about that night."

Patience managed a smile, but somehow it wasn't that easy. "Thanks. I appreciate that."

He helped her down from the truck and walked her over to her pickup. "So where'd you learn to play cards?"

"My dad. I watched them playing poker in the movies when I was little and I begged him to teach me. He learned just so he could. When we were growing up, he played with me and my sisters all the time."

Dallas chuckled at the image. "What about your mom?"

"She died when I was eight." Patience stared off toward the grassy square in the center of town. "Sometimes it's hard for me to remember what she looked like."

Dallas followed her gaze. "My mother died when I was twelve. I remember everything about her."

Patience studied his face, read the loss that flickered in his eyes. "What was she like?"

"My mom? She was Charlie's sister, you know. A real Texas cowgirl. She was born and raised right there on the Circle C Ranch. The Carsons were ranchers all the way back to the days of the Alamo."

"We both lost our mothers," she said. "I guess that means we actually have something in common."

Dallas reached out and touched her cheek. "So who are you, P.J. Sinclair?"

"What do you mean?"

"Tell the truth—you write for some sleazy tabloid and you're doing an article about aliens who disguise themselves as cowboys."

Patience grinned. "I hadn't actually considered that but maybe you've got an idea."

"I know—you write a lonely hearts column and you're doing a series about sex on the rodeo circuit."

She laughed. "Wrong again. Definitely not a lonely hearts column." She cast him a speculative glance. "Even if I were, you wouldn't be much help. What would you know about being lonely?"

His smile slipped a little. "You're right. How could a guy like me possibly ever get lonely?" But she thought she saw something in his face that said there were times he was very lonely indeed.

He opened the door of her truck and she climbed up behind the wheel. Dallas closed the door and she fired up the engine. As she pulled out from the curb, she could see him in the mirror, standing on the sidewalk, watching as she drove away.

CHAPTER 9

In rodeo, the Fourth of July weekend was one of the biggest of the year. Charlie and the Circle C were producing the show in Greeley, Colorado, a big-money rodeo where Dallas would be competing before he flew out to St. Paul, Oregon, then on to compete in the Cody, Wyoming, show.

Patience was glad he was leaving.

She needed to concentrate on her thesis. She was committed to finishing it by the end of summer and whenever Dallas was around, it was almost impossible to work. She hated the way he intruded into her thoughts when he was the last man on earth that she should be thinking about.

Sitting in the booth in the dining area of the trailer, Patience worked for a while, then decided to call her father. As usual, Tracy answered.

"Patience! Good Lord, your father is practically ready to board the next plane for Arizona. Is everything all right?"

She sighed. After Tyler, she understood her father's worry; still, she wasn't thirteen anymore. "If he flies to Prescott, he'll be wasting his time. I'm in Greeley, Colorado."

"Colorado!"

"I've got to say, I really didn't realize what a grueling life rodeo people lead. They're on the road every week, heading for one show after another. One of the bronc riders said he'd done twenty shows in the last eighteen days."

"Good heavens."

"Lucky for me, Shari's schedule isn't quite that bad." Though Dallas's was definitely rough, with his public relations work and making three shows in one weekend, as he planned to do over the Fourth.

"Hang on a minute, your dad's reaching for the phone."

"Take care, Tracy."

"You, too."

Her dad's voice came on the line. "I'm glad you called. I was starting to worry."

"Everything's okay. If you're worried about Tyler, I haven't seen a trace of him. Did the police find out if he was involved in the burglary?"

"Tyler denied knowing anything about it. They didn't find any fingerprints so there's no real way to tell. But a couple of days ago, your friend Molly Jansen called the house." Patience's best friend at B.U., Molly, knew about her problems with Tyler. Patience made a mental note to drop her an e-mail the next time she got the chance.

"Molly says rumor is, Tyler has taken a trip out of town. His friends say he went to Bermuda with some girl, but no one seems to know for sure. Molly and I . . . well, we both thought you ought to know."

A little shiver ran through her. Tyler wasn't in Boston. For an instant, her paranoia rose up. He had found out where she was and he was coming after her. God knew what he planned to do if he found her. Then her common sense took over. Tyler had no way of knowing where she was—half the time, even her parents didn't know. Besides, he had never really done anything to hurt her. Scared her pretty bad the night he had come into her bedroom and threatened her, but never physically hurt her.

"I'm glad you told me. I don't think he's trying to find

me. It's been weeks since I broke off with him. Still, if he does show up, I have a dozen of the toughest cowboys in the country to look out for me."

It was true, though she'd never really thought about it until now. Most rodeo cowboys grew up with an old-fashioned sense of right and wrong that included a protective attitude toward women. She was traveling with Shari, a member of their world, therefore she fell under their protection. Just like the day she had landed in the pen with the bulls.

She didn't mention that to her dad, however.

"Everything okay with you and Tracy?" she asked instead and could almost see her father smile.

"Everything's fine. She'll have her master's by the end of summer. I'm so damned proud of her." *And so much in love with her.*

Her father had loved Patience's mother that same way. They had met in college and married shortly thereafter. They'd had a fairy-tale life, until Faith Sinclair had suffered a rare kind of stroke and died.

Losing her had nearly destroyed Ed Sinclair. Then he'd met Tracy. She was six years younger, an assistant in the admissions office at B.U. They had so much in common, just as he and Faith once had. The marriage had worked, and after fifteen years, the two of them were still deeply in love.

Patience sighed. Her father had been lucky—not once, but twice. Why couldn't something like that happen to her?

"Give Snickers a hug for me," she said at the end of the call, thinking it was a pretty sad state of affairs when her house cat was the most important man in her life.

She couldn't help thinking of Tyler Stanfield, wondering if there was any chance he had gone in search of her. Surely not. Their brief relationship had never been good. She hadn't the slightest idea why he had become so obsessed with her.

Unless it was the sex.

Maybe he felt even more inadequate than she. Maybe secretly he blamed himself for the fact she hadn't been responsive. He was, after all, Tyler Stanfield, the golden boy. Women usually fell all over him. Whatever the reason, she didn't have time to worry about it.

Patience unfolded her glasses, slid them up on her nose, and opened her laptop. Entering the Word file titled *Cowgirls,* she started typing in the notes from the interviews she had done. When she finished, she reviewed some of her thesis work, then closed down the machine. In an overhead cupboard, she found her great-grandmother's journal, and set it down on the table.

She was reading it slowly, enjoying the odd connection she felt to a woman who had died twenty years ago at the age of eighty-one. Adelaide Holmes was dead and buried and yet with every page, every word, Patience could feel her presence as if she stood just a few feet away.

As if they shared some bond, some secret method of communication. Which, with the journal, in a way, they did.

> *Met a gal in Wyoming. Her name is Lucille Sims but everybody calls her Lucky. She's the new relay rider on the colonel's team and she's a darned good one. She and I got along right off, since she's from down Texas way, Wichita Falls, which is close to Oklahoma, not far from where I come from.*

As Patience read over the next few pages, Addie and Lucky began traveling together, their friendship growing, two unmarried young women braving a world almost totally dominated by men. In Portland, one of the horses pulled a tendon coming down the homestretch and Addie's team lost the race.

Patience would have kept on reading if a knock at the door hadn't interrupted her. "Come on in," she called out, figuring it was probably Stormy.

She didn't expect to see Dallas Kingman's black hat poke through the door. He grinned when he saw her.

"I didn't know you wore glasses. Kind of reminds me of my fifth grade teacher."

Patience snatched them off her face and sat up a little straighter in the booth. "I usually wear my contacts."

He smiled as he pulled his hat off, ducked his head, and came in, absorbing the last of what little space there was inside. "Actually, that was a compliment. Mrs. Lovell was a total fox." He grinned. "I had a crush on her for years." He glanced down at the computer sitting on the Formica-topped table. "You working on your article?"

Patience gazed up at him, thinking how terrific he looked. "Actually, I was reading my great grandmother's journal. She was an early rodeo cowgirl."

"No kidding."

"That was back in 1912. I think she did a little trick riding once in a while, but mostly she competed in the cowgirl relay races."

The grin reappeared. "So you've actually got a little red, white, and blue rodeo blood pumping through you."

Patience set the tapestry-covered volume on the table. "I suppose so, though it's pretty diluted by now." Mixed with the ice water Tyler believed ran through her veins. Patience glanced up at Dallas, wishing the last thought hadn't popped into her head. "I didn't even know I had relatives in Oklahoma until last year."

"That must have been quite a shock for a Boston-bred, city girl like you."

He was laughing at her. She should have been insulted but his eyes were twinkling and somehow she wasn't. "Is there something you wanted?"

He fiddled with his hat. "Charlie's talking to a couple of old-time cowgirls over at the VIP stand. He thought you might like to meet them."

She brightened. "Definitely. I'll pack things up here and head over that way right now."

Dallas turned the hat in his hands. They were large and calloused but when he had held her, they had been gentle.

"I'll be flying out after the show. After I'm through in Cody, I'm headed to Calgary. I guess I won't be seeing you till we meet up in Sheridan."

"I guess not." After Shari and Stormy left Greeley, they were traveling to a Circle C rodeo down in Pecos. Afterward, Charlie was going home to his ranch in the Hill Country to see his wife.

"I got a whole week off," Charlie had said. "I been missin' my woman somethin' fierce. I can't wait to get back home."

Patience returned her computer to its usual spot on the table, then turned to Dallas. He was dressed for the evening performance, wearing his trademark blue western shirt and hand-tooled black and gold metallic fringed chaps. They rode low on his hips, framing the zipper on his jeans and a substantial male bulge that brought a rush of color to her face.

Dallas must have noticed. He made a rough sound in his throat and when she looked up, his eyes were a deeper shade of blue and even more intense. Her cheeks felt hot. She kept her gaze on his face.

Dallas's fingers tightened around the brim of his hat. "I . . . um . . . I better get going."

"Good luck with your ride."

He just nodded and turned to leave. She thought she heard him curse as he descended the steps of the trailer.

In Greeley, Dallas rode well and won some money. In St. Paul, he rode like a boob. He drew a good horse but got sidetracked on the first jump out of the chute, dropped a boot behind the horse's withers, and took a no score. In Cody, he was determined to make up for the poor showing in Oregon and made one of the best rides he had made all year. The good news was he took home first-place money, which was a respectable chunk in Cody.

The bad news was, his dismount was faulty and he went into the fence, wrenching his shoulder again and ripping the skin off the back of his hand.

His hand scabbed over. In Calgary the following week, he wrapped the shoulder in an Ace bandage and took a third in the overall. Roy Greenwood showed up and though he grumbled that the judges scored the ride too low, he seemed happy that Dallas had landed in the money.

After the perf, Roy took his entire entourage out to supper: three hot-looking Vegas showgirls who had accompanied him on his private jet—a sleek little Citation that Dallas had ridden in a couple of times—Roy's brother, Bob, always up for a party, and a small group of men and women who worked at a Greenwood Enterprises branch office in Calgary.

One of the showgirls, a leggy brunette named Cherry, slid into the red leather booth beside him at supper and Dallas saw Roy grin. Apparently, Cherry was a gift. She was nearly as tall as Dallas and built like the proverbial brick s-house. What was that old saying? Never look a gift horse in the mouth?

They went back to the River's Edge Inn where Roy had rented a bank of rooms, drank for a while in the bar, then Dallas and the brunette went upstairs.

She was good. He had to give her that. She must have sensed a hint of reluctance or indifference or whatever it was he was feeling, because the next thing he knew she was taking charge. Cherry knew what she wanted and she took it.

No strings attached.

Not like the Boston blonde he had left in the tiny trailer. Sex with her would be ridiculously complicated. She'd want promises he couldn't give. Commitments he couldn't begin to make.

He didn't know how much time passed, but when they

were finished, Cherry smiled, pleased with the job she had done.

"Anything else I can do for you, cowboy?"

He wanted her to leave. His shoulder was aching, she had done her work, and he had to get up early in the morning. And all the time she had been working him over, he had been thinking of Patience. "Tell Roy I owe him one."

She looked up at him through heavily mascared lashes. "Are you sure you don't want me to stay?"

Dallas shook his head. "Sorry, darlin'. I got work to do tomorrow."

He sent her away, thinking of Patience, wishing she had been the woman in his bed, cursing the fact that he wanted her and didn't really understand why. She was getting under his skin and he couldn't let that happen. He couldn't afford commitments, couldn't afford to get involved with a woman. Romance didn't fit into the life he led, the plans he had made for the future.

From this moment on, he told himself, he wasn't going to think of Patience Sinclair. When he got back to Sheridan, he'd do whatever it took to get her out of his system for good.

Dallas rolled over in the bed, exhausted but oddly restless, even after his bout with the brunette. Spotting the bottle of whiskey she had left on the nightstand, he reached over, unscrewed the cap, and took a long drink, hoping it would help him fall asleep.

Dallas woke up with the mother of all headaches. He groaned as he cracked open his eyes and tried to will away the pounding between his temples. The alarm clock was buzzing. He grimaced as he leaned over to shut it off.

Six a.m. Roy's plane would be leaving at eight, giving him a first class ride to Sheridan, and Dallas needed to be on it. He rolled toward the edge of the mattress, fought down a wave of nausea, and swung his legs over the side of the bed.

At least he was alone.

He didn't remember what time the showgirl had left, but he was damned glad she was gone. He didn't realize he had drunk so much. Now he was stuck with one helluva hangover. He swallowed against the bile that rose in his throat and forced his feet to move toward the bathroom. He grimaced when he looked in the mirror, stared into his whiskery face and bloodshot eyes.

Fleetingly, he wondered how much longer he could keep up the pace.

Long enough to get what you want.

To win the All-Around title again in December and a good chunk more money stashed away toward buying his ranch.

Aside from that, getting more rest would help. He could sleep on the plane, be rested by the time he got to Wyoming. As he turned on the hot water in the bathroom, drew the curtain and stepped under the spray of steaming hot water, a couple of things were clear.

He was through partying for a while.

And it was time he started focusing on his work.

Which meant he was going to do everything in his power to avoid Patience Sinclair.

"God, I hate to leave." Charlie tightened his hold on Annie. They were standing in the kitchen, in front of the old white enamel stove that his father had bought his mother when Charlie was a kid. It sat next to the big white side-by-side refrigerator he had bought for Annie for Christmas last year. She was baking an apple pie, his favorite, with others and the fragrance of apples and cinnamon filled the cozy kitchen.

"I wish I could go with you," Annie said, "but the way things have been going, I think I'd better stay here."

When they were younger, Annie had traveled with him all

the time, but in the last few years, the constant moving, the uprooting every week to head off for another rodeo, had just become too much for her.

Annie preferred to stay on the ranch, to tend her chickens and grow things in her garden and generally keep things running smoothly at home.

"I hated to see you sell those horses," she said, her arm around his waist. "They were some of our very best."

"Yeah, I know. Lem paid top dollar for them, though."

"He and Jack still after you to sell?"

Charlie chuckled. "They've never really stopped. We beat them out of the contract for the Greeley Stampede this year. I think it rankled them plenty."

Charlie released his hold so Annie could check on the pies. When she bent over, he noticed the curve of her hips beneath her jeans, felt the twinge of desire he always felt for her, and found himself smiling.

"The sheriff says he'll keep an eye on things here while I'm gone," he said, though so far no more Circle C stock had been stolen in the time he had been gone.

"Oh, I forgot to tell you. Sully called about an hour ago." Malcolm Sullivan was their nearest neighbor, the owner of the four-thousand acre spread, the Double Arrow, that bordered the Circle C.

"What'd he want?"

"Wanted to talk to you about those cattle thieves. He's been out of town, I guess. Wanted to know if you'd talked to Sheriff Mills lately and if he'd turned up anything new."

Charlie hadn't lost any more cattle, but according to Mal, the Double Arrow had lost some twenty head. "Mills hasn't found anything that I know of."

"Sully's cows turned up missing about a week after ours. Nothing's happened since then. Maybe whoever did it has headed somewhere else."

"I sure hope so."

Annie turned off the oven, pulled out two golden-brown

apple pies, and set them on top of the stove. Charlie walked over and inhaled the cinnamon fragrance, then turned and kissed the side of her neck.

"Charlie!"

He grinned at the flush that rose into her cheeks. They only had one night left and he meant to make it a good one. They usually ate early. After they were finished and he'd had time to let his pie settle a little, he intended to take her upstairs and spend the evening showing her just how much she meant to him.

"I wish Dallas could have come home with you," Annie said wistfully. He was the son she never had and though the boy called at least once a week, Charlie knew she missed him.

"He's been busy. Maybe he'll come home with me next time."

She untied the apron around her waist and tossed it onto the table. "I worry about him. He works too hard. He tries to ride in too many shows and then he still has to do all that darned publicity. He needs to come home and rest for a while."

"What that boy needs is a good woman," Charlie grumbled. "By the time I was his age, you and I had been married four years."

"I think he'd make a really good husband. He loves kids and he's good with them, and you taught him the right way to treat a woman."

Charlie grunted. "If he ever makes up his mind to settle down with just one."

Annie shoved the pies a little farther back on the stove. "He just hasn't met the right girl, that's all."

"I guess not." But an image of Patience Sinclair flashed in his head. She was not the sort of woman Dallas usually went for, the flashy types like Jade. She was sweet and thoughtful and sincere. She was intelligent, too, the way Dallas was.

Still, they didn't have much in common. A high-tone Boston

gal would hardly make a suitable wife for a Texas cowhand. And that was all Dallas ever wanted to be.

Charlie thought of his sister, Jolene, and her ill-fated marriage to Dallas's father, Avery Kingman. The pair was doomed from the start, no matter how much they were in love. Avery came from old-money Houston society while Jolie was raised on a ranch. Though they never divorced, in the years before Jolie died, they grew further and further apart and neither was ever truly happy.

Charlie sure didn't want that to happen to his boy.

"Supper's almost ready." Annie pulled open a drawer and started taking out silverware for the table. "Maybe we'll go for a ride or something after we finish eating."

Charlie flicked her a look and his eyes twinkled. "Yeah, maybe we will."

Patience couldn't stop thinking about him. No matter how hard she worked, no matter how deeply she immersed herself in her thesis, Dallas was always there, hovering at the edge of her mind.

At first she told herself she was acting like a fool. She wasn't the kind of woman who went for guys like him. Guys who wanted only one thing from a woman and made the fact more than clear. No-strings sex was fine for Dallas, but for Patience, sleeping with a man without any sort of relationship was out of the question.

Or was it?

Day and night, the notion haunted her.

The hard truth was, she wanted to sleep with him, wanted it more than anything she could remember in a very long time. She began to think, *why shouldn't I?* She was a modern, liberated woman. Besides, traveling the rodeo circuit was supposed to be her grand adventure. Why not just give in, go to bed with him and get it over with?

She remembered the way it felt when he had kissed her. No man had ever stirred her that way. Dallas knew women. He had made love to dozens of them. He would know how to make a woman respond. She thought of the men in her life. In high school she had been the shy, bookish Sinclair sister with short hair and glasses. Hope had had to bribe a friend to take her little sister to the prom.

In college she'd had a couple of dates, then began to see a guy in her psychology class. She was tired of being a virgin, the last one at the U., she began to believe. Danny Shepard wanted to make love to her and eventually she said yes. The first time had hurt and the second time wasn't much better. Danny was gangly and not much fun. She wasn't really that attracted to him, so she had ended the affair.

Her relationship with Tyler wasn't much better.

But Dallas . . . Dallas was the sexiest man she had ever met. Her heart started knocking the minute he walked into the room. Her legs felt shaky when they danced. Maybe with Dallas it would be different. Maybe afterward, she could banish her low self-image where sex was concerned, go out and find a man who was right for her.

By the time Dallas rejoined them in the little western town of Sheridan, Wyoming, Patience had made up her mind. She was going to bed with Dallas Kingman. If one night was all he wanted, well, there was every chance one night would be more than enough for her.

"You hungry?" Shari stuck her head inside the trailer. They had arrived at the fairgrounds late in the afternoon. It was nearly seven o'clock in the evening and her stomach was making an embarrassing rumble.

"I'm starved."

"You might want to grab a sweater. As hot as it was today, this high up in the mountains, sometimes it gets cold in the evenings."

"All right." She reached into the tiny closet next to her

bunk and dug out a lightweight cardigan, reached over and grabbed her purse. "We're out of here."

They weren't going far, just over to Kendrick Park to the rodeo Welcome Barbecue being given by the local Kiwanis Club. She was hungry enough to eat roast mule, and besides, Dallas would be there, or so Stormy had said.

Patience's stomach contracted. She wasn't sure she could go through with this. It wasn't her nature to be aggressive when it came to men, but this was different. Dallas had made the first move. The next move was up to her.

"Dallas isn't back yet," Stormy told them as he walked her and Shari toward the big black Dodge dually he'd been driving while his partner was gone. "He's doing a local TV show. He'll meet us at the park as soon as he's finished. I think he's missed seeing everybody."

Patience couldn't help wondering if Dallas might have missed *her*. Probably not. He had probably been too busy.

The chuck wagon barbecue at Kendrick Park, where there were acres of grass and big, leafy cottonwoods, was in full swing when Stormy drove the pickup into the parking lot. Once they reached the picnic area, they grabbed bottles of ice-cold beer and wandered toward the old-fashioned chuck wagon that was about to start serving up food.

"Hey, Stormy!"

Patience turned at the sound of the gruff, unfamiliar voice. It was the grizzled old cowboy Patience recognized as one of the Circle C crew who worked behind the chutes.

"You seen Dallas?" he asked. "Charlie's lookin' for him." He was slightly stoop-shouldered, his cheeks sunken in and rough with stiff white whiskers. Sun-browned skin stretched like rawhide leather over his bone-thin arms.

"Dallas had a TV interview," Stormy said. "He'll be here as soon as he's finished." Stormy's hazel eyes flicked to Patience then back to the old man. "You two know each other?"

" 'Fraid I ain't had the pleasure."

"Salty Marvin, meet Patience Sinclair. Most of us call her P.J."

Salty tipped a dusty, battered felt hat that looked about a thousand years old. "How do, ma'am?"

"Hello, Salty. It's nice to meet you." A second man walked up just then, average height and build, dressed in the usual scuffed boots and faded jeans of the rodeo world.

"And this fella here is Junior Reese. He's clowning the show with Cy Jennings. Junior, this is P.J. Sinclair."

She smiled. "Nice to meet you, Junior."

"Same here."

He didn't say more and neither did she. In Flagstaff, Shari had mentioned the clown who would be taking Ritchie Madden's place until Ritchie got back on his feet. Patience had watched him perform, mostly working the barrel, but he had been wearing his clown makeup then.

He looked far different now.

Shari had told her the story, that years ago, as a young bull rider, he'd gotten hung up on his rope and been trampled by a bull. The Brahma had kicked him in the face, breaking his nose and jaw, leaving a scar that bisected his eyebrow, and crushing his cheekbone. In profile, Junior looked perfectly normal. When he turned, half his face was caved in.

"Anybody seen Cy?" Junior asked. "I want to go over tomorrow's routine."

"Haven't seen him," Stormy said. "He may be downtown, doing that interview with Dallas. Dallas mentioned something about the station asking him if he could get one of the clowns to come along."

"Thanks." Junior wandered away as they moved toward the chuck wagon line, which stretched half a block across the grass. Wes McCauley walked up to join them.

"I'm so hungry I could eat the ass end out of a skunk," Wes said, making them laugh.

Wes hadn't been at the Greeley show, but he had com-

peted at the rodeo they had been to in Pecos. Wes had wrestled his steer to the ground in three point four seconds, the
fastest time of the night, and taken home first place money.
To celebrate, he had invited them all out to dinner at the
Caramba Cafe. Wes had asked her to go out the following
night and finding no good reason to decline, she had said
yes. They had doubled with Stormy and Shari and gone to
see a movie.

Afterward, Wes had kissed her. Though she hated to admit
it, she had been hoping for a rousing, blood-stirring, Dallas-
Kingman-sort-of-kiss, but it hadn't been even close.

Patience sighed, thinking there was only one man who
could excite her the way Dallas did, and if she were going to
explore her sexuality, no other man would do.

"Boy, that looks good." Stormy eyed the thick, perfectly
grilled New York steak and heaping pile of barbecued beans
that passed by on a plate in the hands of Reno Garcia.

The line moved forward. They drank another beer and inhaled the rich aroma of roasting meat and thick slabs of but-
tered, toasted garlic bread. They were all loaded up with
heaping plates of food, plastic silverware, and red-checked
paper napkins, heading for one of the empty picnic tables
when Dallas showed up.

"Get your plate and join us," Stormy called out as he set
his plate on the table. Dallas flicked a quick glance in the
group's direction and shook his head.

"I'm sitting over there with Cy and a couple of his
friends. I'll catch up with you later." He turned away without
so much as a hello, how are you, kiss my backside—nothing.
Patience's chest tightened with disappointment. Obviously,
he hadn't missed her.

"Wonder what's got into him?" Shari asked.

"He was fine when I talked to him earlier," Stormy said.
"He's probably just tired after being on the road for so long."

Not too tired to sit with a couple of little blond buckle
bunnies, Patience noticed. Not too tired to fetch one of them

a beer then take her over to meet Charlie and some of the local VIPs before they joined Cy and sat down to eat.

After all the restless nights Patience had spent pondering whether or not to sleep with Dallas Kingman, after the tug-of-war she'd had between her conscience and her brain, Dallas didn't even want her anymore. Maybe he never really had.

She finished her second beer and set the empty long-neck down on the picnic table, angry at Dallas, even more angry at herself. What was it about him that made her act like a fool again and again? She took a deep breath, shoved her hands in her pockets as she rose from the picnic table.

"I'm really wrung out. I think I'll see if I can catch a ride back to the trailer."

Wes stood up beside her. "I'm packin' it in, too. I'll give you a ride home before I head back to my motel."

She nodded. "Thanks."

As they walked toward his dark green Ford pickup, she noticed Salty Marvin leaning up against the trunk of a cottonwood tree. He watched them as they passed and she made a mental note to see if she could interview him about rodeo life in the past.

Wes opened the door of his big 250 diesel and helped her into the cab. "I don't see how you guys do this, year after year," Patience said as Wes fired up the motor. "All of the travel, I mean."

" 'Less you rodeo some yourself, you'll prob'ly never really understand."

"So, explain it to me."

He shrugged a set of linebacker shoulders. "It's jus' what we do."

She noticed the way he had begun to slur his words. She didn't say more as they drove back to the rodeo grounds, just watched Wes gulping his beer and casting her sideways glances. There were six empties rolling around at her feet and she realized he had drunk more than she'd thought.

He shouldn't be driving. Not until he sobered up. She decided she would make him a cup of thick black coffee when they got back to the trailer and insist he drink it before he set off for his motel.

CHAPTER 10

Dallas tried not to look for her. He had made up his mind to stay away from her, but the minute he had seen her standing next to Wes, a knot had tightened in his gut.

He finished his steak and excused himself from Cy and his friends. Dumping his empty paper plate in the trash, he picked up his beer and took a long, thirst-quenching swallow. A glance at the picnic table where Patience had been sitting told him she was no longer there. Neither was Wes McCauley.

Hey, she was single and over twenty-one. She could go out with any man she wanted. But the thought of her with Wes spawned a sick feeling in the pit of his stomach. He glanced around to see if she might be sitting somewhere else, all the while telling himself to forget her, reminding himself she was nothing but trouble.

In the distance, he could hear western music pumping over the speakers at the edge of the picnic area, but saw no sign of Patience. He wondered if Wes's truck was gone, too. Giving in to the urge to find her, he wandered toward a cluster of cottonwood trees near the parking lot. Up against the rough bark of one of the towering trees, Salty Marvin sat in the shadows, his brown, weathered hands forming a hand-rolled cigarette.

"If you're lookin' for that pretty little gal I seen you starin' at, she left with Wes." The knot in Dallas's stomach turned into a ten-pound rock. "Heard someone say he was givin' her a ride back home."

"That so?"

"I was you, I'd make sure she got there okay."

Dallas fixed a hard look on Salty. "What are you talking about? She's Wes's problem, not mine."

"Maybe so. But Wes was drinkin' pretty hard tonight. He gets liquored up, he don't always listen too good when a lady says no."

A thread of worry slipped along Dallas's spine. He had heard stories about Wes, that sometimes the big steer wrestler had been known to press a woman a little too hard for what he wanted. Rumor was, it had happened at Roy Greenfield's party. Dallas didn't believe Wes would actually force a woman to have sex, but he was big and sometimes he didn't know his own strength. He didn't want Patience having problems with Wes.

"How long have they been gone?"

"Fifteen, twenty minutes."

Dallas started walking toward his truck. Using his own set of keys, he clicked open the door, climbed behind the steering wheel, and started the engine.

It didn't take long to reach the rodeo grounds. He spotted Patience's little white travel trailer hooked up to her brown Chevy pickup. Wes's Ford sat in the shadows not far away. Dallas turned off the motor but didn't get out of his truck.

You do this, you're gonna make a damned fool of yourself.

But the door of his truck cracked open as if it had a mind of its own. Dallas climbed down from the seat and started walking, cussing himself all the way. When he reached the trailer, he heard voices inside. Then the lights went off and the trailer fell silent.

Sonofabitch. He knew what was going on in there. He knew and it and it royally pissed him off.

You'll probably think I'm old-fashioned . . .

Old-fashioned? Ha! His hands balled into fists. Fine, he told himself. She wants Wes, she can have him. He started to walk away, but something just wouldn't let him. He turned to look at the trailer. He thought he heard them talking again.

Calling himself ten kinds of a fool, Dallas strode over and banged on the door. "Patience?"

Wes's deep voice answered. "Hey, buddy, we're busy in here."

Dallas swore foully. He started to turn away, even madder at himself that he was at her, when he heard the sound of glass breaking inside the trailer. Combined with the instincts screaming inside his head, he reached for the knob and jerked open the door.

A Coke bottle whizzed past his head, smashing against the door frame.

"Get out of here, Wes McCauley! And don't you ever come back again!"

Everything happened at once.

Wes dragged Patience against him and crushed his mouth down over hers. She jabbed an elbow into his ribs and kicked him hard in the shins.

"Shit!" Wes swore, and a red haze of fury dropped over Dallas, unlike anything he had known.

"You son of a bitch!" He caught the front of Wes's shirt and spun him around, dragged him toward the door, and heaved him down the stairs. Wes landed in the dirt and Dallas went after him, hauling him up and smashing him in the face. Wes spun around and swung a punch at Dallas, who dodged the blow and punched Wes in the stomach, doubling him over.

"What the fuck are you doing?" Wes slurred. He was a taller, heavier man, but he was drunk and disoriented. He staggered to his feet and Dallas smashed a fist into his jaw that sent him sprawling. He went down like a stone and this time he didn't get up.

Adrenaline pumped through Dallas's blood. His jaw was locked, his teeth clenched. The scab on the back of his hand had been ripped away and he saw that it was bleeding. He turned toward the trailer, found Patience standing at the bottom of the metal stairs.

"I-I needed a ride back to the trailer," she said as he walked toward her. "Wes volunteered. I didn't . . . I didn't realize he had drunk so much until we had already left the picnic." She glanced over at the big lump sprawled on the ground. "I was worried about him driving back to his motel. I insisted he come in for coffee."

Dallas said nothing. He was still so mad, he couldn't speak.

Patience took a shaky breath. "Wes started kissing me and I couldn't make him stop." Her face looked pale. He saw that she was trembling and a band seemed to tighten around his chest.

Dallas reached for her, drew her into his arms. "It's all right, darlin'. It's over and you're okay."

Patience slid her arms around his neck and seemed to melt against him. "Dallas . . ." She said his name with a soft sigh of relief and it was suddenly hard to breathe. He held her for long moments more, until her trembling eased and she began to compose herself.

"I'm sorry." She eased a little away, straightened the front of her shirt. "I think I could have handled him." She shook her head. "He's just so darned big. He's damned pushy but I don't think he would have forced me." She flicked a glance at Wes, who now lay there snoring. "It's just . . ."

"Just what?"

"Something happened before I left Boston. A man I briefly dated became obsessed with me, a guy named Tyler Stanfield. He started stalking me, wouldn't leave me alone.

One night, he broke into my apartment while I was in bed. I guess he made a copy of the key on my key ring. He threatened me, scared the living daylights out of me. I had to get a restraining order to keep him away."

Dallas drew her back against him, pressing her into his warmth, angry all over again. "He hasn't bothered you lately?"

"No. Aside from bumping into him once at the supermarket, it's been months since I've seen him. I don't think he even knows where I am. I guess that's why Wes scared me so much."

"Wes is through scaring anyone. He isn't going to bother you again." No, Wes McCauley wasn't going to bother her. He'd beat the bastard senseless if he ever came near her again.

She leaned closer, stood there in the darkness with her cheek nestled into the hollow of his neck, her hair brushing his temple. She felt so good in his arms. So good. He had tried not to think of her, tried to satisfy himself with other women. But God, he had missed her.

"It's all right," he said again, stroking her hair, holding her until the stiffness left her body. Patience drew a little away and he noticed the marks left from Wes's late-night beard. His temper shot back up and he wanted to smash his fist into Wes's face again. "My cell phone's in the truck. I'm going to call the sheriff."

Patience straightened, caught his arm. "Wait a minute, Dallas. Please don't do that. He just kissed me. He didn't really hurt me."

Some of Dallas's anger shifted onto her. "Look, Patience. I don't know what's been going on between you and Wes the last couple of weeks, but tonight I lost a friend because of you."

Her chin went up. "So now this is my fault?" She started to turn away, but he caught her arm.

"Hold on—I didn't mean it that way. This isn't your fault.

I'm sorry. I guess I'm just a little . . ." *Jealous.* He bit back the word. "I'm sorry." Very gently, he reached out and touched the whisker marks on her cheek. "Damn him."

She caught his hand, then spotted the bloody scabs on the back. "You're hurt!"

"It's nothing. Just a scratch. No big deal."

She wouldn't let go when he tried to pull it away. "It'll be a big deal if it gets infected. Let me put a bandage on it for you." She rushed back inside and came out a few minutes later with a gauze pad, a roll of adhesive tape, antibiotic ointment, and a pair of scissors. Her hands were gentle as she worked over him, spreading the ointment, fitting the gauze just so, carefully applying the tape. Her fingers brushed his and a thread of desire slipped through him.

Dallas ignored it. "Are you sure you don't want me to call the sheriff? A night in jail might do Wes some good."

"I don't want to get involved with the police. I had enough of that in Boston."

The light from inside the trailer outlined her slender figure and long, jean-clad legs. He wanted to scoop her into his arms and carry her off somewhere safe from guys like Wes McCauley and Tyler Stanfield.

"If you're sure about that, I'll talk to Charlie about Wes. We'll put the heat on him, make sure he understands what will happen to him if he ever pulls this kind of stunt again."

Patience nodded. "That sounds like a good idea."

"Will you be all right?"

She flicked a glance at Wes. "What about him?"

Dallas flexed a muscle in his jaw. "I'll drive him back to his motel. I promise you, Wes McCauley won't bother you again." He walked over to the man lying in the dirt and nudged him with his boot. Wes grunted but didn't wake up.

"Dallas?" He turned toward the sound of Patience's voice. "Why did you come here tonight?"

Why did he come? Because he couldn't stay away. "Salty said he thought you might need some help."

She gave him a tremulous smile. "So you were playing Sir Galahad again?"

The corner of his mouth edged up. "It's kind of a cowboy thing." He bent to haul Wes to his feet but Patience's voice stopped him one more time.

"I wish I could figure you out."

He looked at her there in the moonlight, her hair mussed and her clothes rumpled, and thought how pretty she was and how much he wanted her. "I wish I could figure myself out."

Turning away, he went back to the not-so-small task of hauling Wes over his shoulder and carting him off to the truck.

She hadn't seen Dallas all day. The evening performance was just about to begin. This far north, it stayed light until well after ten. Standing outside the trailer, she looked up at the vast Wyoming sky, so big and blue it hurt her eyes. The weather was warm, almost hot, the heat seeping through her clothes and into her skin. As she made her way toward the arena, the smell of hay and horses mingled with the hot dry air and the sound of the wranglers' shrill whistles.

She needed to see Dallas, to thank him for helping her with Wes last night. She spotted his tall, broad-shouldered frame the minute she arrived, riding comfortably in his heavy leather saddle, warming Lobo up in the arena. As she walked toward the fence, she watched him loping the big, muscular palomino in lazy circles, appreciating his easy manner with the horse, the effortless way the two of them worked together, just a light tug on the reins or the press of his knee conveying his wishes.

Dallas spotted her just then, turned Lobo in her direction, and rode toward her, reining up on the opposite side of the fence.

"Well, you don't look any the worse for wear," he said

from astride the horse, his gloved hands resting on the saddle horn. "Are you feeling okay?"

"I imagine I'm feeling a whole lot better than Wes." She smiled. "I didn't really thank you last night. I wanted to tell you how much I appreciate your coming to my rescue."

Dallas swung down from the horse and led the big gelding closer to the fence. "Charlie and I had a talk with Wes this morning. Charlie told him if he heard even a whisper that Wes was behaving as anything less than a gentleman where a woman was concerned, he would make sure everybody on the circuit knew about it. I can tell you, none of these guys want anything to do with a guy who would press a woman that way."

Her fingers curled around one of the cables that formed the fence. "I went to the movies with Wes once, that's all. It was a double date with Stormy and Shari. Last night . . . I wouldn't have left with him except . . ."

"Except what?" He gazed at her with those intense blue eyes that seemed to look at her differently than other men.

"The truth is, I watched you flirting with those women last night and I just . . . I didn't want to be there. Wes volunteered to take me home and I said yes. I would have left with the devil himself if he would have taken me out of there."

Something shifted in Dallas's features. "I didn't want any of those women, Patience. The truth is, since the day you drove up in your little red car, I haven't wanted any woman but you."

Her heart seemed to slow. She thought it might completely stop beating. Surely she had heard him wrong. Surely the great Dallas Kingman wasn't saying those words to her. She almost looked over her shoulder to see if another woman stood behind her.

"If that's one of your usual lines, Dallas, it really isn't—"

"It isn't a line." He shoved up the brim of his hat. "You're driving me crazy, Patience. I've stayed away on purpose, drank too much whiskey, forced myself to be with other women. But even when I'm with them, all I can think of is you."

Her legs started trembling. He couldn't possibly mean it. But she couldn't image Dallas lying about something like that.

"I don't understand any of this," she said. "You're not the kind of man I'm attracted to—I only just started to like you. Still, I can't stop thinking about you. When I see you with all those women, I wish I'd never met you. Other times . . . all I want is for you to kiss me the way you did that night in Vegas."

She shrugged her shoulders, wishing she could really explain. "I know it's insane. I know you're the worst possible thing that could happen to me, but I can't stop thinking about what it would be like if we made love."

Dallas just stared. His eyes were as blue as she'd ever seen them. Finally, he sighed. "Well, at least I'm not the only one who's going out of his mind."

It was true. As much as she wanted to stay away from him, she was drawn to him as she had never been to another man. She had never been jealous a day in her life and yet when she saw him with other women, she wanted to tear out their hair. It was time to do something about it.

Patience took a shaky breath. Dallas wanted her. And God knew she wanted him. It was now or never.

Courage, she told herself.

"I think we should . . . um . . . make love. Maybe if we sleep together, we can get over this . . . this . . . whatever it is that's driving both of us nuts."

Those intense blue eyes grew hotter, burned like the tip of a flame. His gloved hand covered hers where it rested on the fence. "God, I'd like to kiss you right now."

That deep Texas drawl washed over her. Her heart did a slow sort of roll. He wanted to kiss her. She wanted that, too. More than anything she could think of. It was a little impractical, considering there was a fence between them and a grandstand full of people watching.

Patience grinned. "I'd love to take you up on that, cowboy, but I don't think we have time. The rodeo's about to begin."

As if to prove it, Lobo nosed him in the back, nudging him toward the fence. Dallas smiled. "I guess you're right." He stroked the white strip on the horse's nose. Patience watched his hands moving with such gentle care and her stomach quivered. The tips of her breasts began to throb.

"I'd better get going," he said. "I'll see you after the show." He gave her a last warm smile, then turned and walked away.

Dallas surprised himself that night and took a first in the calf roping. He wasn't all that good, but he only had to win a little to qualify for the All-Around title, which required earning money in more than one event. Fortunately, Lobo was a damned good cow pony, a registered quarter horse gelding, officially Doc's Lobo, out of Doc's Bandit, raised right there in Texas on the Circle C Ranch. Dallas mostly gave the horse credit for the win whenever he landed in the money.

Tonight he was amazed they had done so well, considering that on and off all evening his mind had wandered to the woman who had been driving him crazy for weeks. He still couldn't believe she had suggested they make love.

Desire slid through him and his groin tightened. He hadn't lied. He had wanted her from the moment he'd first seen her, but traveling together, his gut warning him this wasn't a no-strings lady, he had forced himself to stay away.

Now he thought that maybe she was right. Maybe once they slept together they could get over their unwanted attraction and get on with their lives.

He hoped so. Tonight, just as he was climbing down into the chute, settling himself in the saddle aboard a big blue roan named Hellfire, an image of Patience had popped into his head. For an instant, he had forgotten where he was and nearly got unseated in the chute.

He'd forced himself to concentrate as the horse exploded out the gate. The cheering snared him then, the whistles, the rumble of feet in the stands, and he'd been determined to give them what they'd paid for. It was a decent ride, though he'd made better. He scored an eighty-four, high enough to keep him in the overall.

Still, thinking of Patience had affected his concentration. And he'd had Charlie on his mind, as well. His uncle had been brooding ever since his return from Texas. He didn't like being away from Annie so much and the lawsuit he was involved in seemed to be heating up. Dallas wished there was something he could do, but Charlie was a proud man and aside from moral support, there didn't seem to be any way to help.

The announcer's voice drew his attention. "Well, ladies and gentlemen, boys and girls, we hope you enjoyed the rodeo— the greatest show on dirt!" The old Roy Rogers tune, "Happy Trails," blared out of the speakers and the crowd began to stand and start moving toward the exits.

Dallas spotted Patience leaving the auxiliary stands near the chutes and started walking toward her. For a minute or two, he followed her, watching the nice way her bottom filled out her jeans, his own beginning to fit too snug. He caught up with her, fell into step beside her. Together they walked back to his trailer to put Lobo up for the night.

"You made a great run in the calf roping," she said.

"Yeah. I guess I got lucky. Most of the credit goes to Lobo." She stopped as they reached the spot where the big palomino stood next to the trailer, but Dallas kept walking, pulling her into the shadowy darkness just beyond.

"What about your horse?" she asked as he hauled her into his arms.

"You first; then, we'll worry about Lobo."

She laughed the instant before he kissed her; then, she

sort of melted against him and made a soft little mewing sound in her throat. She kissed even better than he remembered, her lips so damned soft, the taste of her filling his senses. He loved the way she sort of gave herself over to him, letting him take and take until he found himself wanting to give and give. She was slender but lusciously curved and she fit against him as if they were made for each other.

He nibbled the corners of her lips, slid his tongue inside her mouth, let his hands slide down her back to cup her bottom and pull her even closer. He was hard—uncomfortable in his jeans—and the buckle on his chaps was pressing in exactly the wrong spot.

He shifted, trying to find a better position, kissed her again, gently cupped her breasts, and felt her tremble. Her nipples were diamond hard and he desperately wanted to taste them. Damn it, he wanted to drag her into his trailer and down on his bed. He wanted to peel off her jeans and bury himself so deep she would never forget the first time he had taken her.

But he had waited weeks for this. And after the way Wes had treated her last night, he didn't want her thinking he was anything close to that kind of guy.

A couple of cowboys walked by and he forced himself to let her go, though it was the last thing he wanted. "Easy, darlin'. Unless you want an audience, I think we'd better stop."

She reached up and gently touched his lips, her big green eyes fixed on his face. "How do you do that?"

"Do what?"

"You just kiss me and I feel . . . kind of like I'm melting."

Dallas laughed. "Honey, if that's what happens when I kiss you, we'll probably set the room on fire when we make love."

She flushed. In the moonlight, he could see the color creep into her cheeks. Maybe she really was old-fashioned. The notion was strangely intriguing.

"What are you doing tomorrow?" he asked.

"Traveling, I suppose."

"I'm going to Houston for a couple of days. It's my father's sixtieth birthday. My stepmother is throwing a party for him. She called and asked me to come." That was putting it mildly. Rachael had pressured the hell out of him to be there and after four years of staying away, he'd felt guilty.

Patience nervously wet her lips and he went instantly hard again. He ground his jaw against the subtle ache and tried to think of other things.

"I don't know, I . . ."

"We wouldn't be staying at the house with them. My father and I aren't on the best of terms. The truth is, I haven't seen him in quite a while. If you came along, it might make things easier. In a way, you'd be doing me a favor."

She smiled. "Well, I certainly owe you a favor or two."

"Great. I'll take care of your plane ticket. We'll fly down tomorrow morning."

She nodded and smiled and it was all he could do not to haul her back into his arms. He didn't dare. He liked sex—a lot. And he wanted to have it with her.

Instead, he walked her back to her little white trailer. Tomorrow they would take off for Houston. By tomorrow night, Patience Sinclair would be sharing his bed.

The Saturday night perf was over and Charlie was bone tired. Tomorrow he and the crew were hitting the road again. He wished he could squeeze in a couple days off and go home, but July was one of the busiest months of the year and he was feeling the pinch for money.

As soon as he could get away, he headed for the crew trailer, went inside, and picked up his cell phone. He punched an autodial button and a few seconds later, Annie answered. Damn, it felt good just to hear her voice.

"I sure do miss you, honey," he said after the small talk that always helped him relax.

"I miss you, too. You're coming home after Cheyenne, right?"

"A herd of wild elephants couldn't keep me away." They talked about the ranch, then caught up on what had been happening with the Circle C rodeos.

"How's Ritchie doin'?" Annie asked. "I hear Junior Reese is fillin' in for him till he's back on his feet."

"Ritchie's doing all right, considering. He's home, I hear. His wife'll be glad about that. Where'd you hear about Junior?"

"You know I'm not about to reveal my sources." But a lot of her old friends still rode the circuit and she pretty well kept up on what was going on. "So, what about Junior?" Though the words were light, he could hear the worry in her voice. Annie didn't like Junior Reese any more than Charlie did.

"Junior's all right. There's no love lost between us, but as long as he does his job, we'll do just fine."

Years ago, Junior Reese had been one of the top bull riders in the country. Charlie had been young back then, riding broncs and clowning a little. Then, at a rodeo in Kansas, Junior got hung up in the rigging. Charlie was clowning that day. He tried to get him free, but he was inexperienced, mostly just working the barrel. When Junior finally got loose, he fell under the big bull's hooves. Beneath his makeup, his face was badly disfigured.

And he blamed Charlie for it.

"Promise me you'll keep an eye on him," Annie said.

Charlie grinned into the phone. "Yes, ma'am," he said, wishing more than ever he was home.

CHAPTER 11

Patience got up early Sunday morning. Dallas stopped by for a couple of minutes after breakfast, said the plane would be leaving at 12:02 and that he would pick her up at ten so they would have plenty of time to get to the airport and get through the security check.

Shari was sitting in the dinette when he arrived. She didn't say a word until he left.

"You're actually going to Houston with Dallas? I can't believe it."

Patience tried for nonchalance. "Why not? We're two adults. We're attracted to each other. Why shouldn't we do something about it?"

Shari looped a red curl behind her ear. "You know very well why you shouldn't. Because Dallas is Dallas and you are you—and don't pretend not to know what that means."

Patience sighed. "Okay, I know what it means. But just this once, I've decided to be somebody else for a little while."

Shari laughed. "Someone who has the hots for Dallas and plans to do something about it."

Patience grinned. "Exactly." As if to prove it, she knelt in front of her bunk and dragged out her suitcase, which was never completely unpacked in the tiny trailer. She took out the items she didn't need, then tossed in several pairs of lacy underwear, a lavender shorty nightgown and a pair of low-heeled sandals.

"I'm meeting his father and stepmother. I wonder what I should wear. Do you know anything about them?"

"Not much. Dallas never talks about them. His father's got money, though. That's why he and Dallas don't get along. He doesn't approve of Dallas rodeoing. I get the impression he thinks rodeo people are beneath him."

"Great. I can tell I'm going to love him." She folded a pair of slacks and put them in the suitcase. "You'd think he'd be proud of what his son has accomplished."

"From what Charlie says, Dallas takes after his mother's side of the family—a long line of Texas ranchers. I guess that's why his dad and mom never got along. Dad was a city boy. Mom was a country girl. There were just too many differences to make it work."

The words put a damper on the morning. There were never two people more different than Patience and Dallas. A cowboy and a professor—or soon-to-be, at any rate. Inwardly she groaned.

At least she had a good idea what to take with her on the trip. She tossed in a pair of strappy, black high-heeled sandals, took out a short black sheath dress—one of her few concessions to fashion—and the string of pearls her mother had left her.

Shari was gone by the time she finished packing and she still had an hour or so to work. Her thesis was coming along nicely. She slid her glasses on, cracked open her great grand-mother's journal—the most interesting part of her research—and immediately became engrossed.

Lucky and Adelaide Holmes were still traveling the circuit together and their friendship seemed to be growing. Addie's horse came up lame, but the colonel found her another mount and she seemed happy with his choice. After that, several pages were missing, or appeared to be. When the writing resumed, Addie talked about racing in a couple of smaller rodeos and Sam Starling's name appeared again.

> *I really like him. I wish I didn't. Sam's a cowboy and most of us gals know what that means. Cowboys are like tumbleweeds. Tryin' to hold onto one of 'em will only leave you with a passel of stickers. They're the very best sort of men—long as you don't fall in love with one of 'em.*

As she read the words, Patience felt an odd sort of connection. She liked Dallas Kingman—more than liked—though she definitely didn't want to. Whatever she felt, she wasn't about to let herself fall in love with him.

She turned the page, started reading, then sat forward in the booth.

> *There's a man who's started following the show. I saw him last weekend in Billings and I remember seeing him somewhere even before. Now it looks like he's come to this rodeo, too. He's always in the front of the crowd when the women are competing. I don't like the way he looks at us. There's just something about him.*

Patience's heart started beating. She flipped to the back of the journal and carefully removed the page that had fallen out the first time she had opened the book.

> *He was out there again today. I saw him when I got ready to race. I don't like the way he watches me. Sometimes when I go into town with some of the gals, I feel like he's there behind us. I keep telling myself I'm being a fool. Surely, I am. I guess it doesn't matter. It won't do a lick of good to worry about it.*

The first entry appeared to have been made right before the passage in the torn-out page.

Parts of the journal were dated but not all. The earlier page was marked *July 27*. Patience read the next several entries. The man continued to appear at a number of different rodeos, but the girls had become convinced that whoever he was, he was harmless.

> *Lucky says we should be flattered to have such a faithful fan.*

But none of them knew his name and he always seemed to disappear as soon as the rodeo was over. Addie still had misgivings. Having been in a similar situation, Patience had misgivings of her own. She wanted to keep reading, wanted to find out what happened, but Dallas would be there to pick her up any minute and she needed to be ready when he got there.

Patience put the journal away and finished getting ready for the trip to Texas. She was excited, determined—and growing more and more nervous. She prayed she was doing the right thing.

The plane landed at Houston International Airport at 7:06 p.m. They hadn't flown first class, though Shari said that on occasion, some of Dallas's sponsors flew him around in their private jets. Shari said Dallas saved as much as he could, so she didn't know what sort of weekend was coming up.

She certainly didn't expect to see a black-haired chauffeur standing in the baggage area holding up a sign with Dallas's name on it. Dallas walked over to talk to him and the man came over to the luggage carousel to help them carry out their bags.

As Dallas pushed open the terminal door and they stepped out onto the sidewalk, a gust of thick, damp air hit her, surrounding her in a solid wall of heat. It was definitely summer in Texas and this close to the gulf, Houston suffered unbearable humidity. Her hair began to curl in the dampness, forming ringlets around her face.

They crossed the asphalt and the chauffeur opened the door to a long black Cadillac limo.

"My stepmother sent it," Dallas explained. "She told me she'd arrange for a car to pick me up."

"Nice choice," Patience said, sliding onto the deep, gray leather seat.

"Yeah, Rachael's always had expensive taste."

But Patience wasn't complaining. As the All-Around champion, Dallas might be used to living high on occasion, but Patience rarely had the chance. She leaned back against the seat and smiled when she noticed a silver ice bucket holding a bottle of champagne.

"My, your stepmother treats you extremely well."

"It's taken her four years to convince me to come home for a visit. I guess she figured that was cause for celebration."

Patience turned to look at him. "Four years? That's how long it's been since you've seen your family?"

Dallas reached over and plucked the champagne, an icy bottle of Dom Perignon, out of the bucket. "My father and I had a major falling out when I dropped out of college." He wrapped a towel around the bottle and deftly popped the cork.

"You went to college?"

He flicked her a glance. "Pretty hard to believe, huh?"

But maybe it wasn't. Dallas had never struck her as dumb. "Where did you go?"

"Texas A and M. I was on the collegiate rodeo team. That's how I first got started riding broncs—that and Charlie, of course. He rodeoed when he was younger, before he met Annie."

Questions swirled through Patience's head. She opened her

mouth to ask what subject he had majored in and why he had dropped out of school, but he pointed to the glasses and she held two of them up for him to fill. Dallas nestled the bottle back in the ice and Patience handed him one of the flutes.

"To us," he said, clinking their rims together with a crystalline ring.

"To us," Patience repeated and both of them took a sip. The questions returned to mind. "What about your father? Will you tell me about him?"

Dallas moved closer on the seat. Bending his head, he pressed his lips against the side of her neck, and a shiver went through her. "Yes—since it seems you're going to meet him—but not tonight. Tonight I don't want to think about my father or anyone else. I don't want to think of anyone but you."

He tipped her chin up with his finger, lowered his head, and very gently kissed her. The kiss grew hotter, deeper. He didn't rush, didn't hurry, just kissed her and kissed her. Patience forgot her questions.

At least for the night.

In her apartment in New York, Hope dragged her mind from the words she was typing onto the screen of her laptop, the ringing of the phone beginning to penetrate her senses. She lifted the receiver, coming out of her writer's daze, and pressed the phone against her ear. "Hope Sinclair."

"Hello, Hope. . . . It's Tyler."

Hope stiffened at the unexpected name. "Hello . . . Tyler. What can I do for you?"

"I was wondering if you could tell me where I could find your sister."

Hope snorted a laugh. "Oh, sure, Tyler. I'm really gonna do that." She had met Tyler Stanfield once when she had been visiting her family in Boston. She knew the trouble he had caused. "You've been driving my sister crazy for months. Why don't you just leave her alone?"

It was late in New York City, the lights in the buildings outside her apartment window were beginning to wink out one by one. She'd been working on a human interest story for *People* magazine when the phone had started to ring.

"I love her, Hope," Tyler said.

"You hardly even know her."

"We're perfectly suited. Both of us are graduate students and our interests lie in teaching. We like the same kind of people. Like to do the same things. She just hasn't realized how good we are together."

"That's total bullshit, Tyler."

"It isn't bullshit, Hope. Deep down, I know she still cares."

Hope sighed into the receiver. "Patience doesn't give a damn about you, Tyler. You just can't stand being dumped. Stay away from her or I'm going to call the police."

"I hear she's doing her rodeo thing, traveling with some female hillbilly from Oklahoma."

"You knew what she planned to do this summer. In case you haven't figured it out, there are hundreds of rodeos all over the country. You haven't got a snowball's chance in hell of finding her."

"Yeah, well, maybe I'll surprise you."

"You do, and maybe I'll surprise *you*. Leave her alone, Tyler, I'm warning you."

". . . You really don't think she cares?"

She gentled the tone of her voice, hoping she might actually reach him. "Look—be honest with yourself. You two only dated a few weeks. It just didn't work—at least not for her. Do yourself a favor and find a woman who really does care about you."

A long pause on the line.

"Listen, Tyler. You're a good-looking man. You've got a

great education, a promising future. You keep this up, you're going to spoil everything you've worked for."

"You really think so?"

"Yes, I do."

"I'll give it some thought."

"You do that. You'll be doing yourself *and* my sister a favor if you just get on with your life."

The phone went dead on the other end of the line and Hope released a slow breath. She should probably telephone Patience. But if she did, it would put a major damper on her sister's summer. Traveling, moving around as much as Patience was, odds were Tyler wouldn't be able to track her down even if he tried.

And even if he found her, aside from being a royal pain in the ass, he seemed to be pretty much harmless.

Hope decided to wait. If he called again, she would warn Patience he was still on her tail. In the meantime, she would let her sister have the adventure she deserved.

Houston rose like the Emerald City out of the flat Texas landscape, a sea of tall glass buildings lit by beams of multi-colored lights. As they stepped out of the limo in front of the Four Seasons hotel, the humidity hit her as it had at the airport, making it hard to breathe and reminding her they had arrived in the southern portion of the country.

"Did you know that before this was Houston, it was a place called Harrisburg? It was a maritime trading post founded in 1824."

"You don't say."

"Years later a couple of men tried to buy it, but the owners wanted too much money so they settled the actual town of Houston a few more miles up the bayou from the gulf."

Dallas grinned. "Having you around is like having my own personal travel guide."

Patience flushed. "I didn't mean to—"

"Hey—I like it. I think it's great you know all that stuff."

They started walking toward the door of the hotel. The closer they got, the more her stomach churned with nerves. "The Four Seasons," she said. "Pretty swanky." Dallas pushed open the glass doors and she stepped into the marble-floored lobby. "This your stepmother's doing as well?"

Dallas smiled. "This one's on me. Rachael offered. I refused. I don't like being indebted to them." He glanced around the elegant interior, done in subtle shades of beige with Asian accents and huge bouquets of fresh flowers. "I wanted this to be special. I thought you might like it."

She liked it, all right. She loved it. And it was very thoughtful of Dallas to choose a place like this. "I heard you were trying to save money."

He shrugged his shoulders. "We're only staying a couple of nights. I used Roy Greenfield's name. Roy's company gets a rate. It wasn't really all that bad."

It wasn't cheap, either, but the ambiance was lovely, the hotel elegant and refined. Their room was equally spectacular, a small suite with Chippendale furnishings and huge bay windows that overlooked the city.

"It's beautiful, Dallas."

"I'm glad you like it." There was another bottle of champagne in a silver bucket on the table in the living room. He went over and opened it, poured them each a glass, and handed one of them to her.

"You're not trying to get me drunk, are you?"

"Do I need to?"

Actually, yes, but she didn't say that. Every minute they were together, her nerves seemed to crank up a notch.

"Why don't you go unpack and I'll order us something for supper."

"Supper?"

He smiled. "You thought all I was going to feed you were those awful snacks we got on the plane?"

She laughed. "I guess food wasn't my highest priority."

He gave her one of his intense blue-eyed stares. "If that's the case, maybe we should forget the food until later."

"No! I-I mean, no, I'm really very hungry. I'd love something to eat."

"Steak all right? This is Texas, after all."

"Steak sounds great. If you don't mind, while you're calling downstairs, I think I'll shower and change."

"Good idea. Maybe I'll join you."

"No! I mean, I'd rather you didn't." She took a big gulp of champagne. "I'll be out in a minute."

Dallas noticed the tremor in the hand that held the glass and frowned. "You're not nervous, are you?"

Patience forced herself to smile. "Why on earth would I be nervous? It's not like I haven't slept with a man before."

"Are you sure?"

"Well, I'm certainly not a virgin."

He chuckled. "I meant are you sure you're not nervous."

She felt like a fool. He seemed to have a way of doing that to her. "Well, maybe I'm just a tiny bit nervous, but I'll be fine—I promise."

She left him there in the living room and headed for the bedroom. The valet had left her garment bag in the closet. She unzipped the bag, took out a simple apricot cotton sundress that, except for two tiny straps, left her shoulders bare, and a pair of sandals, then picked up her carry-on bag and took it into the bathroom.

Like the rest of the suite, it was elegant, all beige marble and mirrors, a big marble tub, and a clear-glass shower. She laid out her toilette articles, took off her travel-stained clothes, wrapped her hair in a towel, and stepped into the shower.

She was dressed in less than fifteen minutes, her hair swept up in a twist. She smoothed the skirt of the sundress, took a deep, fortifying breath, opened the bedroom door, and walked into the living room.

"You look terrific." Dallas walked toward her, his gaze running over the short, slim skirt of the sundress, down the length of her legs, then back to her bare shoulders. "Good enough to eat."

She flushed as he bent his head and very thoroughly kissed her.

"Now it's my turn," he said. "I'll be out in a minute." He paused at the door to the bedroom. "The food should be up any time. Feel free to nibble until I get back."

But he showered even faster than she had and reappeared in a pair of black slacks and a crisp white shirt. She had never seen him in anything other than western clothes and the change was startling. He looked as if he had stepped straight off a page in *GQ* a difference that made him seem strangely remote.

Her nerves inched up. By the time dinner arrived, she had downed another glass of champagne, which didn't seem to help. The waiter rolled a white-draped table into the room, and the smell of broiled meat hit her. Mixed with the champagne and her unsteady nerves, her stomach rolled. She was afraid she wouldn't be able to eat a single bite of the meal.

Dallas signed the check, waited till the man was gone, then walked over to where she stood behind one of the chairs.

He was studying her face and frowning. He reached down and caught her hand, laced his fingers with hers.

"You're skin's like ice and your face is pale. Tell me what's wrong."

She tried to smile. "Nothing's wrong. I told you I'm fine."

"That's what you said. Now tell me the truth."

She glanced away, tried to collect herself. A heavy weight seemed to settle on her chest. "I'm sorry." She shook her head. "It's just . . . I'm just not good at this kind of thing."

"What kind of thing is that? Eating supper in a man's hotel room?"

"Having sex. Making love. I've always been a complete and utter failure. My last relationship, brief as it was, was a total disaster. Tyler said . . . well, he said I was a terrible lover. There's even a chance . . . Actually, Tyler thought I might be frigid and I think . . . I'm afraid he might be right."

Her hand was trembling. Dallas pressed their linked fingers against his mouth, then led her over to the sofa. He urged her down on the cushion and sat down beside her, his trouser leg brushing against her calf.

"All right, you're nervous. I can understand that. But being frigid—that's something else altogether. Are you telling me you've never had an orgasm?"

She could feel the heat creeping into her face. Once, in an intimate moment, her sister Charity had confided that she had multiple orgasms with her husband, Call. Patience had been wildly envious, but she had kept her silence. Sitting here now, she didn't want to tell Dallas the awful things Tyler had said. She didn't want to mention her past disastrous relationships. She had been so hoping that tonight things would be different.

Maybe they could be . . . if she somehow found the courage.

Taking a deep breath, she fixed her gaze on the table in front of the sofa and plunged in. Patience told him about the first time she had made love and about the psych student in college and how she hadn't really liked sex from the start.

And then there was Tyler. She admitted that at first she had been attracted to him. She liked his blond good looks and the fun places he took her. But making love had been a disaster and after that things had gone straight downhill. She just couldn't seem to enjoy sex the way her sisters did.

"You've been with so many women." Patience blinked against the unexpected sting of tears. "I can't stand to think of being a disappointment to you."

The strong hand holding hers tightened ever so slightly.

Something shifted in Dallas's features, turning them dark and fierce. Suddenly he looked like the cowboy who had rescued her that night from Wes McCauley.

"I'd like to take a swing at that guy Tyler Stanfield—and any other man who's made you feel the way you do. Like you said, I do know something about women and about making love. And as for being frigid . . . You probably won't believe it, but there's a question as to whether or not there even is such a thing."

Patience just looked at him.

"We're going to take things nice and slow tonight, okay? There's no rush, no reason to hurry. I know what I'm doing, Patience, but I need you to trust me. Do you think you can do that?"

She bit her lip, then nodded.

"Then everything's going to turn out fine. And even if you don't reach a climax, I'm not going to be disappointed. I'm going to love just being inside you."

To punctuate his words, he bent his head and gently brushed his mouth over hers. "That sound okay to you?"

She felt the pull of a smile and a small stirring of excitement. "That sounds perfect."

He kissed her again, very slowly, just the slightest melding of lips. Then he captured her face between his palms and deepened the pressure, kissing her first one way and then the other, nibbling the corners of her mouth, sliding his tongue inside.

The stiffness melted from her body. She could feel herself beginning to relax. She might not trust Dallas Kingman with her heart, but she trusted him completely with her body, and she gave herself up to him in a way she never had with a man before.

Dallas must have sensed the change. He shifted on the sofa and kissed the side of her neck, lazily ran his hands up and down her back. "I think supper can wait, don't you?"

Before she could answer, he started kissing her again, and

every place his mouth touched seemed to burn. Slowly the pressure began to build, a hot ache that tugged low in her belly and sent gooseflesh over her skin. Dallas kissed her and kissed her until she was squirming on the sofa, wanting him to touch her, wanting him to peel away her clothes and his own.

A faint moan escaped as he lowered one of the straps on the sundress, baring her breast, then bent his dark head and took her nipple between his teeth. He nipped and tasted, pressed soft kisses over her skin, drew the fullness into his mouth. Heat tugged low in her belly, floated out through her limbs. When he lowered the second strap and curled his tongue around her nipple, Patience's head fell back and she moaned.

Oh, dear God! She didn't feel frigid. In fact, her body seemed to burn.

"Lovely," Dallas said, easing away a little to look at her. "I knew you would be." He lowered his head and sucked on her nipple and unconsciously her body arched up to give him more.

"Dallas . . ." His name whispered out with an urgency she had never felt and her fingers dug into his shoulders.

"Easy, darlin'. Like I said, we've got all night."

But she didn't want to wait all night. She didn't want this feeling to end and she was afraid that it would. "Can't we just—"

"Not yet. Not until you're ready."

"But—"

He silenced her with a kiss that tasted of champagne and the raw masculinity that was Dallas. God, she was more than ready by the time she felt his arm beneath her knees, lifting her against his chest. He carried her into the bedroom and set her on her feet beside the bed. She heard the buzz of her zipper, felt the apricot fabric sliding down over her hips into a soft heap at her feet.

She had dressed for seduction: no bra, only a tiny white satin thong bikini that revealed more than it covered.

Dallas's hot gaze ran over her and she heard his harsh intake of breath. "So damned beautiful." Reaching up, he pulled out the comb holding up her hair, letting it tumble down around her shoulders, then gently ran his fingers through it.

Her heart was thundering, her hands shaking. Dallas returned his attention to her breasts, laving her nipples, making them ache and distend.

"You promised to trust me," he said, his mouth moving over her skin, trailing moist kisses along her rib cage, down toward her navel. "Remember?"

"I . . . remember." She wasn't likely to forget. Already she was more aroused than she had been in her entire twenty-seven years.

He knelt in front of her, slid his tongue around the hollow of her navel. She was embarrassingly hot and wet. The last thing she expected was the feel of his mouth against her sex.

His hands moved over her hips and he cupped her bottom, holding her immobile where she stood. Patience gasped at the feel of his tongue sliding gently inside her. Her heart raced and her knees shook. The promise she had made was all that kept her from pushing him away. She stood there trembling while he laved and tasted, closed her eyes against the delicious sensations, laced her fingers in his silky dark hair.

The unexpected climax hit her so hard her legs nearly buckled beneath her. She tried to push him away, but Dallas held her steady and continued his assault. Waves of heat washed over her, little pinpricks of light burst behind her eyes. The sensations seemed to go on forever. She didn't notice when he picked her up and settled her in the middle of the big king-size bed.

Every muscle in her body completely limp, she looked up to see Dallas stripping off the last of his clothes. Naked, he climbed up on the bed to join her, a tender, oddly possessive smile on his face.

"Trust me," he said, reminding her again of her promise. She noticed the empty foil wrapper on the nightstand, one of a sizeable stack. She jerked her eyes away, back to his beautiful body, vee-shaped and athletic, lean yet ridged with muscle. His shoulders were wide and hard, his biceps well defined, his forearms veined and corded.

Dallas came up over her, leaned down and kissed her, and a fresh wave of desire washed through her. She could feel his erection, big and incredibly hard, pressing against her thigh. Still, he didn't move to take her, just kept kissing her mouth, her breasts, his hands moving over her tingling skin. He slipped his fingers between her legs and began to stroke her. The sensations she had felt before rose up with even more force and she shifted restlessly beneath him on the bed.

"Dallas, please . . . I need . . ."

"Easy, darlin'. I'll give you what you need."

But the heat was building, becoming nearly unbearable. Her breasts felt sensitive where they brushed against his chest and a hot ache throbbed between her legs. In the moonlight streaming in through the window, Dallas's eyes looked incredibly blue and intense.

His lips claimed hers, more urgently now, more demanding, his tongue sliding in, stroking the inside of her mouth. She kissed him back and the kiss grew even hotter. Dallas parted her legs with his knee and she felt the heavy weight of his sex as he eased himself inside. He took her slowly, carefully, filling her completely.

"God, I want you so much." Still, he held himself back, bracing himself on his elbows, giving her time to adjust to the heavy length inside her, kissing her again and again. Then he started to move.

Heat rolled through her. Desire spiraled up, thick and delicious. A moan built in the back of her throat, seeped from between her lips. Nothing had ever felt so good, so perfectly right as making love with him. Her body was burning, flaming out of control.

In a far corner of her mind, the thought occurred, *there is nothing the least bit wrong with me. I've just been making love with the wrong men.*

The rhythm increased, his strokes deeper and harder. She wrapped her legs around his, matching his rhythm, and he groaned. He was losing control, she realized, and some deep, feminine part of her reveled in her power. She met each of his thrusts, arched up for more, and started coming again.

She couldn't believe it. It was so easy, so natural. So good. She felt as if she were flying, spinning into a world she had never known before. Dallas drove into her a few more times, then his muscles went rigid and he followed her to release.

Their heartbeats melded. Very slowly, they began to spiral down, Dallas's skin slick with perspiration, matching the dampness of her own. His weight shifted off her as he settled himself on the bed, then pulled her into his arms.

Neither of them spoke. She could feel his pulse begin to slow, feel the tension in his muscles seep away. She didn't want to move, just wanted to stay where she was forever. She turned to look at him, saw the hint of a smile on his lips.

"I guess we don't have to worry about you being frigid."

Her soft laughter drifted across the room. "I guess we don't. Thank you, Dallas."

"My pleasure."

She laughed at the pun. "I ruined our supper."

"Are you kidding? I'd rather eat—"

She clamped a hand over his lips. "Don't you dare—"

He grinned. "I'd rather eat late anyway."

Both of them laughed.

"Are you hungry?" she asked.

Dallas turned his head and nipped the side of her neck. "You wouldn't believe how hungry. Just not for food." He came up over her, captured her mouth again, and she felt his arousal, as big and hard as it had been before.

He slid inside her but he didn't rush, and she thought that

this was the perfect way to make love. Perhaps that was really the difference.

Love.

It was a terrifying thought.

CHAPTER 12

They ate at two in the morning. Cold filet mignon wasn't bad, Dallas thought, slicing off a chunk and popping it into his mouth with his fingers. And the shrimp salad was hardly wilted at all.

Dressed in the fluffy white terry cloth robes they found hanging in the bathroom, they sat at the table in the living room, picking through the food, trying to salvage what they could of their ruined meal.

Not that he was complaining. He glanced at the woman sitting across from him. In the light of the candle in the center of the table, she looked radiant and utterly luscious. Her skin glowed and her cheeks bloomed a soft shade of rose. Her lips were slightly kiss-swollen, her long, golden hair rumpled and sexy.

His groin tightened. He could hardly believe it. They had made love three times already and he wanted her again.

He smiled as he watched her eating, plucking the shrimp out of the wilted lettuce and plopping them into her mouth.

"I can see you aren't the least bit hungry," he teased, since it was obvious she was even hungrier than he was.

Patience stopped eating long enough to look up at him.

"I'm ravenous." She grinned. "Somehow I worked up an appetite."

He smiled. "Yeah . . . somehow."

A hint of color washed into her cheeks. He found it completely charming. Once they were finished, he would take her back to bed. He should probably let her sleep. For himself, he would give up sleep for the chance to be inside her.

In a way it was scary. It had been years since he'd been so hungry for a woman. Maybe never.

Still, this was new to them both and they had waited for weeks. By the time they left Houston, hopefully the newness would have worn off. He didn't want to think about what would happen when they got back. Having a serious relationship was out of the question and both of them knew it.

Whatever they decided, he wasn't going to let it ruin the time they had together.

Dallas took a last bite of steak. Over Patience's shoulder, he could see the rumpled bed, and heat pooled in his groin. Every time she slid the fork into her mouth, his erection throbbed.

"I'm finally getting full," Patience said.

"I'm still hungry."

Her head came up. "Then why did you stop eating?"

Dallas grinned. "It's time for dessert." Shoving back his chair, he stood up and walked around to where she sat.

Patience stood up and turned into his arms. "I can handle it if you can, cowboy."

There was no mistaking the desire in her eyes. That fool Tyler Stanfield had convinced her she was frigid. Dallas chuckled to himself as he scooped her into his arms.

"You still haven't told me about your dad." Patience sat beside Dallas in the same black stretch limo that had picked them up at the airport, heading for Avery Kingman's sixtieth birthday party. "What does he do for a living?"

"Dear ol' Dad is a plastic surgeon."

"You're kidding."

"As a matter of fact, he's a doctor of some renown. He even does the occasional movie star and politician. You'll see why when you meet my stepmother."

"Your stepmother? You mean your father worked on her face?"

"Rachael's forty-eight but she looks thirty. She's a walking advertisement for my father."

"You don't like him much, do you?"

Dallas seemed to mull over the question. He still hadn't answered by the time the limo pulled up in front of an elegant, two-story red-brick home in an exclusive neighborhood north of Houston. Patience waited while the chauffeur opened the door and Dallas climbed out to help her.

He was dressed *GQ* again today, a navy blue double-breasted suit, white shirt, and power tie, though his feet were encased in polished black ostrich boots. He had left his hat in the hotel room, a concession to his father, he had said, but she could tell it didn't sit well with him.

"I feel half naked without it," he had grumbled.

Patience just laughed.

She walked in front of him up the wide brick stairs, in through the double white-painted front doors, and stepped into the foyer, where his mother and father stood greeting their guests.

"David!" An exquisite dark-haired woman hurried toward them, enveloping Dallas in a hug. She was every bit as strikingly beautiful as Dallas had claimed, with perfectly sculpted cheekbones, full red lips, and big dark eyes. Dallas hugged her briefly then stepped away. "Avery, look! David is home."

"David?" Patience hadn't realized she had spoken the word out loud until Dallas answered.

"My parents couldn't agree on what to name me. My mother wanted Dallas, after her father. My father wanted to call me David, after his grandfather. They compromised. My full name is David Dallas Kingman."

"I see." She saw that his parents couldn't agree on even so basic a thing as the name of their son.

"Hello, David." Avery Kingman was almost as tall as Dallas, an attractive man with dark brown hair, silver at the temples, and eyes the same striking blue as his son's.

"Happy birthday, Dad. It's good to see you."

"It's good to see you, too, son. Thank you for coming." The two men shook hands. She noticed no hugs were exchanged, just stiff formal greetings.

"I'd like you both to meet a friend of mine," Dallas said. "This is Patience Sinclair."

Rachael Kingman managed a smile as she scrutinized the simple black silk sheath dress Patience wore and the string of pearls around her neck. "A pleasure to meet you."

"Patience is from Boston," Dallas added.

A look of interest came into Rachael's dark eyes. "Boston?"

"Yes." Patience managed a smile. "I'm traveling the rodeo circuit this summer. I'm working on an article about early and modern-day women in rodeo."

"I see." Some of the interest faded. "Which magazine do you write for, dear?"

Don't say it, a little voice warned, but the condescending tone of Rachael Kingman's voice forced out the words.

"Actually, I'm working on my doctoral thesis. I'm in the graduate program at Boston University."

Next to her, Dallas's whole body went rigid. Patience didn't dare look at him. All she could think was *oh, God, what have I just done?*

But Rachael Kingman was smiling, looking at her with approval and a cunning light in her eyes. "How interesting." She shot a look at her stepson. "That's quite something, isn't it, David? Her doctoral thesis?"

"Yeah. It's something, all right." The words sliced right through her. She should have told him. She knew it, but she had been afraid of his reaction. There were already enough differences between them without adding more.

"When will you be ready to take your final examination?" Rachael asked. In the light from the hanging chandelier, her upswept dark hair shone like onyx and the street-length black and white floral designer gown she wore must have cost a fortune.

"It's scheduled for the end of summer. I've already accepted an assistant professorship at a small college outside Boston, starting this fall."

Rachael oozed a smile. "That's wonderful, dear." She flicked a glance at Dallas. "Isn't it, David?"

"Yeah, terrific."

Rachael reached over and took Patience's arm. "I think most everyone is here." She cast a conspiratorial glance over her shoulder at her husband. "Why don't we go in and join the others? There are some people I'd like the two of you to meet."

Avery fell into step beside his son. Patience recognized the moment he noticed Dallas's boots, for his mouth thinned in disapproval.

"I thought maybe your coming here tonight might mean you had finally decided to stop playing games and settle down to a real sort of life."

Dallas stopped just inside the archway leading into the spacious living room. It was done in a traditional style with camelback burgundy sofas and beige wool carpets. Dark wood cabinets lined one wall and expensive beige draperies hung at big bay windows.

"Look, Dad. I just got here. If you're going to start this whole thing up again, I'm going to turn around and leave. I told you before—my life is my own. I made my choice when I quit school and nothing you say is going to change my decision. I was hoping your invitation meant you had decided to accept me the way I am."

Rachael cast Avery a look of warning. With a sigh of defeat, he made a stiff nod in Dallas's direction. "You're right. The past is the past. Tonight is my birthday. Let's enjoy ourselves."

But as the evening progressed, Patience didn't think Dallas was enjoying himself at all, and with the dark looks he continued to toss her way, neither was she.

Dallas knew a number of the guests, the cream of Houston society, and his stepmother introduced them to others. There were several Texas politicians, including a senator and a congressman, Houston's mayor, a number of professional people, and of course, the wealthy couples able to afford the doctor's expensive services. After each introduction, Rachael mentioned that Patience was writing her doctoral thesis, and Dallas grew more and more remote.

He was angry, she knew. She wished she had told him the truth a long time ago.

"You ready to get out of here?" It was only just past ten and the party didn't seem to be winding down, but Patience could see the tension in his shoulders.

"I'm ready if you are." She hoped she could make him understand the reasons she had kept her silence, but it didn't look like it was going to be easy.

They said their farewells to his parents. Dallas had given his father a commemorative bottle of Oban, his favorite single malt scotch, for his birthday. Not exactly personal, but the doctor seemed to like it well enough. He and Rachael tried to get Dallas to stay in Houston a couple more days, but Dallas declined the invitation.

"I've got to go. I'm riding in Salinas this week, then catching up with Charlie in Cheyenne."

"Charlie," Avery repeated, the word almost a growl. "Don't mention Charlie Carson's name to me. If it hadn't been for your mother's brother, you never would have dropped out of school. You would have graduated by now and be living a responsible life, instead of gallivanting all over the country, acting like some Wild West cowboy."

"I am a cowboy, Dad. And I need to win all the money I can if I'm going to make the Finals in December."

Avery grunted. "Charlie Carson is a fool. He always has been. I should have put a stop to you staying with him at the ranch, but your mother was gone and I was working long hours. I should have known better. As far as I'm concerned your uncle is responsible for ruining your life."

A muscle flexed in Dallas's jaw. "I made my own choices. None of it was Charlie's fault. Someday maybe you'll understand."

His father's mouth flattened out and Rachael's winged, dark eyebrows drew together. Avery let the subject drop and Dallas seemed relieved. They said very formal farewells and Dallas turned to collect Patience as he made his way toward the limo. They rode back to the hotel in silence, Patience trying to think what she might say to lighten his dark mood.

They were entering their suite by the time she had worked up the courage. She waited until he closed the door.

"I'm sorry things didn't go better between you and your dad."

"Yeah? What about the nice little surprise you sprang on me tonight? *Ph.D. Assistant professor.* Christ, I should have figured you for something like that."

"I didn't tell you I was working on my thesis because I thought you would look down your nose at me if you thought I was some sort of academic. I thought it would only make things harder between us."

A muscle flexed in his jaw. His eyes looked dark and angry. "Is that so?" Rudely, he grabbed her wrist and pressed her hand against the fly of his slacks. "Well, things couldn't get any harder."

He was aroused. Angry and aroused, and for an instant it frightened her. Then he backed her against the door, slid his hand up into her hair, knocking out the little pearl combs that kept it swept up, and took her mouth in a rough, demanding kiss.

Her body flooded with heat. In the past two days, they had made love again and again. She knew what it would feel like to have him inside her, knew the delicious sensations, how incredibly turned on she would get. She wanted it—wanted him—just as she had each time before.

Dallas kissed her fiercely, took her with his tongue, kissed her until he had her moaning.

Then he turned her a little and she felt the arm of the sofa beneath her stomach as he bent her over. He slid up her narrow black skirt and ripped off the black silk thong panties she wore underneath. She was hot and wet, her body quaking with desire. She didn't resist when she heard the buzz of his zipper, felt the heavy thickness of his erection as he thrust himself fully inside.

He took her hard, holding her hips in place, pounding into her and setting her on fire. Patience arched her back, taking all he could give, silently demanding more. She didn't know what the future held for either one of them. She couldn't let herself love him, but she wanted him, wanted everything he could give her and more, wanted him for as long as she could have him.

They both came fiercely, their bodies heaving, trembling with the effort. Dallas eased her dress down over her hips and gently drew her back against his chest.

She heard his sigh whisper into the darkness. "I didn't hurt you, did I?"

She shook her head. "No." She could feel the tension still running through his body.

"We're just so different," he said gruffly.

"I know."

"My father and mother were that way. You saw what he's like. Can you imagine him married to a rancher's daughter? It didn't matter that she'd had three years of college. They had nothing in common. There was just no way it could possibly work."

Patience made no reply. Her throat was aching. She could imagine what he must have endured as a child, living with two such unhappy people. She knew he was thinking that the two of them were equally different—and it was the truth.

She turned into his arms and they tightened around her. She felt the brush of his lips against her hair.

"Let's get some sleep," he said, an odd sort of weariness in his voice. "We've got to get up early in the morning."

Patience nodded. But her heart was hurting, her throat tight. She didn't think she would get much sleep that night.

And she would feel even worse when he left her in the morning.

The following day, as they had planned, they parted ways at the airport, Patience heading back to Wyoming to meet up with Shari and Stormy, Dallas flying off to California for Salinas, one of the biggest rodeos of the year.

Dallas's flight left half an hour earlier than hers. Patience walked him to the C terminal, down to his departure gate. She tried to be upbeat, tried not to think that their few brief days were over and now things would return to the way they were before.

She had told herself she was in lust, not love. She was a modern, independent woman—why shouldn't she make love with a man she desired?

But she hadn't counted on this hollow ache around her heart, hadn't thought how she would feel when she watched him leave, knowing that in Salinas women would line up just to get a glimpse of him, that there was every chance he would go to bed with one of them.

The passengers were moving toward the gate, showing their boarding passes, and beginning to disappear down the ramp to the plane.

"We don't have much time," Dallas said. He'd been remote since the party last night. They hadn't even made love this morning, though they'd awakened curled pretzel-like together and Dallas was fully aroused.

She pasted on the brightest smile she could muster. "Thanks for a terrific time. And for the . . . well, you know."

His mouth barely curved. "Therapy?"

"Yes."

"You didn't need therapy. Just a man who would take his time with you." He looked down at the toes of his boots, then back into her face. "I guess I'll see you in Cheyenne."

She swallowed. "Right. Cheyenne." She gave him her too-bright smile. "Good luck in Salinas."

Dallas didn't answer. For several long moments, he just stood there. Then he slid a hand around the nape of her neck and dragged her mouth up to his for a quick, hard kiss.

Patience kissed him back, desperately fighting back tears.

"Stay away from Wes," he said gruffly.

"Bye," she said, hating herself for caring so much, reminding herself it was lust, not love.

Knowing it was a lie.

Dallas's eyes touched hers one last time. He tugged down the brim of his black hat, turned and walked briskly away.

Patience went into the ladies' room and wiped away the wetness on her cheeks.

"Hey! Welcome back, partner." Shari's warm smile cut through some of the gloom Patience was feeling. The pickup idled at the curb out in front of the Casper airport. Patience tossed her luggage into the back and climbed into the passenger seat for the short ride to the rodeo grounds.

"How did it go? Did you two have a good time?"

Patience slumped down in the seat. "Terrific," she said glumly.

"Uh-oh."

"Actually, we were doing just fine until Dallas found out about my thesis. He doesn't seem to think a cowboy and a professor go together very well. Neither do I."

"You probably should have told him."

"I suppose so. Twenty-twenty hindsight and all that."

"He'll get over it. Besides, I don't see what the big deal is. I mean, the guy went to college himself."

"Yes, but he didn't finish."

"He finished four years—graduated with honors. He just didn't finish medical school."

"Medical school?" Patience shot up in the seat. "What are you talking about?"

"I figured you knew. I mean, the way everybody's always coming up to him and asking him for advice."

She remembered Wes asking him to take a look at Hotshot. And the day she had fallen into the pen with the bulls, he had checked her over to be sure she didn't have a concussion. Even the little girl with the broken leg had received a cursory exam.

"His father wanted him to follow in his footsteps," Shari explained. "Dallas went along with him for a while, his mother being dead and all, but he hated every minute of med school. After his second year, he just flat quit. Said he wanted to go into ranching. He had no desire to be a doctor and never would. I guess his father went completely insane."

"From what I could tell, Avery's still mad about it." A lightbulb went off in her head. "That's what Dallas's license plates mean. H P P Y N O W. *Happy Now.* He's happy, now that he's doing what he wants."

Shari slowed the truck and flicked on her turn signal. "The man surely does love to rodeo—and he's the best there is. He's saving his money to buy that ranch he wants. He says he won't stop until he gets it."

They made the turn into the rodeo grounds, and livestock barns and rows of horse trailers passed by outside the window. Dallas had been in med school but he had quit. He hated college. He wanted to be a cowboy. Patience loved every minute of school, loved the learning, loved the books.

Just one more difference.

She sighed as Shari pulled the truck over to their little white RV and turned off the engine.

It was Sunday night. The Casper rodeo was over. Shari had placed in the barrel racing and Stormy had taken a second in the calf roping. To celebrate, Patience was cooking Sloppy Joes. Stormy and Shari would be there any minute.

Shari opened the door of the trailer just as Patience's cell phone rang. She grabbed it up and pressed it against her ear, still stirring the sauce.

"Hello?" No answer. "Hello, is anyone there?"

"I miss you."

Her stomach instantly knotted. Her face must have gone white because Shari started to frown.

"How did you get this number?"

"I've got friends in the computer department at B.U. It wasn't all that hard. Do you really mind?"

"Of course I mind." Her hand shook as she took the wooden spoon out of the pan and set it on the counter. "Listen, Tyler. You know the way I feel. It's over between us. I don't want to see you anymore. I want you to leave me alone."

"I've started seeing someone."

"Good for you. I'm happy for you."

"I'd rather be with you."

She closed her eyes. "We've been through all this a hundred times. If you call me again, I'll get a new cell phone and it won't be under my name." She hung up and sank down on the bench in the dinette.

"Who was that?"

"Tyler Stanfield." She had never mentioned Tyler to Shari.

She didn't want to think about him. But now that he had phoned, she thought her friend ought to know. "I dated him for a few weeks." She told her about his pursuit, how he had dogged her every step, sent her postcards and letters, clogged her inbox with dozens of e-mails, and finally broken in to her apartment, come into her bedroom, and threatened her in the middle of the night. "I finally got a restraining order. I was hoping the problem was over."

"Does he know where you are?"

"He knows I'm following the rodeo circuit. He doesn't have the slightest idea where I am."

"He isn't dangerous, is he?"

"I don't think so, but you never know with a guy like that. I'm not taking any chances. If he shows up, I'm calling the police."

"I don't blame you. Does Dallas know?"

"I told him I hadn't heard from Tyler in months."

"Dallas isn't going to like this."

The trailer stairs rattled just then. "It's me," Stormy said, pulling the narrow door open. He ducked his head, made his way over to the small dinette, and squeezed himself in next to Shari. He looked from one serious face to the other. "All right, what's going on?"

While Shari filled him in on the phone call and told him about Tyler Stanfield, Patience returned to stirring the Sloppy Joe sauce boiling on the little propane stove.

"So you think this guy might be a problem?" Stormy asked Patience.

She started stirring the sauce again. "I hope not."

Stormy looked over at Shari. "Dallas isn't gonna like this."

Patience almost smiled. Dallas was protective of his friends. No matter how things turned out between them, she supposed they could call themselves that.

"As a matter of fact, he just called," Stormy said. "He's flying into Casper instead of Cheyenne. He wants me to pick him up at the airport in an hour."

The spoon in her hand stopped moving. Dallas was coming back.

"I wonder why he changed his plans," Shari said.

Patience couldn't imagine. She just kept thinking, *Oh, God, Dallas is coming back.*

A knot tightened in her stomach. She knew the kind of life he led. He had never made any secret of it. But she wasn't the sort to share a man, and if Dallas thought he could just waltz in and expect her to hop back into bed, he had a big surprise coming.

In the week he'd been gone, she'd had plenty of time to think and most of it wasn't good. It was one thing to have a brief fling with America's top cowboy, another thing entirely to be counted among his numerous female admirers.

"I don't want you to worry about this Stanfield fella," Stormy was saying. "I'll put the word out. Anyone comes around asking questions, we'll tell him we never heard of you."

"Thanks, Stormy."

He tossed his hat on the bunk, and ran a hand through his sandy brown hair. "I'm starved. Boy, that sure smells good."

"Nothing too tough about making Sloppy Joes," she said, trying to sound cheerful as she filled them each a paper plate loaded with the tomato-hamburger concoction poured over a toasted bun.

Everyone dug in, falling silent as they enjoyed the meal. They washed the food down with Diet Cokes, eating hurriedly so Stormy could get to the airport in time for Dallas's flight.

There wasn't much clean-up, just disposing of the paper plates and washing the saucepan. As soon as they finished, Shari left to work with Button while Patience stayed behind and tried not to think of Dallas, with very little success.

What would he say? Why had he come back to Casper instead of meeting them in Cheyenne? Though he knew her cell number, he hadn't called from Salinas, and she hadn't really expected him to. Dallas had never made her any promises. In truth, it was her suggestion that they make love.

Had she really believed it would help them get over their unwanted attraction to each other?

Well, it might have worked for Dallas. It sure hadn't worked for her.

The minutes crawled past. She had to do something to keep her mind occupied. Glancing around, her gaze lit on her grandmother's journal. She picked it up, sat down in the dinette and opened it to where she'd left off. It didn't take long to become absorbed in the pages.

Sam kissed me last night. Never in my life have I ever felt anything like it. Like falling off a cloud—that's the way it felt. He's trouble—no doubt about it. But when he looks at me with those beautiful green eyes, I just can't seem to resist him.

Patience smiled. The more things changed the more they stayed the same, her father always said. There were loose pages after that, some out of sequence, Addie writing about earlier shows. Then a yellowed, tattered page caught her eye.

Lucky didn't come back to the room last night. She went out to supper with Betsy and Star, but they said she left early. Her things are still here this morning and it's time for us to leave. I'm going to see the colonel. I'm really worried about her.

The entry was dated August 7. No pages seemed to be missing, but there wasn't another entry until August 15.

No sign of Lucky. Colonel Howard spoke to the sheriff back in Cheyenne but he says she never turned up at the hotel. Probably ran off with some cowboy, the sheriff said. Said they were holding her things at his office till she got the good sense to come back and pick them up.

Lucille Sims was my best chum and I don't believe for a minute that she up and run off that way. I think something terrible bad happened to her.

A little chill slid down Patience's spine. Though she really didn't want to, she thumbed ahead in the journal. A couple more passages mentioned Lucky, but Addie never saw her again and no one ever found out what had happened to her.

Patience set the book away, feeling oddly depressed. She couldn't help wondering if there was a connection to the man who had been following the rodeo circuit and the disappearance of her grandmother's friend. It made her think of Tyler Stanfield, made her wonder how far his obsession would push him and if she were in any sort of danger.

With a sigh, she got up from the dinette and started for the door. Dusk had settled over the prairie, the sun a bright orange ball sinking behind a row of distant hills. Streaks of orange and pink fanned out through a fading blue sky and she thought that no matter what happened, she was glad she had come on this, her great adventure.

As she walked toward the rear of the trailer, she caught a glimpse of Dallas's big black Dodge. The men would have been back for at least an hour, but he hadn't made an effort to see her. It probably hadn't occurred to him. Dallas wasn't interested in a relationship with a woman. He had made that clear from the start. She told herself it was better this way, better that they'd ended the affair that morning at the airport in Houston. Apparently Dallas felt the same.

The crunch of boots on gravel alerted her. She turned to see a tall shadow walking toward her, knew it was Dallas by the long, purposeful strides and the width of his shoulders.

He was wearing his usual jeans, boots, and hat, and he looked so good her heart turned over.

She took a deep breath to calm the pounding in her chest, then remembered the passage Addie had written about Sam—*he's nothing but trouble*.

"Hello." The soft drawl stirred a longing deep inside her.

Patience ignored it. "Hello."

"I . . . um . . . decided to come back and drive down to Cheyenne with Stormy."

"That's what he said. How was Salinas?"

In the fading light, his features subtly tightened. "Not so good."

"What happened?"

"I got bucked off. I needed to make some extra earnings so I entered both bronc riding events. Bareback is tough. You lean way back. Puts a lot of pressure on your spine. If you screw up, it's kind of like you've been in a car accident."

He reached up and rubbed the back of his neck and she realized he was hurting. Unconsciously, she moved closer, her protective instincts kicking in. Then her brain interceded and she forced herself to stay where she was. "Are you all right?"

"Just a little sore, is all. And a little pissed at myself."

"You'll do better in Cheyenne."

He nodded, looked away, out onto the endless prairie. "I . . . um . . . I thought about you a lot while I was gone."

I thought about you, too. But this isn't going to work and we both know it. "Look, Dallas. We had our little fling and now it's over. It was fun while it lasted, but—"

"Fun while it lasted?"

He was getting mad. She remembered what had happened the last time he'd gotten angry and desire slid through her.

"What I mean is, you have your life and I have mine, and they just don't fit together. I'm not interested in becoming one of your groupies. I'm not the sort of woman who is willing to share a man with a dozen other women."

Her heart was beating, thundering away, just because he was standing so close. It was terrifying to realize how much she wanted to touch him.

Dallas moved toward her, his eyes still fixed on her face. "You think I slept with someone else in Salinas."

Her chest hurt. It was exactly what she thought. "It's none of my business who you sleep with. You never made any promises. I'm just saying—"

"I didn't sleep with anyone. I wouldn't do that. Not as long as I'm involved with you."

Her head came up. She couldn't believe she had heard him correctly. "Are you? Involved, I mean."

"I must be. I tried like hell to put you out of my mind, but I couldn't make it happen."

Patience shook her head. She wasn't sure she should believe him and even if she did, what was the use? "What are you saying, Dallas? You know this . . . thing between us can't go anywhere. Even if I stay through the summer, once it's over, I'll be returning to Boston. We'll probably never see each other again."

He glanced down. "I suppose that's true. Even if it is, I think we should ride this thing out, enjoy what we're feeling, take advantage of the time we have together. Odds are, all this heat will start to fade and by the time you're ready to leave, we'll be able to say good-bye like good friends."

In the fading light, she could see his eyes beneath the brim of his hat, as blue as the big Wyoming sky. Maybe they could. Or maybe she would fall for him even harder and Dallas would break her heart.

"I don't know, Dallas. I need some time. I've got to think this over."

"All right. If that's the way you feel, I won't press you. Just think about it, okay?"

She nodded, wondering why she wasn't relieved. "There's something I should probably tell you."

"Yeah? What's that?"

"Remember that guy I had trouble with in Boston . . . Tyler Stanfield?"

He straightened. "I remember. What about him?"

"Somehow he got my cell number. He called me tonight. I don't think he'll actually try to find me, but since we're all traveling together, I thought you ought to know."

She could see the faint tightening of his jaw. "What did he say?"

"He said he missed me. The usual stuff. I told him if he called me again, I'd get a new phone under someone else's name."

"That's probably a good idea. In the meantime, I'll put the word out. That guy comes near you, I'll—"

She laughed. "I know. I saw what you did to Wes McCauley."

Dallas slid a finger beneath her chin and tilted her face up. "You've got friends here, Patience. You don't have to be afraid." Bending his head he softly kissed her. "Think about what I said."

Dallas turned and started walking, his shoulders hunched forward, his hat pulled low. Patience watched him disappear into the darkness and wished that she could go with him.

CHAPTER 13

Patience and Shari got an early start in the morning, leaving the rodeo grounds in the wake of the stock trucks, following Dallas and Stormy in Dallas's fancy black rig. Patience drove the pickup and trailer as they headed down I-25, making the short, hundred-eighty-mile haul to Cheyenne, a weeklong rodeo with more than six hundred thousand dollars in prize money that attracted the top cowboys in the nation.

"I've read a lot about Frontier Days," Patience said to Shari. "The first one was held way back in 1897. People came by train from a hundred miles away. You could sit in the bleachers for free but it cost thirty-five cents to sit in the grandstands. The papers called it 'The Great Cowboy Carnival at Cheyenne.'"

Shari laughed. "I love all that stuff you know about the West. You're really going to make a great professor."

"You think so?"

"Yeah, don't you?"

"My dad is a really great teacher. The students love him."

"He teach history, too?"

"American history. One of his courses is called Outlaws, Renegades, and Lawmen. It's completely filled every semester."

"Sounds like something I'd like to take."

"Are you looking forward to going back to school?"

Shari fiddled with a curl of red hair. "Actually, it's amazing how much I am. I love rodeos. I guess I always will. But I'm tired of the travel, of staying in cheap motels and eating in crummy cafes. I want a real life, you know? With a husband and kids and a house of my own. You're going to be a professor. I was thinking, once I got through college, I might try teaching, myself. I'd rather work with little kids, though. Kindergarten or first graders."

Patience had noticed Shari with the kids who came up to look at Button. Shari encouraged them to pet him, but she was always careful to make sure they didn't get hurt. "I think you'd be a terrific teacher."

They talked for a while about their future plans then both of them fell silent. Patience was thinking of her return to Boston at the end of the summer and she figured Shari was thinking of having to leave Stormy. They stopped for a fresh cup of coffee at a little cafe in the Best Western motel in Douglas, parting ways with Dallas's rig and the livestock trucks, then pulled back onto the highway stretching across the vast Wyoming prairie that went all the way to Cheyenne.

"What's that up ahead?" Shari asked, sitting forward, pointing toward a collection of flashing lights that appeared on the horizon.

"I don't know. Looks like an accident or something." Patience slowed the pickup as they drew closer, falling in behind the line of slow-moving cars in front of them.

"Oh, my God!" Her fingers tightened on the wheel as she recognized one of the Circle C livestock trucks lying on its side, flipped over in a dry, shallow ditch along the edge of the road. The trailer had been ripped open as if it were tinfoil and she could see several big bucking horses lying in the back.

"Oh, God, what could have happened?" Shari stared at the accident ahead. The pickup seemed to crawl forward, each moment an hour as the cars rolled in single file toward the wreckage.

Patience frantically searched for any other vehicles that might have been involved in the incident, but no other damaged autos appeared anywhere in sight. As soon as they reached the overturned trailer, she pulled the pickup off the road, out of the lane of traffic, and turned off the engine, her hands shaking as she reached down to pull on the emergency brake. Dallas's Dodge sat on the shoulder ahead of them, and several other cars and trucks had also pulled off the road.

The chaos around them was a scene from a nightmare. Patience's chest tightened as she cracked open the door and jumped down from the cab, started toward the terrible sight in front of her.

On both sides of the road, injured horses roamed aimlessly, their eyes glazed with fear and pain, some of them limping, others cut and bleeding. Horses shrieked and whinnied, others thrashed on the ground, digging up the earth with their hooves. The police had slowed traffic to a crawl and some of the officers were trying to help the Circle C cowboys corral the terrified animals that remained on their feet.

A big buckskin mare wandered along the interstate, the side of her neck torn and bloody. A rawboned sorrel dragged his back leg, while a tall pinto gelding bled from a gash on its forehead.

A lump swelled in Patience's throat. She couldn't stand to see the animals suffering. If only there were something she could do. Then she spotted the blue roan Dallas had ridden in Sheridan—Hellfire, she remembered—thrashing on its side at the edge of the road. Tears blurred her vision and her throat ached so hard she couldn't swallow.

Dallas knelt beside the horse, his shirt spattered with blood, trying to calm the animal and stop the blood flowing out of a wound in its chest. Speaking softly to the horse, Patience knelt beside him and gently stroked his neck.

"Easy, boy. You're gonna be all right."

The horse neighed softly, its head jerking up, then falling back to the ground.

"Easy," she said.

Charlie walked up just then, looking more haggard than she had ever seen him. "He gonna make it?"

Dallas slowly shook his head.

"Go ahead, then. No use lettin' him suffer."

Patience turned away as Stormy handed Dallas a needle and he slid the long thin, stainless shaft into the animal's neck. The blue roan thrashed a couple more times, then went still, its eyes staring sightlessly ahead.

Tears rolled down her cheeks. She looked away from the horse and felt a tug on her arm.

"Come on," Shari said softly. "Let's go see what we can do to help."

Patience swallowed and nodded. Steeling herself, she fell into step beside her friend. As Dallas moved from horse to horse, sewing them up, administering shots to ease their pain, she and Shari joined some of the men who were driving the loose horses into a circle in a wide spot on the side of the road.

An hour went by before a tan veterinarian's van pulled up and two white-coated doctors climbed out. Charlie led them toward the circle of horses. The worst of the lot had already been singled out and the two men set to work. Dallas continued to help, doing his best with the limited medical supplies the Circle C crew kept on hand.

It was nearly noon when another stock truck arrived to carry the injured horses into the large animal veterinary hospital in Cheyenne, even later that the remaining horses were coaxed into another trailer and hauled off to the rodeo grounds.

Patience spotted Dallas and Stormy, their clothes covered with blood, walking toward the big diesel truck that had been hauling the livestock trailer. Dallas's face was lined with fatigue and Stormy's features looked eerily grim.

"Are you okay?" Shari said to Stormy.

Stormy shook his head. When he turned, Shari put her arms around him and he just stood there holding on to her.

"I'm so sorry," Patience said to Dallas. "I've never seen anything so terrible."

A knot formed in his jaw. Dallas just kept walking. She knew he must be hurting as badly as she, probably worse. She wished there was something she could say, something she could do. Silently, she fell into step beside him, wondering where he was going, keeping pace with his long strides until he stopped at the rear of the diesel truck and began to examine the hitch.

"Poor Charlie," she said. "It doesn't seem fair. He's just had so much trouble lately."

"Too much trouble," Dallas said darkly. "Way more trouble than he should have." He studied the bent, twisted piece of metal that had torn free of the fifth wheel hitch, causing the tractor to disconnect from the trailer, and she wondered what he saw.

Salty Marvin walked up just then, the lines of his weathered face etched even more deeply. "Charlie wants me to drive the rig on into town. We'll be needin' to get this hitch fixed."

Dallas looked down at the hitch. "When you get to town, I want you to take this truck straight to the sheriff's office. I'll meet you there. I want those guys to go over this rig from top to bottom."

"You think they're gonna find somethin'?" Salty asked. "You think somebody done somethin' to cause this?"

"Yeah, I do. I'm beginning to think these accidents Charlie's been having aren't accidents at all."

Patience's eyes widened. "Surely you don't think some-one would do a terrible thing like this on purpose!"

Dallas's features looked carved in stone. "That's exactly what I think—and I'm going to find out who it is."

Dallas pulled up in front of the Laramie County Sheriff's Office on Pioneer Avenue. It was his second trip in two days. Yesterday, he had spoken to Sheriff Auggie Harden about the accident on the interstate and his suspicion that it wasn't an accident at all. Dallas had told the sheriff about the problems the Circle C had been having over the past several months, a string of bad luck that led him to believe someone was out to make trouble for Charlie Carson.

Big trouble, it seemed.

Sheriff Harden had called the next day. He had asked Dallas to bring his uncle down to the office. Charlie had grudgingly agreed.

"I still think you're crazy," Charlie said to Dallas as he turned off the engine of his truck in front of the big brick building. "I may have pissed off a few people over the years, but not enough to do something so bad as what happened out there on the road. The hitch was faulty, is all. It's the kind of thing that happens."

"I hope you're right. Let's see what the sheriff has to say."

They pushed through the doors of the three-story brick and glass building that housed both the sheriff's department and jail. Dallas led the way down the corridor to the reception area, and a few minutes later, they were shown into Sheriff Harden's private office.

It was neat and orderly, partially wood-paneled, his L-shaped desk organized, a computer handy on his left. Dallas introduced Charlie, who shook the sheriff's hand.

"Why don't you both have a seat?" Harden said. He was a little taller than average, dark-haired, with a thick mustache and glasses. He had the kind of face a politician needed, the kind that said he was a man you could trust.

"Have your people had a chance to go over the tractor hitch?" Dallas asked the minute the three men were seated, the sheriff once more behind his desk.

"I'm afraid they have."

"And?" Charlie asked.

"The mechanic didn't see it at first. According to him, a lot of trucking companies have the damned things removed so something like this can't happen."

"I'm afraid I'm not following you," Dallas said.

"According to Joe—he's the mechanic—most of the new trucks are equipped with a switch inside the cab that can release the fifth wheel to unhitch the trailer. It's a cylinder, activated by air pressure. This one's been tampered with."

Dallas's jaw knotted. "Sonofabitch."

"How was it done?" Charlie asked, leaning forward in his seat.

"Like I said, Joe didn't see it at first. But he kept on looking. Found a little hole drilled in the valve. It caused the mechanism to leak a small amount of air. The hitch worked fine until the truck was driven a while, but the leak caused the pressure to slowly build. Finally, it released the hitch. Joe figures when the truck was going down that grade, the pressure was off the movable side of the hitch and it came open. When the truck started back up the hill, the trailer came loose and drifted away. It could have hit another car or jumped into the oncoming traffic. It's lucky no one was killed."

No one besides three of Charlie's prized bucking horses. Dallas closed his eyes against a flash of blood and dying horses, the screams of injured animals lying on the road.

"Do you have any enemies, Mr. Carson?"

"A few. Most men do who've lived as long as I have."

The sheriff shoved a yellow pad across the desk in Charlie's direction. "Write down their names and where they can be found. We'll start running a check, see what we can find out."

Charlie wrote a couple of names and addresses, then the pen stilled. Dallas read the names and tapped on the page.

"Write down Junior Reese," he said.

"He only just come aboard the last couple weeks. We was havin' problems way before that."

"He doesn't like you. Write down his name."

Charlie complied.

"And put down Wes McCauley."

Charlie's head came up. "Wes may have his faults, but he ain't the kind to do something like this."

"I think you're probably right, but I didn't believe he was the kind who'd try to take advantage of a woman half his size, either."

Charlie wrote down Wes's name, along with those of a couple of other cowboys he'd had run-ins with over the years, including a few he'd helped to blacklist from professional rodeo, either for writing bad checks, not paying entry fees, or not having paid a fine. Abusing animals could also get a cowboy blacklisted, but Charlie couldn't think of anyone he'd clashed with in that regard.

"I gotta tell ya, sheriff. Ain't a soul I can think of would kill a bunch of poor defenseless horses."

The sheriff removed his glasses, set them down on the top of his desk. "Someone damaged that hitch, Mr. Carson. According to your nephew, you've had other problems as well. An unusual amount of breakdowns and delays, bulls getting loose on the midway, an expensive lawsuit. He says you've even had some cattle rustled at your ranch back in Texas."

"Now wait a minute. Even if something *is* going on, all those problems happened while we've been on the road. Texas is a long way from Wyoming, and in the ranching business, every once in a while, cattle get stolen. There's no way the two are connected."

"Odds are you're right. For now, we'll concentrate on the problems your rodeo company has been facing. Can you think of anyone who might profit from causing you this kind of trouble?"

"Not really."

"Lem Wilkins," Dallas said. "He and his partner, Jack Stiles, are Charlie's biggest competitors in the rodeo business. They've been trying to get him to sell out to them for years. Recently, they bought three of Charlie's best bucking horses. After yesterday, with Charlie's bucking stock out of commission, the Flying S will be the company supplying the horses for the show."

The rest of Charlie's stock was headed back to the ranch. Even the horses that had come out of the wreck unscathed were skittish and hard to handle. They balked at going back in the trailer and Dallas didn't blame them. Charlie had a second string of animals in Texas. If he spent the money for a couple more good buckers, he'd be able to make it through the rest of the year. Barely.

"We'll check the two of them out." The sheriff stood up behind his desk. "In the meantime, I'd suggest you both keep your eyes and ears open for anything out of the ordinary. It seems to me these attacks might be escalating. So far no one's been hurt, but that could change in a heartbeat."

Dallas flicked a glance at Charlie, whose features looked drawn and grim. Charlie didn't want to believe any of this. He was a man whose handshake was his bond. He'd never do anything so underhanded and it was hard for him to believe that someone else would.

They said little on the way back to the arena, Charlie riding in the passenger seat in silence, looking like the weight of the world rested on his shoulders.

Dallas clenched his jaw. If Charlie had trouble, then so did he. Dallas was determined to do whatever it took to protect the man who was more of a father to him than his real dad ever would be.

* * *

It was early the following morning. Patience couldn't sleep so she rolled out of bed just a few minutes after Shari, pulled on jeans and a tank top and left the trailer. She'd been thinking of Dallas and Charlie. Dallas believed the hitch on the truck had been tampered with, that the wreck was intentional. He and Charlie had spoken to the sheriff.

She found herself wandering toward Dallas's trailer, wondering what the sheriff had said, hurting for him and Charlie. She came to a stop when she saw him standing outside the door of his RV. He was looking into a mirror hanging above the fender of the trailer, shaving from a metal bowl filled with water. He wore boots and jeans, no shirt, the jeans unsnapped, his silver buckle hanging open. The jeans rode low, beneath a ridged, six-pack belly. Curly brown hair dusted a chest that was every bit as solid as it looked.

Desire filtered through her, a warm sticky heat that made her skin feel flushed and damp. She had never thought of herself as a particularly sensual woman. In fact, just the opposite. But looking at Dallas stirred images of raw, uninhibited sex and it was all she could do not to walk over and drag him off to bed.

She didn't, of course.

Dallas wanted to continue their affair through the end of summer. Part of her wanted to agree, to enjoy more of those hot, wicked nights she had sampled in Houston. The other part warned she would be putting her heart in danger. She was attracted to Dallas Kingman in a way she had never been to a man before. That attraction could grow into something even deeper, something that would wind up breaking her heart.

Accepting his proposition was far too risky. Still, the idea was tempting. More than tempting. It slithered through her mind like the snake in the garden of Eden, taunting her every minute of the day.

Not that she intended to let him know.

Managing a casual smile, she started walking toward him

just as he wiped the last of the shaving soap from his face. "Good morning."

He surveyed her bright orange tank top and jean-clad legs and his eyes lit with appreciation. "You're up early."

She didn't tell him she'd had a restless night—he might offer a sleeping aid she couldn't refuse. "It's a really nice morning. Cheyenne is hot in the daytime, but the mornings and evenings are perfect."

"Stormy's gone someplace with Shari. There's coffee on inside. You want to come in for a cup?"

"Sure."

There wasn't much room inside the RV, even less than in her trailer. Just a pair of bunks at one end, a one-burner stove, tiny fridge, a table with two stools, and a minuscule bathroom.

"All the comforts of home," Dallas said, pouring her a steaming mug of coffee and setting it on the table in front of her. She noticed a laptop, out of place among the cowboy clutter—boots, ropes, chaps, gloves, spurs.

"A computer man. I never would have guessed." Dallas was still bare-chested. She kept her eyes on his face.

"Are you kidding? This is the twenty-first century. We've got cell phones and e-mail—the whole enchilada." He grabbed a shirt off a hook beside the door, shrugged the cotton fabric over his shoulders, but didn't bother with the snaps. "Actually, I use that thing mostly to keep up on the standings . . . who's ahead in the overall and how much each man has won. It'll even tell you the rank of the horse or bull you've drawn."

"That's pretty amazing."

He poured a mug of coffee for himself and sat down on the stool across from her. "Your great grandmother sure would have thought so."

"That's the truth." Patience blew on her coffee, took a scalding sip. "How's Charlie?"

Dallas raked a hand through his still-damp hair. "Worried. So am I."

"What you did yesterday . . . at the accident, I mean. you were incredible. Shari told me you went to medical school. I guess I wasn't the only one with secrets."

"It's hardly a secret. I figured you knew. Everybody else does." He wrapped his fingers around the mug, lifted it and took a drink. "I never wanted to be a doctor. I only went to medical school to please my father. I'm glad for the years I spent, for learning as much as I did. A rancher needs to know how to take care of his stock and I know more than most. But I have no interest in that kind of career."

"Shari says you only have a couple more years to get your degree. What about becoming a veterinarian?"

Dallas shook his head. "I want to raise cattle. I want to own my own place and someday I will. That's all I've wanted since the first time I set foot on Circle C land."

"*Happy now.* Right?"

The edge of his mouth curved up. "Right."

Patience blew on her coffee, took another sip. It was dark and slightly bitter, but she liked it that way, and the punch to her system felt good. "What did the sheriff have to say?"

"He said the hitch was tampered with."

Her head came up. "Just like you thought."

"Yeah, just like I thought. Someone drilled a hole in the pressure release valve, which caused air to leak out and build up pressure. When the pressure got high enough, the hitch came loose and the trailer drifted away."

A memory arose of dying and injured horses, and a chill swept through her. "Sounds tricky. Whoever did it must have known a lot about trucks."

"Or hired someone who did. The guys on the Circle C crew are pretty versatile. Most of them have worked off and on at different jobs to earn extra money, truck driving among them."

"Any idea which of them might have done it?"

"I know most of those guys. I can't imagine any of them doing something like that, but the cops are looking into it."

"They're bound to turn up something—sooner or later."

Dallas's gaze slid out the window. "I'd rather it was sooner," he said.

Cheyenne Frontier Days. Nine days of ass-kicking, ball-breaking rodeo, the cowboys said. The Daddy of 'Em All, they called it. After more than a hundred years of attracting the top performers in the country, Patience figured the show deserved the name.

Cheyenne was an old-time celebration, with pancake breakfasts, western art auctions, street dances, and parades.

"Come on, P.J." Shari tugged her away from the keyboard of her computer. "Let's go downtown and see what's going on."

"I probably ought to work," Patience said halfheartedly, wishing she could go.

"Come on—this *is* work. Your thesis involves the history of rodeo, right? This is Frontier Days. You can't get more historical than that."

They caught a ride into town with the barrel racers, Ruth Collins and Bonnie Sweeney. There was a big parade that morning. It took a while to find a parking spot for Bonnie's bulky Suburban, but eventually they got lucky. They climbed out of the vehicle and the four of them walked along the route until they found a good vantage point to watch the parade.

It was already underway, an all-American affair with high-school marching bands, John Philip Sousa songs, flags and banners, and horsemen dressed as outlaws, bandits, and Indians. A mounted sheriff's posse rode past, the uniformed men all on matching palomino horses with silver-mounted saddles.

Patience grinned as the Golden Angels baton-twirling school marched past, twelve darling little girls all dressed up in white satin angel outfits glittering with sequins. Their baton twirling wasn't much to watch, but their enthusiasm made up for it.

Junior Reese and Cy Jennings paraded past, decked out in full clown regalia. Cy wore his usual red tights, knee-length fringed red chaps, and smiling clown-face makeup, while Junior's makeup was applied the opposite way, to look like a big ugly frown. Cy ran back and forth across the street tossing candy to the children while Junior rode past on the little donkey with long floppy ears he used in his act. Cy spotted the women and waved, tossed them a handful of brightly wrapped candy, which the four of them laughingly scrambled to catch.

"Look! There's Dallas!" Shari waved at the '58 Cadillac convertible Dallas rode in, a collectors' automobile, pale pink with tons of chrome and a huge pair of longhorns mounted on the front. Dallas sat next to a couple of rodeo bigwigs on top of the backseat, waving to the crowd. Having the world's champion cowboy join in the festivities was good for the rodeo, and his sponsors liked the added publicity it got them.

Dallas smiled and continued to wave, but even from a distance, Patience thought he looked a little distracted. He was worried about his uncle and what the sheriff had discovered. Patience hoped he'd be able to concentrate on his performance during the show. If he didn't, he might get hurt.

The morning drifted past, the sun beating down overhead, the air growing thinner and hotter. The parade was winding down. When the fire truck at the rear of the last marching band appeared in the distance, they decided to slip away before the traffic made it hard to get back to the rodeo grounds.

The afternoon performance began at one P.M., an hour from then. This was Cheyenne and there was something different in the air, a competitive spirit that seemed to heighten the excitement. Already cowboys gathered behind the chutes, limbering up. There was a lot of money at stake in Cheyenne and these cowboys wanted to win, but it was more than that.

Cheyenne meant real, old-fashioned rodeo. The unspoken challenge was there. *Cowboy up! This is the reason you do it. This is because you love the sport.*

Shari led Button up just then and Patience reached out to pet him. The sleek little sorrel nickered softly and nuzzled his head against Shari's shoulder while Patience stroked his neck beneath his reddish mane.

"Would you do me a favor?" Shari asked.

"Sure. What is it?"

"Warm Button up a little. You said the other day you missed riding. Hell, you're right here in the middle of cowboy country. I know you ride English, but there can't be that much difference."

"I'd love to ride him for you." Patience reached up and rubbed the horse's ears. "I've been itching to get in the saddle since the day I got to Rocky Hill."

But there were matters of trust where valuable animals were concerned. She and Shari knew each other now. Apparently, Shari felt her horse was safe in Patience's hands.

"Stirrups are gonna be short. We could let 'em down, but it's a lot of trouble and we don't have all that much time."

"Don't worry about it. I'm just going to ride him around the arena a little."

"Thanks. I got a couple of things I need to do. I'll see you before the show starts."

Patience nodded and accepted the reins. The strips of worn leather felt good in her hands. She was reaching for the saddle horn, looking forward to the pleasure of riding again, when Wes McCauley walked up behind her.

"Well, look who's here."

She stiffened at the sound of his voice. She hadn't talked to him since the wrestling match they'd had in her trailer. She would have been happy if she never saw him again.

She let go of the horn and turned to face him. "What do you want, Wes?"

"Nothin' much. You know, you caused me considerable trouble back there."

"Is that so? Well, you caused me considerable trouble when you mauled me around in my trailer. Do anything remotely similar to that again, and you'll find yourself on your way to jail."

Wes's jaw tightened. "You invited me in. What did you think was going to happen?"

"I thought I was going to make you a cup of coffee so you would sober up a little before you drove home."

Wes glanced away. "I was drunker than I thought. Maybe I got my signals crossed."

"Yes, I guess you did. I told you to leave and you refused. You were all over me like a rash and I don't appreciate being treated that way."

"You were putting out for Dallas. I figured—"

"She wasn't putting out for anyone," Dallas said sharply from a few feet behind her. "And if you ever do more than smile and say hello to her again, the beating you got that night will only be a sample of what you're going to get the next time."

Wes's gloved hand fisted. "Don't threaten me, Kingman."

"That's not a threat, Wes. It's a promise."

Wes's jaw locked and color rose beneath the bones in his cheeks. "You think that scares me? I was drunk that night. Next time you'll be the guy left lying in the dirt." He turned and spit on the ground as if to emphasize his point. "You got a knack for stickin' your nose into other people's business, Dallas. I'm warning you not to do it again."

Patience watched Wes stalk away and dragged in a shaky breath. "I'm sorry about Wes. You've got enough trouble without having to worry about me."

Dallas's eyes remained on the man who had once been his

friend. "That's all right. Better to discover a snake in the grass than to wind up getting bit."

She felt the pull of a smile. "I presume you're riding today."

He nodded.

"What horse did you draw?"

"Timber Rattler." He grinned. "I guess it's my day for snakes."

Patience laughed. "Good horse?"

"A Final's horse. One of Jack Stiles's best."

He was dressed to rodeo, wearing his trademark blue shirt and black and gold metallic-fringed chaps. God, she loved a man in chaps. "Will you promise me something?"

Those incredible blue eyes slid down to her mouth, and there was no mistaking his thoughts. "Pretty much whatever you name."

She ignored the coil of heat that tightened in her stomach. "Until the rodeo is over, I want you to forget Wes McCauley and everyone else. I want you to go out there and ride like winning is all that matters in the world. I want you to knock 'em dead this afternoon."

From beneath his black hat, Dallas looked at her and his lips curved up. "Yes, ma'am," he said.

CHAPTER 14

Button danced with impatience as Patience collected the reins, shoved her boot into the stirrup, and swung up on the sorrel's back. She had never ridden western style before and the saddle felt strange beneath her, but the cantle curving against her bottom felt solid and reassuring. Shari was so petite the stirrups were inches too short, but riding hunter-jumpers required a shorter stirrup so it didn't feel all that awkward.

Patience walked the horse, letting him stretch his legs, then went into a trot, posting in the English manner. A slow canter followed, guiding the horse in lazy figure eights at the end of the arena. Button settled down right away, performing like the perfectly trained animal he was, responding to her silent commands as if they had ridden together a hundred times.

She was grinning when she left the arena, exhilarated by her brief return to riding, enjoying the bond between horse and rider as she always did. She dismounted outside the fence, led Button back to the trailer, and returned his reins to Shari.

"That was wonderful. You've got yourself some horse there."

"Thanks." Shari patted Button's neck and spoke to him gently. "You ready to do your thing, sweetheart?"

Button nickered as if in reply and Patience laughed. Western music drifted toward them, the Charlie Daniels Band's "The Devil Went Down to Georgia." Then the distant sound of the announcer's voice boomed over the loudspeaker. Applause from the grandstand said the rodeo had begun.

The show started with a patriot display of fireworks, then a flag-waving run up and down the arena by two local rodeo queen contestants mounted on big white horses. A loud, swelling version of the National Anthem filled the crowd with rodeo excitement.

The show clicked along without a hitch, Charlie doing his usual good job behind the scenes, keeping things running smoothly. With the Circle C bucking horses out of commission, he was forced to use Jack Stiles's Flying S stock—for a fat fee, of course. But the horses were working well and so far there hadn't been a problem.

Dallas had told Stormy and Shari about the sabotage that had been done to the trailer hitch and asked them to keep their eyes open for anything out of the ordinary, but Charlie had insisted they keep the information to themselves. The sheriff had sent a couple of extra officers out to the rodeo grounds but so far the afternoon had been peaceful.

The rodeo progressed. In the steer wrestling, Wes brought down his steer in three point six seconds, which was a damned fast time and put him in the lead for the money. The saddle bronc section followed. Patience looked around but didn't see Dallas. She spotted Junior Reese running into the arena and turned to watch him do his skit.

In big, baggy, size fifty-plus Wranglers and a red striped shirt, he told the crowd, "Me and my wife was drivin' by a field full of pigs and mules. 'Them your relatives?' I asked. My wife just nodded. 'Yeah,' she said. 'Them's my in-laws!' "

The crowd roared with laughter and Patience joined in. Behind her, cowboys walked up and down the row of chutes, getting ready to make their rides. She was used to the activity by now, the shuffle of scuffed leather boots, the jangle of spurs, the big Brahmas grunting in the pens behind them. Dust hung in the air, tinged with the smell of alfalfa and manure.

She turned back to the arena just as a boot slammed down on the fence rail beside her. Spurs jingled, fringe slapped against a man's long leg. She looked up and for an instant, she simply felt drenched in cowboy—there was no other way to describe it.

"Good show so far," Dallas said, but he was looking at her, not into the arena, and she felt suddenly breathless. His gaze traveled the length of her, over her breasts and down her jean-clad legs, and her mouth went dry. "How about afterward we go out and get something to eat?"

She swallowed. He was asking her out to supper but looking at him, food was the last thing on her mind. *How about we just go straight to bed?* she thought, then mentally kicked herself.

What she needed least in the world was a deeper involvement with Dallas Kingman.

Then again, this was supposed to be an adventure, something to remember the rest of her life. She ran her tongue nervously over her lips and watched the hunger creep into his eyes.

"If I say yes, will you promise to think about riding and not what you're thinking right now?"

He laughed. "If you say yes, thinking with anything other than my little head is going to be almost impossible."

"We *are* talking about supper here, aren't we?"

"Sustenance of some sort, at any rate."

"Dallas . . ."

"All right, supper, then."

"Concentrate on your ride and I'll give you my answer once you're safely back on the ground."

He nodded. "Okay. I guess that's fair enough. I'll ride this one for you, darlin'." Tugging on the brim of his hat, he leaned down and grabbed his saddle. "Don't move. I'll be right back."

Hoisting the saddle over his shoulder, he started walking away, the fringe dancing on his chaps as he moved along the line of chutes being filled with bucking horses. Patience tried not to stare at the worn seat of his jeans.

She watched him climb up on one of the chutes. From a distance, she could see him working with Lee Henderson, the Asian cowboy she had met some weeks back, trying to get the big spotted horse saddled and ready to go.

"Ladies and gentlemen," the announcer said, "please turn your attention to chute number three. Our first contestant is the current World Champion All Around Cowboy—Dallas Kingman. He's the top saddle bronc rider in the world and he's drawn a horse called Timber Rattler. This is a National Final's horse and, man, he's got a mean look in his eye this afternoon."

Settling himself deeper in the saddle, Dallas tugged on his glove, then took a slightly shorter grip on the braided rope attached to the horse's halter. He jerked his hat down, turned to the boys on the ground, and nodded.

The gate swung open. Fifteen hundred pounds of horse-flesh burst out of the chute as if it had rockets attached to its hooves.

"When he rides they call him The King!" the announcer shouted, and once more Dallas lived up to the name.

He might have been sitting in a rocking chair instead of on the back of a plunging, bucking, wildly twisting bronc. Rattler leaped, kicked his back feet straight up in the air, then all four feet hit the ground with a jolting, bone-jarring impact. The horse twisted right, bucked and twisted left. Dallas countered his every move as if he knew them before they occurred.

The crowd thundered its approval. Feet stamped, hands clapped, people cheered. Even the hot dog vendors roaming up and down the stands stopped to watch Dallas's ride. The eight seconds ticked past but the horse never slowed, a keg of dynamite exploding beneath the man on top of him. Dallas stayed glued in the saddle, his left arm in the air all the way to the whistle. He pulled leather and rode a few seconds longer while the pickup men caught up and boxed the horse in.

Dallas leaned over the pickup man's horse and caught hold of the big cowboy's shoulders. He slid out of the saddle and landed neatly on his feet.

He grinned and waved his hat in Patience's direction, then turned and waved at the crowd. It occurred to her that she hadn't seen him smiling that way since the livestock truck had been wrecked and sympathy for him tightened her chest.

"You saw it, ladies and gentlemen. The judges saw it, too. Ninety-two points for a championship ride on a championship horse. That's gonna be the number these cowboys have to beat."

Dallas appeared at her side a few minute later, still smiling, obviously pleased with himself.

"Congratulations."

"You brought me luck." Bending down, he brushed a kiss over her lips. "Now let's see if it was good enough to win the money."

Standing together, they watched the rest of the bronc riding. Lee Henderson was the only other contestant who came close to Dallas's score, riding a horse called Jughead for eighty-nine points, putting him in second place. A Wyoming cowboy ended up in third, but there would be more riding after the show when they bucked off the slack, so it was too soon to tell if Dallas's score would win.

The calf roping followed. While Junior clowned in the center of the ring, Dallas headed off to collect Lobo and get ready to make his run.

"That was some ride Dallas made." Blue Cody walked up

beside her, lean and black-haired, handsome as sin. He propped a boot up on the fence and his spurs jingled, but the sound didn't make her heart stumble the way it had before. Blue shoved his black felt hat back, revealing his striking Navajo features, the smooth dark skin and dark eyes, the high, carved cheekbones. Women flocked after Blue the way they did Dallas, though he didn't seem to notice it much.

"He was incredible, wasn't he?"

"He's been off a little lately," Blue said. "Worried about Charlie, I guess. Hard to ride when you got problems on your mind."

"I imagine it is."

Both of them heard Dallas's name just then, blaring over the loudspeakers, and turned their attention toward the calf-roping chute. Hat pulled low, Dallas sat in the saddle, Lobo collected and ready to go. He nodded toward the gate. It sprang open and the calf shot out. An instant later, the big palomino leapt forward. Hooves pounded. Dallas's arm swung up, whirling the loop above his head.

The same instant his hand shot out, he glanced in her direction. The rope stalled an instant longer than it should have. The calf veered left and the rope glanced off its shoulder, flicking backward to land in the dirt.

Dallas muttered something only he could hear and pulled back on Lobo's reins. He didn't go for a second loop, just sent a dark look in Patience's direction and started collecting his rope. Blue chuckled as Dallas turned his horse and trotted out of the arena.

"I think you distracted him," Blue said.

"Me! I didn't do anything!"

Blue just grinned. "On second thought, I guess it was me." He turned to see Dallas riding toward them, the dark look still on his face. "I think I'll catch you later." Grinning, Blue sauntered off whistling. Not long after, Dallas walked up, holding onto Lobo's reins.

"Where's Blue?" were the first words out of his mouth.

"Blue? He left a few minutes ago. Why?"

"What'd he want?"

"He didn't want anything. He said you made one helluva ride and I agreed. Why are you frowning? What's the matter with you? What happened out there?"

He took a deep breath, exhaled it slowly. He wasn't wearing chaps, just his faded blue jeans. He slid his hands into his back pockets, then pulled them out again. "I don't know what happened. Whatever the hell it was, I don't like it."

"Dallas, you aren't making sense."

"You're telling me," he grumbled. Reaching over, he caught her hand, started tugging her away from the fence. "Come on. You can keep me company while I unsaddle Lobo."

"But—"

He glared down at her from beneath the brim of his hat. "Unless you'd rather stay here and wait for Blue."

"Blue? Don't be ridiculous. Blue is just a friend."

"Fine." He started hauling her forward. "I just hope Blue is smart enough to know it."

The following morning, Patience sat in front of her computer, still wearing the borrowed Every Woman Loves a Cowboy—or Will T-shirt she usually slept in. Lately, it was beginning to annoy her.

Yesterday, after the rodeo, once Dallas had officially won first place, they had gone to supper at a restaurant called The Cattle Company to celebrate. It was packed to the rafters— an hour wait to get in—but the steaks were hot and medium rare and she had enjoyed the time with Dallas.

Still, when they returned to the trailer, she wound up sleeping alone. Well, *sleeping* was a stretch. More like tossing and turning, having erotic dreams of Dallas that left her covered with perspiration. But Dallas hadn't pressed her last night, and though Shari and Stormy had a room at the edge of town, Patience hadn't invited him in.

Whether or not to resume their affair was a monumental decision—at least for her.

Still, she was beginning to wonder who was torturing whom.

As the morning wore on, she worked on her thesis, then read a few more entries in her great grandmother's journal. Lucille Sims's disappearance still bothered her, just as it had Adelaide Holmes. It occurred to her that Lucky had disappeared during the rodeo in Cheyenne and an idea crept into her head.

Shutting down her computer, she picked up her purse, dug out the keys to the pickup, and left the trailer.

It didn't take long to reach downtown Cheyenne. Patience smiled as she drove past the old brick buildings along the railroad tracks, remnants of a town that had once been called "Hell on Wheels."

Back in the late 1860s, the first businesses to arrive at the railhead followed the track of the Union Pacific, a motley collection of false-fronted tents, mostly gambling halls or houses of prostitution—thus the name. It was a different, more modern town now, but hints of the old Wild West remained.

Patience headed for the local newspaper office, the *Wyoming Tribune Eagle* on Lincoln Street, and parked the Chevy truck in the parking lot.

The *Tribune,* she discovered, had been in Cheyenne, under myriad names, since 1867. Its archives were numerous, some of the oldest newspapers bound in volumes, wrapped, and stored away in a room that smelled of dust and printing ink. But old papers didn't hold up very well and most of them were now on microfilm. She was told they'd been moved to the state archives downtown.

It didn't take long to get there. Patience spoke to the desk clerk, flashed the press pass Charlie had given her that first day in Texas, and a chubby little woman named Rose led her into a back room lined with drawers and files.

"You know how to work one of these?" Rose asked, leading Patience toward a row of microfilm reader machines.

"Yes, thank you. I've done a considerable amount of research over the years."

A blunt hand reached over and flicked on the machine. "Film is in those metal file drawers over against the wall. They're all in chronological order. There's also a master index for each decade that sorts by names and places, that kind of thing. You need help, you let me know."

"Thank you, I will." Eager to get to work, Patience walked over and began to examine the four-drawer metal files, her eyes lighting on the drawer that contained the newspaper records for the period from 1910 to 1913. She checked the index under the last name Sims, found only one entry, and located a brief article dated the tenth of August, 1912.

> *The disappearance of a woman named Lucille Mae Sims has been reported by the sheriff's office. The twenty-one-year-old Miss Sims, a resident of Wichita Falls, Texas, was a participant in the annual Frontier Days Rodeo, competing in the cowgirls' relay races. According to the report, she has blond hair and brown eyes, stands approximately five-foot three inches tall and weighs one hundred and thirteen pounds. Any person with information regarding Miss Sims's disappearance should contact the sheriff's office.*

There was nothing else in any of the papers during that period and no other word of Lucky Sims. Patience returned the film and grabbed the next roll, which carried her through the period ending December 31, 1918. Still, no mention of Lucille Sims. She tried a third roll, ending the decade, but again had no luck.

She tried to think what other indices might hold clues to the disappearance. Addie Holmes believed something terrible had happened to her. Patience went back to the first three years of newspapers on the film. She considered looking under the reference Jane Doe—a woman who had died but never been identified—but it was probably too modern a term. Instead she went through the police blotter, a section of the paper that reported anything that had been filed by the police.

In the first three-year period, three unidentified bodies popped up. Two of them were men, transients who died at the local county hospital. The third was a woman who was trying to hop a freight train and was killed when she fell beneath the wheels. None fit the description of Lucky Sims.

It wasn't until June of 1918 that Patience found something of interest. Two fourteen-year-old boys reported finding the badly decomposed body of a woman in a ravine not far from an old, closed-down theater at the edge of town. It appeared the earth and branches under which the body had been buried had been eroded away by flooding over the years.

In those days, with forensic science still in its fledgling stage, not much could be told about the victim. But the sex was known, her height estimated at somewhere between five-foot-two and five-five. The authorities guessed her age between eighteen and thirty, and her hair appeared to have once been blond. There was no way to determine the manner of death, but the report estimated it had happened five to ten years earlier—which could fit the time Lucky had disappeared.

Patience searched ahead, her heart pounding, trying to find out if the sheriff had ever connected the unidentified body to the disappearance of Lucille Sims. But six years had passed and according to her grandmother's journal, most people believed Lucky had run away with one of the rodeo cowboys. Like a lot of the women performers of that day, Lucky had no family, no one to really pursue the matter.

Though Patience searched the records for two more hours, she never found another reference to the body that was found, or to Lucille Mae Sims. It really wasn't surprising. When Lucky went missing, Cheyenne had been a small, isolated country town.

Patience's chest felt heavy as she drove the pickup back to the fairgrounds. The case might have been left unsolved, but Patience believed she had found the answer to the mystery of her grandmother's friend's disappearance.

She thought of the man who had been following the show and couldn't help wondering if he was the man who had murdered Lucky Sims.

There were only two days of rodeo left. All of the cowboys were tired, exhausted by the long days of tough competition. Yet when the time came for them to compete, each man continued to give it his all.

Dallas had ridden well all week. He was ahead in the standings for the overall and determined to take home the money. After his ride that afternoon on a big black bronc called Indigo, he was in the lead again today, but he had reinjured his shoulder on the dismount and twisted his knee when he hit the ground. He hobbled out of the arena, favoring his left leg, but refused to stop by the ambulance and let the EMTs take a look at him.

"I'm fine," he said. "Just wrenched it a little, is all."

"You hurt that same shoulder before," Patience said. "If you don't take care of it, you might do permanent damage."

He looked down at her and smiled. "I think I like it when you worry about me."

Patience gave up a frustrated sigh. "Dammit, Dallas—"

"I'll be fine," he repeated. "I promise." His injuries were just one more thing for him to worry about. All week he'd been on edge, concerned about Charlie and constantly on guard, watching the arena and the area behind the chutes for any sign of trouble. He'd been gruff and a little bit short with everyone.

Everyone but her.

Instead, whenever they were together, he was amazingly sweet, surprisingly thoughtful, and subtly relentless.

He wanted her. He made no secret of it. Whenever he wasn't competing, doing rodeo publicity, or speaking for one of his sponsors, he took her out to eat or sat with her during the show. Dallas wasn't a man to take no for an answer and he was completely determined in this.

Mounted on Button, cooling the horse down for Shari after the show, Patience spotted him walking next to Charlie. Ever since the wreck, he'd been staying as close to his uncle as his busy schedule allowed. Even with his bad dismount, Dallas had scored well today. Stormy had taken a third in the calf roping, so he was happy.

Unfortunately, Shari hadn't fared nearly so well. She'd made a solid, third place run in yesterday's perf, and come in second one day earlier in the week, but today, Button had taken the second barrel wide and her time wasn't fast enough to place in the money.

Today, Jade Egan had won.

The rodeo was over but Jade was still there, sitting on the fence next to Reno Garcia, getting ready to watch the last of the bull slack being ridden. Patience made a final circle of the arena and rode out of the ring. Jade didn't wave and neither did Patience. But Reno grinned and waved as she rode past. Handlebar mustache waxed to a sheen, he said something to Jade, then left to prepare for his ride.

Patience turned Button around to watch. Cowboys, cowgirls, and die-hard rodeo fans remaining after the show returned to the grandstands or climbed up on the fence to watch the last bulls being ridden, the most dangerous event in rodeo. Reno paused to rosin-up his rope and glove, then grabbed his gear and headed for the chutes.

He'd had some bad luck so far. His thigh was wrapped in an elastic bandage, and day before yesterday, a rank bull named

Texas Red had knocked out one of his teeth. But Reno was a cocky little cowboy, a good bull rider, and today he wanted to win.

Patience reached down to pat Button's neck. The horse blew as she sat in the saddle, watching from behind the fence in an area enclosed by another lower fence beyond. She wouldn't stay long, but she was rooting for Reno. She hoped he had drawn a good bull.

And that this time he stayed on.

Minus his face paint, dressed in a T-shirt and jeans but still wearing his knee pads, Cy Jenkins waited anxiously in front of the chute, his lean, muscular legs splayed apart, his concentration fixed on the gate. Junior Reese stood farther away, but close enough to rush in if he were needed. The clowns were the best athletes in rodeo, the fastest, the toughest, the most agile of the men. They were the cowboys' lifeline and there wasn't a man out there who didn't know it.

Patience sat forward in the saddle as the gate jerked open. A big black bull, Ace of Spades, surged up and out, taking Reno with him. The animal bellowed and tossed its head, flinging slobber and twisting its massive body from one side to the other. Reno clung to his back like a thorn.

It was a plunging, whirling ride but Reno made it to the whistle. His dismount was shaky. He tripped when he hit the ground and landed on his head. For a second, he didn't seem to know where he was and then Ace of Spades was on him.

Patience's heart froze. The crowd let out a terrified roar and Cy rushed forward. He threw himself in front of the bull just seconds before the big black Brahma stomped Reno into the dirt, turning the bull away at the very last instant.

Junior hurried toward Reno. Along with several other cowboys, they helped him to his feet. Reno staggered, then straightened, shook his head and appeared to be all right. Patience sagged with relief as he limped away, but Ace of Spades wasn't finished. The big bull paced the arena, nostrils flaring, horns in the air, looking like he wanted to stomp every cowboy he saw into the ground. He circled the arena, ignoring the mounted cowboys trying to shoo him into the gate leading back to his pen and instead increased his speed.

Ace of Spades roared down the fence line in front of the nearly empty grandstand, thundering like a locomotive toward the end where Patience sat on Button, acting as if the fence weren't even there. Or if it was, it didn't matter. He hadn't the slightest intention of stopping no matter how high the fence was.

Her pulse speeded up. She told herself the big Brahma would turn, that he was just making a show of being tough, but when she saw his head go up, saw his front feet lift off the ground, she whirled Button, pressed her boots into the horse's ribs, and hung on for dear life as Button leapt forward, as eager to escape the raging bull as she was.

Ace of Spades sailed over the six-foot fence, his back hooves knocking down the top rail, his big body crashing to the ground on the opposite side right behind her. Still, he didn't slow. She and Button were picking up speed, the bull still on their tail. The second fence loomed ahead, shorter than the first, maybe three and a half feet high.

Button was sleek and fast and he wanted out of there, too. Patience came up over him, leaning forward, letting him collect himself, giving him the help he needed to sail over the fence. They made a perfect, four-point landing on the opposite side, smooth and controlled, not a single missed beat. Patience grinned, her heart still racing. She patted Button's neck as she slowed him a little, thought again what a magnificent horse he was.

Strangely enough, when she looked back over her shoulder, she saw that the bull had refused to jump the second fence and now trotted back toward the arena, trying to find a spot to get in. A couple of cowboys herded him toward the gate and he slithered back around the corner. The alley leading to his pen apparently looked good to him now and he headed in that direction, bellowing and eager to get there.

Patience gave Button another grateful pat. "Weren't you a brave, good boy?" Smiling, she swung down from the saddle just as Jade Egan, Reno Garcia, Stormy, Charlie, and half a dozen cowboys rushed up.

Jade got there first. "Well, what do you know."

"Yeah," Dallas said, walking up just then. "What do you know." He turned a hard, blue-eyed stare in her direction. "I thought you said you couldn't ride."

Patience shrugged. "Jade said that. I just didn't bother to correct her." She flicked a glance in the black-haired woman's direction. "Actually, until I started exercising Button, I'd never ridden Western before. I teach English riding to children in the summers."

A muscle bunched in Dallas's jaw. "How many more secrets you keeping, P.J. Sinclair?"

A few feet away, Charlie grinned. "Well, it ain't no secret she can ride—not now. You did good, honey. Real good."

"That was one mean-ass bull," Reno said, knocking the dust off his hat. "He sure made short work of that fence."

Shari raced up just then, breathing hard, her eyes darting worriedly from Patience to her horse. "I heard what happened. You two okay?"

"We're fine." Patience rubbed the star on the sorrel's forehead. "Button was great. If barrel racing doesn't work out, maybe you can take up show jumping."

Shari laughed and several of the cowboys joined in. Then the group began to disperse back toward the chutes. Jade cast a long glance at Dallas, turned and went with them. There were more bulls waiting, more cowboys yet to ride, and a little thing like an angry Brahma was all in a day's work.

Dallas still stood there frowning. "I think you took ten years off my life when you charged that fence with that bull right behind you. Dammit to hell, why didn't you tell me you could ride like that?"

She grinned. She couldn't help it. "You didn't ask."

"I swear, woman, you never cease to amaze me."

Her grin went wider. "Well, good for me." She linked her arm with his. "So you were worried, were you?"

"Damned right I was." He turned her to face him, bent his head, and very thoroughly kissed her. "Don't scare me that way again."

But if that kind of kiss was her reward, she might have to make a habit of it. They started back toward the trailer, Dallas favoring his leg as he walked along beside her, following Shari and Button.

"How's your knee?" Patience asked.

"Better."

"Yes, I can see that." To a cowboy, better meant he could manage to walk at all.

"You missed part of the show today."

Her mind slid back to the information she had found in the archives. "I went to town. There was something I wanted to check out." Dallas knew about the journal and about Lucky Sims. Now she told him her theory about Lucky being murdered.

"So you think it might be the guy your grandmother mentioned? The one who seemed a little too interested in the women in the rodeo?"

"I think there's a chance it might have been him."

"Might have been a lovers' quarrel or something. Crime of passion, you know."

"According to the journal, Lucky didn't have a boyfriend."

"People didn't know about stalkers back then, but it doesn't mean they didn't exist." He didn't mention Tyler, but she knew he was thinking about him, and a little chill went through her. "If it *was* the guy who was following the rodeo, I wonder if he killed any other women over the years."

"I didn't see anything mentioned in the journal, but Addie only rodeoed for a couple of years."

"Well, if Lucky really was murdered, I hope the bastard got what he deserved."

"So do I," Patience said. But she wondered if he ever really did.

CHAPTER 15

It was the last day of the Cheyenne rodeo and the exhausted cowboys all looked forward to the end of a long, grueling week. They were tired and battered, a number of them, like Dallas, sporting injuries they had picked up in the tough competition.

During that final performance, Stormy took a second in the calf roping, adding to the money he had won earlier in the week, but he'd pulled a muscle in his roping arm and he was taking Advils by the handful. In the saddle bronc riding, Dallas drew a horse named Snowball who was a straightaway bucker, making the ride look pretty good. But the judges were savvy and not all that impressed with the difficulty and he only scored seventy-eight points, not enough to win the day money, but enough to keep him in the lead for the overall average.

By the time Frontier Days was over, he had collected another silver buckle and a pocketful of winnings toward a spot on the top fifteen and an invitation to the Finals.

The bad news was, he had trouble again on his dismount and landed hard on his shoulder and Ace-bandaged knee. Stormy and Reno raced into the arena, hurrying to where

Dallas lay on his back in the dirt. Stormy must have realized how serious the problem was. While Reno held him steady, Stormy braced a foot against Dallas's ribs and jerked on his arm, popping his dislocated shoulder back into place. Stormy helped him to his feet, bracing him up as he limped out through the arena gates.

The crowd applauded and Dallas turned to give them a reassuring smile. Reno retrieved his hat and gave the crowd a wave, but when the men turned, their smiles slid away. Deep lines etched into Dallas's forehead and his jaw was knotted against the pain. He didn't protest when Stormy helped him over to the ambulance and sat him down on a bench so the EMTs could take a look at him.

Hurrying from her seat in the press area, Patience rushed to where the ambulance was parked. Her chest ached with fear and her hands felt damp. She wondered what Dallas would say if he knew how important he had become to her.

She stopped next to the white and orange van with the word AMBULANCE printed backward on the hood, watched the men pull off Dallas's boots, take off his chaps, then cut away the leg of his jeans. Patience stood anxiously as the EMTs worked over his injured knee.

"Looks like you twisted it pretty good," one of them said, a cadaverish little man with short black hair. His homely features didn't inspire much confidence, but he seemed to know what he was doing. "I don't think you tore anything. How's the shoulder?"

"Aches like hell, but I think it's okay, thanks to Stormy."

The tech just nodded. "A dislocated shoulder's a real bitch. Looks like it slid back in okay."

Dallas closed his eyes. "Thank you, God."

They gave him a couple of Vicodin, pain pills he downed with a slug of bottled water while they laid an ice bag over his knee and wrapped it in place with a clean Ace bandage.

"I know you probably won't listen," the second man said, bulkier than the first, wearing a pair of horn-rimmed glasses, "but you ought to take some time off and give yourself a chance to heal up a little."

"Good idea," Patience chimed in, knowing it wouldn't do a bit of good.

Dallas flicked a glance in her direction. "Actually, Charlie and I were talking about that just before the show. He thinks I ought to go back to the ranch with him, stay through the end of the week."

"You better," the skinny tech said. "You don't stay off that knee, sooner or later you're gonna do some permanent damage."

"Yeah, well, I was thinking that maybe I'd go . . . if I could convince this lady here to come with me."

Patience's eyes widened. "To Texas?"

Dallas smiled. "Yeah, what do you think?"

A week with Dallas on Charlie's ranch. How romantic was that? She flicked a glance at Dallas, her head filled with erotic thoughts she'd never had until she met him.

"You'd have your own room and all," Dallas said a little gruffly, though his eyes promised something else entirely. Accepting the pair of crutches the EMT handed him, he hauled himself to his feet. "Annie's kind of old-fashioned. I guess you know what that means."

She took a deep breath, let it out slowly. She was tired of pretending, tired of arguing with herself. She wanted to go with him. Heck, she just flat wanted him.

"If it'll keep you off the back of a bronc and give your body a chance to heal, I guess I owe it to your fans to say yes." She smiled. "I'd love to see the ranch, Dallas."

When he looked at her, his eyes seemed bluer than they were before. She recognized the hunger, the wanting. Suddenly she couldn't get to Texas fast enough.

"That's great," he said, his eyes still on her face. "You're really gonna love it."

"Are you sure it'll be all right with Charlie?"

"Not a problem. There's plenty of room in the house and Annie always enjoys the company."

"Especially you, I'll bet."

"She never had kids. She's been mothering me since the first time I came to stay on the ranch when I was twelve years old."

They made their way back to his RV, the pain pills starting to kick in, Dallas using the crutches like a pro.

"You're awfully good with those things. How many times have you had to use them?"

He shrugged. "A few times, I guess. I'll be better by tomorrow."

Better. That meant he'd be able to walk on his own. Cowboys. They were all a little crazy.

"Were you really going to Texas, even before you hurt your knee?"

"Yeah. Charlie got a phone call from Annie. I could tell something was wrong. He says another forty head of stock were stolen from the ranch last night."

"Oh, no."

"It's probably not related to what happened with the trailer, but it still makes me nervous. I want to go back and check things out myself, see what's going on."

She paused at the door of his RV. "I'm glad you asked me to go."

He looked down at her from beneath the brim of his hat. "If you knew how much I wanted you, you might not say that."

She reached up and touched his cheek. "I'd still go. I should have said yes to you sooner."

Dallas's gaze sharpened. He bent his head, settled his mouth over hers, and Patience swayed toward him, encouraging him to deepen the kiss. His crutches slipped and his foot hit the ground. Dallas jerked away and a groan of pain rolled up from his throat.

Patience steadied him so he wouldn't fall. "Oh, God, I didn't mean to hurt you. Are you okay?"

He nodded, but sweat popped out on his forehead. Stormy ran up just then. "Easy, buddy. Remember that knee." Together, the two of them helped him into the trailer and up on his bunk.

"We're leaving tonight," Dallas said, his voice beginning to slur from the drugs. "Just as soon as Charlie can get the crew packed up. We'll be riding with him . . . driving straight through."

"All right," Patience said. "You get some rest. I'll tell Shari what's going on and get my stuff together." She and Stormy left him on the bunk, his eyes drifting closed.

"They gave him some pretty strong stuff," Stormy said. "He'll probably sleep halfway to Texas."

"Rest is exactly what he needs. I can help Charlie with the driving."

"He'll be taking his pickup, not one of the stock trucks. He's eager to get back home."

"I think that's nice," Patience said a bit wistfully. "It's obvious how much he loves his wife. My dad has that kind of marriage. I think they're both lucky men."

Stormy look away, off toward the little white trailer that Shari called home. "Yeah. I think so, too."

Charlie glanced over at the woman asleep on the passenger side of his truck. Dallas slept in the cramped backseat, awake off and on only briefly since they had left Wyoming. The boy was hurting and he was tired. Flat, bone tired. Charlie had rodeoed enough to know what that felt like. He also knew, hurting or not, his nephew wouldn't quit until he had won enough money to earn himself a place in the Finals.

Charlie couldn't help feeling proud of the boy, as close to a son as he would ever have. Two years after he and Annie had married, she had miscarried their first child and the doctors had discovered a growth on her ovaries. They had done a complete hysterectomy. There would be no children for two people who had always planned to have a passel, so when Dallas had arrived on their doorstep—twelve years old, his mother dead and shunted off by his father—Charlie and Annie could only feel grateful to God for sending them a child to fill the hole in their hearts.

The road stretched ahead. Charlie blinked against the grit in his eyes and kept them focused on the broken yellow line dividing the lanes. Patience had done her share of driving, maybe a little bit more. Seemed like she was the sort who never backed away from doing her share of the work.

He liked her for that. Hell, he liked her for a lot of things. Still, he was worried. He had never seen Dallas this way with a woman and it didn't bode well.

Carsons loved hard and usually only once, and Dallas was a Carson on his mama's side. If the boy fell in love with Patience Sinclair . . . well, Charlie only had to recall his little sister, Jolene, to know the consequences of a match like that. Patience and Dallas were as different as Jolie and Avery, no matter that she could ride and seemed to like rodeo.

This summer was a lark for her, an adventure. She had told him that herself.

The fact was, a Boston professor and a cowboy—even one who dreamed of someday turning rancher—just didn't suit. Charlie and Annie were proof of the kind of marriage a man could have with a woman who fit into his life, his dreams. It was the kind of marriage he wanted his nephew to have, the kind Dallas deserved.

The good news was, no matter how involved the boy got with Patience, Dallas wasn't a fool. Charlie didn't think the girl was, either. They were infatuated with each other, yes. But there was a lot at stake. He didn't think either one of them was crazy enough to make the same mistake Dallas's mother and father had made.

At least Charlie hoped not.

Patience stirred on the seat beside him, opened her eyes and yawned. She stretched and rotated her head, trying to work the kinks out of her neck. "Must be my turn to drive."

"Not yet," Charlie lied. "You can sleep a little while longer."

"You sure?" She was a pretty little thing, even with her blond hair rumpled and her eyelids a little puffy. And she had grit. He could see why Dallas liked her.

"I'll wake you up when we stop for gas."

Patience didn't argue. It was a long trip from Wyoming to Texas. She curled up against the window and almost instantly fell back asleep.

Charlie noticed again how attractive she was and his worry returned. On top of the problems with the production company and the cattle rustling on the ranch, he was concerned about Dallas's future. Charlie prayed the boy was smart enough to tell the difference between a woman who fired your blood and one you could make a life with.

But he wasn't all that sure.

The Texas hill country was so green it made your eyes hurt. Tall green grasses, thick green shrubbery, big green trees. Flowers bloomed along the road and fanned across the lush, rolling hills, adding bright splotches of color. The air was damp, hot and thick this time of year, and yet Patience thought that compared to the wet cold of Boston, perhaps it wasn't so bad.

"So what do you think?" Dallas asked, driving now, awake and alert after his long hours of slumber.

"It's pretty. So lush and green. I can see why you like it so much."

He smiled. "It shows, does it?"

"In every line of your face."

Charlie slept scrunched up in the backseat and Patience heard him stir. He had driven for hours last night, letting her and Dallas sleep. He was a sweet man, and she was beginning to think that under all the alpha-male toughness and buckets of testosterone, so was the man he had adopted as his son.

"Texas is my home," Dallas said. "I like everything about it. The rivers that wound through the fields, the cottonwoods shading the banks of the creeks." Flocks of birds flashed out of the trees, winging their way upward, and a deer tripped daintily toward the stream.

"We're almost there." Dallas pointed up the narrow paved road they traveled. "The Circle C gate is just past those two big sycamore trees."

Behind him, Charlie stirred again, sat up and blinked himself awake, as if the nearness of home drew him as well. He stretched in the backseat, and picked up the plastic bottle of water that rolled around under his feet. He took a long drink, swished it around in his mouth, and swallowed.

She could see the anticipation on Charlie's face as they pulled through the tall wooden gates of the Circle C and drove down the tree-shaded lane to the house. They passed a pasture full of horses, who kicked up their heels and raced along beside the truck. Then Dallas stepped on the brakes in front of a white, two-story wood-framed house with bright red shutters and a white picket fence around the front yard. It looked like a storybook home, and Patience thought that it perfectly fit the image she carried of Charlie and his wife.

Annie came through the front door just as the dust began to settle. They all got out of the truck and Charlie made straight for his wife, hauling her into his arms and kissing her until she looked embarrassed. She wasn't very tall, maybe five-one or two, trim and gray-haired, a woman who carried her sixty-odd years without apology, which added to the attractiveness of her face.

"Honey, this is Dallas's friend, Patience Sinclair."

Annie smiled. "It's a pleasure to meet you. Charlie's told me all about you."

"It's a pleasure to meet you, too," Patience said, meaning

it. "Charlie talks about you all the time, so I feel like I already know you."

"Well, good, then we won't have to be formal. Come on in and I'll show you upstairs to your room. It's nothing fancy, but I think you'll be comfortable."

"I assure you it'll seem like a palace compared to my bunk in the trailer." She followed Annie inside, Dallas and Charlie trailing in behind them. Annie led her up a wooden staircase, into a bedroom with white-ruffled curtains and a handmade red and white quilt over a bed with an old-fashioned white-painted iron headboard. A hooked rug in matching colors warmed the wide-planked oak floors.

"It's charming, Mrs. Carson. I especially love the quilt."

"It's Annie, dear, and thank you. I made it myself."

"Along with the curtains and the rug?"

She smiled. "Helps to pass the time. Gets a little lonely out here sometimes with Charlie gone."

"Yes, I imagine it does." She glanced out the window, to the horses and cattle in the rolling green fields. "Still, I imagine you have plenty to do, keeping a ranch this size running smoothly."

Annie sighed and shook her head. "Ain't been runnin' all that smooth lately. I'm real glad Charlie and Dallas come home."

Dallas walked in just then, carrying Patience's suitcase. "Any place special you want this?"

"Just put it on the bed."

"It's near to lunchtime," Annie said to her. "Be ready in about half an hour. Give you time to unpack and settle in."

"Thank you. If there's anything I can do to help—"

Annie smiled. "I appreciate the offer. You can help with supper. I'll see you downstairs in a while." She turned to Dallas. "You coming?"

Dallas just smiled. "Yes, ma'am." He cast a regretful glance at Patience and followed his aunt from the room, closing the door behind him.

Watching them leave, Patience felt the tension ebb from between her shoulders. She wasn't quite sure what to make of Annie Carson. She liked what she knew of the woman, admired her for the way she handled the problems of running the ranch, but Patience was fairly sure Annie wasn't thrilled to have her there. Patience figured it had something to do with her relationship with Dallas.

She couldn't help a smile. Her dad would probably react the same way if she ever brought a cowboy home with her to Boston.

The Circle C Ranch stretched across the vast Texas landscape, eight thousand acres of lush Hill Country land. But someone was rustling Circle C cows and stopping them was Dallas's first priority.

As soon as they finished lunch, a delicious spread of smoked ham, fried potatoes, vegetables from Annie's garden, and homemade cornbread with her delicious honey butter, Dallas phoned Max Mills, the sheriff of Bandera County.

Max wasn't in his office. Instead of returning the call, he drove up in front of the house that afternoon.

"Good to see you, Charlie, Dallas."

"You, too, Max," Dallas said. All three men shook hands. Max was ten years older than Dallas, but like a lot of Texas men, he had rodeoed during his youth, team roping with his dad mostly, riding bulls till he got enough sense to quit. He was tall and athletically built, an attractive man even though his blond hair was slowly turning silver and thinning so much he was nearly bald.

He glanced down at the bandage wrapped around Dallas's leg. "How bad you hurt?"

"Not too bad. Just a twisted knee. I'll be able to ride again by the end of the week."

"Glad to hear it," Max said, knowing from experience that *not too bad* meant the knee hurt like blazes.

"So tell us what's going on," Dallas said, cutting straight to the point. "You come up with anything useful this time?"

Max filled them in on the latest raid and any new information his deputies had picked up—which wasn't much—then he suggested they climb into his car and drive out to the area where the cattle had been stolen.

"Whoever's behind this has a pretty fair notion of what's going on around here," Max said. "Sully lost a couple dozen head that same night. He was away in Austin on business at the time. Seems like maybe they knew Charlie would be gone as well."

"Sounds like," Dallas said.

The men combed the upper pasture where the cattle had been taken. They found tire tracks, but they were a fairly standard Goodyear model, a Uni-Steel ll R 22.5, the sheriff said. The tracks showed the truck was fitted with a pair of dual wheels on the back, the sort of vehicle commonly used to transport horses and cattle. There were boot prints, indicating several different men were involved, evidence that might come in handy later on, but nothing that would help the sheriff discover exactly who was behind the theft.

"They've got to be selling those beeves somewhere," Dallas said. "Anything turn up along that line?"

"Not so far. We figure maybe they're hauling them out of state but we haven't got anything concrete."

"If they did go out of state," Charlie said, "maybe they'll stay there. They've got to know the risk increases every time they hit the same place."

"That's what we figured before. As it turned out, that wasn't the case."

"Maybe we could lay a trap for them," Dallas suggested. "Move some cattle into one of the more accessible pastures, then let it be known around town that Charlie and I are going back on the road. We could stake out the pasture, see if our cattle thieves turn up."

"That might work, except it was weeks between the first

strike and this one. We can't have deputies out there every night. We *can* try to patrol the area more often whenever you two are gone."

"We'd appreciate that," Charlie said. "And I can hire another hand or two, set up some kind of rotating night patrol."

But of course that would cost money, an additional expense that right now Charlie couldn't afford.

As soon as they got back to the ranch house and the sheriff went on his way, Dallas pulled Charlie aside. "Let me help you with some of these expenses. I've got money put away—you know that. If you won't accept the money straightaway, I'll make it a loan."

But Charlie was already shaking his head. "Not gonna happen, son. These are my problems, not yours. I'm the one who's gonna solve them." Charlie turned away, but Dallas caught something in the grim set of his features.

"You're not thinking of selling that southern acreage to Sully?"

Charlie refused to look at him. "He's offered to buy the piece a couple of times before. It butts right up to that dogleg section he owns along the creek. Annie says he asked about it again the other day, offered her a good price for it, too."

Dallas felt a sinking in the pit of his stomach. The Circle C had been in the Carson family for over a hundred years. Until now, Charlie had adamantly refused to sell off even a few acres.

"Don't do it, Charlie. There's got to be some other way."

Charlie finally looked at him. "I ain't sold anything yet. Even if I do, it's not for you to worry about. You just get well, then git yerself back to ridin'. You win at the Finals, that's the best thing you can do for me and Annie."

Dallas said nothing more. He loved his aunt and uncle, but sometimes they frustrated the hell out of him. He sighed as Charlie headed back to the house, caught up, and started limping along beside him. For a while, at least, he would do as Charlie asked. He needed to rest and mentally prepare himself for the difficult months of competition ahead.

He glanced toward the kitchen, saw Annie and Patience through the window over the sink, at work on the evening meal. Patience laughed at something Annie said and the sound went straight through him. His loins tightened and his pulse spiked up. She had drawn her blond hair back into a single, no-nonsense braid, but he knew how silky it would feel if he untied the ribbon at the end and ran his fingers through it. He knew how luscious those long legs would look if he stripped away her jeans, remembered exactly how sweet it felt to be inside her.

His groin thickened and filled. He needed to heal, all right, but he needed something else even more. He had waited long enough for Patience Sinclair.

CHAPTER 16

Annie handed the last of the supper dishes to Patience, who dried the plate carefully and put it on top of the stack in the cupboard.

"Well, now that we're through with the chores, let's go see what the men are up to."

Dallas and Charlie were sitting in the living room, Dallas reading the *Daily Times,* the local area newspaper, Charlie in his recliner, his feet up, watching the evening news. This was a ranch and the chores were clearly divided. The men might not wash dishes, but looking around the ranch, it was obvious they did their share.

Annie stopped in the doorway leading into the room. "All right, you two—now that you're stuffed full as ticks, what do you say we all sit down and play a little cards?"

Dallas laughed as he folded the paper and set it aside. "I don't know if that's such a good idea, Aunt Annie. The last time I played with Patience, she wound up with all my money and everyone else's."

One of Annie's gray eyebrows went up. She cast Patience a look that clearly said she was impressed. "Well, then, we'll only count points, how's that?"

"I don't think I'm up for it tonight," Dallas said. "It's still plenty light outside. I thought I'd saddle a couple of horses, show Patience a little of the ranch." He cast a look at Patience, whose eyes locked with his, then he turned and smiled at Annie. "Tomorrow night, I promise you can kick my butt at Hearts, the way you usually manage to do. That okay with you?"

Annie didn't looked thrilled, but she nodded. "Just make sure you don't stay out too late. You need to get your rest."

Dallas grinned. "Yes, ma'am."

Patience watched the smile slide away as his attention returned to her. "That all right with you?" His eyes were a brilliant shade of blue and she knew he was planning a lot more than a sight-seeing tour.

"Are you sure you're well enough to ride?"

A spark of mischief crept into his eyes. "I'll be able to ride just fine—I promise."

Patience felt the heat climbing into her cheeks. Her stomach tightened with anticipation that she prayed didn't show on her face. "I'd love to see the ranch," she said softly, and watched those hot blue eyes turn downright scorching.

"Come on, then." He reached out and caught hold of her hand. "We're burnin' daylight here."

She was certainly burning something. Her heart jumped, and her skin tingled wherever those blue eyes touched her.

Dallas kept hold of her hand as they left the house. As soon as they reached the barn and stepped inside out of sight, he pulled her into his arms.

"I've been dying to do this all day." Bending his head, he kissed her, his lips brushing lightly over hers, then sinking deeper.

"Hey, Dallas!"

She thought he whispered a curse as he jerked away and dragged in a calming breath of air.

"Hey, Ben—it's good to see you." Dallas reached out and shook the man's outstretched hand, then turned to where she stood in the shadows. "Patience Sinclair, meet Ben Landers, foreman of the Circle C Ranch."

Patience stepped into the light and Ben touched the brim of his hat, looking faintly embarrassed to discover that Dallas wasn't alone.

"Pleased to meet you, ma'am." A slight flush shaded his cheekbones, which were lean, the skin across them dark and leathery. He looked like a cowboy should, tall and spare, his legs slightly bowed.

"It's nice to meet you, too," Patience said.

"We were just about to go for a ride," Dallas told him. "I thought I'd show Patience a little of the ranch."

Ben nodded. "Good idea. I'll saddle you a couple of horses."

"Thanks." Dallas ran a finger along her cheek, turned, and walked over to help Ben with the horses. A few minutes later, he led a pretty little bay mare and a big-chested sorrel gelding over to where she stood next to one of the stalls.

"Take your pick. Gigi walks out a little faster than Outlaw, but he's got a really smooth gait."

She opted for Gigi. The mare was just too pretty to pass up. Dallas adjusted the stirrups and they left the barn, heading off down a narrow trail along a small running stream. The breeze picked up, lifting some of the humidity and cooling the damp summer air. Puffy white clouds drifted by overhead, lending occasional shade as the evening continued to cool.

They didn't ride all that far. She smiled when he pulled the horses to a stop in a shaded, secluded meadow next to the creek. Dallas tied the horses, reached up and pulled her down from the saddle and straight into his arms.

His kiss wasn't gentle. Maybe he had meant it to be but the minute their lips touched, something happened. Both of them just seemed to lose control. His tongue was in her mouth and she was sucking on it, hard. One big hand cupped the nape of her neck, dragging her closer, at the same time moving her backward, up against the trunk of a tree. He shoved up her T-shirt, slid his hands inside her bra to cup her breasts, molded them, rubbed her nipples.

He was big and hard against the front of his jeans, and she arched against him, heard him groan. Her body was on fire, her breasts aching, throbbing against his palms. She was wet, her thong panties rubbing places she had never noticed before, her nipples hard and erect.

"Dallas . . ."

He kissed the side of her neck, kissed her deeply again, yanked her tank top up over her head, unfastened her bra and filled his hands with her breasts. She was shaking all over and on fire, wanting him so much it was frightening.

"What . . . what about your knee?"

"It's fine."

That meant he had taken a pain pill and wrapped it really well, but she knew better than to argue. Dallas kissed her again and slid his tongue into her mouth. He kissed her one way and then another, kissed her and kissed her and kissed her. The snap popped open on her jeans. He slid his hands inside to cup her bottom, felt the naked curves, the thin silk thong between the globes, and groaned.

The husky sound sent a wave of desire flooding through her. She felt hot and dizzy, teetering on the edge of climax. Dallas pulled her tighter against him, fitted his erection into the notch formed by her thighs, rubbed himself against her. All the time he kept kissing her, kneading her breasts, using his tongue in an erotic imitation of what he meant to do to her body. He tugged the ribbon off her braid, sank his hands into the ripply strands of her hair, fisted them, dragged her head back, and kissed her again.

"God, I hope I'm not scaring you," he said between ragged breaths, voicing the thought she'd had just moments before.

Patience pressed her mouth against the side of his neck,

went up on her toes and lightly bit his earlobe. "I'm not the least afraid."

She felt his muscles tighten, straining with his effort at control. "God, I want you. I want to tear off your clothes and bury myself so deep you start coming and never stop." Kissing her shoulders, he moved lower and began to feast on her breasts. She felt his teeth scrape against her nipple and heat washed over her, so fierce she swayed on her feet.

"You make me feel . . . so good," she whispered, and Dallas kissed her savagely again. She had never met a man who could kiss the way he did, or seemed to enjoy it so much. He stopped only long enough to strip her jeans down her legs, then bent and tugged off her boots. The jeans were gone, leaving her in only her red thong panties. He slid his fingers inside the damp satin, began to stroke her, and her body went up in flames.

Lifting her, he shoved the panties aside, wrapped her legs around his waist, and buried himself to the hilt. She came almost instantly, her head falling back, clamping down on her bottom lip to keep from moaning his name. The pleasure had barely begun to fade when he surged even more deeply and she started coming again.

Dallas kept a tight grip on her bottom, holding her in place to receive his heavy thrusts. She could feel the thick weight of his shaft as he drove into her several more times, then allowed himself to reach his own release.

For long seconds neither of them moved. Patience's head rested on his shoulder, her legs still circled his waist. Dallas released a weary sigh as he let her go and she slowly slid down his body. He stripped away the condom she had no idea he'd put on, zipped himself back inside his jeans, then bent his head and kissed her one last time.

"Now maybe I'll be able to think straight around you for a while."

Patience gave him a catlike smile, feeling feminine and

sexy as she never had before she met him. "Don't count on it, cowboy."

Dallas laughed. Shaking his head, favoring his leg only a little, he walked over and untied the blanket behind his saddle, spread it out on the grass. Then he caught her hand and tugged her down beside him.

Leaning back, he propped himself on his elbows and cast her a serious glance. "I wish I could figure out what it is about you that drives me so crazy."

One of her eyebrows went up. "You think *you've* got a problem? Until I met you, my life was neat and orderly—everything planned out way ahead. I never did anything without thinking about it first. And I never would have believed I could share a strictly sexual relationship with a man."

His eyes locked on her face. "Is that what this is? A strictly sexual relationship?"

Patience swallowed against the lump that began to form in her throat. "You know it is. It has to be, Dallas."

He nodded, dragged his gaze away. "Yeah, I know." He didn't say more and neither did she. Both of them were thinking that the summer was slipping away and summer was all they had. They were just too different. It could never work between them. It was a fact that neither of them could change.

Patience reached up and cupped his cheek. "Dallas?"

He had put his hat back on—a dusty white straw in deference to the heat—and he smiled at her from beneath the brim. "What is it, darlin'?"

"Would you think I was greedy if I asked you to make love to me again?" He was already hard. She could see the heavy bulge at the front of his jeans, but he went harder still.

"I'd think you were almost as greedy as I am." Bending his head, he nibbled her lips, then very softly kissed her. Patience took off his hat and tossed it away, pulled his head down for another lingering kiss. They made love on the blanket, more slowly this time, then curled up next to each other to watch the sun slowly sink behind the hills.

It was time to leave, and so, regretfully, they did. Patience rode Gigi along the narrow trail behind Dallas, who led the way back to the house. She loved the way he looked on a horse, so tall and broad-shouldered, so casually straight in the saddle. His hat rode low and butter-soft jeans molded to his thighs.

It was impossible not to be attracted to a man who looked that good, that male, one who was also such a wonderful, considerate lover. It was hard not to fall in love with him.

She had to take care, she told herself, had to be wary, but a nagging voice warned that it was already too late.

Dusk settled in as they neared the big white, wood-framed house, turning the sky a soft pinkish purple. She could see the glow of the TV through the window of the family room, where Annie and Charlie sat watching a *Seinfeld* rerun, both of them laughing, curled up next to each other on the sofa.

A pang went through her. She would love to share that kind of closeness with a man. Maybe someday she would find someone who fit into her life the way Annie and Charlie fit together. Patience refused to think of Dallas in the role, knowing how impossible it would be. The fact was unbearably depressing.

Instead of joining the couple in the family room, she pled a case of travel weariness, said a brief good night, and headed upstairs to her room. She could feel Dallas watching her but he didn't ask her to stay and she wondered if his thoughts might be the same.

Annie watched Patience Sinclair leave the family room and head for the stairs. There was no mistaking the flush in her cheeks, or the satisfied male smile on Dallas's face when he walked into the room, hung his hat on the rack beside the door, and sat down in one of the brown leather chairs in front of the TV.

It was none of her business, Annie told herself. Both of

them were adults. They had a right to live whatever kind of life they wanted. Annie just hoped Dallas didn't make the same mistake his mama had.

Not that she didn't like Patience. She was one smart little gal—getting herself a Ph.D., Charlie said, gonna be a professor at some fancy college in the East. But that was just the point. A professor and a cowboy. It just wouldn't work, even if the two of them wanted it to.

Annie had seen what had happened when Jolene married Avery. A rancher's daughter and a highfalutin, big-time Houston plastic surgeon, though, of course, he was still in medical school back then. What a disaster that turned out to be. Nothing but arguin' and fightin' about every little thing, one of them wanting to live the high life in the city, the other feeling out of place, begging to move back to her home in the country.

Far as Annie was concerned, it had driven Jolie Carson Kingman into an early grave, and it was the last thing she wanted for the boy she thought of as her son.

Annie sighed and clicked off the TV. Next to her, Charlie snored lightly. She nudged him a little and he grunted, blinked his eyes, and sat up on the sofa.

"Gettin' late," Annie said. "Time to go on up to bed."

Charlie's gave her a sleepy-eyed grin. "Bed, is it? Well, honey, you know I can't resist that kinda invitation."

Annie laughed and elbowed him in the ribs, but she didn't say no and she didn't mind at all when his hand went around her waist as they started up the stairs. Annie loved Charlie Carson, had loved him from the first time she had met him, right here on his daddy's ranch. Her mother had worked cleaning the house once a week, and on that summer day so long ago, Annie had come with her mama to help.

She remembered the exact moment Charlie Carson had walked in, wearing his worn jeans and boots, a battered straw hat, and a big, warm smile. Annie remembered thinking how handsome he was and that any man with a smile like that had to have a good heart. She had thought that if he did, Charlie Carson was the man she wanted to marry.

Annie shook her head, letting the sweet thoughts slip away. Charlie loved her. They were happy together, one of the most blessed couples that God had put on this earth. That's what she wanted for Dallas.

And it wasn't gonna happen with a city gal like Patience Sinclair.

Patience slept deeply. It was the clean country air and the quiet, she thought, combined with a mind-blowing, stress-relieving round of sex.

Dallas took her riding after breakfast that morning and this time he actually showed her some of the ranch. It was beautiful, a lot of wild, untamed hill country, as well as some really great cattle grazing land. Pride sparkled in his eyes as he talked about ranching and his dream of owning a place like the Circle C.

"I've been saving ever since I started rodeoing. Eventually, I'll have enough money to buy a spread of my own." He grinned. "All I have to do is keep winning."

But winning wasn't always easy, even for a champion like Dallas. His leg and shoulder were healing, but it wouldn't take much to injure them again and put him out of the running, at least for the rest of the year. She hoped he would be able to make the Finals, earn a chance at the really big money. Dallas deserved to be happy.

But then, so did she.

She watched the easy way he swung down from the saddle, the way his eyes swept the grassy meadow, the faint smile that edged his lips.

"You seem different out here." Patience swung down beside him. "More relaxed."

Dallas took her reins and tied both horses to a cottonwood tree. "This is the life I want, Patience. The life I've always wanted. I'm at home in the country. I could never feel that way in a city. It's something my father could never understand."

"Annie says your mother felt that way, too."

"Yeah, I suppose she did. She was never really happy in Houston. I used to feel sorry for her. I think her depression caused the cancer that finally killed her."

Patience reached over and linked hands with him and the sadness eased from his face. "I can see why you love it here so much. It's beautiful and in some way oddly compelling."

"It's the vastness, maybe, or the fact the land is still so untamed."

"You're right, there. Back in the old days, Comanche raided this area until almost 1880. It was a favorite hunting spot and also a source of paint."

"You mean like war paint?"

She nodded. "They found blue and yellow clay south of Bandera, red and white northwest of here."

Dallas chuckled. "Still full of trivia, I see."

Patience smiled. "Sorry."

"Don't be. It's interesting."

Patience squeezed his hand. She looked out over the open green fields. "You'll have your ranch someday, Dallas. I know you will."

He carried their linked fingers to his lips, kissed the back of Patience's hand. They made love there on the grass and afterward swam naked in the stream. It was a beautiful day she would always remember, followed by a memorable week. Except for a slight reticence on Annie's part, she was treated as if she were part of the family, joining easily into their way of life.

As Dallas had promised, they played cards a couple of nights. Patience thought she gained a little respect when she shot the moon playing Hearts, burying each of the other players in unwanted points. They played a little Texas Hold 'Em, and she was smart enough to let Annie win.

Apparently the woman wasn't fooled, which for some strange reason seemed to gain Patience another couple of Brownie points. Still, Annie was worried about Patience's involvement with Dallas. She didn't want him in a relationship with nowhere to go and that was exactly the sort they had.

Patience sighed as she headed downstairs. It was morning—but not by much. She wasn't normally an early riser, but this was a working ranch and for the people here, work started at the crack of dawn. Today the men would be rounding up Charlie's second string of bucking horses. They'd be loading the stock trucks sometime in the afternoon.

As she reached the bottom of the stairs, she caught a glimpse of Dallas through the living room window, dressed in his worn jeans and boots, heading for the barn, looking so sexy a little curl of heat slid into her stomach. Annie might be worried about Dallas, but Patience wasn't. With the number of women who flocked around him at every rodeo he attended, he would hardly have time to miss her.

Dallas's life would return to normal, but Patience wouldn't forget him anytime soon. Leaving Dallas was going to hurt and she knew it. Still, he was hers for the present and she was determined to enjoy whatever time they had left.

The men returned to the house for the breakfast Patience and Annie prepared—pancakes, bacon, and eggs—then went back to work. They were headed toward the barn when a light beige Buick sedan drove up in the front yard. From her place next to Annie at the kitchen window, Patience watched Charlie and Dallas walk over to greet their visitor.

"That's Mal Sullivan—everyone calls him Sully." Annie wiped her hands on her apron. "He owns the Double Arrow Ranch. Borders our spread a little southwest of here. Sully had some cattle rustled the same night we did. I guess he's come over to talk to Charlie about it." He was an average-looking man, brown-haired, late forties, well-dressed in tan slacks and a white pullover shirt and a pair of polished brown cowboy boots.

"I really feel bad about all the trouble Charlie's been having."

Annie shrugged her shoulders. "Happens that way sometimes. We've had a lot of good luck over the years. Guess this just sort of evens things out."

It occurred to Patience that perhaps Charlie might not have mentioned his conversation with the Laramie County sheriff, or told her that the destruction of the stock trailer hadn't been accidental. Both he and Dallas were the protective sort. Charlie probably hadn't wanted Annie to worry.

They watched Mal Sullivan give a final wave, climb back in his car, and drive away.

"Charlie's thinkin' about sellin' a chunk of land to Sully," Annie said. "Or maybe takin' out a second mortgage." Annie fiddled with the apron she wore around her waist. "I don't much like the notion, but it's better than selling the land, I guess." It wasn't like Annie to discuss private matters, which showed just how worried she was.

"Maybe Dallas can help."

"He's offered. Charlie won't have it and I don't blame him. The boy's worked too hard for the money he's earned."

"Maybe they'll catch the men who stole your cattle and things will settle back down."

"I hope so. I surely do."

But stolen cows were the least of the problem. There was also the matter of the sabotaged truck and the potential danger the rodeo company faced until whoever did it was apprehended.

Thinking of Dallas and Charlie, Patience helped Annie finish the breakfast dishes, then went out to watch the men bring in the first batch of fresh bucking horses the Circle C Company would be taking on the road.

Tomorrow, she, Dallas, and Charlie would be leaving the ranch, heading for the rodeo Charlie was producing in Lawton, Oklahoma. As soon as Dallas finished his ride Saturday night, he and Patience were renting a car and driving to Colorado Springs for the final day of the big Pikes Peak or Bust Rodeo.

It was a grueling life, not the sort she would ever want to live. But it was certainly exciting. And definitely an adventure.

Patience tried not to think how soon that adventure would end.

CHAPTER 17

The good news was Dallas won in Oklahoma. His ride went off without a hitch and his knee held up. He wrapped it good before he rode and it was healing very well. He rotated his arm, trying to work the soreness out of his shoulder. It was still a little stiff, the muscles across his chest kind of tight, but his body was improving every day.

As soon as the Saturday night rodeo was over, he rounded up Patience and they left for Colorado Springs in the Grand Prix he rented from Avis, trading off driving, both of them sleeping in shifts. It was a long trip and he needed to get there as quickly as he could. He was proud of himself for weakening only once, pulling off the road into the darkness so they could make love.

Dallas smiled at the memory, thinking of Patience's hand sliding over his thigh while he was driving. She gave him a come-on look that was both sensual and kind of sweet. Now that she had discovered her sexuality—thanks in large part to him—she was nearly as insatiable as he.

Nearly.

At any rate, they restrained themselves enough to get to Colorado Springs halfway rested. It was almost dawn when he pulled into the rodeo grounds and spotted his big black Dodge rig parked next to Patience's Chevy truck and travel trailer. She was sleeping against the door of the rental car. She roused herself as he drove over the uneven ground and stopped next to his rig.

Dallas turned off the engine. "Well, we made it." Getting out of the car, he rounded the hood to the passenger side and opened the door. "It's early yet. Maybe we can catch another couple of hours sleep. We could both probably use it."

Patience stretched and yawned, climbed out of the car. "I wouldn't turn it down." She looked longingly at her trailer, then glanced toward Dallas's rig. "I wonder which one they're in?" It went unsaid that Shari and Stormy were probably together.

"Maybe they're in mine," Dallas said hopefully, since Patience's bunk was bigger than his. But just then the door of the trailer swung open and a groggy-eyed Stormy stepped out, feet bare, wearing only his half-buttoned jeans.

"Hey, guys!" He scratched the sandy hair on his chest. "Welcome back."

"Thanks. Horses okay?"

"Sure. They're fine." He blinked, seemed to come fully awake, and his carefree smile slipped away. "Everything's okay except . . . we had a visitor while you two were gone. Showed up the first night of the show."

"Yeah? Who was it?"

"That guy, Tyler Stanfield."

Dallas's stomach clenched. "Stanfield was here?"

"He must have known Patience was traveling with Shari. Maybe he tracked down the truck registration or something. I guess he figured if he found the rig he'd find Patience."

Dallas flicked a glance in her direction. Her face looked pale and unconsciously she moved a little closer. Dallas slid an arm around her waist.

"It's all right," Stormy said, "you don't have to worry. Me and Blue and a couple of the boys had a little talk with him.

We told him if he wanted to keep walking on those two legs of his, he'd best leave Patience alone."

"I can't believe he found me," she said softly. "I can't believe he came all this way."

"I don't like this," Dallas said. "This guy just can't seem to get the message."

"I think maybe he did this time."

"Why is that?"

" 'Cause when he showed up again the next morning, Shari called the police. She told them about the restraining order Patience had against him and that he had followed her all the way from Boston. They don't cotton to guys like that around here. They pulled him over a ways down the highway and hauled his ass in."

"They put him in jail?" Patience asked in disbelief.

"Overnight, I guess. He posted bail the next day. When he got out, they drove him straight to the airport."

"So Stanfield's back in Boston," Dallas said with relief.

"Sure is. And he's in a passel of trouble. I don't think he'll be bothering P.J. again."

Patience sighed. "Tyler may be a little obsessed, but he's not crazy enough to get too far on Daddy's bad side. I think Stormy may be right. After his bout with the police, he'll be worried what his father might do. I don't think he'll be giving me any more trouble." She managed a smile, but Dallas thought she looked even more exhausted than she had when they arrived.

"Come on. My trailer's empty. We can still get a couple more hours sleep."

"I need to call my dad first. Let him know what's going on. He can keep us posted on what's happening with Tyler."

She used the new cell she had gotten in Stormy's name in Cheyenne. When she finished the call, they walked arm-in-arm to his trailer. Unfortunately, by the time they got there, sleep was no longer on his mind. Maybe it was Stanfield showing up, or just that he hadn't actually slept with her since their trip to Houston, not in a bed at any rate.

He was hard by the time they reached the door. Dallas told himself she needed to get some rest, but Patience started kissing him the minute they stepped inside, apparently of the same mind as he.

Afterward they snuggled together, Patience curled next to him on the narrow bunk, and he thought how good it felt to have her there beside him. He thought of Tyler Stanfield and his hand unconsciously fisted. The bastard had better not come near her again.

But Patience wouldn't be around much longer. In a few more weeks, she would be leaving, returning to her life in Boston, and he wouldn't be around to protect her. She'd be on her own, gone for good, and knowing that, he'd be a fool to let himself get anymore involved with her than he was already. He might be attracted to her, but that was as far as he could afford to let it go.

It was time he started thinking with the head on his shoulders instead of the one in his jeans, time he started reining in his emotions before he got sucked in any deeper than he was already.

But looking down to where Patience slept nestled so sweetly against him, feeling the brush of her hair against his cheek, Dallas wasn't all that sure he could.

The show went well that Sunday afternoon. Patience watched nervously as Dallas rode a horse called Fan Dancer, worried he might reinjure his knee, but the ride went smoothly and he scored a nice solid eighty-eight points, enough to win him third place money that day. He should have been happy, but instead he seemed moody and out of sorts.

He was worried about Charlie, and Tyler's arrival had only added to the strain. She prayed Tyler had learned his lesson and she thought that after his night in jail, maybe he actually had.

The truck sabotage preyed heavily on everyone's mind. So far Sheriff Harden in Cheyenne hadn't turned up any leads. Dallas was disappointed, but at least nothing new had happened during the week that they had been gone. The Circle C crew was headed for New Mexico. Dallas kept in close touch with Charlie via his cell phone, and they would be joining him as soon as the Pikes Peak Rodeo was over.

Once they reached the next town and got settled in, Patience planned to finish her thesis, which she had been away from far too long. Fortunately, the paper was basically done. She needed to review her research, go over her writing a final time and make any last minute changes, but she hoped to have it finished and ready to submit by FedEx the end of next week. Three weeks after that, she would be eligible to take her final oral exam and apply for graduation in September.

By then she would be back in Boston, teaching her first class at Evergreen College.

Her chest felt heavy. By then, her adventure would be over and Dallas would no longer be part of her life. She told herself it was for the best. Dallas was the wrong man for her and she was definitely the wrong woman for him. It was a fact they had both accepted from the start.

Patience sighed as she drove the pickup and trailer that afternoon the last few miles to Cottonwood Creek. Beside her, Shari seemed equally lost in thought.

"So what did you guys do while we were in Texas?" Patience asked. She hadn't really had a chance to talk to her roommate since she and Dallas had gotten back from the ranch.

Shari turned away from the window. The New Mexico landscape was harsh and forbidding, but also starkly beautiful. Miles of shifting sand and sage, magnificent flat-topped buttes rising hundreds of feet up out of the desert floor, blue skies that went on forever.

"Stormy's got a friend in Colorado. A bull rider named Pete Mathers. Pete asked us to come to his wedding. Since we had a little time before we went to Colorado Springs, we decided to go."

"That sounds like fun."

"I suppose it was. It was only a very small wedding, immediate family and a few close friends, but it was outside in a pretty spot that overlooked the river."

"Nice people, I suppose."

"Real nice. But Marla—that's the girl Pete married—has a couple of kids from a previous marriage. All four of them are living in a single-wide trailer." Shari looked over at Patience. "Of course Pete says it'll only be for a little while longer. He busted his leg real bad at Calgary this year and hasn't been able to ride, but according to Pete, he's going to win big next year."

There was disbelief in Shari's voice.

"I take it you aren't convinced," Patience said.

"You know how cowboys are. The next rodeo is always going to be the big one."

Patience made no reply. After a summer of traveling the rodeo circuit, she knew exactly how cowboys were.

The thought was somehow depressing.

"So what about this guy, Tyler Stanfield?" Shari asked. "How'd he find you?"

"He's got a friend who's into computers. I hear they can track down practically anything these days."

"You think he'll stay in Boston?"

"Actually, I do. His father will have a fit when he finds out Tyler followed me out here. Since Daddy holds the purse strings, I think he'll make sure his son's ridiculous obsession rapidly comes to an end."

Shari didn't say more and neither did Patience. They continued along the road and arrived in Cottonwood Creek late afternoon, Dallas and Stormy having altered their schedule to make more Circle C shows. The first performance didn't start till tomorrow night, but Dallas wanted to be there to help Charlie set up for the rodeo. He'd been edgy all day and oddly withdrawn. Patience figured it was worry over Charlie and left him alone.

It was early the following morning that she finally sat down at her laptop in the cramped little dining area of the trailer, determined to get the final work done on her thesis. Shari was in the bathroom when the phone rang, her dad calling to say Tyler was definitely in Boston and it looked as if he was going to stay there.

She hung up feeling relieved and able to settle into her work, checking and rechecking her research. Then the bathroom door cracked open and Shari stepped out. For the first time, Patience noticed how pale she was, that there were faint purple smudges beneath her eyes.

"Shari? What's happened? What's wrong?"

She gave out a brittle little laugh. "Is it really that obvious? What's wrong is that last night Stormy asked me to marry him."

"Wow! That's terrific!" Patience grinned. "Congratulations."

"Are you kidding? I told him no. I'm not going to marry him. I couldn't possibly do that."

Patience sat up a little straighter in the booth. "Why not? Stormy loves you and you love him. Any idiot can see that."

Tears filled Shari's eyes. "It doesn't make any difference." She scrubbed at the wetness escaping down her cheek. "I don't want to marry a cowboy. I don't want to spend my life in a single-wide trailer or live out of a suitcase for months at a time. I don't want to sit home while my husband's on the road half the year."

Patience couldn't help feeling sympathetic. It wasn't the sort of life for her, either.

"In three weeks, I'm going home to Oklahoma," Shari continued. "I'm starting back to school, just the way I planned."

Patience didn't know exactly what to say. In three weeks,

she would be leaving, too, returning to Boston, beginning the life she had worked so hard for all these years.

In the meantime, she and Shari were living in a crowded trailer, traveling every week. It was fun for a summer, but she couldn't imagine that kind of life with a husband and kids. And she wouldn't want to be left behind, either.

Patience reached over and squeezed Shari's hand. "I wish I could say something that would make you feel better. The truth is, I can't. I'll be leaving, as well, going back to my life in Boston. I understand exactly why you feel the way you do."

Shari sniffed and wiped away the last of her tears. "I'm really glad we traveled together this summer. I'm lucky to have you for a friend."

Patience reached up and hugged her, but neither of the women said more. They were there for each other. Both of them knew it, accepted it without question. No matter what happened when summer was over, Patience had made a life-long friend.

The Cottonwood Creek Rodeo was an old-fashioned, small-town show, not even Pro-Rodeo sanctioned, which meant that the purse was small and even if Dallas won, it wouldn't count toward his yearly total.

Originally he had planned to compete in the big Caldwell, Idaho, rodeo, which had a much larger purse, but he kept thinking of the sabotaged trailer and seeing dead horses, and as much as he needed to add to his winnings, he had decided against it.

At least Cottonwood Creek was a more relaxed show, with lots of locals competing and less pressure than a PRCA rodeo. Volunteers did much of the work, including the check-in and getting the necessary signatures on the liability waver forms from people moving around behind the chutes.

Charlie wound up handling the entry fee money, locking it in a small, fireproof safe in the production trailer. He didn't like the responsibility, Dallas knew, but in rodeos like this one, the rules were made up as they went along.

The rodeo went well, an outdoor night show warmed by the evening summer heat. Big flat-topped buttes surrounded the arena, which nestled at the base of a mountain that had once been the home of ancient Acoma Indians. Ruins of the pueblo remained, their haunting shadows phantom-like in the orange rays of sunset.

Cottonwood Creek was the kind of rodeo Dallas had always loved, the kind you did mostly for fun, but he was a professional rodeo cowboy now and he rarely had time for small shows like this one. It felt good to be there and perhaps that was the reason he won, making a splashy ride on a big spotted horse called Red Dawn. He calf roped well, but not good enough win any money.

As he rode out of the arena, he scanned the contestants' bleachers for Patience but didn't see her. He rode Lobo over to his trailer and unsaddled him, then went in search of her. He was headed for her little RV when he spotted her talking to Charlie near the production trailer. In the circle of yellow light beside the door, Dallas caught the grim look on Charlie's face and knew that something was wrong.

"What's going on?" he asked as he walked up, his adrenaline kicking in.

Charlie's jaw hardened. "Someone broke into the trailer. They stole the entry fee money—over ten thousand dollars."

"Sonofabitch!" Dallas blew out a breath and shoved back his hat. "Anybody see anything? Somebody going in or out of the trailer?"

"I've been asking around," Patience said. "So far no one's seen a thing."

"How'd they get in?" Dallas glanced up the metal stairs to the trailer door.

"Crowbar, looks like. Bent the latch pretty good. Noise from the crowd would have covered the sound."

Patience walked over to where they stood. "I'm going to keep asking around. Someone must have seen something."

Dallas watched her walk away, wishing he didn't like the view so much, his mood sliding even farther downhill. "Will your insurance cover this?"

Charlie shook his head. "It wasn't my money, so no, it's not covered."

Dallas muttered a curse. Another problem for Charlie. More money he would have to come up with. Coincidence? There was always the chance. But Dallas didn't think so. "You called the sheriff yet?"

Charlie nodded. "Got on my cell as soon as I saw the door pried open."

Both of them climbed the stairs to inspect the broken latch, then opened the door and went in. The fireproof safe appeared to be the only thing missing. It was heavy, but not so heavy a man couldn't haul it out.

"Probably threw something over it and just carried it down the stairs," Charlie said.

"I can't believe no one saw him."

"Hey, guys!" Patience's voice rang from the bottom of the stairs.

Dallas headed in that direction, Charlie close on his heels.

"I think maybe we got lucky." Patience turned to a slender young woman who stood beside her. "This is Rae Ann Bonner. She lives here in Cottonwood Creek. She was one of the contestants in the barrel racing tonight. Rae Ann was leading her horse back to her truck when she saw a man coming out of the production trailer."

"That's right." Rae Ann was no more than twenty, with light brown hair pulled back in a coil at her nape that fit neatly under the brim of her straw cowboy hat. "The guy was carrying something heavy, but I couldn't see what it was. It was covered by a canvas tarp that hung down over the sides."

"Would you recognize this guy if you saw him?" Charlie asked.

"Yes . . . no . . . not exactly. I mean I saw him real clear and all, but he was wearing baggy pants and grease paint. It was one of the rodeo clowns."

Dallas's adrenaline shot up. Charlie flicked him a meaningful glance, thinking exactly what Dallas was.

"We'll, I'd say that narrows it down," Charlie said.

Down to Junior Reese. With the bad blood between him and Charlie, it couldn't be anyone else.

"Do you know which clown it was?" Dallas asked, hoping the woman could be more specific.

"I heard the announcer mention his name, but I don't remember what it was. He's the one with the smiley makeup. I remember the other one wears a painted-on frown."

Dallas couldn't believe it. Cy wore the smiling face. Junior wore the frown. "Are you absolutely sure of that?"

"That's the man I saw. It's kind of hard to forget a guy in a clown suit."

"And you're sure the clown wore a painted on smile."

"Yeah. I thought it was kind of funny, considering he was carrying such a heavy load and all."

The sheriff's car pulled up just then. The door cracked open and a short, well-built, dark-skinned deputy got out. His badge read *Raul Santiago.*

"Thanks for coming," Charlie said.

The entire scenario was repeated for the deputy's benefit, while the young officer took notes on a water-stained spiral notepad.

Santiago flipped the pad shut and turned to Charlie. "I guess we'd better have a talk with that clown."

"Good idea," Dallas said. He started walking next to Charlie, and Patience fell in beside him.

"Where do you think you're going?" He stopped and turned toward her, effectively blocking her way.

"I'm going with you—what did you think?"

"The hell you are. If Cy really took that money, there might be trouble. If there is, I don't want you anywhere near."

"What are you talking about? I found Rae Ann, didn't I? If she's going, then I'm going."

"No way. You're staying here where it's safe. I won't be long. Stay out of trouble until I get back."

Patience opened her mouth to argue, then clamped down on whatever she planned to say. She didn't like taking orders and especially not from him. She didn't say anything more, but her face was red and he could see blood in her eye. Dallas ignored her. He wanted her here, where nothing bad could happen. He'd smooth her ruffled feathers later.

Leaving the production trailer, they made their way over to Cy's camper. By now, the rodeo was over. Cy had washed off his face paint by the time the deputy approached with Dallas and Charlie but still wore his red-striped shirt, knee-length red leather chaps, and cleated running shoes. Santiago stood protectively next to Rae Ann Bonner and seeing him, Cy paused in the act of stashing his gear behind the front seat of his truck. His gaze went from Dallas and Charlie to the armed, uniformed officer.

"What's up?"

"The entry fee money was stolen tonight," Charlie told him, "sometime during the performance. A witness put you at the scene."

"Me!" Cy looked thunderstruck. "What are you talking about? I was busy working the show."

"Not all the time," the deputy said. "Isn't that right, Mr. Carson?"

Charlie looked apologetic. "The clowns are in the arena off and on but they're behind the chutes during the events—all except the bull-riding, of course."

"I didn't steal any money. Come on, Charlie—you know me better than that."

"Is that the man?" the deputy asked Rae Ann.

"I-I don't know. I told you he had his clown makeup on."

"Did you happen to notice what he was wearing?"

"I remember the red-striped shirt. But I couldn't say what else."

"Maybe it was Reese," Cy said. "He's a clown. He had the same opportunity I had."

"The lady says the clown she saw coming out of the trailer wore the same face paint as you—a smiling face, not a frown. According to Mr. Carson, her description doesn't fit the other clown."

Cy looked stricken. "I didn't do it, Charlie. I swear it."

"Do you mind if we take a look inside your camper?" the deputy asked.

Cy shook his head. "No, go ahead."

Santiago opened the camper door and went in. He came back out a few minutes later. "I didn't see anything. If he took the box, it's not here."

"I didn't take the goddamn box or anything else."

"I'm sorry, Mr. Jennings. It looks like you'll have to come down to the station. There are a few more questions I need to—"

"Hold on a minute," Charlie said. "I've changed my mind. I've decided not to press charges."

Cy's whole body seemed to sag with relief. The deputy looked uncertain, but knowing Charlie as he did, Dallas wasn't all that surprised.

"Are you sure that's what you want to do, Mr. Carson?"

"I don't believe Cy Jennings stole that money. I've known the man for years and if he says he didn't do it, then I believe him. Besides, I've had other problems lately. I got a hunch this is just one more."

Dallas had to agree. Someone wanted to cause trouble for Charlie and it was highly unlikely the man was Cy Jennings.

"If anything turns up, we'll be in touch," Dallas said. "Thanks for your time, Deputy Santiago."

"No problem." He turned to Rae Ann Bonner. "I've got your phone number. If we need you again, we'll be in touch."

Rae Ann nodded and left with the deputy, heading back to her pickup and horse trailer.

As soon as the pair was gone, Cy turned to Charlie. "I didn't steal that money, Charlie. I hope you believe that."

"If I didn't, I would have let him cart you off to jail."

"Keep your eyes open, will you, Cy?" Dallas put in. "Somebody stole that money and whoever it was, tried to lay the blame on you."

"I'll keep my eyes open," Cy said darkly. "You can count on that."

Dallas clapped him on the shoulder. "Thanks." He and Charlie walked away from the camper, only to come up on Patience, who stood in the shadows just a few feet away. Recognizing the hard glint that appeared in Dallas's eyes, Charlie gave him a wave and kept on walking.

"What happened?" Patience asked.

"I told you to stay away from here, dammit."

"Well, you're not my boss, Dallas Kingman—in case you didn't know—and I was worried. Tell me what happened."

Reining in his temper, Dallas lifted his hat and raked back his hair, then settled his hat back over his forehead. "Charlie doesn't think Cy stole the money and neither do I."

"But Rae Ann Bonner said—"

"We think someone was trying to frame him."

"Like who?"

"Probably the same guy who rigged the hitch on the livestock truck."

Patience seemed to ponder that. "That makes sense. Although it could have been one of the locals. Or a competitor who figured out where the money was being kept and decided he could use it more than Charlie."

"Maybe."

"But you don't think so."

"The guy dressed up to look like Cy. He had to know the business and he had to have this pretty well planned out."

"True." They walked together back toward their trailers. "There's another possibility, you know."

"Yeah? What's that?"

"It's hard to keep secrets around here. A lot of people know that livestock trailer didn't turn over by accident. Shari says they're saying Charlie's troubles might be more than co-incidence."

"So?"

"So maybe whoever stole the money was just jumping on the bandwagon—taking the cash, laying the blame on Cy, and making Charlie think it was the same guy who sabotaged his truck."

Dallas tossed her a long, discerning glance. "That's not bad. Sometimes you're even smarter than you look."

Patience smiled. "So you think I might be right?"

"It's possible. Definitely possible." And if that was the case, Dallas had a good idea where to start looking. The same place his instincts had led him the moment he had heard about the theft.

Junior Reese.

Reese would have known how to copy Cy's makeup and owned very similar clothes. And he hated Charlie with a passion.

The big question was, if Junior *was* guilty, how the hell were they going to prove it?

CHAPTER 18

The sun was well up, beginning to heat the inside of the trailer. According to her father, Tyler was still in Boston so she could stop worrying. Patience finished working on the next-to-last section of her thesis and leaned back in the padded vinyl booth.

The paper was basically done. Next to it, the journal beckoned. She hadn't tuned in to her grandmother's adventures in over two weeks, not since her digging had lead to the discovery of what she believed to be Lucky Sims's murder.

She had skimmed the pages, of course, looking for more information, but Addie had rarely mentioned Lucky again, except to say how much she missed her. And she never found out what had happened to her friend.

Patience cracked open the faded tapestry covers of the book, savoring the connection to a long-dead relative she admired. The month was September. Addie's life was changing now, heading in a new direction, her words filled with the first glow of love.

Sam Starling. Patience turned the pages, saw the name again and again.

Sam and I went to a moving picture show. It was called The Lonely Villa *and my favorite actress, Mary Pickford, was the star. We had the most wonderful time.*

Sam took me to supper at this funny little restaurant, the Cat's Paw Inn. A man was strumming the guitar while we ate, and afterward, Sam went up and borrowed it for a while. He can really play that guitar.

Patience smiled as she submerged herself once more in Addie Holmes's journey.

Me and Sam took the train together, all the way to Dodge City, Kansas. I should have gone with Betsy and Star. They were leaving with the rest of the gals the next day, but Sam was so darned persistent that I finally said yes. We left a day early just so Sam could ride in a rodeo in Abilene. He won first prize money and bought me a fancy yellow satin western shirt I saw in the mercantile window. I worried a little that if I went alone with him on the train, Sam might get the wrong idea, but he was a perfect gentleman.

I wonder what Lucky would have said if she knew I was falling head over heels in love with him.

The mention of Lucky Sims's name turned Patience's thoughts away from Addie and Sam back to Lucille Sims's disappearance. Had the girl really been murdered? And if she were, was the man who had been following the rodeos the man who had killed her?

Dallas had mentioned the possibility of other rodeo-related murders that might have occurred at the time. More than ninety years ago, information wasn't as accessible, wasn't traded the way it was today. It certainly could have happened.

And it didn't seem right just to let the matter slide. The

first chance Patience had, she would do a little research, see what she could turn up. For years, she'd been studying the cowgirls of early rodeo. Her sources were extensive—in print, over the Net, and through contacts she had made during the course of her work. Perhaps she could find out if any other unexplained deaths in the rodeo community had been reported during, say, the ten-year period following Lucille's death.

She would begin by calling Constance Foster in the historical section of the Cowgirl Hall of Fame in Fort Worth, Texas. She had worked with Connie before. She could also phone Mabel Thompson at the 101 Ranch Museum in Oklahoma. For decades, the 101 was one of the biggest Wild West Shows in the country and Patience had worked a lot with Mabel.

If she got lucky, maybe someone would come up with something. At the very least, they could help her put together a list of towns where rodeos were performed during those years. Perhaps she could get someone in each town to check the police blotter in the local paper of the day, see what might have been reported.

Patience leaned back against the seat of the dinette, feeling a tug of excitement at the prospect of exploring a ninety-year-old mystery.

The journal sat open on the table.

Patience smiled as she returned her attention to the pages, eager to continue reading the virtues of Sam Starling, cowboy extraordinaire—who was stealing her grandmother's heart.

She didn't notice the time, engrossed as she was in the journal. It was perhaps an hour later that a soft knock sounded at the door. Patience set the journal aside, got up, and went over to open it. She was only a little surprised to see Stormy Weathers, hat in hand, standing at the bottom of the stairs.

"Hi, P.J. I was hoping you'd still be here."

"Hi, Stormy. Come on in. Excuse the mess. I've got papers strewn all over the place." Hurriedly, Patience began picking up her research files, moving the journal out of the way, and shutting down her computer.

"I didn't mean to get in the middle of your work." By now, nearly everyone knew Patience was working on her thesis. Surprisingly, most of them thought it was kind of cool.

"You're not getting in the middle of anything. Sit down. I was just about to quit work anyway." Stormy folded his lanky frame into the seat of the dinette and Patience walked over to the stove of the tiny kitchen. "You want a cup of coffee or something?"

"No, thanks. I'm fine."

Patience poured herself a fresh cup, then sat down in the dinette across from him. "I kind of figured you might show up here, sooner or later."

"Yeah, well, I was kind of hoping . . . you know . . . that you might be able to help."

Patience took a sip of her coffee. It tasted bitter now from sitting on the stove for so long. "Shari told me you asked her to marry you. I presume that's why you're here."

Stormy tossed his hat up behind the seat. His sandy hair looked disheveled, as if he had run his fingers through it. There were faint purple smudges beneath his hazel eyes. "So what do you think?"

Patience answered carefully. She loved Stormy like a brother. She could see the pain etched into his features and her heart ached for him. "To begin with, I know Shari loves you and I know that you love her. It's just . . . well, it's just that she has plans for the future that don't include getting married. Maybe in time that will change but right now—"

"So you're telling me that loving each other isn't enough. I always thought it would be."

"Shari wants to go back to school. She wants a different sort of life than you want, Stormy. Maybe after she gets her degree—"

"I love her, Patience. I want to marry her."

"You're a cowboy, Stormy. You love rodeo. Shari says that's all you've ever wanted to do."

"So what? A lot of cowboys get married. They have a home, a couple of kids. My friend Pete Mathers—"

"Your friend Pete Mathers represents everything Shari doesn't want." Patience reached over and caught his hand, felt the tension running through him. "Give her time to do what she needs to, Stormy. If you're still interested after that, maybe the two of you can work something out."

But it was about as likely as working something out with Dallas. It wasn't going to happen. At least she and Dallas knew it.

"So that's it, then? Nothing I say is going to change her mind?"

She sighed. "I'm afraid it isn't."

Stormy swallowed and nodded, shoved himself out of the dinette. He didn't say more, just grabbed his hat and headed for the door. "I appreciate your talking to me."

"I wish I could have helped, I really do."

"Yeah, so do I." Stormy left the trailer and she didn't see him again that day. She didn't see Dallas, either. He'd been keeping to himself more and more. They hadn't made love since the morning she had spent in the bunk in his RV. She had a feeling it had something to do with what was happening between Shari and Stormy.

Patience and Dallas were in the same situation—more so, since Patience's life had never been rodeo, the way Shari's had.

At least she and Dallas weren't in love.

Her stomach squeezed as she admitted the lie to herself. Dallas might not be in love, but Patience was. Deeply, stupidly in love with exactly the wrong man.

Patience took a calming breath. She needed some air, needed to clear her head. She left the trailer and wandered away off toward the flat-topped buttes in the distance, part of her wishing the summer was already at an end.

When he wasn't trying to console his best friend, Dallas was trying not to think of Patience. In the past few weeks, he had let himself get too close. She'd be gone in a couple more weeks and he was already in over his head. Seeing the pain in Stormy's face warned him not to make the same mistake his friend had made.

You've got to pull back, he told himself. *Get things back in their proper perspective.* But it wasn't that easy to do.

Worrying about Charlie helped distract him. Junior Reese and the stolen money loomed heavy on his head. If there had been a shred of evidence, they could have confronted him. But the woman, Rae Ann Bonner, had been specific in her ID, and according to her, the man who stole the money couldn't have been Junior Reese.

Still, Dallas's gut told him it was.

After the robbery, Deputy Santiago had gone to see Reese at the Westward Ho Motel. Junior had denied any knowledge of the theft and refused to let the officer into his room without a search warrant.

Well, Dallas didn't need a warrant. Just a credit card to open the door, or a window Reese might have left unlatched. All he had to do was figure out which room Junior was staying in.

The saddle bronc section was over. Garbed in their clown gear, Junior and Cy rushed into the arena and began entertaining the crowd.

As Dallas headed through the darkness toward his truck, he hastily unbuckled his chaps, opened the door of the pickup, and tossed them behind the seat. Then he slid behind the wheel and cranked the engine.

He was driving across the uneven ground behind the arena when Patience's slim shape appeared in the yellow beam of his headlights. Dallas softly cursed. He rolled down his window, but didn't turn off the ignition.

"Great ride tonight," she said.

"Thanks."

"Where are you going?"

"I've got some business in town."

"I'm kind of hungry. I thought maybe we could go get something to eat."

"Like I said, I've got some business I have to do."

Patience didn't budge, just gave him a long, knowing glance. "You don't fool me, Dallas Kingman. I know the business you're planning to do. You're going to Junior's motel room to look for that money and I want to go with you."

Dallas's fingers tightened around the steering wheel. "How the hell would you know where I'm going?"

"Because I'm beginning to know how you think. And besides, that's what I'd do."

"Yeah, well, even if I am, you aren't going. There might be trouble and I don't want you involved."

"Too bad. If you don't take me, I'll find Junior and tell him where you went."

"Bullshit. You wouldn't do that to Charlie."

Patience gave an exasperated sigh. "Look, if you take me with you, I can help. I can find out which room Reese is in and I can keep watch while you're making the search."

Dallas glanced down at his wristwatch. Time was slipping away. Dammit, he didn't want to take her with him, but she probably would have a better chance of finding out Junior's room than he would. "Get in."

Patience hustled around to the passenger side of the truck and climbed up on the black leather seat. They took off for the motel, which wasn't far from the rodeo grounds, and when the sign appeared, he pulled off the highway into the darkness at the edge of the parking lot.

The light was on in the motel office. Through the window, he could see a dark-haired clerk, standing behind the front desk.

"Leave this to me." Patience cracked open the door and jumped down from the seat.

"Just be careful," Dallas warned, nervous just watching her crossing the pavement.

She wasn't gone long. When she returned, she motioned to him to join her. She was grinning, he saw, dangling a room key from the end of her finger.

"How'd you do that?"

"Told him I was Junior's girlfriend and I wanted to surprise him when he came back to the room after the rodeo."

Dallas felt a tug of admiration. "Come on. Let's go."

They crossed the road and disappeared into the shadows along the building. Dallas waited in the darkness while Patience used the key to open the door. As soon as she stepped inside, Dallas slipped in to join her.

"Close the curtains," he said.

Patience was already in the process. "I'll keep an eye on the parking lot."

He nodded. "If Reese shows up, we'll go out the back window."

Patience leaned forward to peer through the crack in the curtains. The room was inexpensive, just a couple of twin beds with a nightstand in between, a bathroom with a shower over the tub, a water-stained toilet, and rusty sink. As a clown, Junior didn't have much of a name and his pay was minimal.

Dallas quickly scanned the interior. Junior's makeup kit sat open on the dresser, greasepaint gleaming in red, orange, purple, and blue. The dresser drawers were empty. Reese hadn't bothered to unpack and a canvas bag still held most of his clothes. The bag contained clean underwear and socks, a pair of toenail clippers, a few other personal items, and not a dollar of stolen money.

A search of the bathroom turned up nothing, just a toothbrush, razor, and some shaving soap. Dallas moved to the closet and slid open the doors. Metal wheels squeaked as they moved along the track. A couple of shirts and a pair of worn jeans, along with a couple of pairs of oversize Wranglers next to the scuffed boots on the floor.

A pile of dirty clothes had been tossed into a corner. Dallas reached down and rifled through them. A thin white cotton T-shirt caught his eye. He tugged it out of the pile and held it up for closer inspection.

"Take a look at this."

Patience turned away from the window and walked over to where he held up the shirt. "What is it?"

"See this yellow greasepaint on the front? It's kind of smudged, like he got it on there when he pulled the T-shirt off over his head."

"So?"

Dallas smiled grimly. "Junior doesn't wear yellow face paint. He paints his face in darker colors, blue and purple mostly, outlined with orange and red. Cy uses the brighter shades—including yellow."

"Are you sure?"

"Damned right, I'm sure. I've seen him work often enough over the years." Dallas walked over to the makeup kit. "Check it out. Junior doesn't even own any yellow paint. He must have used some of Cy's, then washed it off and redid his face the way he usually does. He would have had plenty of time. There was a full section of broncs, then more time while the barrels were being set up for the racing."

A noise sounded in the corridor outside the motel room. Dallas jerked Patience behind him as a key turned in the lock and Junior Reese swung open the door. He took in the scene, only mildly surprised, and a grim smile curved his lips.

"Well, look who's here. Kind of thought you might try something stupid like this."

Dallas caught the gleam of metal in Junior's hand, looked down and saw the little twenty-five-caliber pistol Reese held. He must have seen the light through the curtains. Junior had wiped off some of his face paint. His hollow, sunken cheek and the scar bisecting his eyebrow stood out starkly in the harsh light of the motel room. Though most of the paint was gone, a wide purple smudge tracked along his jaw and a smear of red tinted his chin.

"Breaking and entering," Reese said. "That's a crime, you know."

"Where's the money?" Dallas said.

"I don't have your money. The police say your witness ID'd Cy Jennings. Why don't you ask Cy where it is?"

Dallas held up the T-shirt. "You don't wear yellow grease-paint, Reese—but Cy Jennings does. You painted your face to look like his in case somebody saw you. Now, what did you do with the cash?"

Junior looked at the incriminating shirt, then his mouth edged up in the parody of a smile. "You want to know what I did with it? I spent it, that's what. Every dime is gone. And if you think that dirty T-shirt is going to prove I stole it, you can forget it. I had a bad couple of years after that bull stepped on my face. Did a little time in the pen. Even if the shirt *was* proof, the court wouldn't allow it as evidence. You aren't the police, and even if you were, you don't have a search warrant."

Dallas softly cursed. The bastard was right. There was no way in hell they would be able to prove Junior was guilty. Dallas took a menacing step forward. He felt Patience's hand on his arm as Junior raised the gun.

"I wouldn't do that if I were you," Reese warned.

Dallas's hands unconsciously fisted. "You may have the money, Reese, but you're ruined in this business. Word will get out—I'll personally see that it does. No one will hire you—nobody in the rodeo world at least."

Junior shrugged his shoulders. "I was thinking about retiring anyway. I'm getting too old for this clown crap. I figured Charlie owed me a little nest egg. You can tell him I said that."

"Charlie never told you to take a suicide wrap when you got on that bull. You can blame him for what happened all you want, but the fact is, if you'd used better judgment, you wouldn't have gotten hung up that day and you wouldn't have gotten hurt."

A muscle knotted in Junior's sunken cheek and his fingers tightened around the handle of the pistol.

"Dallas . . .?" Patience's voice urged restraint and he clamped down hard on his temper. It wasn't smart to go up against a man with a gun, especially when you had illegally broken into his room.

"Get out of my way, Reese." Dallas settled his hand on Patience's waist, urging her forward. They crossed the room and he eased her out the door ahead of him, then stopped and turned back to Reese. "I don't want to see your face again, Junior. Not at a Circle C show or any other rodeo. Your retirement starts today."

Closing the door behind him, Dallas headed for his pickup, his hand still riding on Patience's waist. Beneath his fingers, he could feel her trembling. When he reached his truck, he turned and drew her into his arms.

"You okay?"

She held onto him, pressing herself against him, nodding against his cheek. "I got a little scared in there. I wasn't sure exactly what you were going to do."

The corner of his mouth edged up. "I wasn't exactly sure myself."

"I guess Charlie's money is gone."

"Charlie won't want the hassle of trying to pin Junior down—he doesn't have the time. I'd say it's history."

"What do you think Reese did with it?"

"He's got kin in Alabama. Probably sent some of it to them. Maybe hid the rest. I thought about beating it out of him, but I figured I'd be the one who'd end up in jail, and Reese just isn't worth it."

They drove back to the rodeo grounds. Dallas parked the truck, then walked Patience back to her trailer.

"I'm glad you took me with you," she said.

"Why? Because you were worried I'd make hamburger out of Reese?"

She smiled. "Because if I hadn't been there to stop you from making hamburger out of Reese, he probably would have shot you."

Dallas laughed. He reached out and touched her cheek. "It's nice to know you care."

Patience's expression turned serious. "I care, Dallas. Too damned much."

Dallas stared into those clear green eyes, and something tightened in his chest. Bending his head, he very gently kissed her. It was a tender sort of kiss, the kind that told her the way he felt without saying the words.

Though he hadn't meant for it to happen, he was achingly aroused by the time he broke away, wanting her as he always did.

But Charlie had to come first. "I've . . . um . . . got to go see Charlie, tell him what happened. Maybe if you're awake when I get back—"

"Shari's sleeping in the trailer and Stormy's staying in your RV. And I don't think a room at the Westward Ho is a particularly good idea at the moment."

"No, I guess it isn't." He started to turn away.

"Dallas . . .?"

"Yeah?"

"It's a really nice night. Maybe we could take a blanket and go for a walk up toward those buttes."

He knew he shouldn't. He needed to start easing away, begin to sever the connection. "Yeah, maybe we could. We might have to dodge a rattlesnake or two but I don't mind, if you don't."

"If you're there, I won't mind."

His chest squeezed. "I'll be back as soon as I can." He left her and went to find Charlie. Half an hour later, he returned to her trailer.

It was midnight by the time he brought her home.

CHAPTER 19

Riding on the passenger side of the truck, Patience pressed her cell phone a little closer to her ear. Shari was driving, making the first leg of the trip across New Mexico to the Lea County Fair and Rodeo in Lovington.

"Thanks, Mabel. I really appreciate it. If you come up with anything, no matter how small, please let me know."

"I'm glad you called." Mabel Thompson's voice echoed a little on the other end of the line. "I've never worked on anything quite like this before. It's going to be fun—kind of like trying to uncover the real Jack the Ripper."

"Maybe not quite that exciting. Lucky Sims might not have been murdered at all. And even if she was, the chance that the man who did it killed another of the rodeo women is probably pretty small."

"Maybe not. I watch those shows on TV all the time, you know, like *Law and Order* and *CSI?* If the guy was like those creeps on TV, they get real stoked up. They work in patterns and they kill again and again."

"I guess we'll see. Maybe something will turn up." Patience pressed the end button and stuck the cell phone back in her purse.

"I can't believe you're doing this," Shari said, her eyes fixed on the black strip of asphalt up ahead. "But I think it's really cool."

Patience shrugged her shoulders. "Research is one of the things I do best. I don't like the idea that my great-grandmother's best friend might have been murdered. I like it even less that the guy might have gotten away with it."

"So you're thinking that if he did it again, you might be able to track him down?"

"I'm not exactly sure. Something like that, I guess. I called a friend at the Cowgirl Hall of Fame and a couple of other people I know who are experts in the field. I called my dad, too. He's a real authority on the West. He got kind of excited about it. It's hard to believe but they held one of those early rodeos right there in Boston each year. As far as I know, Addie Holmes never traveled that far east, but Dad said he'd dig around in the Boston archives, see what he could come up with."

"With all that help, maybe someone will find out something."

"That's what I'm hoping. When we get to Hobbs—that's the biggest town around here—I'm going to try to get on the Internet, do a little surfing, see what I might find out."

Shari slowed for a truck up ahead, then pulled out and went around it. "So what's your dad like? He sounds like someone I'd like."

"I think you would. I know he'd like you. He's in his early fifties, handsome, dark-haired, athletic. He and my stepmom have a really happy marriage. She works in the administration department at B.U. That's where she and my father met. They live in a nice two-story house not far from the campus. Tracy's kind of a homebody and since they got married, so is my dad."

"That's the kind of life I'd like to have," Shari said wistfully. "I'm tired of traveling around all the time. I'm ready to settle down."

Shari was beginning to sound depressed and when Patience thought about Dallas, she began to feel that way, too. She turned her attention to the passing landscape, let the vast open spaces and miles of blue sky clear her head.

They were following Charlie and the Circle C stock trucks. Since they'd left Cottonwood Creek, Charlie had made no more mention of the stolen money, accepting it as he did most things, determined to put it behind him.

It was late in the afternoon when they arrived at the fairgrounds and pulled into an area behind the Jake McClure Arena. There were pens for the bulls and a barn for the bucking horses, and the stock trucks headed that way. Patience and Shari stopped to dump their RV holding tanks, refill the water supply, and restock their limited supply of food before traveling the rest of the way to the rodeo grounds.

Patience hoped when they got there she would see Dallas. The summer was almost over and though part of her knew it would only make leaving him more difficult, another part wanted to make every last second count.

But Dallas was busy helping Charlie. She didn't see him the rest of the day. He was busy that evening, as well. She and Shari went to dinner at a Mexican restaurant called La Fiesta, but it wasn't much fun. The two men missing from their lives left an odd hole in the evening.

Both of them were feeling a little lonely by the time they returned to the trailer. They read for a while, then turned off the lights and went to bed.

Unfortunately, Patience couldn't sleep.

After tossing and turning till well past midnight, she finally gave up, pulled on jeans and a thin cotton sweater, and went for a walk around the grounds. Since the rodeo didn't start until tomorrow afternoon, most of the cowboys wouldn't show up until morning.

As she wandered across the open, grassy fields, she could see Dallas's shiny black rig in the distance. She wondered if he was avoiding her and had a suspicion that he was. Perhaps he was feeling the same mix of emotions she was.

Turning in the opposite direction, she strolled off toward the arena. There wasn't much of a moon, but enough to find her way. She could hear the bulls swishing their tails, luffing and snorting and pawing the ground.

She meandered toward the horse barns. They weren't full that night, so Button, Lobo, and Stormy's horse Gus, all had their own separate stalls. Button raised his head and whinnied softly as she walked in. She had been riding him more and more. With Shari's coaching, she had even started working him around the practice barrels before the rodeo started.

"Hello, sweetheart." She reached up and scratched his ears, stoked his soft muzzle. The barn smelled of alfalfa, old wood, and dust, not an unpleasant smell. She checked Button's water and feed, wandered over to check on Lobo and Gus, then left the building.

Still wide awake, she walked a short distance along the deserted road bordering the fairgrounds, then turned back the way she had come. Up ahead, she thought she saw a shadow in the darkness and thinking of Tyler, her senses went on alert, but when she looked again, she realized it was just her imagination. Tired at last, she continued back along the road toward home.

She had almost reached the horse barns when she spotted the first curl of smoke. It crept across the roof, leaked out from under the eaves, curled and rolled skyward, a gray coil reaching up through the darkness. More smoke drifted out through the open barn doors and her chest squeezed with fear. A shot of adrenaline jolted her into action and Patience started to run.

"Fire! Fire in the horse barns!" Her feet pounded over the grass as she headed for Dallas's rig, which sat in the field ahead. Charlie's second string of bucking horses were stabled in the barn. She needed help if the animals were going to get out before the fire swept over them, trapping them inside.

Racing up to the RV, she hammered madly on Dallas's door and a sleepy-eyed Stormy pulled it open.

"There's a fire in the barns!" Turning, she raced off toward the production trailer, but the Circle C crew was already on its feet, pouring out of campers and trailers, the backseats of pickups and cars. As soon as she saw that help was on its way, Patience raced back toward the barn and started opening gates.

The blaze had spread faster than she imagined it would. Long tongues of orange-red flames scorched through the wooden roof in several places, licking relentlessly down toward the animals below. The horses were frantic, neighing wildly, rolling their eyes and rearing, kicking against the sides of their stalls.

Dallas rushed past her, along with half a dozen other cowboys. They raced inside the barn beneath the flaming roof, barefoot and waving their hats, trying to get the animals out of their stalls.

It should have been easy, but the horses were frightened and confused, running in circles, fighting their lead ropes when the men tried to lead them to safety. Thinking of Button, Lobo, and Gus, Patience ran toward the far end of the barn. The flames burned there, too, the fire beginning to eat its way through the ceiling above the horses' stalls. Small bits of burning wood floated down from the rafters, singeing the animals' coats.

"Easy, sweetheart, I'm going to get you out of here." Her hands were shaking as she opened Button's stall and the horse raced out. Shari came running out of the darkness just as the horse bolted past.

"Button!" She turned and ran after him, worried that he might be hurt.

Gus's stall was right next door. Patience ran in that direction. She led him out when he refused to leave on his own, and once he reached the open doorway, he shot out of the barn to safety.

A burning chunk of roof fell down, landed just a few feet away. She needed to get out of the barn before one of the heavy pieces fell on top of her, but Lobo whinnied just then. She could just make out his golden coat in the light of the flame and the whites of his eyes as he rolled them in terror. Coughing, she bent forward and ran toward his stall.

Dallas spotted Shari leading Button away from the fire and hurried toward her. "Button all right?"

"His coat is singed in a couple of places, but otherwise he's fine."

"Where's Patience?"

"She was right behind me. She was bringing Gus out."

Dallas's heart began to beat faster than it was already. "I thought Stormy brought Gus and Lobo out."

Shari shook her head. "Patience went after Gus. I saw him run out behind Button." Shari glanced toward the building, rapidly engulfing itself in flames. "Oh, God, you don't think she went back in after Lobo? You don't think she could still be inside?"

Both of them started to run.

"Have you seen Patience?" Dallas shouted at Stormy above the roar of the fire.

"No! Gus and Button are out! Where's Lobo?"

"I thought you got him out!"

"I thought you did!" Stormy jerked his head toward the barn.

Dallas's gut was twisting. Stormy hadn't brought Lobo out and if the horse was still in the barn and Patience went in to get him . . .

"Give me your handkerchief!" he yelled to Stormy, the crackle of the flames and the shouting of the men making it nearly impossible to hear. Stormy jerked a red bandana out of his back pocket and Dallas grabbed it. "You two stay here."

"You're not going in there?"

"I'll be right back." His pulse was going crazy. He knew she was in there—he knew it. Bending low, he pressed the handkerchief over his mouth and ran into the burning barn. The smoke was so thick he couldn't see. He closed his eyes and tried to remember where Lobo's stall was, but he was disoriented by the darkness and the billowing wall of black. He closed his eyes, got his bearings as best he could, then aimed his steps in what he hoped was the right direction.

He thought of Patience and fear clawed at him, leaving his insides raw. If she was in here, if she was hurt in the fire or even killed . . . He blocked the thought and stumbled blindly on. He had almost reached Lobo's stall when the big palomino came bolting out of the smoke like a fire-breathing dragon.

Lobo ran past him, toward the open barn door, but there was no one with him. "Patience! Patience are you in here?" Fighting for air, he started deeper into the barn, then spotted her stumbling toward him. She was coughing, unsteady on her feet, blinded by the smoke and trying to find her way out.

"Over here!" He caught up with her, hauled her against his side, and together they ran toward the door of the barn. The wooden door frame was blazing. Fire raced across the ceiling overhead and he could hear the crack and snap of burning timbers. They ran toward the bright orange glow, stumbled through the opening, and out into the night.

He didn't stop until they were safely away from the blaze, then they both went down on their knees in the dew-damp grass and dragged in great gulps of air.

In the distance, he could hear the blare of sirens, see the whirling red lights of a stream of fire engines racing along the road. Next to him, Patience shuddered as if she were cold though her skin still felt warm from the blaze.

"Are you all right?" Terrified she had been burned, he turned her face from side to side, checked each of her arms and legs, then her neck and shoulders. She was covered with soot, head to toe, her blond hair streaked with oily smudge. She coughed and so did he.

"I'm okay," she croaked out of a throat rusty with ash and smoke. Still not satisfied, he grabbed her hands and turned them over to check her palms, saw with relief that she really hadn't been hurt.

"Did Lobo get out all right?" she asked.

Dallas closed his eyes. She was worried about his god-damned horse. His chest still ached from his paralyzing fear when he realized she had gone into the burning barn.

"Lobo's fine," he said gruffly. "We got all of the horses out safely—thanks to you."

Shari and Stormy raced up just then. "Oh, God, are you two all right?" Shari knelt beside them, Stormy on the opposite side.

"We're fine," Dallas said a little more harshly than he meant to.

Stormy looked at Patience. "I thought the horses were already out. I thought Dallas had gotten them to safety. Apparently, he thought I had. I'm sorry you went in there." He gave her a crooked smile. "But since you're okay and so is Gus, I'm damned glad you did."

Dallas cast him a glance. "Yeah, well, I'm not." He turned a hard look on Patience. "Dammit, you could have been killed!"

She straightened, pulled a little away. "I got the horses out, didn't I? You would have done the same thing."

Stormy caught the fierce glint in Dallas's eye, tipped his head toward Shari, and both of them slipped away.

Dallas stood up and drew Patience up beside him, held on to her for a long moment. "Come on. We'll stop by your trailer and you can grab some clean clothes. There's a motel just down the street. I've got a room there. I wasn't in the mood to hear Stormy whining about Shari all night. You can stay there tonight with me."

She looked as if she might argue, then sighed and simply nodded. She was exhausted, drained by the adrenaline rush and her earlier fear. He wanted to hold her, make sure that she was all right. He wanted to gather her close and take care of her.

And in some strange way, he needed her tonight in a way he never had before.

In less than twenty minutes they walked into his room at the Pueblo Motel and he set her overnight bag on the floor beside the door. They both smelled of smoke and were covered with soot. It didn't matter. When she turned to face him, Dallas caught the nape of her neck and dragged her mouth up to his for a hard, ravishing kiss.

"You could have died tonight," he said. "You could have been killed in that barn."

Her arms went around his neck and she kissed him back, opening her mouth to accept his tongue, sliding her own over his. As tired as she was, her fatigue seemed to fall away, replaced by the same burning need that Dallas felt.

Cradling the back of her head, kissing her one way and then another, he walked her backward, over to the bed. Her knees hit the edge and she tumbled back, sprawling across the mattress. Dallas came down on top of her, took her mouth again, and savaged it until she moaned.

He wanted her. Now. He needed to be inside her with an urgency that was nearly overwhelming. Unzipping her jeans, he lifted her hips and yanked them down to her knees along with her panties. He parted her legs, positioned himself, and drove himself deep inside.

Patience moaned as her body tightened around him, gloving him so sweetly he nearly lost control. He took her fast and hard, thrusting into her again and again. Something had happened to him tonight when he had seen her in that burning barn. Besides the fear, a primal instinct had arisen, an overwhelming urge to protect her. Now that she was safe, he needed to make her his, to imprint himself on her in some way.

Their coupling was wild and intense. Patience tossed her head and dug her nails into his back. She reached a powerful climax and an instant later, so did he. He waited only a moment, then pulled himself free. Lifting her up, he carried her into the bathroom and set her on her feet. She didn't protest when he started the shower, stripped away her clothes and his own, then helped her in and climbed in to join her.

They soaped each other down and shampooed each others' hair, then rinsed and soaped each other again. Her slim, smooth body felt incredible beneath his hands. He was hard again, but she was exhausted from her brush with death. He meant to carry her straight to bed, curl up beside her and watch her sleep, but her hands closed over his hardness and she began to stroke him.

"I need you," she said, coming up on her toes to kiss him, water sloshing over her face onto his. The tap was getting cold or he would have taken her there, up against the shower wall. Instead he turned off the nozzle and slid back the curtain, dried both of them off, and carried her over to the bed.

She reached for him again, kneaded him, cupped him, and Dallas groaned.

He didn't hurry this time. He wanted to make it good for her, to show her how much she meant to him. He kissed her and kissed her, tasted the inside of her mouth, nibbled his way over her collarbone, made his way down to her breasts, then sucked the fullness between his teeth. Patience wound her fingers in his hair and arched upward, giving him better access. Her skin felt smooth and silky. The smell of some flowery shampoo drifted up from her damp blond hair.

He was hard and throbbing, his body clenching with the need to be inside her. Instead, he returned to kissing her breasts, slid his hand up her thigh, and began to stroke her. He didn't stop until he had her sobbing his name, making soft little mewling sounds in her throat. He parted her legs and slid himself inside her, heard her breath catch in pleasure.

Propped on his elbows, he looked into her face and thought how beautiful she was. He thought of her in the blazing barn and a shudder ran through him. He drove himself deeper, filling her completely, and her eyes met his, heavy-lidded with desire. The stiff peaks of her breasts pressed into his chest and her legs slid over his, forcing him deeper still.

"I want you," she said. "You can't imagine how much."

The words turned his shaft to steel. The blood in his veins burned hotter than the fire they had escaped in the barn. He couldn't get enough of her, and knowing that, he faced another truth.

He was in love with her. Crazy in love.

He hadn't meant for it to happen, wished with all his heart it hadn't. For the sad fact was, loving her didn't change a thing.

"Dallas . . . please . . ."

It was a plea he understood. He started to move, sliding out and then in, stroking deeply, slowly, letting the pleasure build. Patience moaned and arched beneath him and he moved a little faster, a little harder. His muscles strained as he fought for control. Bending his head, he kissed her, felt her soft mouth sinking into his, tasted her on his tongue. He thrust deeper, faster, felt her nails digging into his shoulders, surged again and again until she came.

His own release followed, swift and hard, and seemed to go on forever. Maybe loving someone made it better. He had always thought maybe it would.

Time slipped past. He wasn't sure how long they lay entwined on the bed. Relaxed at last, he moved to her side, reached for her, and eased her into his arms.

He was in love with her, but they couldn't marry. He would only make her unhappy—and himself.

Dallas closed his eyes. He wondered how long it would take him to fall asleep.

Dallas awoke feeling groggy, his throat scratchy, and a pounding in his head. The pounding turned out to be someone knocking at the door. He dragged himself from under the covers and pulled on a clean pair of jeans, then walked over to see who it was.

He opened the door a crack. Behind him, Patience sat up in bed, looking as if she had just been tumbled, which an hour earlier she had.

"You Dallas Kingman?" The man on the other side of the door wore the light beige shirt and dark pants of a county sheriff. He was thin, mid-forties, his hair sandy blond and butched very short.

"Yeah, that's right."

"I'm Sheriff Vance Kendall. I'd like to talk to you about the fire at the fairgrounds last night."

Dallas nodded but didn't open the door. "All right."

"I'd . . . uh . . . also like to speak to Ms. Sinclair. She is in there, isn't she?"

Dallas wasn't sure how the officer knew Patience was in his motel room, but there wasn't much use in denying it. He tossed a look over her shoulder, saw that Patience had heard what the sheriff had said. Her face was red and she was frantically pulling clothes out of the canvas bag she had brought with her last night.

"She'll need a minute to get dressed." Dallas walked back to the closet, grabbed a shirt and shrugged it on, then joined the sheriff out on the porch in front of the motel room.

"What can I do for you Sheriff Kendall?"

"I understand you and your lady friend were there last night during the fire."

"That's right. Patience was the first person to see the

smoke. She woke the rest of us up in time to save the horses. Have they found out how the fire got started?"

"Actually, that's the reason I'm here. It looks as if the blaze wasn't accidental. The fire investigation team found evidence of arson. There were traces of gasoline on the ground around the perimeter of the building and it appears to have been poured on the roof. That's the reason the place went up so fast."

Dallas's mouth went dry. Charlie's troubles were escalating. If Patience hadn't been passing the barn at the exact time she had, there was every chance Charlie's valuable bucking horses would be dead. Worse than that, the way things were going, sooner or later someone was going to get killed. The thought made him sick to his stomach.

"Did you see anything unusual last night?" the sheriff asked. "Anything that could help us figure out who might be responsible for setting the fire?"

"No, unfortunately, I didn't. I wish I could be more help, but by the time I got to the barn, it was already engulfed in flames."

Just then Patience pulled open the door. She had swept her blond hair up with a comb, washed her face, and dragged on jeans and a T-shirt. She gave the sheriff a tentative smile.

"Good morning, Sheriff."

"Good mornin', ma'am. Mind if I ask you a couple of questions?"

"No, of course not."

"According to Mr. Kingman, you were the first person at the scene of the fire last night."

"That's right."

"Did you see anything suspicious? Anyone who might have been involved in starting the blaze?"

Patience's face went a little bit pale. "It was set, then? It wasn't an accident of some kind?"

"No, ma'am, I'm afraid it wasn't."

She drew in a steadying breath. "I didn't see anything,

Sheriff. I wish I had. At the time, all I could think about was getting the horses to safety."

"I spoke to Mr. Carson earlier. He told me about the trouble he's been having. Do either of you have any idea who might be behind these attacks?"

"I'm afraid not," Dallas said.

"Then I guess there's nothing else either of you can tell me." When neither of them replied, the sheriff handed each of them a card. "If you think of anything you might have forgotten, give me a call."

"We will," Patience said.

"Why don't you finish getting dressed?" Dallas gently suggested. "I'll be there in a minute."

As soon as the door was closed, he turned to the sheriff. "I don't know how much my uncle told you. I know he's reluctant to name names, but there are a couple of people you might want to check out." Dallas gave him the same list of names he had given the sheriff in Cheyenne, then mentioned Junior Reese and the robbery in Cottonwood Creek.

"Junior admitted that he had taken the money, but there wasn't any proof. My uncle decided to let the matter drop."

"Cottonwood Creek isn't all that far away," Sheriff Kendall said. "You think this guy Reese might be responsible for the fire?"

"I don't know. He's a real S.O.B. I suppose it's possible."

"But you say he wasn't around when your uncle's troubles first began."

"No, he wasn't. At least not that we know of."

"I'll put out an APB, have him pulled in for questioning. Anything else you can think of?"

He flicked a glance toward the door behind him. "Patience had some trouble with a guy back in Boston. He was stalking her, harassing her. He followed her to Colorado Springs. As far as I know, he's got nothing to do with any of this and he's supposed to be back in Boston but you might want to check it out."

"Will do. You think of anything else, you let me know."

"I will, Sheriff. Thanks."

Dallas returned to the room to find Patience showered and dressed in jeans, a tank top, and boots. He showered himself and they headed back to the fairgrounds. He needed to talk to Charlie, find out what his uncle intended to do.

Whatever it was, the Circle C Rodeo Company had a show to produce. Plans had already been made, people had paid good money, cowboys were there to ride.

The thought made his stomach churn.

CHAPTER 20

As soon as Dallas reached the fairgrounds, he took Patience back to her trailer and went in search of Charlie. His uncle was standing at the bottom of the metal stairs leading up to the production trailer, in the unlikely company of his number one competitor, Jack Stiles.

"Word travels fast," Dallas said. "Or is it just coincidence you arrived at Charlie's door less than twenty-four hours after he suffered a major fire."

"I'm a twenty-first century man," Jack drawled. "I saw it on the Internet. The fire was big news on the Pro Rodeo Web site." Stiles was tall and spare, fifty-one or -two, with thick gray hair and deep lines beside his mouth and eyes. He was a powerful figure in the rodeo world who for years had been trying to steal Charlie's clients. Dallas figured it was only his somewhat oily personality that managed to keep him from succeeding.

"So you just dropped in to voice your concern," Dallas said.

"I flew down from the rodeo in Kalispell. I won't lie about it. I figured with all the trouble Charlie's been having, he might finally be ready to sell."

Dallas's attention swung to his uncle. "Tell me you aren't selling out to Stiles."

Charlie shook his head. "I thought about it—for about five seconds." He turned a sharp look on Stiles. "Fact is, someone's tryin' to run me out of business. Well, I ain't never run from a fight and I ain't startin' now."

Jack Stiles's head came up. "Wait a minute—I didn't have anything to do with that fire. I just figured you was having a run of bad luck and maybe I could capitalize on it."

Charlie seemed to assess him, then he sighed. "It's all right. I never figured you for the criminal sort." He looked at Stiles and the corners of his mouth curved. "Not for the most part, anyhow."

Stiles just laughed. "All right, I won't press you. In fact, I'll do a little digging, myself. A man don't deserve to be cheated out of what he's worked hard for all his life. I hear anything, I'll let you know."

"I'd appreciate it," Charlie said.

Stiles left for the airport, on his way to the twin engine Cessna 414 he often traveled in between rodeos.

"You don't think Stiles might be behind this?" Dallas asked as they watched the man's rental car disappear down the two-lane asphalt road. He had never trusted Jack Stiles, no matter how sincere he might sound.

"I don't know. He's wanted me to sell out to him for years. Maybe he got tired of waiting."

"I don't like this, Charlie. This keeps up, somebody's gonna get hurt."

Charlie stared off toward the blackened remains that were all that was left of the horse barns. "I know."

They left the production trailer and started walking toward the rodeo arena. With the big Albuquerque show coming up next weekend, there were a lot of top cowboys competing here in nearby Lea County.

From the corner of his eye, Dallas saw a familiar, big, thick-chested cowboy walking across the grass and recognized Wes McCauley. Wes ignored him, which was fine with Dallas.

Pulling through the entrance gate, he spotted Jade Egan's fancy gold horse trailer and gold Dodge truck. Jade wasn't driving. Instead she sat in the passenger seat and a young, dark-complexioned cowboy sat behind the wheel, Jade's latest conquest, he figured.

Earlier in the day, Dallas had spoken to Blue Cody, whose name was on the list of competing bareback bronc riders. Reno Garcia would be riding bulls, and Ritchie Madden was back on his feet. With Junior gone, he and Cy would be clowning together again.

Pretty much all of Dallas's best rodeo friends were there and with all that had been going on, Dallas was damned glad to see them. He was walking next to Charlie, thinking about the tough competition he'd be facing, when he spotted the sheriff's white patrol car pulling toward them across the grass.

"That's Kendall," he said. "Maybe he's come up with a lead."

Patience must have also seen the patrol car driving in, for Dallas saw her walking their way. The car pulled up right next to them. The door opened up, Kendall unwound himself from the seat, and the small group converged on him all at once.

"You find out who started the fire?" Dallas asked.

The sheriff shook his head. "Not yet. And I got some more bad news. Seems as though there was someone in that barn last night. Fire department found a body in the rubble."

Charlie's whole body stiffened and a knot of dread tightened in the bottom of Dallas's stomach.

"They figure the guy was probably an itinerant, some homeless person making a bed in the straw for the night."

Dallas flicked a glance at Patience, whose face looked as white as her hat. "So now the man who did it isn't just responsible for arson—he's also wanted for murder."

"That's right. You sure none of you saw anything?"

Dallas looked at Patience and Charlie who were both shaking their heads. "Sorry, Sheriff."

"We'll keep you posted," the sheriff said. "I hope you'll do the same."

"Sure will," Charlie said.

The sheriff returned to his car and they watched the vehicle pull away.

"That poor man in the barn," Patience said. "It was so awful in there. I hope . . . I hope he didn't suffer."

Dallas slid an arm around her shoulders. "He probably died of smoke inhalation, darlin'. Most likely, he never even woke up." He prayed it was the truth. And just as he'd feared, a man was now dead.

Charlie's sigh whispered toward them. "I got this show to finish and I gotta do Albuquerque next week. That's my last rodeo this month. I'd planned to take a little time off after that, go back to the ranch and see Annie. Now, with all that's happened, I'm gonna suspend Circle C productions indefinitely. I can't afford to put other peoples' lives in danger."

Damn. Dallas couldn't miss the defeat and worry in Charlie's face. Closing down was probably the right thing to do, but it would only pose more problems for Charlie.

"What about the money you've already been paid, payments you've received for rodeos through the end of the year? You'll have to pay that money back."

"That's my worry, son. I'll do what I have to."

"If only you'd let me—"

"No." The word echoed with a note of finality. Charlie turned and started walking, his shoulders hunched over, his hat pulled low.

Dallas had never felt more helpless. "Stubborn as a jackass, always has been. Damn, I wish there was something I could do."

But there wasn't. Charlie wasn't the kind of man to risk

people's lives. He was strong and determined and he would do whatever he had to, no matter how painful it was. It was one of the reasons that he had been successful as a rodeo producer, that he'd become a successful cattle rancher. It was one of the reasons Dallas loved him so much.

"I feel so sorry for him," Patience said.

Dallas didn't answer. As he watched his uncle walk away, a rock seemed to settle on his chest the size of a melon. Charlie Carson was the best man he'd ever known. He didn't deserve the things that were happening to him.

Why would anyone want to hurt him? It was the question Dallas had asked himself a thousand times.

But still no answer came.

Patience tried not to think of Charlie or the man who had died in the fire. During the week, she kept herself busy with the project she had somehow found herself involved in. Every morning, she read the journal or made phone calls to the newspapers in towns that had hosted early rodeos. In Hobbs, the nearest sizable town, she found a little Internet cafe and went on-line to surf the Web for sites that might have information on early rodeos.

She was familiar with most of the sources. She had used them in her research. But nothing helpful turned up.

She continued reading the journal, enjoying the special bond she now felt with Addie Holmes. The adventures of Addie and Sam Starling continued, Addie falling deeper and deeper in love.

We're here in Denver. My team won the relay race and Sam took a first on a cantankerous bronc named Bad Medicine. When the show was over, he asked me out to supper to celebrate and we went down to a place called Delmonico's. Oh, it was fancy! With big red

*leather booths and red flocked wallpaper. Sam ordered
thick steaks cooked well done and a bottle of real French
champagne. Afterward Sam asked me to marry him.*

Nothing else was written. Patience got the impression
Addie was too stunned to think of anything to say. It was two
days later, toward the back of the book, that Addie wrote in
the journal again. Apparently Whit Whitcomb, the beau Addie
had left back home in Oklahoma, turned up at the worst possible time.

*I keep seeing Sam's face . . . the way he looked when
he finally worked up the courage to propose. His eyes
were so green and so full of love and I wanted to say
yes so bad it hurt. I knew I couldn't. I knew I couldn't
live on the road for the rest of my life and that's what
marriage to Sam would have been.*

*I guess God was trying to help me be strong be-
cause the very next day, Whit showed up. He'd come in
on the train from Lawton, traveled all that way just to see
me. He looked good, Whit did, better than I remembered.
He was an attractive man in his own way, not handsome as sin, like Sam, but nice-looking all the same.
Whit's strong as a bull and hardheaded as an Irishman,
which is probably why he never gave up on me.*

*They say luck runs in pairs, and maybe it does. That
same afternoon, Whit asked me to marry him. He said
his ma and pa had moved into the smaller house on the
farm and that they wanted us to live in the big house
and raise a passel of kids. He promised he would make
me happy. I thought of Sam and him bein' a cowboy
and before I could change my mind, I told Whit yes, I
would marry him.*

Patience sat back in her chair. She had known from the
start they would marry. Her mother's maiden name was Whit-

comb. Walter "Whit" Whitcomb was her great grandfather. And yet, it made her sad to think of Sam and Addie and that Addie had loved Sam and not Whit, at least in the beginning.

One last entry caught her eye.

> *I had to tell Sam. I'll never forget the look on his face when I said I had up and married Whit Whitcomb down at the county courthouse that morning. I told him I was leaving with Whit, going back to live on his farm. I'll never forget how my heart just purely shattered when I saw tears in Sam Starling's beautiful green eyes.*

The journal picked up a few days later. Whit and Addie left that same afternoon, taking the train back to Lawton, Oklahoma, and his farm on the outskirts of town. Addie never mentioned Sam Starling's name again in the final pages of the journal, but there seemed a wistful note in her words toward the end. Patience wondered how long it had taken her to forget him.

She hoped that Addie and Whit were happy.

She was sorry when the journal ended. She felt as if she, too, had suffered the loss of a beloved friend.

Charlie sat in the chair behind his desk in the production trailer. Usually, he kept the place pretty neat, but tonight papers were strewn over the desk and the trash can needed to be emptied. He'd get around to it, he told himself, but lately he couldn't seem to concentrate on the little things with all the trouble swirling around him.

After Junior had stolen the money in Cottonwood Creek, he'd bitten the bullet, called the bank, and begun the process of taking out a second mortgage on the ranch. Annie hadn't wanted him to, but once he'd explained it was that or sell some land, she'd pitched in and done the paperwork.

His credit was good and the ranch was worth a pretty good

chunk of money, so it wouldn't take long to get the loan completed and collect the funds. He'd figured if he could just hold on until things smoothed out again . . .

But that hadn't happened and now with the fine it didn't look like it was going to. He hated the idea of running from his troubles, but a man was dead. If they didn't catch the bastard who was causing him grief, it just might happen again. Maybe next time it would be Dallas, or someone who worked for him. Charlie couldn't bear the thought.

He leaned back in his chair and picked up his cell phone. For the past half hour, he'd been trying to work up the courage to call Annie. But he didn't feel any better now than he had back then.

He punched in Annie's number. He hadn't told her about the man who'd been killed in the fire. He didn't want to tell her now. He had always tried to protect her from the harsher side of life, but in his heart he knew she was every bit as tough as he was. Maybe tougher.

"Hi, honey," he said into the phone.

She must have heard something in his voice because her breathing hitched on the other end of the line. "Don't tell me it's more bad news."

"I wish I could tell you it wasn't, darlin', but I'm afraid it is." He went on to tell her about the man who had been killed and his decision to forfeit the rest of the rodeos he was scheduled to produce this year.

There was a long pause on the opposite end of the phone. "Jack Stiles and Lem Watkins gonna be able to take on the rest of the shows?"

"I don't know. I imagine they're pretty-well booked, but they're both fairly greedy. I figure they'll find a way."

"We'll have to give back the money we've already been paid."

"I know. That's one of the reasons I called." He took a shaky breath. "I want you to phone Mal Sullivan. Tell Sully we'll sell him that chunk of land he's been wantin'."

"Oh, Charlie, no."

"Look, honey. In a way this might be good. I'm getting' tired of travelin' all the time, bein' away from home so damned much. The money from the sale will give us a cushion. We won't have to go through with that second mortgage and I can make some sort of settlement, resolve that lawsuit with those folks in Silver Springs. Still ought to be enough left so I can stay home and start building up the ranch."

"You told Sully you'd never sell a square foot of the land your great granddaddy worked so hard for. Deep down, I know you still feel that way."

"Maybe I do, but things are different now. Like I said, we could use that money to improve the ranch. It'd be good to spend more time there. Maybe if I'd been home, tending to business, we wouldn't have lost those cows."

"Maybe not." She sighed into the phone. "At least we haven't lost any more."

"How 'bout Sully? They haven't got to him again, have they?"

"Not that I know of."

"Well, that's somethin', I guess."

"You still plannin' to do the rodeo in Albuquerque?"

"Got to. There isn't time to get someone else. It's a big show and I've given my word."

"But after that, you'll be home."

"Absolutely. Believe me, I can't wait to get there."

"You take care of yourself, Charlie Carson. I don't know what I'd do if something happened to you."

"I love you, honey."

"I love you, too."

Charlie hung up the phone. Annie had never been one to use the word *love* overmuch. It was a sign of how worried she was about him. Charlie searched his memory as he had a thousand times, trying to figure out who might have grievance enough against him to try to ruin his life, but no name came to mind.

Charlie sighed into the silence inside the trailer and hoisted himself to his feet. He might be quitting the rodeo business but until he did, there was still plenty of work to be done. Charlie tugged his hat a little lower and headed out of the trailer.

"You ready?" Dallas poked his head through the door of Patience's RV. The rodeo, a night show, was over and he was taking her out for something to eat.

She was a little surprised he had asked her to go. The summer was close to over. She would be leaving next week, right after the final performance in Albuquerque on Sunday afternoon, and knowing their time together was nearly at an end, Dallas had been easing away from her, trying to put some distance between them.

At least he had been until the fire. Since then, he'd been protective of both her and Charlie, keeping an eye on both of them as much as he possibly could.

Unfortunately, his riding had suffered for it. During the saddle bronc riding tonight, he had been pitched off a horse named Locomotive and he was limping a little again.

Patience told herself not to worry. Dallas was a cowboy. Injuries were part of the sport.

"I'm almost ready," she told him. "Just a quick second and I'll be right there."

Earlier in the day and for the past half hour, she had been making a final review of her thesis, getting ready to send it off on Monday morning. It should have felt momentous, an accomplishment that had finally reached culmination after years of hard work, but with all that had been going on around her, she was just glad to finally be done.

Shutting down her computer, she grabbed her cowboy hat off the hook above her bunk and headed for the door. She'd gotten so used to wearing it, she wondered if she'd miss it once she got back home.

"I asked Charlie to come with us, but he says he's got some work to do." Dallas flicked a glance toward the production trailer, saw the light still burning inside. "The sheriff's got a couple of deputies patrolling the area. After the news he delivered this morning, I hired a couple of extra security guards. Charlie thinks they work for the fairgrounds and I didn't tell him any different. You know how he is."

"I think it's a good idea. If whoever started that fire comes back, maybe the guards will spot him."

"Yeah, that's kinda what I was thinking. I also phoned Roy Greenwood in Las Vegas and asked him if he knew a good private detective. He called a guy named Carter Maddox. Maddox is flying out here from Vegas tomorrow afternoon."

"Charlie won't like it."

"I'm not so sure. I'm betting he's tired of sitting around waiting for the other shoe to drop. I think he'll be glad to finally be doing something positive. I only wish I'd done it sooner."

Dallas walked her over to his truck and helped her climb in, then went around to his own side, slid behind the wheel, and cranked up the engine. It was dark outside, just a quarter moon. Patience tried not to think how the smoke and fire last night had filled the sky and made the moon glow blood red.

The big Dodge rolled along the asphalt strip of highway toward town. With only a few cars on the road, darkness seemed to surround them, a pool of black broken only by the twin beams of the pickup's headlights.

Patience looked over at Dallas, determined to turn her thoughts in a different direction. "So how's Stormy holding up?" She had been worried about him ever since he had come to talk to her about Shari.

"Okay, I guess. I think he'll feel better once Shari and Button have left to go home."

"I can see how hard this is on him. I think he really loves her."

Dallas just grunted. "Doesn't seem to bother Shari much."

"It bothers her. She loves him, too, but she doesn't want the same kind of life Stormy wants. You can't blame her for that."

She was reminding him of his own change of career. He hadn't wanted to be a doctor. He simply couldn't be happy in that role. "No, I guess not."

They pulled up in front of the Golden Spur Steakhouse and went in. The place wasn't fancy, just a room full of wooden tables with paper place mats and little red candles in the middle. But the steaks were supposed to be big and juicy and she was surprisingly hungry.

And the place was full of old friends. Blue Cody and Reno Garcia sat with Bonnie Sweeney and Ruth Collins. Patience and Dallas stopped to say hello before sitting down at a table not far away.

They ordered a couple of New York strips that tasted pretty good, a little tough maybe but the baked potato smothered in butter made up for it. When they finished, they didn't linger. She knew Dallas was worried about Charlie and wanted to stay as close as he could.

"We'll see you guys later," Dallas called over to the group of friends.

Blue waved at Dallas and winked at Patience. Dallas tossed him a look, jerked his hat a little lower, and kept on walking. They had just stepped out of the restaurant, headed for the lot where the truck was parked, when a loud clap sounded in the darkness. Just as they walked onto the porch, a chunk of wood splintered away from the doorjamb, missing them by inches.

"Get down!" Dallas shouted, shoving her to the ground, sprawling full length on top of her. Another shot ricocheted off the plaster at the corner of the building. "We've got to find some cover." Grabbing her hand, he tugged her forward. "Let's go!"

Keeping low, they edged over behind the low brick wall

that surrounded the parking lot. Her whole body was shaking, her mouth so dry she couldn't speak. Dallas molded himself protectively around her and she could feel the tension in the muscles across his chest. He jerked off his hat and peered over the top of the wall, scanning the darkness at the edge of the parking lot, trying to locate their assailant, but there was no sign of him.

A noise sounded. Someone running, then a car door closed somewhere down the block.

Dallas sprang to his feet as an engine roared to life. "Stay here!" Tires squealed as the car sped away and Dallas raced after it.

Several minutes passed. When Dallas finally returned, he was breathing hard, a grim look on his face. "He's gone. It was a dark-colored sedan but I couldn't make out what model. I tried to get the license number but I only got the first two letters, A Z something."

Her knees felt wobbly as he helped her to her feet and his arm tightened around her. "Are you all right?"

She stared past him into the darkness but there was nothing there to see. "I can't believe someone was shooting at us."

Dallas turned, his gaze following hers. "Yeah. The question is, why?" Keeping an arm around her waist, he guided her back to the front door of the restaurant. Blue Cody and his group were just walking out.

"You guys still here?" Blue said.

"The good news is we're still breathing. Take a look at this, Blue." Dallas motioned toward the door and the Navajo cowboy turned to see the bullet hole left in the jamb.

Reno whistled and Blue stared in disbelief. "Somebody shot at you?"

"Yeah."

"I'll go call nine-one-one." Ruth hurried back inside the restaurant.

Reaching into the pocket of his jeans, Blue pulled out his

pocketknife, flipped open the blade, and started digging into the wooden jamb. He dug out a bent chunk of lead and held it up in the light from the Golden Spur sign above the door.

"Looks like a rifle. Big caliber. Thirty-ought-six, maybe."

"Let's see if we can find the casing."

Patience waited with Bonnie and Ruth for the sheriff to arrive while the men searched for the shell casing from the bullets that had been fired. They returned a little while later, frustrated and shaking their heads.

"He must have picked them up before he left."

"Why do you think he was shooting at you?" Bonnie asked, looking from one of them to the other.

"He must have been after Dallas." Patience caught his hand and held on tight. "All of these attacks seem to be focused on Charlie. Dallas is the same as Charlie's son. If the man is after some sort of retribution for something he believes Charlie did, killing Dallas would be the perfect revenge."

Other patrons filed out of the restaurant, unaware of the incident that had just occurred. Loyally, the rodeo riders waited with Dallas and Patience for the sheriff to arrive, and a patrol car pulled up to the curb a few minutes later.

As briefly as possible, Dallas explained what had happened while the deputy, an officer named Horn, took notes.

"We've all been briefed on the Carson case," the deputy said, a dark-skinned man who looked to be at least part Native American. "I'll let Sheriff Kendall know about this. He'll want to examine the scene himself." He folded his notebook closed. "He's a big rodeo fan. He's taken a personal interest in this one."

Patience felt Dallas's hand at her waist. "We'll be back at the rodeo grounds if he wants us."

"Keep your eyes open," the officer warned. "It looks like this guy means business. I'd keep a low profile until we can nail this joker down."

"That's good advice. Thanks, Deputy."

"We'll follow you back," Blue said.

Dallas just nodded, grateful, it seemed, to have a man he could trust at his back. Scanning the streets as they went, they drove off toward the fairgrounds.

"Charlie's going to go crazy when he hears," Patience said. "I wish I didn't have to tell him."

"You've got to, Dallas. He might be in danger himself."

"I know." He didn't say anything more the rest of the way and neither did Patience, but her mind kept returning to the sound of gunfire, and she couldn't help thinking how close she and Dallas had come to being killed.

CHAPTER 21

He wanted her to go back to Boston. He thought she should simply pack and leave.

"Look, you're going home, anyway," Dallas said. "What difference does it make if you leave a week early? Once you're in Boston, you'll be safe."

"No."

"You know I'm right. Being around me and Charlie is dangerous. Twice now you could have gotten killed."

He was right. It was stupid to stay and maybe get shot when she could be safe back home in Boston—assuming Tyler Stanfield didn't give her any more trouble once she got there. But her adventure wasn't over and she wasn't ready to leave—not yet. And she refused to behave like the proverbial rat leaving the sinking ship.

"I want you to change your plane reservations," Dallas said gently. "I'm asking as a personal favor. I want you somewhere safe. Will you do that for me?"

"It doesn't seem right just to run away. You won't be safe. Charlie won't be safe. What makes me so special?"

Dallas drew her closer. "Because you *are* special, dammit, and I don't want to see you get hurt."

There was something in those blue, blue eyes . . . something she had never seen in them before. It made her heart squeeze, made her want to leave him even less.

A lump rose in her throat as she imagined how empty her life would be without him once she got back home and wondered how their parting could be so much easier for him.

"It's only one more week," she argued. "After Albuquerque, we'll all be breaking up. Shari will be leaving to go back to Oklahoma and Charlie will be closing down his company and heading back to Texas. I want to stay until then. I refuse to let whoever did this ruin my last few days."

"Dammit, Patience—"

Another male voice spoke up just then. It belonged to a tall, rusty-haired man with hard gray eyes. His name was Carter Maddox and he was the detective Roy Greenwood had recommended. He had arrived in Lea County aboard Roy's private jet that afternoon.

"I hate to get in the middle of a personal dispute," Maddox said, "but I'd advise you to listen to what Dallas is telling you, Ms. Sinclair. Whatever's going on around here seems to be escalating. Being anywhere in the vicinity might be hazardous to your health."

Patience's gaze locked with his, hard gray and determined green. "There are a lot of other people here besides me. If I'm in danger, so are they. I'll give what you've said some thought, but that is the best I can promise. In the meantime, Dallas has to ride. He needs to get ready."

She reached over and caught his arm, started leading him away. Dallas grumbled something about hardheaded women, but didn't resist as Patience dragged him off toward his pickup. Reaching behind the front seat of the truck, he pulled out his black and gold fringed chaps, propped one boot after the other on the running board to buckle them on, then turned toward her.

"At least promise you'll stay away from me until you

leave. Maybe by then the sheriff will have caught the guy who fired those shots."

Patience batted her lashes and said in a too-sweet southern belle voice, "Why, darlin', how could I possibly stay away? Ya'll know how perfectly irresistible ya are ta me."

Dallas shook his head. "You are *the* most irritating female I have ever met." He jerked her against him, kissed her quick and hard. "And I'm crazy about you."

Turning, he strode away, leaving her behind with her jaw hanging open. Dallas was crazy about her? He had never said anything remotely revealing about his feelings for her.

Well, she was crazy about him, too. She was wildly, desperately in love with him. But loving someone wasn't always enough, and in a week they would have to say good-bye. Both of them knew it. Both were resigned to it.

Still, she wanted this last week together, wanted the memories that would have to last her a lifetime.

Now, more than ever, she didn't want to leave.

Dallas couldn't concentrate. The rodeo was a night show and all he could think about was the darkness outside the arena and that maybe someone was out there with a rifle, waiting to shoot him or Charlie or somebody else. The arena lights seemed too bright. The sound of the western music blaring over the loudspeakers grated on his nerves. He took a deep breath, tried to clear his head and concentrate on riding the big horse, Apocalypse, he had drawn for tonight's performance, but it didn't seem to help.

"You ready, Dallas?" Blue Cody strode toward him, ready to help him saddle his horse. Black hair glinted beneath his hat and his chaps flicked out in front of him.

"Ready as I'm gonna get."

They both climbed up on the chute and Reno climbed up beside them, battered straw hat pulled down low. The horse laid its ears back and bared its teeth in challenge, and Dallas figured the way things had been going, there was every chance this was one match the big horse just might win.

They settled the saddle on the animal's back, worked the cinch around, then the flank strap. Dallas straddled the chute, eased himself down into the seat, and shoved his feet into the stirrups.

The announcer's voice echoed over the loudspeakers. "Next up—coming out of chute number two—the current reigning World Champion All-Around Cowboy, Dallas Kingman. He's drawn a horse called Apocalypse and they don't call him that for nothing. The last cowboy who tried to ride him went out of the arena in an ambulance."

The crowd roared at this gruesome bit of news and Dallas settled himself a little deeper in the saddle. Catching his nod, one of the cowboys on the ground jerked open the gate and the horse leapt forward. After the first two jumps, Dallas got into the rhythm and began to feel the adrenaline rush that came when he was riding well.

Then something metal glinted in the lights off to the left and Dallas jerked his gaze toward the possible threat. At the same instant, Apocalypse twisted and bucked, throwing him completely off balance. Two seconds later, unable to get back into position, he went over the horse's head and landed hard in the dirt, sending a frisson of pain up his spine and into his neck and shoulders.

The big bay leapt and snorted, bucking past him with a look that said, *Ha! I told you I was gonna kick your butt.*

Dallas rolled stiffly to his feet. Reaching down, he plucked his black felt hat out of the dirt and slapped it against his thigh, thinking he sure hadn't ridden like The King tonight. More like the king's fool.

He gave the crowd a wave and a smile and they gave him a burst of conciliatory applause. His knee was throbbing but he ignored it. He should have wrapped it before the ride, but in all the commotion, he forgot.

Patience stood waiting as he walked out the gate trying not to limp.

"You okay?" She slid her arm around his waist and leaned a little against him. She felt so good, fit against him so perfectly, he wanted to turn and wrap her in his arms.

Instead, he just nodded. He was fine, except that he felt like an idiot. He hadn't seen a gun or any other sort of threat. He had to stop being paranoid and start concentrating on his riding. If he didn't, he was going to lose his chance at the Finals, or wind up getting seriously hurt.

Once they reached the area behind the chutes, he turned Patience around to look at him. "I thought I told you to stay away from me."

She just smiled and tipped her head toward a cluster of women in hats and jeans bearing down on him with adoring expressions on their faces. "Maybe I don't trust you with all those buckle bunnies."

A corner of his mouth edged up. "You've got no worries there, darlin'. If you haven't figured it out, you've ruined me for other women."

She smiled, but as the group surrounded him, asking for his autograph, her smile slipped away. Dallas knew what she was thinking. He'd had the same thought himself. Even if she stayed through the week, their time together was nearly over. Once she was gone, he would start dating again—and so would she.

He didn't want to think about it. Forcing himself to smile at the women, he accepted the pen one of them held out to him and started autographing whatever they shoved in front of him. Dallas said a silent thanks that this was the final night of the show and that in the morning they would be traveling to Albuquerque.

He just prayed nothing else would happen before they got there.

And as much as he wanted her to stay, he hoped that Patience would go home.

It was four o'clock in the morning. Patience heard the trailer door open and blinked her eyes against the crack of moonlight that illuminated the inside of the little RV as Shari walked in.

Shari made kind of a sniffing sound and blew her nose and Patience realized that she was crying. Dragging sleep-tangled hair out of her face, Patience sat up in bed, reached over and turned on the small light above her bunk. She yawned and tried to wake up enough to make her mouth work.

"From the sounds you're making, I take it you spent the night with Stormy."

Shari nodded and wiped her eyes with a wadded-up tissue. "I knew we shouldn't see each other again—not in a personal way. But he came up to me after the rodeo and said he needed to talk to me. He said it was important, so I went with him."

"What happened?" Patience sat up a little straighter on the bunk.

"We went for a drive up into the hills. The stars were out and the sand was warm so we took off our shoes and sat down on a blanket. It was so romantic. I let him kiss me— he's always been the most wonderful kisser. Kissing led to . . . well, you know . . . and we wound up making love." She sniffed again and Patience caught the gleam of fresh tears. "Stormy still wants to marry me. He says he'll wait for me . . . until I get through school. I told him waiting wasn't the problem. I just . . . I didn't want to marry a man whose whole life was rodeo."

Shari blew out a ragged breath. "My dad was a cowboy, you know. All he ever did was make my mother unhappy. I mean, it was fine when he was home, but he was gone most of the time. Nothing mattered but riding some damned bull."

She shook her head. "He got killed at a rodeo in Kansas City. I don't think I ever told you that. My mom never really got over it and I guess in some ways I didn't, either."

"Oh, Shari." Patience stood up and enfolded her friend in her arms.

"I don't want to go through that again, Patience. I don't want to live that kind of life."

"I don't blame you. I know you care about Stormy. But you have to do what's right for you, no matter how hard it is."

"I know. I just wish Stormy understood. He thinks I don't love him and that just isn't true."

Patience glanced out the small oval window over the dinette. Though it was still early, a gray dawn lightened the horizon. "You want some coffee or something?"

Shari shook her head. "I'd rather just get out of here. I've got one more rodeo before I quit for good. If you don't mind, I'd just as soon we got going."

"No problem. We're both up. We might as well get rolling. We'll stop and get coffee somewhere along the road."

They pulled on jeans and sweatshirts, packed up the trailer, and climbed into the pickup. The stock trucks were in the final stages of loading, Patience noticed as they rolled across the grass toward the gate leading out of the rodeo grounds.

Shari groaned as she spotted Dallas's rig starting up, then rolling toward the gate behind them. "Of all the rotten luck."

"Dallas is always up early. Stormy was probably as eager to leave as you were and the stock trucks are ready to roll. Dallas probably wants to keep an eye on Charlie."

Shari leaned back in the passenger seat as the pickup began to accelerate along the two-lane road. Through the window on Patience's side of the truck, red rock cliffs rose out of the desert, a forbidding wall in the gray light of dawn. She thought of the early cliff dwellers, the long-vanished Anasazi Indians she had read about during her studies, and wondered if perhaps they might have once built homes up there, somewhere in that intimidating wall.

She glanced in the rearview mirror, saw the distant speck of black that was Dallas's rig, followed by Charlie and the livestock trucks.

The speedometer read fifty-five miles an hour when the explosion hit—a huge blast that shook the pickup so hard the steering wheel nearly jumped from Patience's hand.

"Oh, my God!" Shari stared out the back window in horror as Patience fought to bring the truck back under control. "Pull over! Pull over quick!"

Hands trembling, braking with a leg that shook against the pedal, Patience flicked a glance in the rearview mirror and nearly lost control again. The truck bumped several times as it slowed and she pulled onto the side of the road. As soon as the Chevy stopped rolling, both of them leapt out and rushed back to what was left of their trailer, not much more than the axle and wheels. The rest of the little RV and all its contents were strewn like confetti along the two-lane road.

"Oh, my God," Shari said again. "It's completely gone. There's nothing left. Nothing!"

Patience fought to control her trembling limbs. "I know I turned off the propane. Maybe the line broke or something." She swallowed. "Do you realize, if you hadn't come home so late, we would probably still be sleeping? We would have left at our usual time, maybe an hour or so from now. We would have been asleep in the trailer when it exploded."

Shari sank down on the side of the road, her face ghostly pale. Patience surveyed the wreckage strewn over the highway, thought of how close she and Shari had come to dying, turned and heaved behind a cactus at the side of the road.

On shaking legs, she walked over to the pickup and dragged a plastic bottle of water out from under the seat. She rinsed her mouth, then drank deeply and began to feel a little better.

She looked back to see Dallas's truck pulling in behind

her Chevy. Dallas leapt out of the Dodge, not bothering to turn off the engine, and ran toward her like a madman.

Then she was in his arms.

"God, what happened?" He pulled her tight against his chest and she could feel him trembling. "Are you okay?"

"The trailer . . . the trailer blew up."

He looked over the top of her head. "Yeah, I can see that."

"We've lost everything. We don't even have a stitch of clothes."

He stared at the wreckage. "What about your computer and your work?"

She sighed with a hint of relief. "I always carry my computer in the truck, just to be safe. My thesis is in a box behind the seat, printed and ready to be mailed at the first town we come to."

"Thank God for that. And Shari's saddle is in the horse trailer with Button."

Patience looked over at the wheels still attached to her pickup. "If we hadn't left early—"

"If you hadn't left early, you would have been asleep inside when the trailer exploded."

Other cars were stopping. Shari used her cell to call the sheriff while Dallas pulled out his and phoned Carter Maddox at his motel.

Charlie walked up to where they stood at the side of the road. His livestock trucks and the truck that pulled the production trailer were parked along the edge of the highway. His strong features looked haggard, and purple smudges shadowed the pale blue of his eyes.

"Tell me this was caused by a faulty propane tank or something."

"We don't know yet," Dallas said. "I hope to hell it was something like that."

It was twenty minutes later that Carter Maddox pulled his nondescript beige Ford rental car off the road. By then,

Sheriff Kendall had arrived. While the sheriff asked questions, Maddox examined the blown-up bits and pieces of what had once been Patience's travel trailer.

She told the sheriff what had happened and looked up to see the detective returning, carrying a chunk of what appeared to be part of the undercarriage of her little white RV. He held up the burned and melted object in his hand.

"Well, one thing's for sure—this wasn't caused by a propane tank exploding. See that white, powdery substance left on this piece of metal?"

Patience peered down at the spot. "What is it?"

"Looks like traces of C-4 explosive."

"Explosive?"

"That's right. A highly volatile plastic used by the military. It's fairly easy to get—you can even buy it over the Internet. And it's simple to use. It's rubbery so you can stretch it into different forms and it's adhesive, so it will stick to different types of surfaces. And you can make a timer to set it off with a two dollar wristwatch."

Charlie's shoulders seemed to sag. "So the trailer was blown up on purpose."

"That's right. Considering when it was set to happen, I'd say the man who did it knew the ladies' schedule fairly well. Probably been following Circle C shows for quite a while."

Dallas drew Patience protectively against him. "Why would anyone want to kill Patience and Shari?"

"My guess is he was after Ms. Sinclair."

"What!"

Patience stiffened. Her first thought was Tyler Stanfield, but the image just didn't fit. Tyler was a little crazy. This was a lot crazy.

"You aren't thinking this might have been done by Tyler Stanfield?" She knew Dallas would have mentioned him to the detective. He wouldn't leave out any possibility.

"I don't know who's responsible," Maddox said, "but I've

been doing some thinking. After I spoke to you yesterday afternoon, I went down to the Golden Spur. I wanted to go over the scene of the shooting."

"And?" Dallas pressed.

"From what you told me, both bullets were fired well to your right."

"Yeah. So?"

"Both shots barely missed hitting Ms. Sinclair. Because of what's been happening to your uncle, you presumed you were the target, but I don't think so. After what's happened here, I'm pretty sure it was Patience the assailant was after that night."

"But why?" Patience asked. "I realize Tyler made a couple of threats, but he never actually said anything about killing me. Besides, as far as I know, he's still back in Boston."

Sheriff Kendall spoke up just then. "We're checking Stanfield's whereabouts now, but there's another possibility. When something like this happens, I ask the victim if they have any enemies. I also ask if they have something of value that someone might want bad enough to kill them for it. In your case, a third question comes to mind. Considering you were the first person to stumble on the scene of an arson fire that resulted in a homicide, the question is—do you know something you shouldn't?"

"Like who might have set the fire," Dallas said darkly.

Kendall nodded. "That's right. Even if you didn't see the man responsible, he might think you did. Killing you would end any possible threat."

"But I didn't see . . ." Her words trailed off as her mind drifted back to the night of the fire and the shadowy figure she had glimpsed as she walked along the road. At the time, she had believed it was just her imagination.

"What is it?" Dallas asked gently.

"I might have seen someone that night. Until this moment, I thought I was just imagining things. Even if I did, the image wasn't clear enough to do us any good."

"If you did see something," Maddox said, "there might be a way to help you remember."

"If you're thinking of hypnosis," Kendall said, "we're a pretty small county. There's no one around with that kind of expertise. But you might find someone through the police department in Albuquerque."

Dallas's hold on her tightened. "No way. If Patience is the target, I'm getting her out of here."

She turned and looked up at him. "You think I should go back to Boston?"

"No. You could be in just as much danger there. If Stanfield's involved, maybe even more. I was thinking of the ranch. It's pretty remote. We could post some guards around the house, keep watch until the police catch this guy."

Sheriff Kendall didn't look convinced. "Unless Ms. Sinclair helps us figure out who this guy is, that might not be so easy. On the other hand, if she could help us come up with a composite sketch of the man she saw at the scene of the fire— combined with the partial license number Dallas gave us— maybe we could find him. Better yet, once Patience has told us what she knows and it's broadcast to the public, she'll no longer be a threat and he'll have no reason to want her dead."

Dallas shook his head. "I don't like it. She's too exposed in Albuquerque. The guy could be anywhere."

"I can arrange for protective custody," the sheriff offered.

Patience looked at Dallas. "He's right. I have to help if I can."

Dallas lifted his hat, ran a hand through his dark brown hair, then resettled the hat across his forehead. "All right— as long as I go with her."

"I can drive the pickup the rest of the way," Shari offered. "You go with Dallas and Stormy."

Patience just nodded. Her stomach was churning with nerves and her hands still faintly trembled.

She had wanted an adventure.

She certainly had one now—in spades.

CHAPTER 22

Patience sat next to Dallas in a small private office in the Albuquerque Police Department on Roma Avenue. Tyler's alibi had been confirmed. He had been in Boston ever since his return. He could have hired someone to do it, of course, but according to the police psychiatrist, that kind of attack wouldn't be personal enough for someone as obsessive as Tyler. Which put him pretty well out of the picture and meant that all this was probably related to Charlie, just as the sheriff had believed.

Yesterday, Patience had undergone hypnosis. Working with a hypno-therapist in conjunction with a female police artist, she had dug into the recesses of her mind and retrieved a memory of the shadowy figure she had glimpsed before the fire had started. It was amazing how much clearer the image became, the subtle details her subconscious mind had captured that her conscious mind didn't remember.

She studied the composite drawing created from hidden memories Patience hadn't known she had. The sketch sat on an easel on the scuffed linoleum floor, a black and white picture of a man she could still only vaguely recall. His features looked hard, his eyebrows thick and heavy. He had a square-shaped face and solid jaw.

"So what do you think?" Patience asked Dallas. "Does he look like anyone you know?"

Dallas kept his eyes trained on the sketch. "I don't know . . . I'd say he looks a little like Wes McCauley. Same shaped head and jaw."

Patience studied the face, trying to see the resemblance. "I don't think so. This man's features are harder, more intense. Of course, I only got a glimpse. Even under hypnosis, I couldn't remember how tall he was or anything about his build, so I couldn't say for sure."

Dallas turned to the other man in the room, a gray-haired detective named Reardon who had been working with the Lea County Sheriff's Department. "You sure this drawing will make the evening news?" Dallas asked.

Sitting on the opposite side of the desk, Reardon shoved a ballpoint pen into the pocket of his brown polyester suit. "With the rodeo this weekend, this'll be a big story. You'll get good TV coverage and it'll also make the front page of the Albuquerque *Journal,* the *Tribune,* and several other area papers. If this guy's anywhere around, he'll know his witness has come forward. He'll realize he's missed his chance to shut her up and probably just disappear."

"Won't he be worried she might testify against him?" Dallas asked.

"The sketch might not even look that much like him. I think he'll realize how little she really saw. Besides, we have to catch him first, and his real purpose in going after her was to keep from being apprehended. Killing her won't help him now."

"So you figure she's no longer at risk."

"The man who burned that barn is not some psycho. I think it's pretty clear he's got an agenda that is somehow connected with Charlie Carson. His attack on Ms. Sinclair was strictly in the interest of self-preservation."

Dallas looked relieved. "All right, then, if you're finished with us here, we need to get going. We've got a plane to catch this afternoon."

Reardon nodded. "Leave a number where you can be reached. We'll be in touch if anything turns up."

Stormy was waiting for them in the parking lot. They climbed into the pickup and he drove them straight to the airport. Charlie was already there and checked in at the gate. After the explosion, he had made the tough decision to call Jack Stiles and Lem Watkins. The Flying S Rodeo Company was already producing the San Bernardino Sheriff's Rodeo in California this week, but with the loan of Charlie's stock and crew, they agreed to do the Albuquerque Show as well.

Earlier that morning, Patience had said her good-byes to Shari, who would be leaving right after the final performance on Sunday, returning to her home in Oklahoma. Patience had given her the old Chevy pickup as a farewell gift, and Shari had been deeply moved.

"Oh, Patience, are you sure? Don't you want to sell it and get back some of your money?"

"It really isn't worth all that much, and I'd rather you have it. Now you'll have a way to get back and forth to school."

Shari reached up and hugged her. She looked over at the plain brown Chevy that had carried them across the country. "You're terrific. I really needed a car, and now if I rent a one-way U-haul trailer, I can get Button home without having to ask Stormy. Thanks a lot."

The two of them hugged again. Patience felt the sting of tears and noticed the same glint in Shari's eyes.

"Be careful," Shari said. "And keep in touch. I'm really gonna miss you."

"I'm going to miss you, too."

Dallas stood waiting a few feet away. Patience had given her friend a last final wave and let him guide her over to his truck. Though the Albuquerque rodeo was starting that day, Charlie, Dallas, and Patience were flying back to the Circle

C Ranch for the balance of the week. After that, if the police believed it was safe for her to go home, she would return to Boston. Her teaching job started the following week and she needed to be settled by then.

Now, as the plane taxied down the runway, Patience looked over at Dallas, who sat in the aisle seat of the plane, his long legs cramped in the narrow space in front of him. Just a glimpse of his strong, handsome profile made her heart squeeze with longing. She loved him so much. How was she ever going to get over him?

She steeled herself. Thinking of the lonely months ahead would only ruin their last few days together. She reached over and caught Dallas's hand and his gaze swung to her face. He laced their fingers together and pressed them against his lips.

He didn't say anything. He didn't have to.

The look in his eyes made an ache throb in her heart.

Charlie didn't expect his wife to be waiting at the airport, but there she was, standing over at the side of the baggage claim, wearing a pair of beige slacks and a short-sleeved beige and white print blouse. Her silver hair was neatly pinned into a twist and the little pearl earrings he had bought her for Christmas glinted in her ears. She looked so damned pretty a lump rose in his throat.

"Hi, honey. You didn't have to drive all this way. You could have sent Ben or one of the hands."

Annie went into his arms and just hung on to him. When she didn't let go, he realized how frightened she had been.

"I'm so glad you're home," she said as he eased her a little away.

"Me, too, honey. I've never missed anyone so much."

Though it looked a little wobbly, Annie mustered one of her resilient smiles and turned to Dallas, who walked up beside her just then. She gave him the same sort of worried hug, grateful that both her men were safe.

Dallas set her a little away, then frowned as he saw the sparkle of tears in her eyes. "Hey . . . you aren't crying, are you?"

Her gaze dropped and she shook her head, discreetly reached up and brushed away a drop of wetness. "Don't be silly. Of course, I ain't." She turned toward Patience, the third member of their group. "Charlie told me about your trailer and losing all your things. It's not fair we got you involved in this mess of ours. You're welcome to stay at the ranch however long you need."

"Thank you, Annie. I'm only planning to stay through the end of the week. Now that I've done the sketch, the police think I'm out of danger. They're pretty sure the man won't bother me again."

"I hope they're right," Annie said. Charlie walked back up to her and gave her another hug. He found his luggage, then waited while Dallas found his. With Patience's trailer blown six ways to Sunday, all the girl had was a little red duffel to hold the T-shirt, jeans, and handful of other clothes and make-up she had bought at a local Wal-Mart to replace what she'd lost. As soon as the bag appeared on the conveyor belt, Dallas picked it up and they headed for the aging Ford Suburban that Annie had driven to the airport.

It was a quiet ride back to the ranch. Charlie wanted to ask what was happening with the land they were selling to Mal Sullivan, but he hadn't told Dallas about it yet and he knew how the boy would react once he did.

As it was, Dallas appeared just as he and Annie started talking about the deal and it was too late to change the subject. Charlie sighed at the sight of Dallas standing rigidly in the doorway of the living room, a muscle ticking in his cheek.

"You're selling part of the ranch to Sully? I don't believe it."

"Times change, son. I should have told you sooner. This is the best way out of this mess, and for all our sakes, I mean to take it."

"You've already let the bastard behind these attacks drive you out of the rodeo business. Now you're going to let him force you into selling part of the Circle C? This ranch has been in your family for years. Your father owned it and his father before him. How can you even think of selling?"

"I'm not selling all that much, only the southwest section. The property's already in escrow. Even if I changed my mind, I wouldn't back out of the deal. I've given Sully my word."

"You really need money that bad?"

"With that lawsuit about to be settled and everything else that's happened . . . yeah, I'm afraid we do."

"Christ." Dallas turned and stalked out of the living room.

Charlie rubbed a hand over his face as he watched the boy leave. The piece of land they were selling was worth more than a million dollars. Some decisions were hard to make, but there was nothing else to do.

"I knew he wasn't gonna like it," Annie said.

"That land shoulda been his. The rest will be someday." He had never spoken the thought out loud. Now that he had, he felt the rightness of it. He looked down and saw Annie smile.

"It'll all work out," she said. "One way or another. It always does."

Charlie hauled her into his arms and just held her. He hoped she was right. More than that, now that he had closed down the Circle C Rodeo Company, he hoped the troubles that had plagued him would end.

Charlie said a silent prayer he hadn't just brought them home with him.

Patience walked over to the desk in Charlie's office. He and Dallas were out making a check of the ranch and Annie was working in her garden. A couple of men were posted outside the house, just to keep an eye on things, but she felt fairly certain that she was out of danger.

She settled herself in the old oak swivel chair, pleased to have discovered last night that the Circle C had actually made its way into the twenty-first century. On a corner of Charlie's desk sat a fairly modern computer hooked up to a DSL line. While the house was empty, she decided to go on-line, drop a note to Mabel Thompson and a few other people who had been digging around for her, researching the archives on early women in rodeo.

She got an e-mail back from Mabel almost immediately. *Got news! Tried to call but your cell phone doesn't seem to be working. Call me as soon as you get this.*

Darn! In all the excitement, she had forgotten to give Mabel her new cell number.

Hurriedly, she retrieved Mabel's phone number from the little address book in her wallet. Using a credit card, she picked up Charlie's phone and dialed her friend at the 101 Ranch Museum.

Mabel answered on the second ring and excitement rang in her voice. "God, I've been dying to talk to you. You won't believe what I found."

Her own excitement built. "Another missing female rider?"

"No. One that was clearly murdered. It happened in Denver. A woman named Gracie McGuiness, a trick rider from Belle Fourche, South Dakota. She was killed outside a restaurant called the Frontier Cafe. She was found in the alley out behind the building."

Patience's heart took a leap. "Did they catch him? Did they find the guy who did it?"

"Not that I could discover. But it has to be connected. It happened three years after Lucky Sims turned up missing, on the weekend the rodeo was in town. I tracked down some newspaper articles. I'll scan them into my computer and send them to you over the Net."

"That would be great, Mabel." Patience found herself

doodling the name Gracie McGuiness on the pad beside the phone. "I can't believe it. Another female rodeo performer killed. You don't think maybe it's just coincidence?"

"No, I don't. But then, like I said, I watch a lot of this stuff on TV."

"Well, I'll keep nosing around and if I turn up any more information I'll let you know."

"I'll keep after it, too," Mabel said. "Got my interest up now. I really hope they catch him." Mabel used the present tense, as if the crimes were just now being committed. In a way it felt as if they were.

"Thanks again, Mabel." Patience hung up the phone, then spent the rest of the morning speaking to other members of her research team, filling them in on this latest discovery. The last person she phoned was her father.

Patience had never told him about the shooting or the trailer blowing up. The police had cleared Tyler, so she didn't want to worry him. Now, hearing the cheery note in his voice, she felt guilty.

"Hi, kiddo, how's my number one cowgirl?"

"Pretty good, Dad . . . considering."

The cheerful note faded. "Considering what?"

Taking a deep breath, she told him what had happened and that at present she was staying in Texas.

"I can't believe you didn't call. We could have come out there. We might have been able to help in some way."

"There was nothing you could do, and I didn't want to worry you."

"Well, I'm worried, now. And I think you should come back home now instead of waiting till the end of the week. Your family's here and we could help protect you."

"It isn't that much longer. I've already got my plane reservations made." And she wanted this time with Dallas. "In the meantime, the police are sure I'm not in any danger."

"Well, I don't like it." But he had finally begun to accept that she was a grown woman so he didn't press her. Still, it wasn't half an hour later that her sister, Charity, phoned from her home in Seattle.

"Hi, sis. Dad called. He told me what's been going on. Are you sure you're okay?"

"I'm fine. But things were pretty exciting for a while."

"You're sure that creep, Tyler, isn't involved?"

"I really don't think so. This has something to do with Charlie but no one can seem to figure out exactly what."

They talked for at least an hour. She and Charity hadn't spoken for nearly a month, which was a long time not to hear from her middle sister.

"I gather you and Call have been up North for most of the summer."

"We went up in June. It's great up there that time of year. We finished rebuilding ol' Mose Flanagan's cabin—which turned out really great. It looks just like it used to, only it's all brand new. The place ought to last another hundred years."

"So are you . . . you know . . . pregnant yet?"

Charity laughed. "We're still thinking about it. We wanted to get the cabin done first. And I wanted to give Call a little more time to get used to the idea. But I think he's really beginning to get excited about having a family. Maybe by Christmas I'll be ready to go off the pill."

They talked a little while longer. It was only a few minutes later that her eldest sister, Hope, phoned. She was as worried as Charity had been, but Patience reassured her that she was safe at the ranch.

"Are you sure about that?" Hope said softly. "I have a feeling this cowboy of yours could pose a very serious threat to your heart."

Patience swallowed. Hope had always had a way of sensing her sisters' innermost thoughts. "I'm in love with him, Hope. It's going to kill me to leave him, but both of us realize it could never work out."

"At least you know where you stand." Hope hadn't been that lucky. The man she had loved, Richard Daley, the man she was supposed to marry, had been sleeping with her closest friend. Hope had never really gotten over it.

"I guess I'd better get going," Hope said. "I've got an article to finish and I'm only half done." Hope was a freelance writer. Lately, her career had been going well and she was developing a reputation as a woman who could get the job done. "Take care of yourself and I'll call again soon."

Patience hung up the phone, grateful to finally have time to catch up with her family, though the painful conversation with Hope continued to roll around in her head.

Four more days with Dallas was all she had. Her stomach tightened. Four more days.

Don't do this, she told herself. *Enjoy the time you have left.*

But she thought of Dallas and how much she loved him and knew it wouldn't be an easy thing to do.

It was two hours later that Dallas walked into Charlie's office, looking so handsome it made her ache inside. It was warm in the room, though the ceiling fan made lazy rotations that helped cool the sticky summer air. They hadn't made love since the night they had spent in his motel room. The thought made her realize how badly she wanted him. From the slight darkening of his eyes, she thought that he wanted her, too.

"Any more sign of those cattle rustlers?" she asked, keeping the conversation light, feeling such a mixture of desire and love it made her want to weep.

"Not a trace, I'm happy to say." He sat down on the edge of the desk, one long leg hanging over the side, leaned forward and kissed her. "I missed you. I wish you could have gone with me."

But Dallas had refused to take her along, saying she was safer inside the house.

"Will you be going out again tomorrow?"

He nodded. "Takes more than a day to cover all this ground."

"Good. Tomorrow I'm going with you."

"No way. I told you—I don't want you out there unprotected. What if the guy who tried to kill you followed us here? He might take another potshot and this time he might not miss."

"You heard what the police said. The man was trying to shut me up. Now that I've told the authorities all I know, he's got no reason to come after me."

"You're safer in the house," he said stubbornly. "There are men outside who'll shoot anyone who tries to get near you."

Yes, but she was hundreds of miles away from where the attempts had been made and she believed the police were right and she was safe. And she was going with him tomorrow, whether he liked it or not. They only had a few days left. She was determined to make the most of them.

But she didn't say that and Dallas seemed satisfied, turning his attention to the name she had scribbled several times on the pad beside the phone.

"Who's Gracie McGuiness?"

Her earlier excitement returned. "Gracie was one of the early cowgirls." Glad for a change of subject, she launched into a lengthy discussion of the trick rider who had been murdered in Denver in 1915.

"According to the newspaper articles Mabel sent, it looks like Gracie was strangled. As far as either of us have been able to find out, they never caught the man who did it."

They talked a while longer, then Patience stood up from her chair and slipped her arms around Dallas's neck. "It's nice outside. I think we should go for a ride."

She recognized the hungry look that came into his eyes, but Dallas shook his head. "Not a chance. I'm keeping you safe till the police find the man who tried to kill you."

Patience sighed and let go of his neck. Damn, cowboys

could be stubborn. "Have you heard from that detective you hired? Maybe Carter Maddox has come up with something."

"Actually, he called on my cell phone while I was out in the barn. He's still in Albuquerque. He thinks the guy we're looking for is a pro. That means it isn't likely he's anyone on the Circle C crew and probably not anyone in rodeo."

"You're saying someone hired him to cause Charlie all this trouble? Someone wanted revenge that much?"

"Or someone wanted him out of the rodeo business that much."

She thought of the attempts made on her life. "Enough to kill for it?"

"It sure looks that way."

The following morning, Patience got up at dawn, dressed in jeans, boots, and a tank top, and headed downstairs to help Annie with breakfast. The meal was just about done when the men returned to the house from the barn. They stomped the dust off their boots, sat down, and dug into the sausage, eggs, fried potatoes, and biscuits that she and Annie had prepared.

As soon as the dishes were done, Patience went out to the barn to find Dallas.

"You're riding out again today, right?"

"That's right. Charlie and Ben Landers and me."

"Good, I'm going with you."

"Dammit, I told you I want you here where you'll be safe."

"Look, Dallas. In three more days I'm going back to Boston. Once I get there, you won't be around to protect me. In the meantime, we only have a little time left. I want us to be together."

Dallas looked at her and she could see the turmoil in his face, worry mixed with the same need she was feeling.

"I'm not stupid, Dallas. If I really believed I was in danger, I wouldn't go. The police don't think so and they ought to know."

Dallas lifted his hat and blotted his forehead with the sleeve of his shirt. "All right, you win, you can go. I'll tell one of the hands to saddle Gigi for you."

Patience gave him a flirty perusal. "I promise you won't be sorry."

For an instant, his eyes turned hot. He smiled, then turned and walked away. He headed for the barn and came back a few minutes later, leading their horses and carrying a rifle in his hand.

"You're bringing a gun?"

"Thirty-thirty." He shoved it into a scabbard behind his saddle. "If there's trouble, I want to be prepared."

She didn't really mind. She'd been shot at and barely escaped being blown to bits. "Good idea. Let's go."

CHAPTER 23

It was a good day to ride, a little cooler than it had been, a little less humid. A cleansing breeze tugged at the back of Dallas's neck and ruffled Patience's hair. Charlie and Ben rode up ahead, keeping an eye out for trouble and checking for any sign of cattle thieves.

Dallas looked over to where Patience sat casually in the saddle beside him. Over the years, he had dated a lot of women, some of them movie-star gorgeous, but none of them attracted him the way Patience did. Beneath the brim of her cowboy hat, her eyes were a soft sea green. The sun had pinkened her cheeks, and wisps of golden hair framed the fine bones in her face. Her loved her lips. They were beautifully curved and when he kissed her they sort of melted into his.

His belly clenched and blood pulsed in his groin. An instant later, he was hard against the zipper of his jeans and damned uncomfortable.

He couldn't think of Patience without getting turned on, but what he felt for her went way beyond lust. In the months he had known her, he had come to admire her. She was smart and determined and a damned fine horsewoman. He had watched her with the children who came to the rodeo. It was obvious she loved kids, and several times lately he had found himself thinking what a good mother she would make.

But having a family with Patience wasn't going to happen. Not now or anytime in the future. She was about to get her Ph.D. and start a job as an assistant professor. It was a career to be proud of, a goal she had worked all her life to achieve.

He had gotten so used to her upper-class Boston accent, he rarely noticed it anymore, but still it was there, a glaring reminder of the wildly different paths their lives were destined to take. For the past few days, he had tried not to think of that, or how soon she would be leaving. That once she was gone, she would be out of his life for good.

He was a cowboy. A rodeo rider. Cowboys didn't marry professors. And even if he asked her and she was crazy enough to say yes, it would only ruin both of their lives. His parents had proved that. They had married against everyone's advice and destroyed each other's lives in the bargain.

Over the years, his father had become a cynical, bitter man, and his mother had died, driven by her disastrous marriage into an early grave. The differences between the two had simply been too vast to overcome. For Patience's sake as well as his own, Dallas refused to make the same mistake.

Still, he loved her. And looking at her now as she rode beside him, so beautiful in the fading afternoon sunlight, made him yearn to change things, made him wish he could keep her with him forever.

Charlie drew rein on his horse and the rest of them followed. "You two be okay if Ben and me ride up to check that northwest pasture over the hill?"

"We'll be all right," Dallas said. "Been no sign of trouble. Give me a chance to ride down and take a last look at that piece you're selling to Sully."

Charlie's expression shifted, filled with resignation. "All right. We'll meet up back at the house."

Charlie and Ben rode away, and Dallas nudged his horse forward, a big red roan called Brady that was great on the trail. With Dallas's unexpected trip to Texas, Stormy still had Lobo and the black Dodge rig. Dallas needed to catch up with him, get back into the competition. He needed to increase his earnings if he was going to make it to the National Finals this year.

But he wasn't leaving the ranch until he was certain that Charlie was out of danger. He hoped, now that his uncle had closed down his rodeo company, the man behind the accidents had gotten what he wanted and would leave Charlie Carson alone.

A crane flew out of the bushes along the creek and Brady tossed his big, freckled head, jangling the bit in his mouth. Dallas made a quick check of the area, but there was no one around. Beside him, Patience rode at a steady walk, the trail wide enough here so they could ride side by side. He reined off the main path onto a narrower trail that led up to the top of a hill overlooking the southwest section, land Charlie was selling to his neighbor.

It wasn't the most scenic portion of the Circle C, being drier here, more sandy, with stratified ridges and several chalk-like formations marked with an occasional cactus.

"Well, if he had to sell, I'm glad this is the piece," Dallas said.

"It's definitely a different landscape than the other parts of the ranch I've seen, more stark and arid. Why does Sullivan want it?"

"Most ranchers like to increase their holdings whenever they get the chance. Mal's property borders this section to the east. It'll add some acreage and there's a good stream running through it a little farther south."

They rode off down the hill, out toward a sandy flat near

the wire fence that marked the border between the Circle C and the Broken Arrow, Mal Sullivan's ranch.

"Looks like someone's been checking this area over," Dallas said. Drawing rein on the roan, he swung down from the saddle and Patience swung down beside him. Leading Brady, he walked over to examine a set of tire marks in the dirt. "Must have been a pretty big rig to leave tracks so wide and deep."

"Maybe this is where the rustlers drove onto the ranch."

Dallas looked around but saw no cattle tracks anywhere around. "Maybe, but the tire tracks don't go much farther and there are no steer tracks around. Whoever it was, they had to drive across Sully's property to get here."

"Maybe he wanted a closer look at what he was buying."

"Yeah, probably. Or maybe someone trespassed on both of our properties. If that's the case, the sheriff will want to cast those tire marks for comparison against the tracks left by the rustlers' truck."

Handing his horse's reins to Patience, he began a search of the area. A little farther away, he found more tire tracks and signs of the ground being disturbed. It looked as if something had dug up the soil, then filled the hole back in.

"What is it?" Patience led the horses up behind him.

"I'm not sure. Looks like somebody's been digging up the ground."

"Why would they want to do that?"

"I haven't the slightest idea, but the way things have been going, I think we'd better find out." They mounted their horses and headed back toward the ranch house, taking the less used trails, keeping an eye out for anyone who might have been following them, or might be lying in wait somewhere ahead. But they saw no sign of trouble.

As they neared the house, Dallas relaxed his guard a little, letting his mind return to the unsettling discovery he had made. He needed to talk to Charlie, see if he knew anything about who might be trespassing on Circle C land.

Dallas cast a glance at Patience. They hadn't made love in days and he was way past ready. He caught her looking his way and read the same thought in her eyes.

"Charlie's got a couple of pastures to check," he said. "He won't get back to the house for a while. I know a place we can rest and water the horses."

Patience's lips curved into a knowing smile. "Sounds like a plan to me."

Once they reached their destination, Dallas led the horses into the slow-moving stream and both animals drank deeply. He tied them to a tree, giving them enough room to graze, then spread a blanket in the grass and drew Patience down beside him.

There was no one around. He heard the sound of insects and the breeze luffing through the trees as Patience reached over and touched his cheek.

"I've missed you," she said and he knew exactly what she meant. Though they had been living under the same roof, he had missed the closeness, the intimacy.

They made love there on the blanket, hidden by the deep green grasses, their naked skin warmed by the sun slanting down through the branches of the trees. He tried to go slow, but she felt so good beneath his hands and he wanted her so badly. He kissed her breasts, her belly, found the place between her legs and pleasured her until she cried out his name.

She climaxed as he entered her, surging deeply, driving into her harder than he meant to. He clamped down on his need, determined to please her again, holding back, kissing her instead of pounding into her as he wanted. He loved her. He wanted her to know it. He kissed her breasts and she moved restlessly beneath him. Easing out, he drove into her and she arched against him, catching his rhythm, matching it, driving both of them to climax.

Their mating was more fierce than he intended and there seemed a desperation in the act.

She was leaving. He was losing her. He was in love with

her. Though he wanted her again the moment they were finished, he reached for his clothes and so did Patience. They dressed in silence and he guided her back to the house.

Charlie rode up to the corral just minutes after Dallas and Patience arrived. Unfortunately, when Dallas mentioned the signs of trespass he had seen in the southwest section of the ranch, Charlie knew nothing about them.

"Probably just Sully," he said. "He's got a right to see what he's buying."

But Dallas wasn't satisfied. That night after supper, he went into the study and telephoned his father. Avery Kingman made it a point to know everyone who was anyone in Texas, from senators to television personalities, and that included wealthy businessmen and cattle ranchers. Rich men and their wives were the foundation of his hugely successful plastic surgery practice.

His stepmother, Rachael, answered the phone with her usual, effusive greeting, then Avery came on the line.

"Well, I wondered when I'd finally hear from you." The tone of his father's voice grated on Dallas's nerves.

"I'm back in Texas, Dad. Charlie's been having some trouble."

"Is that so?"

Dallas ignored the note of satisfaction. "I was hoping you might be able to help."

A pause. "Go on."

"The guy who owns the ranch next door to the Circle C is a man named Malcolm Sullivan. You ever heard of him?"

"Sullivan . . . yes, I know his ex-wife, Julia. She was a patient of mine some years back. Julia still comes in for the occasional Botox shot or a collagen injection to perk up her looks. She's got two kids, as I recall, a girl in her mid-twenties and a boy several years older, about your age, I think."

That was right. Beth Sullivan was about twenty-five and

Brad was close to Dallas's age, somewhere around twenty-nine or thirty. They were both spoiled rotten, always had been. Dallas hadn't seen either of them in years.

"Sullivan's cut a deal to buy a portion of the Circle C," Dallas said. "I'm trying to find out if he has any special plans for it."

Dallas could imagine his father's face on the other end of the line, his features stern and frowning. "I can't tell you much about his finances, aside from the fact his ex-wife is very expensive to keep and those kids of his are downright bloodsuckers." His laugh held a bitter edge. "That's not something I could ever say about you. You never wanted anything from me, not even the things I wanted to give you—like a college education."

"I have a college education, Dad, in case you've forgotten. I graduated from Texas A&M."

"With honors, I might add."

Dallas braced for the rest of the lecture but it never came.

"Tell you what," Avery said. "I'll put out a few feelers, see if anyone knows anything useful."

"I'd appreciate that, Dad."

"Are you still seeing that attractive young woman you brought to my birthday party?"

Dallas's stomach clenched. "We've been dating. She's leaving on Sunday, going home to Boston."

"That's too bad. Rachael and I both liked her. She seemed to have a lot going for her."

"She does, Dad. That's why I'm letting her go." He hadn't meant to say it exactly that way and he wondered if his father heard the regret in his voice. Maybe Avery did, for he didn't make any of his usual sharp-edged comments, just told Dallas to keep in touch and said he'd call if he turned up any interesting news.

Dallas hung up the phone and swiveled his chair to see Patience standing in the doorway of the office. As he rose from his seat, she walked toward him. She went into his arms and he tightened them around her. She didn't say any-thing and neither did he. Both of them just stood there hold-ing onto each other.

They had the next few days together. At the end of the week, he would drive her to the airport in San Antonio. He had reserved a room at the nearby Embassy Suites Hotel for their last night together, then the following morning, she would leave for home.

The summer was over. As soon as he was sure Charlie's troubles were ended, he would catch up with Stormy, go back to riding broncs, and try not to think of Patience.

He tried to imagine how long it would take him to forget her and wondered if he ever really would.

Patience sat behind the desk in Charlie's office. Dallas was out in the barn, looking over the latest crop of bucking horses Charlie was raising, trying to decide which horses to keep and which they might sell at the stock show in Miles City next spring. The auction in eastern Montana was one of the biggest events in rodeo, a place where bucking horses were actually ridden—or at least cowboys tried—so buyers could see how each animal performed.

Patience used the time the men were working to check in with her research team, bringing up her e-mail for any new in-formation, then phoning Constance Foster, at the Cowgirl Hall of Fame, whom she hadn't heard from yet.

Nothing new surfaced. When she finished, she closed down the computer and headed downstairs, surprised to hear the sound of an unfamiliar voice in the entry.

"The men are out in the barn," Annie said. "They'll be back any minute. Why don't you wait for them in the living room and I'll bring you a nice glass of homemade lemonade."

"Thanks, Annie, that sounds great."

Annie looked up just then and saw Patience at the bottom

of the stairs. "This here's a friend of Dallas's. Her name's Patience Sinclair. Patience, this is Malcolm Sullivan."

Sullivan smiled. "Most folks call me Sully."

Patience stuck out her hand. "It's nice to meet you, Sully."

"Same here."

The only time she had seen Mal Sullivan had been through the kitchen window the last time she had visited the ranch. He had been rather nondescript, she had thought. Now she saw that he had once been a very handsome man, but years of sun and wind had wrinkled his face and time had begun to wear his body down. His shoulders seemed to carry the weight of the world. A general weariness surrounded him.

"So how do you like the Hill Country?" he asked, while Annie went to get the lemonade.

"It's beautiful. It's a whole lot hotter than Boston, but there's something kind of magical about it."

"Last week it was even warmer, and a lot more humid. This week's been pretty nice so far."

She started to say something equally inane when the front door opened and Dallas and Charlie walked in. She didn't miss the faint stiffening in Dallas's shoulders the instant he spotted Mal Sullivan.

"Hello, Charlie . . . Dallas. Heard you two were back. Thought I'd drop by, see how things were going. Figured maybe we might set a date for the closing on that land."

"Figured to see you sooner or later," Charlie said.

"You been up there lately?" Dallas asked. Patience knew he was thinking of the tire marks he had seen and wondering if Sullivan had been digging around on the land.

Sully cast an uneasy glance in his direction. Then he smiled. "My foreman, Pete Russell. He was up there last week. I didn't figure Charlie would mind. I'm thinking of running some cows on that section. Thought I'd have Pete take a look at the water situation."

"No problem," Charlie said, tossing Dallas a look that warned him to tread lightly.

"Cows, huh? Looked to me like someone was doing some digging up there. You wouldn't know anything about that, would you?"

Sully continued to smile. "Like I said, Pete was prowling around. Probably his doing."

Dallas said nothing more. Annie arrived carrying a tray that held glasses and a pitcher of lemonade. While she poured the refreshment, Sullivan and Charlie began discussing a date for the closing on the land.

Twenty minutes later, Sullivan returned his empty glass to Annie, made polite farewells, and left the house.

As soon as he was gone, Dallas turned to Charlie. "I wish you'd hold off on that sale."

"I promised I'd sell the man the land and I keep my word."

"I know, but—"

"Sully's wanted that property for years. Now he's gonna have it and that's the end of it." Charlie stomped off, and Dallas sighed into the silence his uncle left behind. Catching the weary set of his shoulders, Patience walked over and slipped an arm around his waist.

"The afternoon's still early. You promised we could go riding again."

He drew her around in front of him, gave her a soft, lingering kiss. "You're right. We haven't got much time left. We had better make the most of it."

The words made her chest ache. Patience mustered a smile she hoped didn't look forlorn and let him guide her out of the house.

It was late when Dallas's cell phone rang, the sound shrill where it sat in the upstairs bedroom on top of the walnut bureau against the wall. In the process of undressing for bed, he walked over and picked it up, praying it hadn't awakened Charlie.

"I hope you weren't asleep." His father's voice reached him from the other end of the line. Unlike Dallas, whose job got him up early, Avery Kingman was a night owl, often staying up past midnight.

"I was still awake. You got news?"

"Maybe. I spoke to a friend of Julia Sullivan's, a woman named Peppy James, she's married to that golfer—you know—Mickey James? Peppy came in to have her eyes done—long overdue, if you ask me, but then, that's her business. At any rate, I happened to mention Malcolm Sullivan and Peppy gave me an earful. She says Sullivan's gotten into some major financial difficulties. The stock market, I guess, among other things. Peppy says he's threatening to go back to court to get his wife's alimony payments reduced. He cut his kids' allowance in half and they're having a fit about it."

Sullivan in trouble? He never would have guessed. "If he's having money problems, how's he coming up with the money to buy Charlie's land?"

"I have no idea. I just figured this was something you might want to know."

"Yeah, no kidding. I really appreciate the information. Thanks, Dad."

There was a pause on the end of the phone. "Rachael and I . . . we thought maybe you might get a chance to drop by for a visit before you leave Texas."

For a minute, Dallas thought he hadn't heard his father correctly. For years, the two of them had made it a point to stay away from each other. Then Rachael had asked him to come to his father's birthday party. That hadn't gone particularly well, but maybe it was a start.

"Yeah, maybe I can. I'll give you a call once things settle down."

"Great. I'll tell Rachael. I know she'll be pleased." But something in his father's voice said he was the one pleased by the news.

They ended the conversation and Dallas couldn't decide which was more surprising—that his father had asked to see him or that Malcolm Sullivan was in financial straits. He fixed his mind on the latter and two questions popped into his head.

How was Sullivan financing the purchase of the Circle C property?

And what was he planning to do with that land?

Breakfast was over, the morning chores completed when Dallas and Patience headed for the barn. The sky overhead was a bright shade of blue but clouds loomed on the horizon, hinting they might be in for a storm.

One of the hands had already saddled their horses. Swinging up on the pretty little sorrel mare, Gigi, she had been riding since she came to the ranch, Patience trotted along next to Dallas, posting against the cantle while he merely lounged in the saddle. The ranch house disappeared in the distance and rolling green hills stretched out in front of them. Deep green grasses feathered along the edge of the trail, and a little stream tracked through the foliage beside them.

"Let's go this way this time," Dallas said, reining off the path, leading her down a trail she hadn't ridden before. For a mile or so, they wound their way through the trees, then the terrain began to change. Layers of rock pushed up from the earth and the trees became sparse, dwindling until there were only a few in sight. The country was open here, the hills often jagged, with sharp ridges and sheer rock walls.

Dallas had wanted to revisit the southwest section his uncle was set on selling and so here they were. Earlier, he had relayed to Patience the conversation he'd had last night with his father and that Sullivan appeared to be having money problems. Dallas was concerned that Sullivan might be trying to take advantage of Charlie in some way and Patience wondered if he might not be right.

Dallas drew up his horse and Patience pulled the mare to a halt. "What is it?"

"Take a look up ahead. The ground's been disturbed here, too. Someone's been digging." He swung down from his horse, turned and lifted Patience down from her saddle. As he lowered her to the ground, her hands rested on his shoulders and for an instant their gaze met and held. Desire flared in his eyes but there was something more, something deep and turbulent. Then he turned away.

"This is the most remote section of the property," he said. "But there's a road coming in off the highway if you know where the turn is."

They walked over to the base of a stratified layer of rock. In several places, the soil looked powdery, not solid, as if it had been dug up and the hole filled back in. It hadn't rained lately. Once it did, the hole would be hidden and the ground would look the way it had before.

"Ever since my father called, I've been thinking about why Mal might want this land so badly. He needs money, right?"

"Apparently so."

"Last night, after I hung up the phone, I went downstairs and got on the Internet. I did a little research on the oil industry."

"Oil? You think Sullivan's after oil?"

He shoved up the brim of his hat with the tip of his finger. "Years ago, he used to be in the business, a corporate exec with one of the big Houston oil companies. I'd forgotten all about it until last night. He quit when his old man died and he inherited his father's money. That was nearly twenty years ago. Sully bought the ranch, built the house, and he and his family moved in."

"Well, there is certainly plenty of oil in Texas."

"There are lots of big fields, all right, but none in the Hill

Country. Mostly the terrain isn't right. From what I've been reading, oil comes from animal and plant life that died in ancient seas, then decayed into sedentary layers."

"That's right. Over millions of years, heat and pressure turned the organic matter into oil and natural gas."

"Right, and sometimes the layers shifted and the oil got trapped into pools."

"And you're thinking maybe Sullivan believes there's a pool of oil somewhere in this area."

"Maybe. Last night, I stumbled across a Web site that listed all of the Texas oil production by counties. Generally, the Hill Country made a very poor showing, but a little gas was pumped last year in Uvalde County, and eighty-five thousand barrels of crude were pumped in Medina. Even Bandera produced a few thousand barrels."

"So it isn't impossible."

"That was the other interesting thing I found. On a site called drilling.com, I ran across an article about a company named Marshland Oil. They're planning to drill four new nine-thousand-foot wells in Bandera County."

Patience looked up at the striations on the steeply inclined hill. "Those are definitely sedentary layers and the earth has heaved them up on an angle. I remember reading somewhere that one of the ways they find oil is to explode dynamite underground to set up seismographic waves."

"So I read. Apparently, the waves outline areas that might contain pools of oil."

"And the ground in several places in this section has been dug up and then refilled." She frowned. "But wouldn't the explosions have been heard?"

Dallas shook his head. "I don't think so. This part of the ranch is pretty remote."

"Maybe that's why Sullivan has been wanting this property all along. He thinks he might find oil." Patience glanced over at the rough wall of rock. "Sullivan's in financial trouble.

Maybe someone's putting up the money against a percentage of the profits from the wells he plans to dig."

"That's what I've been thinking," Dallas said. "What do you say we pay a little visit to good ole Sully?"

Patience nodded. "Good idea."

CHAPTER 24

Dallas thought about returning to the ranch, dropping Patience off, then driving over to the Broken Arrow. But she would probably pitch a fit if he didn't take her along and he didn't want Charlie to know he was going. Besides, they were more than halfway there already. If he took the shortcut down through Sully's north pasture, it wasn't that long a ride.

And he was damned anxious to hear what Sullivan had to say.

Twenty minutes later, they rode up in front of the sprawling main house, a single-story structure built of wood and stone with two big rock chimneys poking through the heavy shake roof, one at each end of the house. The place sat on a gentle slope, and stone steps led from the circular driveway up to wide, carved double doors.

Since the Double Arrow was actually a working ranch, a hitching rail near the barns allowed them to tie up their horses. Walking next to Patience, Dallas climbed the flagstone steps, heading for the impressive front doors.

A firm knock, and a few minutes later, the portal swung open. "Hi, Rosa. Is Sully around?" The short, dark-skinned

Hispanic woman who stood in the doorway was the live-in housekeeper who worked for Mal.

"*Si, Señor* Kingman. I will tell him you are here."

"Thanks."

Rosa disappeared into the depths of the house, then returned and invited them in. The stone floor in the entry gleamed with polish. So did the wide oak planks running down the hall. Rosa ushered them past the formal living room with its comfortable beige sofas and polished walnut tables, into a wood-paneled den where a deep leather couch nestled in front of a big stone hearth.

Mal's heavy oak desk sat in the corner in front of oak bookshelves lined with leather-bound volumes.

"Dallas! Come on in. What a nice surprise." Dressed in khaki slacks and a white polo shirt, he walked over and extended a hand, which Dallas shook. "It's good to see you two again."

"Your home is lovely," Patience said.

"Thank you. Would you care for something to drink? A soda or a beer? Something stronger, perhaps?"

"Actually, this isn't a social call, Mal. We just came from that southwest section of property you're planning to buy. Kind of got my curiosity working. I thought maybe you wouldn't mind answering a couple of questions about what's going on up there."

"What do you mean?"

"I was wondering if you might have been doing a little prospecting up there. Black gold, though, not the twenty-four-carat kind. I thought maybe you were using some explosives, doing some seismology work? If you were, you were trespassing."

Mal wandered over to his desk. A fancy silver pen and pencil set rested on a dark green felt blotter in front of a black leather chair. Mal straightened a sheet of paper lying on the blotter, setting it on top of the neat pile on the corner of his desk.

He turned back to Dallas and Patience, gave them an indulgent smile. "All right. The truth is, I've always thought there might be oil in that section. After Charlie agreed to sell, I got eager. Knowing he was a man of his word, I hired a seismology company to do a little preliminary work. I didn't figure Charlie would mind. Are you telling me he does?"

He couldn't say that. Charlie wouldn't give a damn what Sully did. Once he had promised to sell, he would consider that the property belonged to Mal.

"The question is, are you sure you did this *after* Charlie agreed to sell? You weren't over there *before* you made your deal?"

Sullivan's features subtly shifted. His friendly smile slid away and a guarded expression appeared. "Of, course, I'm sure. I've offered to buy that land maybe half a dozen times over the years. Charlie always said no. Why would I bother to spend money on land I never really figured to own?"

"You wouldn't," Dallas agreed, the notion in the back of his head growing stronger by the minute. "Not unless you knew that sooner or later Charlie would be *forced* to sell."

Sullivan straightened. "How could I possibly know that?"

Next to him, Patience's eyes swung to his as she realized where the conversation was headed. He had only just realized it himself, though he should have guessed the instant he suspected that Sully was after the oil. But he had known Mal Sullivan since he was a boy and he had always liked him, considered him a good, decent man.

"You couldn't have known," Dallas said. "Not unless you were the one responsible for the *accidents* Charlie's been having."

Sullivan's mouth went thin. "What are you talking about? That's insane."

"Is it? Those accidents have forced my uncle to close down his rodeo company, which cost him thousands of dollars in revenue. They managed to get him involved in a very expensive lawsuit. Then there was the wrecked trailer that killed his horses, the terrible fire in the horse barns, the attempts on Patience's life—oh, and of course there was the cattle rustling, which cost him money, worry, and time."

"You're talking crazy. My cattle were stolen, too."

"Damn straight. A stroke of brilliance, that. All in all, Charlie's troubles drove him out of business and nearly broke him. He was in the process of putting a second mortgage on the ranch when you came along—just in the nick of time—with an offer to buy up his land."

"That is ridiculous. I refuse to stand here and let you continue to make these wild accusations. All I did was take advantage of Charlie's unfortunate circumstances. I thought buying that land would be doing both of us a favor."

The edge of Dallas's mouth barely curved. "Well, Sullivan, maybe you were doing him a favor and maybe you weren't." He flicked a glance at Patience, who looked a little pale, and wished he had left her at the ranch. At the time he hadn't realized the danger she had been facing might live just a few miles away.

"In the last couple of days I did a little checking," Dallas said. "You need money, Sully, and you need it bad. The stock market's down. You've got ex-wife troubles and a couple of spoiled kids you're supporting. Desperate men take desperate measures. That's the reason you trespassed on Circle C land and it's the reason you hired someone to cause Charlie all that trouble. And once he knows the truth, he isn't gonna sell you that land."

"What!"

"You heard me. You can forget it, Sullivan. You should have been straight with Charlie from the start. You should have told him the truth, made some kind of business arrangement, but you were too greedy. Now all you're gonna get is nothing at all." Dallas reached for Patience, slid an arm protectively around her waist. "Come on. We're getting out of here."

They started walking away when he heard a noise behind them from a door leading in from the hall.

"You aren't going anywhere, Dallas. You, either, lady."

Dallas knew that voice. He was only mildly surprised when he turned to see Bradford Sullivan step into the study, lean and blond, with a *GQ* haircut and expensive alligator shoes.

"Dallas, he's got a gun," Patience said, which actually did surprise him, though it probably shouldn't have, and suddenly all of the pieces fell together. As each one clicked into place, a chill slipped down his spine.

"So it was you, not your father."

Brad flicked the older Sullivan a disdainful glance. "He wouldn't have the nerve."

"But he knew what you were doing," Patience said.

"Suspected, maybe. I told him Charlie was having financial trouble. I said there was a good chance he was going to need money. Dad didn't know about Hatch. He didn't want to know. All he wanted was to get his hands on that land."

Patience shifted a little closer to Dallas's side and he cursed himself for bringing her along, for inadvertently putting her in danger.

"Hatch," she said, her eyes fixed on Brad. "That's the man you hired to set the fire? The man who tried to kill me?"

Sully looked stricken, his face gone deathly pale. "My, God, Brad—what have you done?"

"I did what I had to."

"I thought . . . I worried you might have had something to do with stealing those cows. I figured you needed the money. I heard about that awful fire. Surely you aren't responsible for that?"

"I told you—I did what I had to. Now, you just keep your mouth shut and let me take it from here."

The floor creaked. Dallas turned as another man stepped into the study and quietly closed the door.

"That's good advice, Sullivan," the man said to Mal. "I'd advise you to take it." Square face, solid jaw, features harsh and intense. Dallas knew in an instant it was the man in the composite sketch Patience had drawn.

"You're him," she said. "You're the man who tried to kill me."

He smiled but there was ice in his eyes. He reached over and took the heavy automatic from Brad Sullivan's hand, but his hard gaze remained on Patience. "You were the fly in the ointment. After you went to the cops, I figured I might as well let you go, but it never set well with me. I don't like leaving loose ends. Now we can remedy that."

The knot in Dallas's stomach twisted even tighter. "Don't be a fool, Hatch. You can't just kill us. Charlie knows we were on our way over here. If we don't come back, he'll come looking for us." That was a lie, but the men didn't know it.

"Maybe you were on your way," Brad said. "Unfortunately, you never got here. Cattle rustlers in these parts, you know. They've always been a dangerous bunch."

Patience stiffened. She looked more mad than frightened. "You think you've got this all figured out, don't you? Well, you're not as smart as you think you are. Dallas phoned the sheriff before we left the ranch. He's on his way here right now."

Sully just stood there, looking dazed and disbelieving. Brad's features tightened. He tossed a questioning look at Hatch, who gave Patience a wolfish smile.

"I like your style, lady. Too bad we won't have time to get to know each other a little better." The smile slid away. "She's bluffing," he said to Brad. "Let's get this over with."

Brad just nodded. "We'll take them up to the southwest section, use the truck we used before. The tire marks will match the ones from the cattle rustling. It'll look like they stumbled onto thieves and wound up getting killed."

Dallas's hand balled into a fist. He had never liked Brad Sullivan. Still, he never would have suspected Mal's son was capable of murder. Brad left to get the truck, then Hatch motioned for them to leave a few minutes later and they all filed out, the gunman behind Dallas, the pistol pressing into his ribs.

As they walked down the hall, adrenaline poured through him, his senses on alert for the chance to make his move. Rosa was in the back room, but shouting for her to call the police would likely end up getting all of them killed. Better to wait, bide his time, look for an opening.

He was bigger than Brad and in way better condition, but Hatch was lean and solidly built and about his same height. Brad wouldn't be a problem but Hatch was the man with the gun.

Dallas felt the barrel nudge his ribs as the gunman urged him and Patience out the front door. He took a quick look around, but the ranch hands were all off working or somewhere in the barn out in back. The truck, a big enclosed flatbed with a ramp at the back for loading cattle, sat idling in front of the house.

"Keep your mouth shut or I'll shoot the girl right here," Hatch warned.

Dallas clenched his jaw. *Easy,* he told himself. *Take your time and look for the opening.*

As they climbed up into the cab, he bent his head and whispered to Patience, "Keep your eyes open and be ready."

He caught the spark that flashed in her eyes and saw her jaw firm with purpose. "I'll be ready."

"Get in the truck and shut the hell up!" Hatch jammed the gun hard into his ribs, then climbed up beside him, cramming them all together on the front seat, then slamming the door. Brad drove the vehicle away from the house, off down a narrow, little-used dirt road leading up to the portion of the Broken Arrow that bordered the southwest section of the Circle C.

As they drove along the rutted lane, Dallas thought of Patience and how much he loved her. He vowed that no matter what it took, he was going to get her out of there alive.

Patience sat tensely on the seat of the noisy diesel truck, Brad Sullivan's arm brushing against her each time he shifted gears.

On the opposite side, Dallas's heavily muscled shoulder nudged her slimmer one and she could feel the coiled tension vibrating through his body. Perhaps that was the reason she wasn't more frightened. Sullivan and his hired gun meant to kill them. She and Dallas were both determined that wasn't going to happen.

She ran over some of their options as the truck bounced along. If they made any kind of move inside the cab, Hatch would pull the trigger before Dallas could disarm him. Better to wait, look for the best possible moment.

Patience glanced out the window of the truck. The Double Arrow Ranch was more open than the Circle C, with fewer trees and more rolling hills. But it wasn't nearly as arid or as stratified as the southwest section where Sullivan believed he'd find oil.

Perhaps it was there, she thought, but drilling any sort of well was risky and only a handful of wildcatters succeeded. Then again, maybe Brad Sullivan wanted more than money. Maybe he wanted to prove himself, gain independence from a father who had controlled his life far too long.

Whatever his reason, even murder didn't seem to be out of the question.

The truck pulled to a stop in the area where she and Dallas had first found the filled-in holes where the dynamite had been set off. Patience's pulse kicked up, every one of her senses screaming with tension. The clock was running. They had to act soon.

One glance at Dallas and she knew he was thinking the same thing. He reached for her hand as he helped her down from the truck and gave it a purposeful squeeze.

Hatch waved the gun in their direction. "You two start walking. Head over toward that ridge."

Dallas didn't move. "I think maybe we ought to talk this

over, see if we can't reach some kind of compromise. Where money's involved, that's always the smart thing to do."

He kept his gaze fixed on the two men and as he spoke, Patience edged away from him, moving a little closer to Brad, who stood beside Hatch. An inch at a time, she eased a little behind him.

Brad shook his head, a smug look on his face. "We don't have anything to talk about, Kingman. You saw to that when you threatened to blow the deal."

Dallas took an unconscious step, one hand fisted, and Hatch raised the pistol, the big black automatic glinting in the hot Texas sun. "I said, start walking."

It was now or never. Flicking Dallas a glance she prayed he would understand, she took a huge leap forward, hurling her body toward Brad, knocking him into the gunman, whose arm flew up as he pulled the trigger. The sound echoed over the valley, followed by the sound of a fist connecting with bone, Dallas throwing a punch that smashed into Hatch's jaw.

Dallas grabbed the wrist gripping the pistol and they started to struggle for control. On the ground beneath her, Brad fought to shove Patience off him, but she drew back and shot her fist into his face. His nose made a cracking sound and blood spurted out of his nostrils.

"You little bitch!" He finally tossed her off him into the dirt, then captured her wrists to avoid the nails she tried to rake down his face. He pressed her into the ground and Patience bucked beneath him, at the same time bringing her knee up sharply between his legs.

"Shit!" Brad's face leached to the color of sand and he rolled off her into the dirt. Bent double, he clutched his privates as he gagged and tried not to vomit.

Trembling all over, terrified for Dallas, Patience bolted to her feet and began to frantically search the ground for some kind of a weapon. A few feet away, the two men wrestled in the dirt, first one on top and then the other, trying to gain control of the gun.

The pistol fired. Once, twice. Lying in the sand a few feet away, Sullivan made a strangled sound and blood erupted on the back of his custom tailored shirt. Dallas punched Hatch in the jaw and the pistol went flying, landing on the ground, then skidding into the dry shrubs and weeds.

Patience ran after it. By the time she picked it up and whirled to aim it at the gunman, Hatch lay unconscious in the dirt. Dallas staggered to his feet, breathing hard, his hat long gone, blood smeared over his western shirt, the snaps ripped open, the tail hanging out of his jeans. A trickle of blood oozed from the corner of his mouth.

Patience ran toward him. "Dallas!" She threw herself into his arms and he crushed her against him. "How . . . how badly are you hurt? You aren't . . . aren't shot or anything?" She fought to control the shudders ripping through her body and they finally began to subside.

"I'm fine." Dallas reached down and gently removed the gun from her trembling hand. "How about you? You okay?"

She dragged in a steadying breath. "I'm okay. You're the one who's bleeding." She reached down and caught the tail of his shirt, used it to dab the blood from the corner of his mouth.

"Take a look in the truck," Dallas said. "See if there's something we can use to tie these guys up with."

"Hatch shot Brad. I don't know how badly he's hurt."

Dallas turned in that direction, saw Brad lying face-down in the sand and the blood on the back of his shirt. "You get the rope. I'll see what I can do for Brad."

Patience found several coils of rope behind the seat. Hurrying to where Hatch lay sprawled on the ground, she started tying him up while Dallas worked over Brad. Dallas eased him onto his back and she realized that Brad wasn't breathing. Dallas pressed his fingers against Brad's neck to check for a pulse, but the gesture was futile. Hatch's wild shot had gone into his back and out through his chest, a clean shot through the heart.

Dallas walked over to help her finish tying up Hatch, who still lay unconscious. The gunman was just beginning to stir when she heard the blare of sirens screaming over the hill.

"It's Mills," Dallas said, spotting the sheriff's familiar patrol car cresting the rise, followed by a second patrol car racing along behind the first. "I wonder how the hell he knew we were here."

"Maybe Rosa heard the men talking. Maybe she called nine-one-one."

But when the vehicles rolled to a stop beside them, Patience saw Malcolm Sullivan sitting in the sheriff's back-seat. As Sullivan climbed out of the car, his gaze went to the two men on the ground.

Dallas looked at Mal. "I'm sorry, Sully. "I'm afraid Brad's dead."

Sullivan's throat moved up and down. His eyes darted toward the body of his son, lying on the ground. "You . . . you killed him?"

"It wasn't me. I was fighting with Hatch, trying to get the gun. Hatch accidentally shot him."

Sullivan seemed to fold in on himself. His face looked haggard and his eyes filled with tears. Turning away, he wandered off on shaky legs to the place where his son lay in the sand and slowly sank down beside him. Patience felt a surge of pity at the sound of the man's heart-wrenching sobs.

"Sully called us," the sheriff explained. "He told me what had been going on and what Brad planned to do. He said he couldn't let his son kill two innocent people."

Dallas just nodded. He looked over at Patience, reached out and slid an arm around her waist. As the sheriff and his deputies took the prisoner into custody, he led her over to the patrol car and they climbed into the backseat out of the sun.

Patience felt Dallas's eyes on her. "You were really terrific out there," he said.

"You were pretty terrific yourself."

Dallas lowered his head and very gently kissed her. "I love you. I've never said that to any other woman. I know it doesn't change things. I just wanted you know."

Patience slid her arms around his neck and leaned into him. "I love you, too."

They held each other until the sheriff returned to the car. Once they got back to the Circle C, they would send someone to the Broken Arrow to collect their horses, but in the meantime, they just wanted to go home.

Neither of them talked as Mills drove them back to the ranch house, but all the way there, Patience fought back tears. Dallas loved her. She never thought she'd hear him say it. He had also said it didn't change things.

Patience wished with all her heart it wasn't the truth.

CHAPTER 25

They say all good things must come to an end. For Patience, no truer words were spoken. Her adventure was over. Her thesis was written, and it was time to return to Boston, to go back to the world she lived in and the life she had left behind.

After the death of Bradford Sullivan, and facing long years in prison, Gerald Hatch had agreed to cooperate with authorities. He had confessed to being the man behind the "accidents" Charlie had suffered and named Brad Sullivan as his employer, along with—to everyone's surprise—Brad's younger sister, Elizabeth, who, according to the gunman, didn't know about the fire or the attempts on Patience's life, but had been well aware and an equal participant in the scheme to force Charlie into selling his land.

Mal Sullivan's part remained questionable. If he suspected his children were involved and did nothing to stop them, the resulting death of his son would be a burden that would haunt him forever. Charges had been filed against Hatch and both the remaining Sullivans. It was up to the district attorney's office to sort out the truth.

At last, the threat was over. Charlie could return to the

rodeo circuit, Dallas could go back to riding, and Patience could begin her teaching career.

It sounded simple enough.

So why did her heart ache every time she looked at Dallas? Why did just saying his name make her throat clog with tears?

She cast a glance to where he sat next to her in Charlie's pickup, his eyes intensely blue beneath the brim of his hat.

"We're almost there," he said as the truck carried them toward the hotel room he had rented at the Embassy Suites near the San Antonio airport. Earlier, Patience had said her good-byes to Charlie and Annie and was surprised to see tears in the older woman's eyes.

"You're a good girl, Patience. You take care of yourself now, you hear?"

Patience just nodded. Her throat felt tight, and when she went into Charlie's arms for a last good-bye hug, her own eyes filled with tears.

"I was lucky to know you," she said to him. "I was lucky to know all of you."

Charlie gruffly cleared his throat. She thought he might say something about coming back to see them but he didn't. Patience understood why.

"We're pretty modern here these days," he said. "Maybe you'll send us an e-mail once in a while . . . tell us how you're doin'."

She nodded. "I will, I promise."

Neither of them said anything more, just walked out to the pickup and waited while Dallas helped her climb up in the cab. They were getting a late start. The sheriff had wanted to go over the facts of the case one more time and the afternoon had slipped away.

It was evening by the time they arrived in San Antonio. Tonight would be their last night together. Dallas had planned a leisurely dinner at Ellington's, downstairs in the hotel, but in the end, both of them decided against it. She didn't want to waste these last precious hours in a restaurant. She didn't care if they ate at all.

She just wanted to be with Dallas one last time.

The multi-storied hotel appeared in the distance. Dallas pulled up beneath the overhang that protected the entrance to the lobby, handed the car keys to a bellman, and he and Patience went inside. They didn't have much luggage. Hers had been blown to kingdom come and Dallas would only be there one night.

As soon as they finished checking in, they took the elevator up to the fifth floor corridor and he unlocked the door to a large, nicely furnished room with a big glass window and a king-size bed. In silence, he took the canvas bag that was the only luggage she had and set it next to his on the floor of the closet. Then he gently caught her shoulders and drew her into his arms.

The kiss was soft and sweet, as if it were a first kiss instead of one of their last. He kissed her eyes, her nose, the corners of her mouth. For an instant, she thought how much she loved him, how much she was going to miss him, and her chest squeezed.

But she wanted this night, wanted to savor the moments, and she didn't want to spoil it with tears.

She kissed him back, slid her arms around his neck, opened to accept his tongue. He kissed her deeply and heat washed over her, replacing the sadness, at least for a while. Desire slipped through her, made her heart beat faster, made her ache in places besides her heart. He unbuttoned her blouse and slid it off her shoulders, unfastened the serviceable white bra that was the only one she had left and let it fall to the floor.

She stood before him, naked to the waist, and his eyes devoured her. They were hot with need, filled with restless hunger, and everywhere they touched her, she burned. Dallas leaned down and kissed her, filled his hands with her breasts. Such skillful hands, she thought, so gentle and yet so strong.

She opened his shirt, ran a finger over the muscles across his chest, through the tight brown curls, then bent and pressed her mouth against the skin above his heart. They paused only long enough to dispense with their clothes, then he led her to the bed. Sliding his fingers into her hair, he tilted her head back and started kissing her again. She could feel his erection, rigid against her belly, see the rapid pulse beating at the base of his throat.

It was hot tonight and beginning to storm. Heat lightning flashed outside the window. Patience felt the same powerful jolt of electricity as he lowered his mouth to her breast. His tongue found her nipple, circled it, leaving a cool damp ring. His teeth grazed the tip, then he drew the fullness into his mouth.

She wanted to tell him how much she loved him, wanted to hear him say those words to her one last time. But both of them knew it would only make their parting more difficult and the words remained locked away. Still, he said them, speaking through those blue, blue eyes, telling her with each caress, each deep, lingering kiss.

I love you.

If only love were enough.

But it wasn't. Not for her. Not for him. Not for a lifetime. And neither of them would settle for anything less.

Dallas kissed her, long, deep, thoroughly. He laved her breasts and she felt his erection, throbbing with power and need. He carried her over to the bed and came down above her, bracing himself on his elbows. His hard body rested between her thighs and the heavy, masculine weight of him made her tremble. He moved upward, entering her slowly, then filling her completely. He was everything she didn't want. Everything that would make her unhappy.

And she loved him as she never would another man.

"Dallas . . ." she whispered, her throat clogged with tears she refused to shed.

"I love you," he said, moving now, stroking deeper, branding her so that she would never forget him.

She would try. Dear God, she prayed she would succeed. But deep down she knew she would never forget this man who had come to mean so much to her.

Lightning flashed, but there was no thunder. Another flash and another, half a dozen spears of yellow in the darkness all at once, their naked bodies illuminated by the softly muted glow outside the window. It was humid outside and so deathly still. Just the heat and the night and the longing.

Deeply joined, Dallas filled her again and again. She gripped his hips, drawing him deeper still, filled with him as he slid himself out, then surged forward again.

They came together, both of them reaching the pinnacle at once, the force of their need so powerful it left them exhausted, barely able to move.

Afterward, they lay entwined, Patience's head on Dallas's shoulder, his leg draped over her calf. The air conditioner kicked on, humming into the silence, cool air bathing their heated skin.

No more words of love were spoken. Neither of them dared.

They made love throughout the night, mostly in silence, taking comfort in each other's bodies, trying to satisfy a need that seemed to have no end.

In the morning, he drove her to the airport.

"I wish you didn't have to go," he said as he walked her to the gate. "I wish things could be different."

She nodded, her throat too tight to speak.

"I don't suppose we could see each other once in a while. You know . . . just to keep in touch."

She only shook her head. "I don't think it's a good idea, do you?"

Dallas glanced away. "I don't suppose it is." He was wearing his black hat, new blue jeans, and a white western shirt. His jaw was set, his eyes a flat grayish blue. Still, he was so handsome it made her aching heart crack wide open.

The loudspeaker echoed into the waiting area in front of the security gate. "That's my flight. I'd better go."

For an instant neither of them moved. Dallas leaned toward her, caught her face between his hands, bent his head, and very gently kissed her.

"Have a good life," he said.

Patience tried to smile but her eyes filled with tears. "You, too. I know you're going to win at the Finals."

Dallas stared at her a long moment more, memorizing each of her features, just as she did his; then he pulled her hard against him. He kissed her with so much love, so much yearning.

Then he turned and walked away.

Patience watched until she could no longer see him through the hot glaze of her tears; then she turned and started walking to her plane.

CHAPTER 26

Patience's Boston apartment sat ten blocks from the campus, perfect biking distance, except in winter when the snow made the roads icy and the temperature dropped below zero. But most of the year, she enjoyed the exercise and the chance to spend time outdoors.

The two-story building, red brick with white trim, housed six separate apartments. Unit C sat upstairs, a one-bedroom she had decorated herself in navy and white, very traditional with a camel-back sofa and chair, maple tables with doilies under the lamps, and yellow and navy accents in the kitchen.

It was homey, she thought, as she glanced into the living room to see Snickers's furry little black and white body curled up on the sofa. It was homey, but except for her cat, it no longer felt like home.

It was insane to miss a stupid, crowded, pain-in-the-neck RV trailer, but Shari had been there to keep her company, and Stormy and Dallas had traveled with them. She shook her head, not allowing her thoughts to stray in that direction. Her heart ached every time they did, but, oh, it had been a grand adventure.

She had only been home two weeks, but in that short time

she had passed the final oral exam for her Ph.D. with flying colors and now just waited for official word. Tyler had kept his distance. She never found out if he was the one who had burglarized her apartment but she heard he was dating someone new and his friends said he was madly in love. Though the news filled her with relief, Patience pitied the latest object of his affections.

Her job at Evergreen had started a few days after her return and she was enjoying it. Teaching in the upper levels had always been her dream and standing in front of the class instead of sitting in one of the seats hadn't posed as big an adjustment as she had feared.

In that regard, her return had been easy.

Forgetting Dallas Kingman had been impossibly hard.

Patience sighed as the phone rang. It was Saturday, almost noon. The phone line had been ringing off the hook all morning. First Charity, then her stepmom, Tracy. Her father had called, and now, as she pressed the phone to her ear, she recognized the voice of her eldest sister, Hope.

"Hey, kiddo. How's it going?" Hope's cheery voice did nothing to improve Patience's mood.

"All right, I guess."

"Soooo . . . You're saying you still feel like shit." Hope never minced words. And she was usually right on the money.

"Yeah, I feel like shit." Since she rarely swore, her sister had to know how bad she really felt.

"You'll get over him," Hope said. "What else can you do, right? Forgodsake, the guy's a cowboy. He catches cows and things. You're a professor."

"Not quite."

"Well, associate professor, okay? The point is, once you get into the school year, you'll meet some nice guy on the faculty and fall in love all over again. When that happens, you'll have a lot better chance of making it work."

"I suppose." At least that was the way she'd always

thought it would be. When the time came, she would meet someone—the right someone. They would fall in love, get married, and eventually have a family. "It's just that . . ."

"Just what?"

"God, it hurts so much."

Silence fell on the line. Patience figured Hope was thinking of Richard Daley, the man she had loved and lost. But Richard was a major-league rat and Dallas wasn't. Which, in her estimation, made losing him a whole lot worse.

"I know it hurts," Hope said gently. "But you'll get past it—I promise."

But Patience wasn't sure Hope had ever really gotten over Richard, and she didn't think she was going to get over Dallas anytime soon. They hung up the phone and Patience swallowed past the lump in her throat.

She was in love with Dallas Kingman. Still, not once had she considered returning to the life Dallas lived. It wasn't her life. It never would be.

A second sigh escaped. Determined to think of something else, Patience sat down at her computer, which rested on a small maple desk in the corner of the bedroom. Earlier, when she had checked her e-mail, she had discovered an interesting note from Constance Foster, her friend at the Cowgirl Hall of Fame.

Patience clicked on the e-mail from cowgirlone@ Texas.net and reread the note.

> *I've got something for you. Call me as soon as you can.*

Patience had immediately phoned, but Constance worked Monday through Friday and Patience didn't have her home number. She typed in a reply, hoping this was her home e-mail address and not her address at work, put in her Boston phone number, and clicked on *Send*. Three minutes later, the telephone rang.

"Patience?"

"Constance—I'm so glad you got my message."

"Sorry, I should have given you my home number."

"So, what did you find out?"

"I'm not exactly sure if this is connected to the murders you've been working on, but I really think it could be. I ran across an article in the *Colorado Springs Gazette.* In July of nineteen-eighteen, a cowgirl named Bea Crandall, a relay rider, claimed she was attacked by a man who had asked her out to supper after the rodeo."

"He tried to kill her?"

"That's what Bea said. Unfortunately for Purcell—that's the man's name, Barton Purcell—he picked on the wrong woman. Bea was carrying a little pocket pistol, a derringer of some kind. She shot the old boy and killed him right on the spot."

Patience's heart started thumping. "I can't believe it." Was it possible the man who attacked Bea Crandall was the same man who had killed Lucky Sims? "You say this happened in Colorado Springs?"

"That's right. Monday when I get to work, I'll scan in what I've got and attach it to an e-mail."

"That would be terrific, Connie. This is really exciting news. I think there's a very good chance it's connected to the other two murders."

"Do you think there's any way you'll be able to prove it?"

"I don't know. I'm certainly going to try." She hung up the phone and leaned back in her chair. She wished Dallas were here so she could tell him what Connie had discovered and get any thoughts he might have. Since that wasn't going to happen, she opened her desk drawer, dragged out her file on Lucky Sims and Gracie McGuiness, and set to work.

Dallas was bronc riding again. He was calf roping, too, trying to get his winnings up before the slots were filled for the Finals, but doing a damned poor job. It was mid-September. He and Stormy had joined up again in Ellensburg, Washington, then traveled to the Puyallup show. But Stormy wasn't doing much winning, either.

Woman trouble does that to a man, Charlie had said.

This afternoon, they were competing in the Pendleton Roundup, a prior contract Charlie was able to fulfill, now that he was back to work.

Not that he seemed happy about it. Although he was as conscientious as always and the rodeo was going very well, most of the time he grumbled and growled and generally got on everyone's nerves. It was obvious he would rather be in Texas, back at the ranch with Annie.

Dallas had a feeling that once his uncle's commitments were fulfilled through the end of the year, he would probably sell the production company and get out of the rodeo business for good.

Charlie missed his wife. And Stormy was having his share of troubles as well. He had phoned Shari a couple of times, but she always kept the conversations brief. She had started back to school, was doing well in her classes. Once she had cried, Stormy said, and told him that she missed him. Then she wouldn't take his calls again for the rest of the week.

Stormy's mood was as black as Charlie's, and Dallas's was even worse. The one thing he had learned over the summer was how rare and precious real love was. If there was any way in hell he could make things work with Patience, he would have married her.

Or at least, he would have asked.

Even if he had, Patience would have said no, which didn't make getting over her any easier.

"Hey, Dallas!" Jade Egan walked toward him in a flashy, red sequined barrel-racing outfit, this one sporting red fringe. "You seen Stormy anywhere around?"

A muscle tightened in his cheek as his looked at the woman in front of him. "He's over by the trailer, saddling Gus for the calf roping." Jade had her claws bared, hoping to sink them into Stormy, and Dallas didn't like it. With Shari gone, his friend was too vulnerable, his feelings too raw. If Stormy could just take Jade to bed, it would probably be good for him. Lord knew, the woman could make a guy feel ten feet tall. She could also bring a man to his knees, and Stormy didn't need any more heartache.

Dallas headed for his trailer. Lobo needed to be saddled as well. It would be nice to win some money. He focused his mind in that direction and tried to keep Patience out of his thoughts.

In the end, he caught his steer but missed the loop with his pigging string and the calf came untied. No time. No score. No money.

He'd make up for it in the bronc riding, he told himself. But when his horse came out of the chute, he happened to glance toward the announcer's stand where a tall, leggy blonde stood next to Charlie. For an instant, he thought it was Patience and his heart nearly stopped beating.

But the woman wasn't Patience and the horse took a big, sideways leap to let him know how stupid he was for thinking it might be and piled him into the dirt.

Charlie was waiting as he walked out of the arena. "Dammit, boy. What the hell's wrong with you?"

A faint flush rose across the bones in his cheeks. "I got sidetracked, that's all."

"Now you listen here, son. You wanna win that title, you gotta get rid of all that stuff you're carryin' around with you and think about riding. Only riding. You hear what I'm tellin' you, son?"

Dallas nodded. Charlie was right. The problem was, he didn't much care. Somewhere along with losing Patience he had also lost the will to win. None of his goals seemed to

matter the way they had before. He didn't care if he rode or
didn't, didn't care if he won or lost.

And he didn't know if he would ever care again.

Patience couldn't sleep. It had been another long week. It
was late Saturday night, two o'clock in the morning, and she
lay there staring up at the molding on the ceiling. In the
darkness, her mind tumbled with memories, thoughts of
Dallas she couldn't seem to shake. The first time she'd seen
him ride, how hard she had tried to dislike him. She remembered their first kiss and the time he had taken her to Houston,
the look in his eyes when she had told him she thought she
was frigid. The notion brought a smile to her lips.

He had taught her so much about loving. Dallas had
awakened her desires, allowed her to become the passionate
woman she had discovered herself to be, and she would always be grateful to him for it.

She remembered him at the ranch, how different he seemed
there, how much more content. She had loved it there, too,
loved the wildness, the heat, and the lush green rolling hills.
He loved her, he had said, and Patience believed him. A man
like Dallas Kingman did not lie.

Patience blinked into the darkness, trying to force down
the lump in her throat. There was no use crying. She had
done enough of that already. And in time, she would start
feeling better. At least that's what her family said.

Earlier in the day, her father had dropped by to see her.
He had been worried, she knew.

"I know you loved this man. It's obvious losing him has
broken your heart."

"I'll get over it."

"You will, if that's what you want." They were standing in
front of the stove in the kitchen, waiting for the tea kettle to
boil.

"I know Dallas Kingman isn't the man you planned to fall

in love with, that you hoped for the sort of relationship I once had with your mother, the kind I was fortunate again to find with your stepmother. I can't help thinking you're right, that marrying a man who fits into your life the way Tracy fits into mine would make you happier in the long run. But it's possible I'm wrong. Sometimes people who come from different worlds can find happiness together. They find a way to make their marriages work."

"Name one," Patience said.

"Well, let's see . . . How about our friends, Tom Shapiro and his wife, Mary Ann? Tom's a CPA and Mary Ann's an interior designer but they're still one of the happiest couples I know."

Patience rolled her eyes. "I don't think that's quite the same, Dad."

Her father's lips faintly curved. "Well, maybe it isn't, but I know there must be people who are happy. If you love him enough—"

"Please, Dad—don't."

The tea kettle whistled and she reached into the cupboard to get each of them a cup.

"You know all Tracy and I want is for you to be happy," her father said. "That's all that matters to us."

Patience set the mugs down on the counter, leaned up and kissed his cheek. "I know it is, Dad."

Her father meant well, but the visit had only made her feel worse. What if she was wrong? What if Dallas was exactly the right man for her and she was making the biggest mistake of her life? Hours had passed but she was still haunted by the thought.

The red numbers on the digital clock on the nightstand glowed into the darkness. More wide awake than ever, Patience shoved her rumpled hair out of her face and swung her legs to the side of the bed. Padding over to her computer, she sat down and flipped on the switch, waited for the screen to light up, then clicked up her e-mail.

Kat Martin

She hadn't talked to Shari since her return to Boston, but they had e-mailed each other every few days. Patience opened her address book and found exracer@lightning.net, then began to compose a new message:

> *It's the middle of the night. I can't stop thinking about him. Hope you're doing better than I am.*

To her amazement, a few minutes later, a little musical note went off, signaling she had incoming mail. It came from Shari.

> *Can't believe you're up, too. Ain't loving someone a bitch?*

Patience smiled at the words and started typing.

> *I'm glad you're here. I needed a friend tonight. I sure miss the good times we had.*

Shari wrote back. *Me, too.*
Patience typed. *Why did they have to be cowboys?*

The reply came back.

> *Just rotten luck, I guess. We're doing the right thing. Get some sleep. Love ya, S.*

Patience hoped Shari was right. It was good to talk to a friend, but she still wasn't sleepy. Instead of lying there tossing and turning, she spread out the research material she had collected on the two young women who had been murdered and the printout of the old *Gazette* newspaper article Constance Foster had sent.

Both murdered women had died during the summer, three years apart. The attack on the third woman happened—again when the rodeo was in town—three years after that. The miles between the three crimes required lengthy travel, which, by transportation modes of the day, posed a definite problem. Thinking back to the remarks in her great grandmother's journal, she figured most of the female contestants would have been traveling by train.

For the next half hour, Patience scanned the Internet, searching until she found records of old train routes across the western United States. She printed the map, then set it on the table in front of her. As she marked the location of each incident—Cheyenne, Denver, Colorado Springs—she noticed a dotted line connecting the towns. The map showed the Cheyenne and Rio Railroad made a stop at each of the towns.

Perhaps the man was also a contestant who followed the rodeo circuit by train. Whatever the truth, it was a connection. Tomorrow morning, she would continue checking things out.

Patience yawned, beginning to get sleepy at last. She shut down the computer, padded across the room, shrugged out of her terry cloth robe, and tossed it across the foot of the bed. The sheets felt cool and clean as she slid between them.

Still, as tired as she was, she couldn't fall asleep.

Patience was groggy Sunday morning when she awakened to a pounding at her door. Dragging herself out of bed, she pulled on her terry cloth robe.

"Just a minute! I'm coming!" It was only eight o'clock, she saw, as she reached the door. After last night, she could have used a few more hours sleep. Wondering who it could be, she checked the peephole, recognized the man with the salt-and-pepper hair and square-framed glasses standing outside the apartment, and turned the knob to let him in.

"Hi, Dad. This is a surprise. You and Tracy usually go out to breakfast on Sunday mornings."

"She's waiting in the car. I just rushed up to drop this off.

It came in the mail for you yesterday afternoon. I guess your cousin didn't have the address of your apartment."

"My cousin? You mean Betty?"

"No, this is from Irma, one of Betty's sisters. According to the return address, she lives in Louisiana." He handed her the package and shoved his glasses up on his nose. "Got to run. You'll be over for supper, right?"

Patience nodded, her gaze roaming over the small, brown, paper-wrapped box.

"Good," her father said. "We'll see you then."

Patience closed the door behind him and carried the package over to the dining room table. She tore off the paper and opened the box. When she lifted the lid, her heart jumped to life. It was a leather-bound volume with Adelaide Whitcomb's name stenciled in gold letters on the cover at the bottom. There was also a card inside the box.

Dear Patience,

My sister says she gave you one of Grandma Adelaide's journals. I ran across this one up in the attic and thought you might like to have it, too. I think there're one or two more, but I've never seen them and I don't know where they are. Hope this helps in your research.

Your cousin,
Irma

Patience tossed the letter back into the box with a mental note to write Irma a thank you. Hurriedly, she pulled out the leather-covered volume. The book was in far better condition than the earlier volume, since this one covered a period beginning some sixty years after the first.

Apparently, Adelaide Holmes Whitcomb had continued her writing throughout the years of her life. Though the middle volumes seemed to have disappeared, the one Patience held was the final work, written in the waning years of Addie's life.

Patience carried the journal over to the camel-back sofa and settled down to read, the few plans she had for the day flying out the window. Tucking her legs up beneath her, she made herself comfortable and cracked open the book.

She noticed the penmanship first, how much Addie's writing had changed in these later years. Unlike before, the pen strokes weren't smooth and efficient but thin and shaky, revealing her fading health and strength.

Still, it felt good to resume her friendship with a great-grandmother she would only know through the woman's written words. Patience read for several hours before she realized how much time had passed. She set the book aside and went in to shower and dress for the day, but the pull of the pages brought her back as soon as she was finished.

Addie was now a woman in her eighties. She had lost her husband some years back, but still lived there on the Whitcomb family farm. Suddenly curious whether Addie might have discovered anything more about the disappearance of Lucky Sims, Patience skimmed ahead, searching for any sort of reference.

Instead, toward the very end of the journal, Sam Starling's name leapt up from the page.

Patience straightened on the sofa, her gaze riveted to the shaky blue letters scrawled in Addie's hand.

The days have grown long, almost endless. I'm an old woman now and my time on earth is nearly over. As I look back, I know I've been blessed with a full and happy life. As a young woman, during my rodeo days, I knew a freedom few women ever know. In Whit, I had a loving husband, and together we raised four children

*we both could be proud of. But in these private pages,
I have always been honest, and now, as I look back
over the years, I write one simple truth. For all the
blessings I have been granted, I have but one regret.*

*If I had my life to live over, if I were the young, hope-
ful girl I once was, I would marry my cowboy, Sam
Starling. For I have loved him every day of my life and
I shall love him until the last day I live."*

The letters went hazy as Patience's eyes welled with tears.
Her hands started trembling, her chest squeezing. She read
the lines again and fresh tears spilled down her cheeks. Addie
loved Sam. At eighty years old, Addie still loved him. She
loved him and she had given him up, and she had regretted it
every day of her life.

Patience's throat ached as she set the book away. Her
chest felt so heavy it was hard to get enough air into her
lungs.

There were times she had wondered why she had wound
up with the journals. Now she thought that the books were a
rare and precious gift. Perhaps her distant grandmother was
acting as her guardian angel. Perhaps the journals were a
warning not to make the same mistake that she had made as
a girl.

Sheer luck or blessed fate, reading Addie's words had
opened the door to Patience's heart as nothing else could have,
and now that it was open, there was no more doubt what she
should do.

Taking a courage-building breath, she picked up the telephone, called her dad, and told him she wouldn't be there for
supper. She was leaving town, catching the first flight west,
going after Dallas. She just hoped Dallas had meant what he
said and that he missed her half as much as she missed him.

Her father said he loved her and told her he would look
after Snickers while she was gone. He said he looked forward

to meeting her cowboy. Patience's nerves kicked in at the thought. What if she was wrong and Dallas didn't want her? What if he was already over her, maybe even dating someone else?

She felt sick to her stomach.

Remembering Sam Starling and the words in Addie's journal bolstered her courage. She dialed Shari's Oklahoma number and Shari told her Dallas and Stormy were at a rodeo in Pendleton, Oregon. Stormy had a friend who lived there and they planned to get together after the final performance. Shari didn't think the guys would be leaving for at least another day. Once they did, they were headed for the rodeo in Dillon, Montana.

Relieved to know where Dallas was, Patience booked a flight over the Internet. It cost a minor fortune for a last minute ticket, but she still had some savings and Dallas was worth it.

Her last call went to the home of Barry Weinstein, Dean of Faculty for Evergreen Junior College. She was sorry, she told him, but he would have to find a teacher to replace her. Something important had come up and she was resigning her position.

Weinstein said he was sorry to hear she would be leaving, but said it shouldn't be difficult to find someone to take her place. In the meantime, he knew several good substitute professors who would be willing to take over her classes.

On a shaky breath, Patience hung up the phone, waiting to feel the heavy weight of regret. Instead, she felt as if a thousand pounds of despair had been lifted from her shoulders. Her father was right. She and Dallas loved each other. They wouldn't make the same mistakes his father and mother had made. They would find a way to make it work.

Unless, of course, Dallas didn't really love her.

Forcing back the thought, she glanced at the clock. The only flight she could find for Pendleton left at five-seventeen that afternoon. She packed two bags, one that included several pairs of jeans and boots, called a cab to take her to the airport, dropped her dusty white straw cowboy hat into a shopping bag, and headed for the door. She wouldn't be back until she knew where she stood—one way or the other.

CHAPTER 27

Boston's Logan International Airport teemed with travelers. Patience climbed out of the cab, paid the driver, and wheeled her luggage through the glass doors into the terminal. After standing in the ticket line for what seemed hours, she finally reached the front counter where a pudgy clerk punched out the one-way ticket to Pendleton via Portland that she had reserved on the Internet and checked her black canvas suitcase.

The clerk pointed her in the direction of the B Terminal and she picked up her carry-on and the shopping bag with her hat in it and set off in that direction. If for some reason she missed Dallas in Pendleton, she would rent a car and catch up with him in Montana.

She would find him, no matter what it took.

She just prayed he'd be glad to see her when she got there.

Sliding the strap of her leather purse over her shoulder, Patience hurried along the corridor, heading for gate B-17. At the security checkpoint, she tossed the carry-on, shopping bag, and her purse up on the conveyor belt. As the articles passed through the x-ray machine, she walked through the scanning door, fortunately without a beep, went over and retrieved her luggage.

The corridor was filled with people, most of them coming off morning flights just arriving from the West Coast. Lost in thought, she bumped into a short, Asian woman hurrying the other way, pushing a baby stroller with a tiny black-haired child inside. Patience apologized. The woman said something in Chinese and kept on walking.

It was still a ways to the gate. Leaving this time of day, she wouldn't get into Pendleton until nearly midnight. She would have to rent a car, drive to the rodeo grounds, and hope that Dallas and Stormy were parked there for the night.

Her stomach instantly knotted. She tried not to think what she might find when she arrived and prayed once more that Dallas's feelings for her ran as deep as hers for him.

Another planeload of passengers began disembarking, travelers of every shape and size streaming into the long, wide corridor. The walkway filled with people eager to get back to their homes and she wove her way through them, being more careful this time.

It was the cowboy hat that caught her attention, an expensive black felt twenty X beaver with a cattleman's crease just like Dallas's. The man who wore it was tall, dressed in a dark blue western-cut suit and polished black ostrich boots.

Her heart punched to life as her gaze swung to his face. *Dallas!*

His hat was pulled low, his eyes fixed ahead, his mind somewhere else. He kept on walking, almost passed her before she could manage to force out his name.

"Dallas! Dallas, wait!"

He turned at the sound of her voice. The instant he saw her, the bag he was carrying slid from his hand and clattered onto the floor. He stood there staring as if he couldn't believe his eyes, then he took a step toward her, caught her up, and crushed her in his arms.

Patience clung to him, her cheek pressed to his, her eyes

filling with tears. She was trembling, her throat clogged, and she could feel him trembling, too.

"Patience . . . I can't believe it's really you. God, I've missed you so much."

She swallowed past the lump in her throat and tried to blink back the wetness spilling down her cheeks. "I-I was coming to see you. I was hoping . . . I thought . . . if you meant what you said . . . if you really love me—"

Dallas kissed her. "I love you. God, I love you so much." Capturing her face between his hands, he slid his fingers into her hair and kissed her until she felt dizzy. People surged around them, parting to make room for them, creating an island, then closing ranks on the opposite side. Both of them were breathing hard by the time he let her go.

"What . . . what are you doing here?" Patience asked, unable to stop looking at him.

"I was on my way to find you. I left Pendleton on the morning flight. What are you doing here?"

"I was coming to find you. I was leaving for Pendleton on the evening flight."

Dallas's mouth curved up in the sweetest smile she had ever seen. Grabbing her bags and his own, he led her to an area of empty seating. "I came to talk to you. I've got everything all worked out."

Patience slid to a halt. "Worked out? What are you talking about?"

"Look, darlin', I only need one more year of medical school, right? I figure I'll change my focus, get my veterinarian's degree, like you said. Hey, they've got cows and horses in Massachusetts, right? Or small animals, maybe, if you'd rather stay in the city. At any rate, I've got enough saved to finish my schooling and provide for both of us until I get my practice up and running."

Her throat closed up again. "You would do that for me? You'd give up everything you ever wanted? Give up rodeo? Your dream of owning your own ranch?"

"I love you. I don't care about those things if you aren't there to share them with me."

"Oh, Dallas . . ." She went into his arms and stood there trembling, clinging to his neck.

"Will you marry me?" he said against her ear.

A sob escaped. Fresh tears spilled onto her cheeks. "Of course, I'll marry you. I love you. More than anything in the world." She shook her head. "But I don't want you to change your life for me."

She drew away from him, wiped away the wetness, managed a wobbly smile. "I quit my job at Evergreen. I thought you could rodeo for a few more years, till we get enough saved up to buy some land down in the Hill Country. They've got colleges there. I can find a teaching job somewhere in the area. With two incomes we can save even faster. In the summers, I can travel with you, and the rest of the year, you can come home as often as you can manage."

Dallas stared down at her. She had forgotten how small he could make her feel. "You quit your job for me? You gave up your career?"

"I love you. I don't care about my career if I can't be with you."

Dallas dragged her against his chest, kissed her and kissed her and kissed her. "I hope you still have your apartment."

"I didn't have time to sublease it."

"Good. Let's go back and figure all this out."

Patience smiled up at him. Dallas had come for her. He was willing to give up everything important to him—for her. There would never be another man like him. "That sounds good. And now that you're in Boston, tomorrow night you can meet my parents. My dad's really going to like you."

"You think so?"

"He loves the West. You're a cowboy. How could he not?"

They went up to the gate to let airport personnel know she wouldn't be boarding the plane, and the woman there told her she could reclaim the bag she had checked a little later. Tomorrow would be soon enough, Patience thought.

Tonight, she had other plans.

It was nearly noon the following day that Patience lay next to Dallas in the queen-size bed in her apartment, their arms and legs entwined, her head nestled on Dallas's bare chest. The sun blazed in through the bedroom windows and they still weren't up yet. Or actually, they'd gotten up twice and somehow wound up back in bed.

She felt Dallas's fingers, sifting gently through her hair. Beneath her cheek, his heart beat strong and steady. The muscles in his shoulders tightened as he shifted her a little, tilted her head up, and kissed her. It felt so good, so right to be with him. She wondered how she ever believed she could live without him.

"When are we getting married?" he asked, nibbling the side of her neck.

Patience smiled. "How about this afternoon?"

"Good answer."

She laughed. "I was kidding."

"I wasn't."

"All right, how about the end of the week in my parents' backyard? That's assuming we can get them to let us use it."

He smiled down into her face. "Can Charlie and Annie come?"

"Sure. How about your parents?"

"Them, too."

"Perfect." Patience snuggled closer against him. Her eyes widened as she felt his hard length pressing against her hip. "I thought we were getting up this time."

He nuzzled the side of her neck and lifted her a little, adjusting her so that she was lying on top of him. "I thought so, too. Seems there's been a change of plans."

It was nearly two o'clock by the time they had finally

showered and dressed for the day. Dallas sat on the couch absently stroking Snickers beneath the chin while Patience phoned her father and Tracy, who insisted the two of them come over for supper. Tonight she and Dallas would announce their plans to get married. Once her parents got to know him, she had no doubt they would approve.

Next, she called Charity and Call in Seattle. "I'm hoping Dad and Tracy will let us use their backyard on Sunday." With Tracy's love of gardening, the lush green shrubs and beautiful blooming plants, it would make the perfect setting. "I can't wait for you to meet him, but I don't expect you to come all this way on such short notice."

"Are you kidding?" Charity said. "We wouldn't miss it for the world! We'll pick Hope up in New York on the way." Meaning Call would be flying east in one of his fancy chartered jets. Maybe having them there wasn't too much to ask after all.

She phoned Hope next and smiled at her shriek of delight. "I'm thrilled for you, little sister. A cowboy in the family. That's gonna be hard to top."

"Impossible," Patience said, and Hope laughed. Patience told her that Charity would be calling to make arrangements to pick her up in Call's chartered jet.

The last person she phoned was Shari. "It's a long story. I can't wait to tell you. I feel a little guilty when I think of you and Stormy, but I love Dallas, Shari. I don't want a life without him."

"You know I love you both," Shari said, "and I wish you all the happiness in the world."

"Thank you." Patience found it hard to ignore the sadness in her friend's voice, but Shari had her own choices to make.

While Dallas called Charlie and Annie, his father and Rachael, then phoned Stormy, Patience padded over to her computer and flipped it on. Earlier she had told Dallas about Constance Foster's phone call and the man named Barton

Purcell who had been killed in 1918 when he attacked one of the women relay riders.

On impulse she typed in www.google.com, then typed in Cheyenne and Rio Railroad. There was all manner of archive information on the site. Working on an idea that popped into her head, she punched up yearly employee records and was amazed to discover they went back to the early 1880s, when the railroad line first went in.

The Cheyenne and Rio was only one branch of the bigger, Southwest Central Railroad, she discovered, but the records included employees who worked for the various lines. She clicked on the year 1912 and skimmed the alphabetical list of employee names.

"Oh, my God!"

"What is it?" Dallas asked, walking up behind her, resting his hands lightly on her shoulders.

"The guy who got killed in Colorado Springs—Barton Purcell? He worked for the railroad."

She moved the mouse and clicked on the year 1915. The name appeared in the rolls again. He was still employed there in 1918, the year he was shot and killed.

"I can't believe this, Dallas. See these little letters, *con/CR* after his name?"

"Yeah, what do they mean?"

"According to the ledger at the bottom, *con* means conductor. The letters CR signifies the railroad line—in this case, Cheyenne and Rio. The route goes from Cheyenne south across the state line, through Denver and Colorado Springs, all the way to Santa Fe. Purcell probably took time off whenever the rodeo was in one of the towns along the line."

"I wonder why he waited three years between murders . . . or at least before he tried it again."

"I guess we'll never know. But this has got to be the same

guy in all three cases. She turned and looked up at him. "And Bea Crandall killed him."

Dallas reached down and lightly traced a finger across her cheek. "I guess Lucky and Gracie can rest a little more peacefully now. Thanks to you, they know the guy who killed them got what he deserved."

"I think Addie will rest easier, too."

Through the pages of the journal, her grandmother had given her a precious gift—the courage to make the most important decision of her life. Patience hoped that in some small way, she had returned that gift.

Reaching down, she clicked off the computer. "Come on. You've never been to Boston. Why don't I show you around?"

"Okay, on one condition."

"Which is?"

"While we're at it, we shop for a ring."

Patience grinned. "Two rings. You don't think I'd let you go running around the country without a wedding band?"

Dallas laughed and pulled her into his arms. "Two rings," he said, and then he kissed her.

By the end of the week they would be married. A professor married to a cowboy. Before her summer adventure, she wouldn't have believed it could happen.

"I love you," Dallas said, kissing her softly one more time. "Now, before you come to your senses—let's go buy those rings."

EPILOGUE

Dallas won the World Champion All-Around Cowboy title again in December. It took a lot of concentrated effort, since he had gotten so far behind in the earnings he needed to qualify and he spent a lot of time on the road making up for the loss. But his wife had traveled with him those last grueling months, and with her unfailing support, he had no choice but to win.

He had found a woman willing to give up everything for him. Dallas meant to give it all back and a whole lot more, including loving her every day for the rest of his life.

He looked over to where she sat in front of the Christmas tree in her yellow terry cloth robe, her golden hair rumpled from their lovemaking last night. It was Christmas morning. They had returned to the Circle C in mid-December, after the National Finals in Las Vegas, and Patience had begun to look for a teaching job. She already had several interviews lined up and he had no doubt she would get whatever position she wanted. Then they planned to rent a house.

"Come on, Dallas! Get over here, boy." Charlie stood in front of the fireplace, looking like a big gray bear in his robe and slippers. They had awakened at their usual early hour and all raced downstairs to open the packages under the tree. "You and Patience got one more gift to open."

Dallas started toward where Patience sat on the sofa. His knee bothered him a little after the tough Finals competition, and this morning he'd had to take a couple of Advil for his shoulder, but he was off the road for a while, getting in shape to ride in the spring, and he was already feeling better.

Dallas walked over to the sofa. Patience gave him the special smile she reserved just for him and something tightened in his chest. God, he loved her. It still bothered him to think how close he had come to losing her.

Instead, with the money he'd won this year, his savings account was growing by leaps and bounds. In another year or two, he'd have enough to quit riding, buy that ranch, and settle down to the business of raising a family.

It wouldn't be too long before his own kids would be sitting in front of the tree, eagerly tearing through their gifts. He glanced at the tall green pine that glittered with bright-colored lights and red-and-silver tinfoil streamers. Strings of cranberry and popcorn they had made themselves were draped around it, and green, red, silver, and gold balls hung from the branches.

They had all four helped put the tree up, drinking homemade cider and eating Annie's hot and spicy chili one cold Texas night. Now that he was a married man, the atmosphere in the house had changed. Over the past few weeks, watching him and Patience together, his aunt and uncle had realized the two of them were nothing like Avery and Jolene. Unlike Dallas's parents, their marriage came first and no sacrifice was too great to make it work.

"Come on," Charlie grumbled, "me and Annie's gettin' tired of waitin'."

The rest of the gifts had already been opened, a stack that included a fancy new Navajo saddle blanket for Charlie, a pretty robe and matching slippers for Annie. There'd been a bottle of perfume for Patience and a new western shirt for him. Dallas had given his wife a pretty little filly colt that she had gone wild for and she had given him an Australian shepherd puppy, which Dallas figured would be nothing but trouble, but had already weaseled its way into his affections.

Still, one small box remained.

"You open it," Dallas said, handing the package to Patience, who ripped off the pretty silver foil paper and tore open the box to find a sealed envelope inside.

"I did my part," she said, handing him the envelope with their names penned in blue ink on the back. "Now, it's your turn."

Dallas recognized Charlie's bold script, flicked him an assessing glance, and saw his mouth split into an ear-to-ear grin.

"Come on, son, get a move on. I'm startin' to get hungry."

Dallas opened the envelope and drew out a folded document that was several pages thick. He froze as he unfolded it and realized what he held in his hand.

Dallas shook his head. "No. No way. I won't let you do this."

"Take it easy, son. We ain't givin' the place up completely. If you skip down a little, you'll see we're keepin' a life estate on the house and a little chunk of ground around it. We figure you got enough saved up to build a place of your own down the road a piece."

Dallas straightened on the sofa, tried to swallow past the lump that was building in his throat. He opened his mouth, but no words came out.

"The Circle C would have been yours anyway," Charlie said a little gruffly. "You've been a son to me since the first day you come here. Now . . . well . . . me and Annie, we're gettin' too old for all this hard work. We figured the two of you could handle things from here on out. Give us time to enjoy ourselves a little for a change."

"Now your man won't have to be gone all the time," Annie said to Patience, who looked as shaken as he. "And you two can start workin' on those grandkids I been wantin' for so long."

"Thank you." Patience wiped tears from her eyes. "You've both been wonderful to us."

"It won't be easy," Charlie warned. "We've still got that lawsuit to settle and most of the money in the emergency account is gone, what with all the problems last summer. But I figure you can dicker with that oil man, make the deal on the southwest section Brad Sullivan was tryin' to make, maybe find us some oil."

Dallas just nodded, still not quite able to take it all in. With a place of his own, he could quit rodeoing. He could stay home with Patience and build up the ranch.

"There's just one more thing," Charlie said.

"What's that?" Dallas looked up from the papers in his hands.

"Ben Landers is plannin' to retire. He and his wife are movin' out to Arizona. Guess you'll have to find yourself another foreman."

Dallas glanced at Patience and read the same thought in her eyes. "Maybe Stormy would be interested in the job."

"You think that boy's ready to settle down?" Annie asked.

Dallas grinned. "Only if he found the right woman."

"Now, that would be a happy ending," Patience said.

And in the end, it was.

Can't get enough of Kat Martin's unique

blend of romance and suspense?

Keep reading for a special preview of

AGAINST THE WILD,

the latest book in the bestselling *Against* series

by Kat Martin.

The low moaning of the wind awakened him. The old fishing lodge, constructed in the thirties, was built of hand-hewn logs, the chinking between them worn by time and weather, leaving spaces for the air to blow through. An eerie keening echoed inside the house, a chilling sound that sent shivers down Dylan's spine.

Just the wind, he reminded himself. Nothing to do with stories of ghosts and hauntings. Just an inconvenience, nothing more.

Still, he had Emily to think of. Dylan Brodie swung his long legs to the side of the bed, shrugged into his heavy flannel robe, and padded barefoot down the hall toward his daughter's bedroom.

The lodge he'd purchased earlier in the spring was big and sprawling, two stories high, with a separate family wing for the owner, and another for the prestigious guests it had once hosted, back in its heyday in the thirties. The living room was big and open, exposing fourteen-inch logs in the ceiling. A massive river rock fireplace climbed one wall; a second, smaller version warmed the sitting room in the master suite.

Dylan had fallen in love with the place the moment he had seen it, perched on Eagle Bay like a guardian of the two hundred forested acres around it.

Old legends be damned. He didn't believe in ghosts or any of the Indian myths he had heard. He'd waited years to find the perfect spot for his guided fishing and family vacation business, and this was the place.

The wind picked up as he moved down the hall, the air sliding over rough wood, whistling through the eaves, the branches on the trees shifting eerily against the window panes. Dylan picked up his pace, worried the noise would frighten Emily, though so far his eight-year-old daughter seemed more at ease in the lodge than he was.

Frosted-glass wall sconces dimly lit the passage as he walked along. They were original, not part of a remodel of the residential wing done a few years back, before the last owner moved out and left the area.

The four bedrooms and bathrooms upstairs on this side of the building weren't fancy, but they were livable while he worked on the rest of the lodge. The master suite had been updated, but it wasn't the way he wanted it yet. Eventually, he would rebuild this section, as well, bring it all up to the four-star standard he'd had in mind when he had purchased the property.

Dylan paused at the door to Emily's room, quietly turned the knob, and eased it open. His daughter lay beneath the quilt that his housekeeper, Winifred Henry, had made for her as a Christmas gift. It contained princesses and unicorns embroidered in puffy little pink and white squares, all hand-stitched to fit her youth-size four-poster bed.

His gaze went to the child. Emily had the dark hair and blue eyes that marked her a Brodie, but her complexion was as pale as her mother's. Unlike Mariah's perfect patrician features, Emily's mouth was a little too wide, her small nose freckled across the bridge.

She was awake, he saw, her eyes fixed on the antique rocker near the window. It was just her size, fashioned of oak, and intricately carved. She loved the old chair that had been in the lodge when he bought it.

Emily never sat in it, but she was fascinated by the way

the wind made it rock on its own. Dylan found it slightly eerie, the way it moved back and forth as if some invisible occupant sat in the little chair. She was watching it now, her lips curved in the faintest of smiles. She mumbled something he couldn't quite hear, and Dylan's chest clamped down.

It hurt to watch his little girl, see her in the make-believe world she now lived in, forming silent phrases. Nothing he could actually hear.

Emily hadn't spoken a single audible phrase since her mother had abandoned her three years ago. Not a meaningful word since the night Mariah had run off with another man.

Dylan's hand unconsciously fisted. Maybe he hadn't been the husband Mariah wanted. Maybe he'd been too wrapped up in trying to make a life in the harsh Alaskan wilderness he loved. Maybe he hadn't paid her enough attention.

Maybe he just hadn't loved her enough.

Guilt slipped through him. He never should have married her. He should have known she would never be able to adjust to the life he lived here. Still, it didn't excuse her cruel abandonment of their daughter. An abandonment Emily had not been able to cope with.

Dylan forced himself to walk into the bedroom. Emily's eyes swung to his, but she didn't smile, just stared at him in that penetrating way that made his stomach churn.

"Em, honey, are you okay?" She didn't answer, as he'd known she wouldn't. "It's just the wind. The lodge is old. There's nothing to be afraid of."

She blamed him for the loss of her mother, he knew. It was the only explanation for why she had withdrawn from him so completely.

Tucking the quilt a little closer beneath her chin, he leaned down and kissed her cheek. The wind picked up as he walked out of the bedroom and eased the door closed. Emily was his to watch over and protect, his to care for and comfort. But he had lost his daughter three years ago.

When he had driven her mother away.